New Zealander **Alison Roberts** has written more than eighty romance novels for Mills & Boon. She has also worked as a primary school teacher, a cardiology research technician and a paramedic. Currently, she is living her dream of living – and writing – in a gorgeous village in the south of France.

Marion Lennox is a country girl, born on an Australian dairy farm. She moved on, because the cows just weren't interested in her stories! Married to a 'very special doctor', she has also written under the name Trisha David. She's now stepped back from her 'other' career teaching statistics. Finally, she's figured what's important and discovered the joys of baths, romance and chocolate. Preferably all at the same time! Marion is an international award-winning author.

Karin Baine lives in Northern Ireland with her husband, two sons, and her out-of-control notebook collection. Her Mother and Grandmother's vast collection of books inspired her love of reading and her dream of becoming a Mills & Boon author. Now she can tell people she has a proper job! You can follow Karin on X, @karinbaine1 or visit her website for the latest news – karinbaine.com

Saved by a Mistletoe Kiss

ALISON ROBERTS

MARION LENNOX

KARIN BAINE

MILLS & BOON

All rights reserved including the right of reproduction in whole or in part in any form. This edition is published by arrangement with Harlequin Enterprises ULC.

This is a work of fiction. Names, characters, places, locations and incidents are purely fictional and bear no relationship to any real life individuals, living or dead, or to any actual places, business establishments, locations, events or incidents. Any resemblance is entirely coincidental.

This book is sold subject to the condition that it shall not, by way of trade or otherwise, be lent, resold, hired out or otherwise circulated without the prior consent of the publisher in any form of binding or cover other than that in which it is published and without a similar condition including this condition being imposed on the subsequent purchaser.

® and ™ are trademarks owned and used by the trademark owner and/or its licensee. Trademarks marked with ® are registered with the United Kingdom Patent Office and/or the Office for Harmonisation in the Internal Market and in other countries.

First Published in Great Britain 2024
by Mills & Boon, an imprint of HarperCollins*Publishers* Ltd,
1 London Bridge Street, London, SE1 9GF

www.harpercollins.co.uk

HarperCollins*Publishers*
Macken House, 39/40 Mayor Street Upper,
Dublin 1, D01 C9W8, Ireland

Saved by a Mistletoe Kiss © 2024 Harlequin Enterprises ULC.

Single Dad in Her Stocking © 2018 Alison Roberts
Mistletoe Kiss with the Heart Doctor © 2020 Marion Lennox
Midwife Under the Mistletoe © 2018 Karin Baine

ISBN: 978-0-263-34496-7

MIX
Paper | Supporting
responsible forestry
FSC™ C007454

This book contains FSC™ certified paper and other controlled sources to ensure responsible forest management.

For more information visit: www.harpercollins.co.uk/green

Printed and Bound in the UK using 100% Renewable Electricity at CPI Group (UK) Ltd, Croydon, CR0 4YY

SINGLE DAD IN HER STOCKING

ALISON ROBERTS

CHAPTER ONE

'OH, NO...YOU can't be serious.'

'I'm so sorry, Dr Cunningham, but there it is. I'm sure you understand that acute appendicitis isn't something we can plan for. We're doing our very best to find someone else to fill the position but, realistically, that's not going to happen until after New Year. People want to be with their families over the festive season and...it's such late notice. It's the twentieth of December, for heaven's sake. Christmas is only a few days away, you know.'

Of course he knew. There was tinsel in all sorts of odd places in his emergency department here at the Cheltenham Royal Hospital and there was a small Christmas tree in the waiting room. Some staff members had taken to wearing earrings that had flashing lights or headbands with reindeer antlers or little red hats with pompoms attached and he kept hearing people humming Christmas carols. They'd even had a man in a Santa suit come in by ambulance earlier today after suffering a suspected heart attack as he coped with all those small people wanting to sit on his knee and have their photographs taken in the town's largest department store.

And, of course, he knew that people wanted to be with their families. Or felt obliged to be. It was precisely the reason why Max Cunningham always worked right through the holiday season to make sure as many people as possible in his department could have time at home with their loved ones. He'd done it for so many years now he was quite comfortable ignoring the commercial hype that tried to make it compulsory for happy families to gather and have an over-the-top celebration as they enjoyed each other's company. It was as much of a myth as Santa Claus as far as he was concerned—or it was for the Cunningham family, at any rate.

Everybody knew that. He could just imagine how much of a field day any gossips of Upper Barnsley would have when the news of a third December tragedy to hit the Cunningham family filtered out. Talk about history repeating itself.

It's struck again, they'd probably say. *The Christmas Curse of the Cunninghams...*

He'd been too young to do anything but cope the first time when his mother had died. Last time had been gutting when he'd lost his only brother but he'd got through it. Somehow. Life had gone back to normal. But this year was different. This year, his entire world was being tipped upside down and the phone call he'd just taken meant that Max could expect even more disruption. So much more, he wasn't at all sure he knew what to do about it and feeling less than confident was as new and uncomfortable a sensation as any of the changes that were about to happen in his life. Nothing was ever going to go back to normal now, was it?

'Hey...it can't be that bad.' The Royal's senior nurse in the emergency department, Miriam, came into Max's office. 'Here, have a chocolate. I thought I'd bring you one before they all got scoffed by those gannets in the staffroom. Look, how cute are these? Like little plum puddings.'

Max shook his head. 'No, thanks. I'm not really in the mood for chocolate. I've got a bit of a problem, to be honest.'

Miriam's face creased in sympathy. 'I did hear that something was going on. To do with your brother? And his children…?'

'My brother Andy died just over a year ago. A car accident.' It was a testament to how Max managed to keep his private life private that nobody here was aware of the full story but Miriam was trustworthy—the kind of motherly type that inspired confidence from both her patients and her colleagues. A great listener, too, with enough life experience to offer sage advice in almost any situation. Max could do with some advice.

'It was his wife, this time,' he added. 'Or, I should say, his ex-wife. I haven't seen his children since his funeral. I didn't even know that there was a third one.'

'Oh?' Miriam's eyebrows rose as she sank into the chair in front of Max's desk. 'Why ever not?'

Max sighed. 'His marriage had broken down and he was dealing with difficult custody issues. He didn't know that his wife was pregnant when she left and she obviously wasn't too keen to keep in touch with the rest of his family after he died. She moved all the way up to somewhere north of Glasgow.'

'And she's the one who's just died?'

'Yes. She was taking the oldest one to school. Ben. He's six. Icy road and an elderly driver must have panicked when he went into a skid and put his foot down on the accelerator. She managed to shove the baby's pushchair out of the way but got killed instantly herself. There was an elderly aunt or someone who made funeral arrangements but she couldn't take care of the children. They were all put into foster care while they tried to track down any other family.'

'And you're the children's guardian?'

'So it would seem. Maybe it was a legal document that got overlooked in the separation and then Andy died so a formal divorce never happened. It's a good thing. It would have been appalling if Andy's kids had been left in foster care when they've got an uncle and grandfather who are quite willing and able to take care of them.'

Well…being willing was one thing. Being able could prove to be a lot harder.

'Your dad's the GP in Upper Barnsley, isn't he?'

'Yes. And he lives in a house that's ridiculously big for one person, but the house has been in the family for generations and he says the only way he's leaving it is feet first when they carry out his dead body.' Max found a smile. 'That's also a good thing because there's plenty of room for the children. His housekeeper is happy to help out a bit more than doing her usual weekly shop and clean and I'd made arrangements for a live-in nanny who was going to get here tomorrow, in time for when the children arrive.'

'Sounds like you've got things well under control.'

Max rubbed at his jaw. 'I thought I had. But I've just had a call from the agency and the nanny got rushed into hospital a couple of hours ago with acute appendicitis. She's probably on an operating table as we speak…and they have no one else available until after New Year.'

'Oh…no…' Miriam's despairing tone was an exact

echo of the one he'd used on receiving that news. 'I wish I could offer to help but I've got family coming from all over the country this year. Christmas dinner for fourteen people and I've only got one day off to do the rest of the grocery shopping. It's going to be a bit of a nightmare.' But the older woman's smile suggested that she was rather looking forward to the chaos.

'I do have an idea, though,' she added a moment later.

Max was open to any ideas because he had none of his own. He could even feel an edge of panic hovering—as if he was about to go into a skid that he wouldn't be able to control—like the unfortunate one that had killed his ex-sister-in-law a few weeks ago. Who was going to get injured by this one? Himself or his father? His nieces or nephew? He was about to become the father figure to children who had suffered unimaginable loss of both their parents and their home. Their whole world. Was he about to stumble at the first hurdle of this new journey? No...he couldn't allow that to happen.

'What's your idea?' he asked.

'There's an agency we've used before. London Locums. They're a specialist medical recruitment agency and they might be worth a try even with such short notice and at such a difficult time of the year. I could ring them if you like?'

'But I need a nanny, not a locum doctor.'

Miriam's smile was gentle. 'Don't you think it would be better for those poor children to have family looking after them instead of strangers? Why not get a locum to cover *you*? That way, you could be with the children to help them settle in. They must be so scared by all the changes happening around them.'

Max swallowed hard. He was a bit scared himself,

to be honest. It wasn't that he didn't like children. He had enjoyed being an uncle and welcoming his brother's first two children into the world and he got on very well with the small people who came through the doors of his emergency department. He just hadn't ever planned to have any of his own.

Ever.

The disintegration of his own happiness when he was a child, after losing his mother—the sun of their family universe—had left an indelible stain. He had watched his father grapple with a sadness that meant he had no resources to provide for the emotional needs of two young boys and it had been Max who had tried to help his younger brother. That the sadness had morphed into a lasting depression that his father would never admit to or seek help for had cemented the deeply absorbed knowledge that the fallout of a family breaking apart for whatever reason was simply not worth the risk.

Max Cunningham had finally discovered the delicious balance of his passion for working hard and as brilliantly as possible with playing just as hard outside of work hours and that time almost always included a beautiful woman as a playmate. Max was confident that he had honed his skills in making a woman feel very, very special but only for a limited amount of time, of course. He wasn't ever going to get caught in the trap of having his happiness depend on a family, only to have his world destroyed. If his own childhood memories hadn't been enough, his brother's death last year had more than reinforced his belief that the risk was far too great. He hadn't ever intended to be responsible for the happiness of others either, by trying to create and protect the safety of a family unit or to patch up the fragments of a world that had been irreparably broken.

But, here he was, about to attempt exactly that and the responsibilities about to land on his doorstep were more than daunting. Who knew how traumatised these children already were? The girls might be too young to remember losing their father last year but little Ben was six and maybe he was already trying to wear the mantle of the oldest child and look after his siblings and Max knew how hard that could be. And Miriam was right. The children had been in the care of total strangers since they'd lost their mother and that wasn't acceptable. Max might think his world was being upended but for his nephew and nieces the only world they knew had just vanished for ever.

'And it's *Christmas*,' Miriam added softly, as she got to her feet—as if that settled the matter. 'They're family. And they need you.'

'Emma?'

'Hi, Julie.' Emma Moretti paused beneath the bare branches of trees in London's Hyde Park as she answered her phone, watching a squirrel race up the trunk of the nearest tree. 'I hope you've got some good news for me?'

Julie was the manager of London Locums, the specialist medical recruitment agency that Emma had been employed by for the last few years.

'You're not going to believe it. After telling you there was absolutely nothing on the books for the Christmas period, I just got a call from someone at the Royal in Cheltenham. They're desperate for someone to take over from their emergency department HOD. Seems he's got some family crisis happening until some time in early January.'

'ED? My favourite.' Emma's outward breath was almost a sigh of relief. She was desperate to get out of London for a few days. At least until Christmas was over. There were too many memories here and it felt harder this year, for some reason. Maybe she hadn't got past things as well as she thought she had. Or maybe it was because, at thirty-six, her last birthday had reminded her that the window of opportunity for having the family she'd always dreamt of was beginning to close. Worse, she still wasn't sure she was ready to do something proactive about that. Even after nearly five years, she hadn't ever given serious thought to changing her single status.

'Are you sure, Em? I don't think the Royal really expects us to be able to provide someone at such short notice and you know how crazy emergency departments can get over Christmas. People drink far too much and there's all those weird accidents you hear about, like people falling off the roof because they're trying to change the bulb on Rudolph's nose or something. You could just go on holiday if you wanted to escape. Somewhere nice and warm like the Maldives. Or Australia? Goodness knows you've earned a break and they're talking snow here. Possibly a white Christmas for once.'

Going on holiday alone would be the worst thing to do. It would give her far too much time to think. To remember things that were better left in the past.

'You know me,' she reminded Julie. 'I kind of like crazy.'

'What about Italy, then?' Julie was a good friend as well as her employer. 'When did you last have Christmas with *your* family?'

A long time ago. But not quite long enough, it would seem, because she still wasn't ready for a full-on Italian-style family gathering. Or perhaps it had just become a habit because locums were always in such demand over holiday periods.

'Are you kidding?' Emma tried to keep her tone light. 'My cousin has just had twins. My mother will be crying in the corner because her only child is thirty-six and still single and maybe she'll never get any grandchildren of her own. They'll probably drag in every eligible male in the village and try and arrange a marriage on the spot. You have no idea the kind of pressure that will entail.' She managed a laugh. 'Give me medical chaos any time. Please, I need to be in Cheltenham. My family won't mind. They know I always work over Christmas.'

'Well…if you're sure. It does have accommodation on offer as well. A modern apartment near the hospital. Let me see…a suburb called Montpellier.'

'Sounds French. *Trés chic*.' Emma drew in a deep breath. 'It's perfect, Julie. When do I need to be there?'

'Early tomorrow afternoon by the latest. Someone called Miriam will give you an orientation tour and supply the keys to the apartment. I'll text you the details.'

It was no more than a brisk walk to the compact basement apartment where Emma lived alone. It wouldn't take her long to pack. She'd been with London Locums long enough to know exactly what she needed to take and to be ready to leave the city at a moment's notice if necessary. It had been a huge lifestyle change to leave her secure position as a junior consultant in a paediatric ward, but it had been the perfect choice at the time. There was an adrenaline rush to be found, never knowing what kind of job would be around the next corner. She could be taking over a general practice in a remote area to give a sole GP a proper holiday, doing aeromedical retrievals from some exotic location with a seriously ill or injured person who needed to come home or plugging a gap in a hospital roster like this time. And an emergency department really was her favourite place to work—maybe because it was a bit like her lifestyle. You got to do all sorts of exciting, satisfying things but only for a brief time. Patients got moved on to other departments. She got to move on to other positions and that was the way she liked it.

If you never put down roots or formed deep attachments, there was no danger of having the pain of them getting ripped out, was there? Life was so much easier this way.

A busker, just outside the park gates, was—predictably—singing a Christmas carol. Emma increased her pace as she tried to escape the lyrics of 'Mary's Boy Child' because it never failed to bring tears to her eyes every time. Just those four words—*born on Christmas Day*—could still potentially rip a hole in her heart.

It was five years ago now, though. She would have expected it to be getting easier year by year and it was... except for Christmas. Sometimes it felt as if the whole world was conspiring to remind her in agonising detail of how hard it had been to have coped as well as she had. Especially being here, because the hospital where it had happened—and where she'd worked at the time—was just on the other side of the park.

Thank goodness she could head out of town first thing tomorrow.

Emma couldn't wait. She made a mental note to make sure she had some chains in the back of her SUV. Just in case. A town as big as Cheltenham was highly unlikely to get snowed in but it was surrounded by winding country roads and isolated villages. A white Christmas with all the extra chaos that could bring to an emergency department?

Bring it on...

'She's here, Max. With an apology for being a bit late but she said the traffic on the M40 was diabolical. There'd been a crash.'

'No problem. At least she's here now. Thanks, Miriam. Can you give her a really quick tour of the department to get her up to speed to start her first shift tomorrow morning and then bring her in here? I've got a couple of things I must finish but then I'll be heading off to Upper Barnsley. I'll need to be there when the children arrive.'

'Of course. You'll be wanting to give her the keys and any instructions for your apartment?'

'I think it would be polite to actually show her the apartment myself. It's only a few minutes' walk away, after all. It's not going to hold me up. Oh...' Max lifted an eyebrow. 'What's her name?'

'Emma...something. Sounded Italian but I can't remember. She looks competent, though.' Miriam's mouth twitched. 'I'm sure you'll approve.'

Max cringed just a little at the inference he couldn't miss. Yes, he appreciated good-looking women and there never seemed to be a shortage of contenders to fill the inevitably changing position as his out-of-work-hours companion but there was something in his senior nurse's expression that made him think his reputation might not be something to be proud of. Well, it was irrelevant now, anyway. Even if he had any opportunities to meet someone new in the foreseeable future, he wouldn't be able to take advantage of them. He had other, far more pressing, responsibilities that were due to land on his doorstep in—he swallowed hard as he glanced at his watch—only a hour or two from now.

He turned his attention back to the computer screen in front of him. There were a few last-minute adjustments to make to the rosters to ensure that this department ran as smoothly as possible while he couldn't be here. He needed to give this Emma his personal mobile number as well so he could be on call to give her any advice if she needed it.

An Emma with an Italian-sounding surname was ringing a vague bell in the back of his mind as he pulled up a spreadsheet. It came with an image of a laughing young woman surrounded by children, holding a baby that had his hands tangled in her long ponytail. A quintessential 'earth mother' type, which, of course, had made her an absolute 'no-go' type for Max—no matter how gorgeous those generous curves and dark eyes and that smile had been.

Good grief…that had been ten years ago but the memory was astonishingly clear, now that he had dredged it up. They'd both been junior doctors on a paediatric ward at the same time. And her name was Emma…dammit… what had her surname been?

'Moretti.'

Max's gaze flicked up to the figure standing in the doorway of his office. He'd been totally lost in thought and the fact that the answer to his internal query was being answered in person had just thrown him completely.

'I'm Emma Moretti,' she said, coming further into the small space. 'Miriam said to pop in and see you?'

Was it really the same woman? This Emma Moretti was nothing like the one Max had just been remembering. She was slim and smartly dressed and had short, spiky dark hair like a brunette pixie. She wasn't smiling but her eyes were certainly dark enough. Almost as black as her hair. And she was staring at him with just the same astonished intensity that he knew he was subjecting her to.

'*Max?* No way...' Her lips were curving into a smile now and, suddenly, Max could see the woman he remembered. The life and soul of any party, especially if there were children involved. And that thought led straight to another party he couldn't help but remember. The Christmas function for the staff of that paediatric ward. That sprig of mistletoe he'd held over Emma's head. That kiss... The way they'd both laughed and blamed it on the prosecco because they couldn't have been more wrong for each other.

Emma was still smiling. 'I knew the HOD was a Dr Cunningham, but I never for a moment thought it might be you. I would have imagined you to be living in a place like New York by now. Or Sydney, maybe.'

A large, vibrant city that would be a perfect social playground for someone with a reputation like himself? That cringeworthy moment he'd had earlier came back to bite a little harder. Ten years on and he hadn't changed much, had he?

Unlike Emma.

'And I would never have imagined you working as a locum. I would have imagined you to be completely settled in one place by now. With a husband and half a dozen kids.'

He was genuinely curious about what had happened

in her life but he knew he'd just stepped over a boundary of some kind. He saw the instant the shutters went up.

'Nobody has half a dozen kids these days, Max. How irresponsible would that be, given global resources?'

Max cleared his throat. 'Precisely why I haven't contributed to the population statistics myself.' He shuffled some papers on his desk to cover the slightly awkward atmosphere. 'Did Miriam give you enough of a tour? Are you happy to start your first shift at seven a.m. tomorrow?'

'I'm happy.' Emma's nod was brisk. 'I've had a lot of experience working in unfamiliar surroundings and I can quickly get a feel for how helpful the staff are going to be. You've obviously got a great crowd here and I don't anticipate any problems at all in covering for you. I assume you have a trauma team on call as well? With specialists from other departments?'

'Yes. I can't guarantee there'll be a consultant from every department available on the bank holidays but there should be someone from orthopaedics, general surgery and neurology who'll get here as fast as possible if the alert is activated. We only do that if we know there's major trauma coming in. Otherwise, we assess and call in consults as needed. Same goes for medical or obstetric emergencies.' Max closed down his computer and got to his feet. 'I'll be available by phone at any time. Don't hesitate to call. I can probably come in if there's a real crisis. I'll be just outside of a village that's halfway between Cheltenham and Cirencester, which is only twenty minutes away—unless this forecast for snow is accurate.'

'I'm rather hoping for a white Christmas,' Emma

said. 'Especially seeing as I've got accommodation that's within easy walking distance.'

'Speaking of which…let's go.' Max headed towards Emma to reach for his coat that was hanging behind the door. He caught a faint scent of something clean and crisp as he got closer. Lemons, maybe? Or mandarins…?

'Sorry?' Emma was blinking at him. 'Where are we going?'

'To the apartment.' Max held open the door of his office. 'I thought I'd show you around, seeing as it's mine.'

The HOD of the Royal's emergency department was making his own apartment available for his locum?

And the HOD was Max Cunningham?

Emma was still getting her head around both of these startling pieces of information as she followed him out of the emergency department via the automatic doors that led to the ambulance bay.

It would probably be a swanky penthouse apartment, she decided. Very modern and luxurious and not at all to her taste but perfect for a brief stay. Unless…oh, help… could there be something really tacky like mirrors on the bedroom ceiling?

Everybody had known what Max Cunningham was like back in the day of their junior rotations. Not that that stopped women from joining the queue. And why not? Max was drop-dead gorgeous, totally charming and knew how to make any woman feel special. He'd had a catchphrase, hadn't he?

Oh, yeah… Emma bit back a smile as they turned out from the hospital grounds and waited for a set of traffic lights to change so that they could cross the busy main road. She remembered it now.

We're here for a good time, not a long time...

Playboys had never been remotely Emma's type but she had understood the attraction. Felt it herself, in fact, even though she wouldn't have touched him with a bargepole as far as a relationship went. The man had actually kissed *her* once, at that Christmas party and… and…good grief… How was it possible to remember a moment like that with such astonishing detail after so many years? She could feel her toes trying to curl themselves up inside her shoes so it was a relief to start walking swiftly across the road. She certainly wasn't going to start wondering if the toe-curling was due to embarrassment or the intense desire that kiss had generated. There were decorations overhead, she noticed, trying to distract herself further by looking up. Long strings of icicle lights that would look very pretty at night.

'Five minutes' walk, that's all,' Max was saying. 'And the place should be perfectly clean. My housekeeper went in a few days ago and gave it a thorough going-over and changed the linen and so on. I'll make sure you have her number as well, in case you need anything else.'

'That's great. Thank you very much. I usually end up in a hotel or something when I'm doing a short locum like this.'

'We did think of that, but a quick check told us that there was nothing available. For some reason, Cheltenham seems like a very popular destination for the festive season.'

'No room at the inns, then?' Emma caught Max's sideways glance. 'Quite appropriate, really.'

His smile hadn't changed at all. Or the way the corners of his eyes crinkled to make his appreciation appear completely genuine. Ten years had given him a few grey hairs and deepened those lines a bit but, if anything, they had just made Max even more attractive.

'Here we are…' Max keyed a code into the front door of a very modern building and led the way to an elevator. He pushed a button that wasn't the top floor.

'Not the penthouse?' Emma murmured. 'You surprise me, Max.'

He shook his head. 'Was I really that much of a plonker in those days?'

'Not at all. From what I remember you were a brilliant doctor. You just had a reputation for playing as hard as you worked, I guess.'

'Those days are over.' He didn't sound too happy about that, Emma thought, but he wasn't about to tell her why. 'The penthouse here is very nice, I believe,' he added. 'But it's empty most of the time. The guy who owns it is something high up in a bank and has to travel a lot.'

Emma followed him out of the elevator. She watched as he unlocked the door but then her gaze dropped.

'What's that?'

'What?'

'All that water.'

The carpet outside the door was soaked. As Max lifted his foot, his shoe was dripping. 'Oh, *no*…' He pushed the door open and stepped in. The tiled entrance-way to his apartment shimmered like a small lake. 'Stay there,' he warned Emma. 'This doesn't look good.'

But she followed him in, looking over his shoulder as he checked a bathroom to see whether taps had been left on. There was a bedroom that had water dripping from the bulb in the ceiling light.

'It's coming from upstairs,' Max muttered. 'A burst

pipe, perhaps...' He sighed. 'I've been staying with my father for the last few days or I might have noticed this happening soon enough to prevent this much damage.'

So that was the family crisis? His father being ill? He certainly didn't need this complication on top of other worries. Emma felt very sorry for Max but it was very clear that she wasn't going to be able to stay here. It was the main living room that was the real disaster. Enough water had seeped into the ceiling to make the plaster-work too heavy. Large sections had fallen to cover the couches and a glass-topped coffee table.

To give him credit, Max was very calm as he took control of the situation. 'I'll have to call the building manager,' he said. 'Give me a minute.'

As soon as he'd made the call, he turned back to Emma. 'You can't stay here, obviously,' he said. 'We'll find a hotel nearby—there'll probably be somewhere we overlooked before. I'll pay for it.' He was focused on his phone again. 'Let's just see what's available on one of those comparison sites.'

Emma had taken out her own phone. A minute or two of silence and then they both looked up.

'Not looking good, is it?' Emma said. 'As soon as I put the dates in there's no availability at all.'

'There'll be something.' Max was obviously trying to sound reassuring. 'We might have to look a bit further afield, that's all.' He hesitated, glancing at his watch. 'That could take a bit of time but don't worry, I'm not going to leave you in the lurch. You can come with me for the moment. As I said, the place I'm staying is only twenty minutes away so, even if we can't find you a suitable hotel room tonight, it won't be a difficult com-mute tomorrow morning unless the weather turns nasty.'

'I've got chains,' she told him. 'But...this is your father's house you're talking about, yes?' A hotel room would be preferable. Perhaps Emma should just stay in town and keep trying to find something.

'He'll be just as concerned as I am that my locum is well looked after,' Max said. 'It's a big house and there's more than enough room for visitors. It was probably built to cater for a Victorian couple who had twelve children.' He gestured for Emma to lead the way out of the apartment. 'They weren't so worried about global resources in those days.'

He might be making a joke but a glance at his face suggested to Emma that the hypothetical camel's back might have just been loaded with the last straw.

'I should keep trying to find a hotel,' she said. 'I wouldn't want to intrude. Not if your father is so unwell.'

'Unwell?' Max's eyebrows rose. 'He's as fit as a fiddle.' He looked at his watch again and stifled a groan. 'Come on, you'll have to follow me to Upper Barnsley in your car. We don't have that much time before the children arrive.'

Children?

But hadn't Max said that he hadn't personally contributed to the population statistics? Emma was curious but the look of fierce concentration on Max's face was enough to stop her asking any more questions as they hurried back to the hospital car park. Besides, the mention of children had reminded her of that assumption he'd voiced—that she would have a husband and a tribe of children by now—and there was a sting in that assumption that needed to be dealt with. Back in those days, she had assumed exactly the same thing so it was no wonder he was surprised. She had been more than surprised herself, of course. Having her life derailed like that had been devastating but at least she was well past the toughest time of her life, when working only with children and babies as a specialist paediatrician had proved hard enough to have dimmed the joy and she'd been tempted to change the direction she had chosen for her career. She could cope with children.

As long as she didn't get too close to them...

Life had a habit of upending plans sometimes and it appeared that it was happening again, Emma decided, as she followed Max out of town and into the pretty countryside of the Cotswolds with its narrow roads and tiny villages full of trees and stone-built cottages. Her most recent plans had already gone more than a little awry, with her accommodation proving uninhabitable. The person she was replacing was unexpectedly someone she had once been more than a little attracted to, even though she would never have gone there, and she was now being whisked away to some unknown but large house by this still very attractive man and there were children involved, which didn't make any sense at all. Unless Max had acquired an instant family by marrying someone who already had children? Or this house with far too many bedrooms was being run as some kind of foster home or orphanage?

She hadn't even started her new locum position and they still had several days before Christmas arrived but it seemed like the chaos had already begun. As a few fat flakes of snow drifted gently onto her windscreen, Emma found she was smiling wryly.

Almost grinning a few moments later, in fact.

She had needed a distraction and it would appear that the universe was providing one.

CHAPTER TWO

UPPER BARNSLEY WAS bigger than other villages they had driven through, with its high street full of shops, a village green and a market square with a tall Christmas tree as a centrepiece. Moments later, Emma was following Max's vehicle down a long, tree-lined driveway to stop in front of a house that took her breath away. She was still blinking up at the huge, three-storeyed gabled mansion with imposing chimneys and ivy creeping up its stone walls as Max opened the heavy wooden front door and waited for her to go inside.

'You grew up here?' Somehow it didn't fit with the image of the contemporary 'man about town' she'd met in that London paediatric ward a decade ago. She gazed from one side of the entranceway to the other. There was probably a library in here. And a drawing room like they had in those period dramas on television with dogs lying in front of an open fire big enough to roast an ox. 'This is amazing.'

Max simply nodded. 'It's been in the family for more than a hundred years. Known locally as Cunningham Manor.' He raised his voice. 'Dad? You here?'

A woman who looked to be in her late fifties appeared from a doorway at the far end of the entrance foyer. 'He's in the west wing,' she told Max. 'Oh…who's this?' She was wiping her hands on her apron and beaming as she came towards Emma. 'I'm Maggie—Dr Cunningham's housekeeper. Dr Cunningham senior, that is,' she added.

Max took pity on her. 'The west wing is a private joke. Dad's the GP for Upper Barnsley and the lower level of that side of the house used to be the stables, I believe. It was converted to be a clinic years before I was born.' He turned to the housekeeper. 'This is Emma Moretti,' he told her. 'She's the locum who's taking over from me at the hospital until we get the nanny situation sorted. She also happens to be an old friend of mine. We worked together in a paediatric ward a very long time ago.'

Emma wasn't about to contradict him publicly but calling her a friend was stretching things a little. They had been colleagues and she'd totally respected his abilities as a doctor but she'd never trusted him enough to think of him as a friend. Or maybe she hadn't trusted herself? If they'd got close, she might have given in to that major attraction she'd felt for Max and how embarrassing could that have been? It had only taken one kiss for him to laugh about how she was 'so not his type'. She'd agreed, of course, and laughed along with him. How else would one save face at a time like that? Besides, he'd been right. He was 'so not her type' as well, but it had been a bit of a put-down to find out that the attraction hadn't actually been mutual.

'Oh…wonderful.' Maggie was still smiling. 'You'll need all the expert help you can get with these babies.'

Babies? A chill ran down Emma's spine. Max had said children, not babies.

Children were so much easier to be around than babies.

Especially newborn babies. She could work with them, of course, but preferably in a clinical setting rather than, say, an accident scene. And never in a private home. Even in a medical situation, being present at a birth or close to a tiny baby made the scars on her own heart ache. She might have built barriers to protect herself enough to live with the pain of only ever having a few hours with her own precious baby but she had no desire to deliberately test how strong those protective walls might be.

'I didn't bring Emma here to stand in for the nanny,' Max told Maggie. 'She's supposed to be using my apartment but there's been a small catastrophe with an upstairs flood and she needs to stay here until we can sort that out.'

'It's okay.' Emma found her voice. 'I'm sure I can find somewhere in town. It sounds like you're going to be very busy if…if you're expecting…babies?'

What on earth was going on? she wondered. Was Max sharing custody for stepchildren of a failed marriage? Had he married someone who had already been pregnant with twins, perhaps? Or triplets? The thought of multiple newborn babies made Emma want to head straight out of the door and keep on going. She even looked in that direction, only to find a broad-shouldered older man coming in through the front door, with a small, scruffy white dog at his heels. It was a vision of what Max would look like in about thirty years' time, she realised. Except that this man didn't have the same charming smile. If anything, he was glowering at Emma.

'What's going on? Who's this? A new nanny?' He shut the door, turned and made an irritated sound. 'Pirate, come here.'

But the small, scruffy dog had made a beeline for

Emma, was sitting at her feet and staring up at her with black button eyes. She guessed that he was mostly a West Highland White terrier but it was easy to see where his name had come from because he had a black patch covering one eye and ear. He was very cute. And he was wagging his tail. It was impossible not to bend down and offer him her hand. The small black nose felt cold and damp as it touched her skin.

'Look at that,' Max said. 'That doesn't happen very often. Pirate likes you. And no,' he told his father. 'This is Emma, who's going to be my locum at the Royal. I told you about that plan.'

'I thought she was staying at your place.'

'My place is wrecked. I'll explain later. The kids are due to arrive any minute. Maggie, could I ask you to make up another bedroom for Emma for tonight, at least? It seems that there aren't any hotel rooms to be easily found.'

'No, really... I should go.' Emma actually took a step towards the door. 'If I can't find a hotel room in Cheltenham, I could try Gloucester...?'

'Nonsense.' Maggie's hand was on Emma's elbow. 'We've got ten bedrooms here and I got an extra one ready in case the children wanted their own rooms later but I'm sure they'll want to be together at least for now. Come with me.'

So they were children now? Emma was becoming increasingly confused.

'It's snowing out there,' Max's father said, coming towards her. 'You don't want to be going anywhere if you don't have to. You might get stuck until they come to clear the lanes. I'm James, by the way. James Cunningham. Max seems to have forgotten his manners.'

Max shrugged and offered Emma a crooked smile but there were frown lines on his forehead. And some kind of plea in those dark eyes? The tension in the air here was palpable and Emma suddenly felt trapped but she couldn't run away if someone needed help, could she?

'And you're most welcome to stay,' James continued. Yes, there was a hint of the same kind of smile that Emma remembered his son using to devastating effect. Even a short-lived twinkle in his eyes. 'Pirate is a very good judge of character.' He snapped his fingers at the dog, who instantly went back to his master. 'I'm going to make sure the fire's going properly in the drawing room. Central heating is one thing, but you need to see some flames to feel properly warm when it's snowing.'

Maggie was pulling gently at Emma's arm. 'Come upstairs,' she invited. 'You'll love this room. So much better than a hotel, I promise.'

Perhaps it was best if she stayed for one night, Emma thought. It might only be mid-afternoon but it was already looking a lot darker outside and what if she went hunting for a hotel room and couldn't find one? She would hardly want to start her first shift in an unfamiliar emergency department having slept in her vehicle overnight. Besides, she had to admit she was curious. She wanted to see more of this impressive house. She also couldn't deny that part of her wanted to know what was going on in Max Cunningham's life. It almost felt like they had something in common here, in that their lives weren't turning out how they might have anticipated—or wanted—when they'd last been in each other's company.

The sweep of the wide staircase was dramatic enough to conjure up images of women making a grand entrance in exquisite ball gowns. The first part of the hallway it led to looked down over the entrance foyer. Emma could see Dr Cunningham senior disappearing through a door with his dog by his heels. She could also see Max, who was simply standing still as if he was taking a breath in order to size up an accident scene, perhaps. Or what looked like it might be a complicated resuscitation.

The way he cradled his forehead in his hand a heartbeat later, rubbing both his temples with his thumb and middle finger, added to the impression of a man out of his depth, and it was enough to touch Emma's heart. She knew, better than most, how life had a habit of side-swiping you sometimes and it never hurt to offer kindness.

Sometimes, it could save a life.

'Here you are.' Maggie stopped at one of several doors further down the hallway. 'This one's got its own bathroom so it will be perfect for you, I think.'

Emma followed her into the room. She could actually feel her jaw dropping. A four-poster bed? A massive wardrobe and dressing table that looked like museum pieces, an ornate fireplace with leather armchairs positioned in front of it and a cushioned window seat set into the mullioned window. The floorboards were polished wood but there was a large rug with a Persian design.

'I hope it doesn't smell musty,' Maggie said. 'I've only had a day or two to change linen and try and air things out. Some of these rooms haven't been used since Max and Andy left home and that's a very long time ago, now.'

'Who's Andy?' Emma was still gazing around the room. Her earliest years had been in a small Italian village. Her recent years had been in a cramped one-bedroom flat in central London. She'd only ever been in houses like this when she'd paid an entry fee and stood behind the braided red ropes.

'Max's younger brother.' Maggie had been leading the way to an interior door that must lead to the en-suite bathroom but now she paused. 'He hasn't told you what's going on, has he?'

Curiosity battled with an odd sense of…what was it? A desire to protect Max—or at least his privacy—perhaps?

'It's probably none of my business,' she said quickly.

'Nonsense.' Maggie flapped her hand. 'You're part of it for the time being, anyway, so you may as well know. The children that are arriving here any minute are Andy's children. They're orphans now and Max is their legal guardian.'

Wow… No wonder Max was looking like he was about to face a daunting situation. Everybody had known that he was a diehard bachelor even a decade ago. And while he'd been great with the children on that paediatric ward, he'd confessed more than once that that was because he could hand them back to their parents. Or get a nurse to change a nappy or deal with any tears and tantrums. That he'd never want to have any of his own.

And he'd just lost his brother?

'I'm so sorry,' Emma said. 'I really shouldn't be intruding. Not when the Cunninghams have just lost such a close family member.'

Maggie shook her head. 'Andy died just over a year ago. And his marriage had fallen apart a year or more before that. They did try and work things out, and that must have been when Alice was conceived, but then it turned nasty and lawyers got involved. Simone moved away, broke a court order and took the kids with her and broke Andy's heart at the same time. He died in a car accident not long after that. He'd been drinking and drove straight into a tree.'

'That's tragic...'

'Mmm.' Maggie hesitated for a moment and Emma wondered if there was more to that accident than simply drink-driving but if the housekeeper had been about to voice her own opinion, she obviously changed her mind. 'Even worse, Simone wouldn't let the family have anything more to do with the children after Andy was gone. She was living up in Scotland and Dr Cunningham didn't even hear about her death until after her funeral. Until someone in Social Services had tracked down legal documents that gave Max guardianship.' Maggie was moving again. 'Come and see your bathroom. There should be everything you might need.'

Emma took in the clawfoot iron bath with its brass tapware, separate shower and shelves piled with fluffy towels. 'It's beautiful.'

'It is.' Maggie smiled. 'This was the master suite in the early days when the boys were little ones. Dr Cunningham senior couldn't bear to stay in it after his wife died and then he decided he'd just stay in the Green Room. Oh...is that a car I can hear?' She walked swiftly to the window and peered down. 'It is. I'd better go and help. There was supposed to have been a nanny here already to be with the children but she got sick and that's why you're here. To cover Max at work so that he can stay home to look after them all.'

Unsure of what she should do, Emma followed the housekeeper. Her head was spinning slightly with the tales of tragedy this family had experienced. What had happened to Max's mother? she wondered. And how old

had Max and his brother been when she died? She was
also trying to do a bit of maths in her head. If Andy had
died over a year ago and his ex-wife had already been
pregnant, then this baby Alice had to be at least several
months old now. Not a newborn.

She could cope with that. For one night, it shouldn't
be any problem at all, even if this wasn't exactly the
kind of clinical situation that was part of her protective walls. As for Max—she had no idea how he was
about to cope. He had years and years ahead of him as
a guardian. Remembering the way he'd been cradling
his head in his hands when he thought he was not being
observed, Emma couldn't believe that he'd magically
changed his attitude to children in the last ten years and
would be quite happy to be sharing his life with them
from now on.

'Where are they?' Maggie opened the front door but
there was no sign of a car. 'Oh, no…they must have gone
through to the clinic parking.'

'There's another car.' Max was standing beside her.

James Cunningham had come into the entrance foyer
to see what was going on but Emma hung back, near the
staircase, wondering if she should, in fact, go back upstairs for a while. How terrifying would it be for small
children to arrive and be faced with so many strangers?
Even if they'd met these members of their extended family it had apparently been more than a year ago and they
would still be traumatised by the loss of their mother.

Through the wide gap of the open front door, she
could see a large people-carrier type van that had parked
a little way away from the entrance to the house and
someone was getting out of the driver's seat. Max walked
out into the snow that was still falling to greet the new-

comer. But someone else was running towards the front door of the house from the opposite direction. A middle-aged woman who was looking very anxious.

'Dr Cunningham? Is the clinic closed already?'

'Surgery finished an hour ago, Jenny.' But James was frowning. 'What's wrong?'

'It's Terry. He's got terrible chest pain and his spray isn't helping. He wouldn't let me call an ambulance. It was all I could do to persuade him to come and see you and he only did that because you're right next door.'

Behind Jenny, Emma could see that children were being helped out of the van. A boy who might be about six or seven. A smaller girl. The driver was opening the back hatch which looked to be full of luggage and items like a pram and cot. Max was unclipping a baby seat. Emma's mouth went a little dry. Maybe this was going to be harder to cope with than she'd thought.

James looked towards where his grandchildren were being ushered towards him. He turned his head to look in the other direction, presumably to the 'west wing' that housed his general practice clinic. His duty lay in both directions, with the professional one clearly more urgent than the personal.

And, suddenly, Emma knew exactly how she could help everyone here, including herself. Years of honing her skills to be able to work to the best of her ability in unfamiliar places made it automatic to take charge but, as a bonus, it felt as if her protective walls were suddenly strengthening themselves around her and keeping her in her safe space. She walked towards the anxious woman.

'I'm Dr Moretti,' she told her. 'I can help you.'

* * *

Only a couple of minutes later, Emma was opening the door to the clinic with one of the keys on the ring James had given her.

'There's a twelve-lead ECG machine in the treatment room,' he'd told her. 'If it looks like an infarct, call an ambulance and then let me know.'

'I can handle it,' Emma had promised.

Jenny and her husband, Terry, followed her into what was clearly a waiting room.

'How's the pain level, Terry? On a scale of zero to ten, with zero being no pain at all and ten being the worst you could imagine?'

'Seven,' Terry told her. 'It's like a knife in my chest. It's hard to breathe, even.'

'Let's get you lying down so I can have a good look at you.' Emma walked ahead, opening one door and then another. There was a small kitchen, a storeroom, a consulting room and…yes…what looked like a treatment room, well set up for minor procedures or more extensive assessments. She recognised the machine for taking a twelve-lead ECG, spotted an oxygen cylinder in the corner of the room and was relieved to see a defibrillator on another trolley. If Terry was having a heart attack and in any danger of an imminent cardiac arrest she had the means to deal with it. She also knew that one of the keys on the ring she was holding was to open a drug cabinet that James had told her was well stocked.

On first impressions, Terry didn't look like a man who was in the middle of having a heart attack. His colour was good, he wasn't sweating and he seemed to be clutching the side of his chest rather than a more clas-

sic sign of pressing his hand to the centre. He'd also told
her that he wasn't feeling sick in any way but Emma
wasn't about to make assumptions. She helped her patient climb onto the bed and lifted the back so he wasn't
lying completely flat.

'Let's get that coat and jumper off and unbutton your
shirt, Terry.' Emma opened the drawer on the ECG trolley and took out electrodes. 'So you've been getting angina for a while?'

'Just a bit. And only when I'm doing too much.'

'He's taken up jogging,' his wife told Emma. 'I told
him he's going to kill himself but he's determined to
lose the weight.'

'And you were jogging when the chest pain came on?'

'No…' Terry lifted his arm out of the way as Emma
stuck the final electrodes on the left side of his chest.
'I was getting the damned turkey out of the freezer in
the barn.'

'It was far too big to go in the freezer in the house.'
Jenny nodded. 'And it takes days and days to thaw.'

'It was like carrying a giant, slippery rock,' Terry
complained. 'And then I started to drop it and almost
tripped over something at the same time and it went
flying.' He gave a huff of something like laughter that
turned into a groan. 'So to speak… Anyway, it was
when I bent down and picked the turkey up that the
pain came on. By the time I got it into the laundry tub,
I could hardly stand up.'

'Does anything make it worse?' Emma asked, still
smiling at Terry's attempt at humour. 'Like taking a
deep breath?'

Terry tried to breathe in and groaned. 'Yep…that
really hurts.'

'And you used your angina spray?'

'Didn't do a thing.'

'Okay.' Emma was becoming more confident that she wasn't dealing with a critical cardiac event. 'Keep really still for me for a few seconds, Terry. I'm going to do the ECG.'

With the sheet of graph paper in her hand a short time later, Emma smiled at the anxious couple in front of her.

'Good news,' she told them. 'This all looks absolutely normal. There's no sign of your pain being due to angina and certainly no indication that you're having a heart attack.'

'Oh...' Jenny started to cry. 'I was *so* worried.'

'What is it, then?' Terry asked.

Emma handed Jenny the box of tissues. 'I suspect you pulled a muscle between your ribs while you were wrestling with that frozen turkey,' she told him. She put her hand on the left side of his chest. 'Tell me if this hurts...'

Jenny stayed by the head of the bed, watched the thorough examination her husband was receiving and listened to the advice about cold and heat packs and using anti-inflammatory medication.

'Are you sure it's not a heart attack?' she asked.

'Quite sure.' Emma smiled. 'But you did the right thing in getting it checked out. I'm going to take your blood pressure while you're here too, Terry.'

'Imagine if it *had* been a heart attack.' Jenny reached for another tissue. 'Right before Christmas. I know it's terrible at any time of year but there's something about Christmas, isn't there?'

'Mmm...' Emma stuck the earpieces of a stethoscope into place as a hint for Jenny to stop talking. She didn't need a reminder of how much worse it was to have a tragedy at Christmas time. She placed the disc of the stethoscope over the artery in Terry's elbow as she pumped up the blood pressure cuff.

Jenny hadn't taken the hint. 'It's like the poor Cunninghams. Ruined Christmas forever for those poor boys. They used to call it "the Cunninghams' Christmas Curse" in these parts.'

Emma knew she shouldn't encourage gossip but it wasn't as if she'd asked a question aloud. Her startled glance had been enough to prompt Jenny to continue.

'Their poor mother,' she said sadly. 'Fought off the cancer for such a long time and all she wanted was one last Christmas with her little boys but they didn't even get the decorations up.' She lowered her voice. 'And they've never been put up again, from what I heard. Not in that house…'

Emma let the pressure out of the cuff slowly. Concentrating on the figures as she heard a pulse begin and then disappear again didn't stop part of her brain absorbing the information she'd just been given. What a sad house this must have been for Max—especially that first Christmas without his mother.

'Your blood pressure is on the high end of normal,' she told Terry. 'Are you on any medication for that?'

'Yes. Dr Cunningham looks after me well, don't you worry about that. Can I get dressed again now?'

'And then there was last year.' Jenny handed her husband his jumper as he finished buttoning up his shirt. 'Losing poor Andy like that. It shouldn't have happened at all, but to have it happen in December. Another Christmas funeral…' She clicked her tongue. 'And now…those children… What sort of Christmas is this going to be for those poor wee mites?'

Terry's head popped out of the jumper's neck. 'That's enough, Jen,' he said quietly. 'I'm sure Dr Moretti isn't interested in hearing all this gossip.'

'It's not gossip,' Jenny said defensively. 'We care about each other in Upper Barnsley, that's all. Especially our closest neighbours.' She smiled at Emma. 'Are you here to help Dr Cunningham, then? It's about time he had another doctor to help him in this clinic. Young Max is brilliant but he's always been one for an exciting life. He doesn't want to leave that big emergency department at the hospital.'

'I'm actually here to help at the hospital,' Emma told them. 'But, right now, I'm going to go and show Dr Cunningham your ECG, Terry, and let him know that you're okay.' She held the door open for the couple. 'Have you got plenty of anti-inflammatories at home?'

'Oh, yes.' Jenny nodded. 'And don't go bothering Dr Cunningham with my Terry's problems right now. I suspect he's got enough of his own...'

'You need to follow the directions on the tin for how many scoops. Level scoops, like this...' Maggie scooped the formula and showed Max how to level it off with the back of a knife. 'Put it into the bottle of warm water. Attach the nipple and ring and cap like this...and then shake it.'

Maybe baby Alice could smell the milk being prepared and she was sick of waiting. Or maybe she didn't like the unfamiliar male arms that were holding her right now. Whatever the reason, her unhappy whimpers were steadily increasing into shrieks that were pulling the tense knots in Max's gut tighter by the second.

'Are you sure you can't stay, Maggie?'

'I'm sorry, Max, but it's impossible. I've got my daughter, Ruth, arriving and she's nearly eight months pregnant and on her own. She'll be exhausted after that long drive up from Cornwall and I haven't had proper time with her since that bastard of a boyfriend walked out on her a few weeks ago. We've got a lot of talking to do about how she's going to cope.' Maggie took the cap off the bottle and upended it. 'Shake a few drops onto your wrist, like this. If it's the right temperature it won't feel either hot or cold. There…that's perfect.' She held the bottle out to Max. 'Try that. She's probably eating solids now as well and there's plenty of baby food in with all that other shopping that's in the pantry but she'll be wanting her milk for comfort right now, I expect.'

He took the bottle and offered the teat to the baby. Alice turned her head away and arched into his arm as if she was trying to escape.

'Take her into the drawing room with the others,' Maggie suggested. 'This is all new and strange for her too, and it might help if you're sitting in a comfy chair with her brother and sister nearby.'

Max walked out of the kitchen and into an entrance-way that looked like it had exploded into a collection point for a children's charity over the last thirty minutes or so. A portable cot had a few stuffed toys and books in it. There were car seats and a pram and even a high chair, along with boxes of baby supplies like nappies and formula and suitcases that he'd been told were full of clothing. The social worker who had delivered the children and their belongings had been apologetic but in a hurry to get away before the snow started settling on the country roads and Maggie, who'd done far more than anything her part-time position with the Cunninghams had ever expected of her, was obviously worried about leaving the men to cope but also anxious to get back to her own family.

'You go, Maggie,' Max told her. 'I've got this.'

The older woman gave him a searching look. 'Are you sure?' she asked quietly. 'I don't want to leave you in the lurch. Ruth would understand if...'

Max shook his head. 'These children are my responsibility,' he said. 'Between us, Dad and I will figure it out.' He joggled the baby in his arms and, for a merciful few seconds, the howling seemed to lessen.

'You've got that lovely Emma to help, for tonight at least.' Maggie was heading for the coat rack. 'If you're sure, then... I'll come back as soon as I can in the morning if the roads are clear enough.'

As she opened the door, Max could see a car disappearing down the driveway. Emma had spent a good deal of time assessing that unexpected patient who had turned up but she hadn't summoned an ambulance or come to find his father so he had assumed things were under control. Some things, anyway. Baby Alice was crying again as he went into the drawing room.

His father was sitting in his usual chair by the fire but Pirate had disappeared beneath the chair, which was highly unusual. On the sofa next to the chair were the two older children, Ben and Matilda. They were both sitting silently, side by side, holding hands. Six-year-old Ben was clutching a very small artificial Christmas tree in his other hand that was devoid of any decorations. Four-year-old Matilda had a toy rabbit with long legs and rather chewed-looking ears clamped under her arm. They both looked accusingly at their uncle when he came in carrying their miserable baby sister.

Max sat in the matching leather wing chair on the other side of the sofa, settled Alice into the crook of his elbow and tried to get her to accept her bottle again. Her renewed cries were so loud he didn't hear the door opening. He didn't notice that every other head in the room had turned to see who was coming in or that Pirate had wriggled forward enough to peer out from under the chair.

What he did become aware of was that fresh lemony scent he'd noticed when Emma had come into his office in what was beginning to feel like a previous lifetime. And when he looked up, it felt like the depth of understanding in Emma's eyes told him that she knew exactly how far out of his depth he currently was. That, no matter how determined he was to do the right thing for his nieces and nephew, it felt like he was drowning. But there was something else in her eyes that looked as though she was tapping into something much deeper. Darker.

Fear…

But why would Emma Moretti, of all people, feel afraid when faced with a miserable, hungry infant? She'd been the first to offer cuddles or bottles to their small patients in that paediatric ward, the first in line to be present at a birth or do the newborn checks on those slippery, squiggly little bundles that Max had found quite alarming at the time. If anything, he would have expected her to scoop Alice out of his arms and rescue the situation like some sort of Christmas angel, albeit with dark eyes and hair and olive skin instead of peaches and cream and blue eyes and golden hair.

But she was just staring at him and…yes…he was sure he could see fear in those astonishingly dark eyes.

What on earth had happened, he wondered, to have changed her like this?

The curiosity was fleeting, however, because despite Alice's cries still increasing in volume, he could hear the landline of the house ringing from the hallway. His father seemed oblivious, slumped in his chair as if he had no idea quite how to deal with what was going on around him. Emma had clearly heard the sound of the telephone and the way she raised her eyebrows was an offer to go and answer the call but Max acted without really thinking. He could handle a phone call far better than what he was trying to cope with right now.

He walked towards Emma and shoved Alice at her, knowing that she would instinctively hold out her arms to take the baby. Then he passed her the bottle of milk, turned away and walked out of the room.

CHAPTER THREE

EMMA WATCHED IN horror as Max walked out of the room and left her—literally—holding the baby.

And maybe Alice was significantly older and heavier than a newborn but, for a heartbeat, Emma simply froze because this baby wasn't sick and she wasn't standing here in the capacity of a doctor. This baby needed feeding and she had just been forced into the position of being a surrogate mother—something she wouldn't have volunteered for in a million years.

Turning away from watching Max leave, Emma found herself looking at the two small children who were sitting on the couch and staring at her. They both looked scared. That something terrible was happening with their baby sister, perhaps?

'It's okay,' Emma heard herself saying calmly. 'I think she's just hungry.'

She could do something about that, she realised, and that was the only thing she needed to think about right now. Anything else, including how this was making her feel, would simply have to wait but, as she moved to sit down, it seemed that the shock of having the baby shoved into her arms was receding enough to make it bearable. She would certainly not have volunteered to take the baby and feed it but, now that it was happening, Emma found that it hadn't smashed through her walls the way she might have feared that it would. This was someone else's baby, not her own. A healthy baby that just needed to be fed. Surely she could cope with this?

She chose to sit on the couch beside the other children, not wanting to take over the chair Max had been using. Or maybe she thought it might comfort the infant in her arms to be near her brother and sister. She settled Alice into the crook of her arm and offered her the nipple of the bottle, sliding it into her mouth that was opening for a new wail. Surprised eyes stared up at her and then, mercifully, that little mouth closed over the teat and Alice began sucking vigorously.

In the sudden silence that fell, Emma was aware that the older children were still watching. Max's father had turned to peer at her from behind the wing of his chair and even the dog had wriggled forwards far enough to see what was happening beyond the safety of being beneath his master's chair. She could hear the fire behind its screen, crackling softly in this new silence, and then she could hear Max coming back into the room. Or maybe she could feel the change in the atmosphere as he entered—that kind of electricity that charismatic people radiated.

'That was the builder,' he said. 'They've fixed the leak in the apartment above mine but it's going to be a big job to get things fixed and cleaned up. It certainly won't be happening before Christmas.'

James Cunningham grunted. 'Can't say I'm surprised. It's hard enough to get tradesmen in a hurry at the best of times.'

Max sat down in the other wing chair, his gaze fixed

on Alice. 'You always did make it look easy,' he murmured. 'You're just a natural, aren't you, Emma?'

Emma said nothing. She couldn't say anything. Not with that damned lump that had just formed in her throat. Breathe, she told herself. You only need to breathe.

The silence returned and then Max sounded like he was making an effort to break it.

'Is that your special Christmas tree, Ben?'

Emma glanced sideways to see Ben nod solemnly. 'You've got to have a Christmas tree,' he told his uncle. 'It's a rule.'

'Oh?'

Emma could understand the note in Max's voice— as if he was wondering what other 'rules' Ben might be holding as sacrosanct.

Ben nodded again. 'That's how Father Christmas knows where to leave the presents. It should go near the chimney.'

Emma lifted her gaze to look around the huge room they were in. She wondered what this little boy might think of those paintings in their ornate frames, the ornaments on sideboards and the baby grand piano in the corner. Was he used to this kind of house or was it making this an even more frightening experience for him?

But Ben was sounding worried rather than frightened when he spoke again.

'Where's *your* Christmas tree, Grandpa?'

This time, the silence in the room was filled with a tension that made a knot start to form in Emma's stomach. There was level upon level of misery here that she could feel as if it was her own. Some of it *was* her own but she had learned long ago how to shut that away and it was actually quite empowering to find she could hold and feed baby Alice without falling apart in any visible manner. Looking down, she met the fixed gaze of those dark baby eyes on her own and could be confident that all was well in this tiny human's life for the moment, at least, as she sucked down the rest of her milk. It wasn't the case for anyone else in this room, was it?

Emma looked at the children beside her on the couch. The little boy was still staring at his grandfather, waiting for an answer to his question about the missing Christmas tree. The little girl seemed to sense Emma's gaze and returned it with such a solemn one of her own that, if her arms weren't full of baby Alice and her bottle, she would have instinctively wanted to gather this child to her as closely as she could to give her a big hug. James was stroking an imaginary beard as if it might help him find an answer and Max...

Well, Max was looking at *her*.

As if he knew that she knew why Christmas hadn't been celebrated in this house for probably decades and why a simple child's question was creating such tension. As if he had no idea how to defuse it and as if he was trusting her to help in the same way that she had managed to conquer the difficulty he had faced in getting the baby fed.

Just for a heartbeat, Emma could see something she was quite sure she'd never seen before in Max Cunningham's eyes. Bewilderment, almost. The look of someone who'd lost something very important and had absolutely no idea where to start looking for it. There was something sad in that gaze as well and that made her realise he must know exactly how his nephew must be feeling right now and that could be what was making it so hard for him to find the right thing to say. A tragic history had repeated itself and a small boy had lost his mum just before Christmas.

The squeeze on Emma's heart was so tight it was painful. Painful enough to set off alarm bells that suggested a potential breach in any protective walls that needed maintaining but she had to ignore that for the moment. She was an adult and she had had plenty of time to develop coping mechanisms she could tap into a bit later. Doing something to try and make these children look and sound a little less sad was far more urgent.

'Sometimes,' she told Ben, quietly, 'things happen that can get in the way of remembering rules. I'm sure your Uncle Max or your Grandpa will know where to find a Christmas tree.'

James leaned forward to pick up a poker and prod the fire, making a grumbling sound that could have been disapproving but Max was nodding as if this was, indeed, the solution.

'A real one,' he said. 'We can go and look in the woods tomorrow, Ben. You can choose a branch and I'll cut it off. Or, if we can't find one, we can drive into town and buy one.'

'How old are you, Ben?' Emma asked.

'Six.'

'That's old enough to make decorations for the tree, then. Like silver stars. I can show you how to do that.' She offered a smile. 'My name's Emma.'

The little girl was wriggling closer. 'I'm four,' she whispered, 'and I like stars…'

'You can help too, sweetheart,' Emma promised. She just had to hope there would be a supply of cardboard and silver foil somewhere in the house.

'That's Matilda,' Max said. 'But she likes to be called Tilly.' He was smiling at Emma.

And it was such a genuine smile... Nothing like the charm-loaded curl of his lips with that mischievous edge that had always won him so much attention from women. This time, that automatic hint of flirting that Emma had remembered so clearly was completely absent and it changed his face. It made him look a little older. Softer—as if he was perfectly capable of providing the care and commitment these children were going to need so badly even if he used to say it was the last thing he ever wanted to do.

Alice had finished her bottle and felt sleepy and relaxed. Emma shifted her to an upright position and began to rub her back. Seconds later, the loud burp broke both the new silence and quite a lot of the tension in the room.

'I'm hungry,' Ben said.

Emma caught the slightly panicked glance that was exchanged between the two Cunningham men.

'Maggie's left a pie in the oven,' Max told his father. 'And chips.'

'I like chips.' Ben slid off the couch. He stood there, waiting for one of the grown-ups to move as well.

But, for a long moment, nobody did and Emma could understand why. This was it, wasn't it? The first step into a life that was never going to be the same again for either of these men and it was huge and daunting and they'd been thrown into the deep end. None of it was Emma's responsibility, of course, but the people who were going to suffer if it turned into a disaster were only children and these children had suffered enough, hadn't they?

It seemed that Max was thinking the same thing because they both got to their feet in the same moment.

He stepped towards Emma and took the sleeping baby from her arms.

'It's okay,' he said. 'I can manage.'

'I'm here,' Emma reminded him gently. 'I may as well help you manage for tonight, yes?'

There was always something about a man holding a baby that tugged at the heartstrings. But there was something else about this particular man holding a baby that actually brought a lump to Emma's throat. This had to be his worst nightmare, inheriting a ready-made family including a baby, but he was stepping up to the challenge and determined to do his best and that was courageous and kind and…it tugged at her heart so hard she couldn't look away from his eyes.

She hadn't remembered them being quite such a dark blue.

Or quite so…intense.

It almost felt as if he was seeing her…*really* seeing her…for the first time ever.

Man…

Those eyes… So dark they looked bottomless. You could fall into eyes like that and get totally lost. And, just for a heartbeat, that was exactly what Max wanted to do. The rollercoaster of emotions he was currently riding was proving even more overwhelming than he'd feared it would be.

His heart had gone out to his nephew and nieces the moment he'd seen them but he was little more than a stranger to them and, oddly, that hurt. There was so much stuff that had come with the children and he wouldn't have even known how to make up a bottle if Maggie hadn't helped. He might have failed in feeding

Alice if he hadn't forced Emma to help so he could add a sense of failure into the mix. He was worried about how his father was coping, especially after that question about the Christmas tree. They hadn't put a tree up in this house since his mother had died, leaving a huge pine tree undecorated and a shattered family that barely noticed the showers of dead needles that came weeks later.

On top of that, there were feelings of heartbreak for these children. Part of him just wanted to gather them all into his arms and somehow let them know that he was going to protect them for ever, but he could sense their shyness and knew he would make things worse if he tried to force closeness. He felt gratitude to Maggie for all her extra work and, currently, he was just so, so glad that Emma was here in the house. Trying to convince her that he was up to this task was giving him a lot more courage than he might have otherwise found in the face of such a daunting challenge.

There was also the way she'd been looking at him after Ben had asked about where the Christmas tree was. It had made him think that she knew the answer to that innocent question, which was not unlikely given that she'd spent time with Terry and Jenny. Jenny wasn't a gossip by any means but she was one of the villagers who all knew the Cunninghams' history and she was a woman who loved to chat. Max didn't mind if Emma did know because there was also something in that look that gave him the impression that she understood how much it might hurt and, in turn, that was giving him the oddest feeling of connection. Something that was disconcerting because he'd never associated a feeling like that with any woman. It had to be just another side effect of this strange situation. It was also something that was irrelevant because the children were the only people that mattered right now.

'What's first?' he asked. 'Shall I feed the children?'

'How 'bout you and your dad sort some of their things out? Find things like pyjamas and toothbrushes? You could put Alice in her pram for the moment while she's asleep. Show me where the kitchen is and I'll sort out the pie.'

'And chips.' The small voice came from right beside Max's leg and he looked down to find Ben standing close by. 'And sauce. Red sauce.'

'Is that a rule?' Max asked. 'Red sauce for chips?'

Ben nodded. He was holding out his hand towards Matilda. 'Come on, Tilly,' he said. 'It's time for tea.'

'It is,' Emma said, as Matilda slid off the couch. 'And after that it will be bath time and…what happens after bath time?'

'Storytime,' Ben said. 'And…and then…'

His small mouth wobbled as it turned down at the corners. It was painfully obvious that the prospect of bedtime in this new, scary house was too much even for a very brave child who was doing his best to look after his younger sister himself. The squeeze in Max's chest was so sharp it made the back of his eyes prickle. He bent down so that he could say something quietly, just for Ben.

'It's going to be okay,' he whispered. 'I promise.'

Ben's eyes were a dark blue. Like his father's had been. Like all the Cunningham men, for that matter. They were also far too serious for a six-year-old boy.

'It's a new rule,' Max added gravely. 'And I try very hard to never break rules.'

* * *

Having so much to do to start getting the children settled into what was going to be their new home was helpful for the next few hours. Having Emma there to answer the questions James and Max kept coming up with was also very helpful.

'Should we put Alice's cot in the same room as Tilly and Ben?'

'It might be better to put it in your room to start with. That way, if she wakes up, she won't wake up the others.'

'But…what will I do with her if she does wake up?'

Emma's smile was kind enough not to make Max feel inadequate in any way. 'Give her a bottle of milk. Change her nappy. Cuddle her.'

Ben and Matilda ate enough of their dinner for Emma to be looking pleased when Max went to tell her that he had unpacked the suitcases to find pyjamas.

'Shall we go up those big stairs?' She made it sound like an adventure. 'I know where there's a bath that's got feet.'

Ben shook his head. 'A bath doesn't have feet,' he told Emma. 'It can't walk.'

'No. This one just stands there but it really does have feet. Like a lion's paws. Do you want to see?'

Max watched her go up the stairs with a child on each side of her, holding her hands. Ben still had the little Christmas tree in his other hand, he noticed. And Tilly was holding her rabbit by one foot so that its head, with those chewed ears, was bumping on every tread. James was coming down as they reached the halfway curve.

'Have you got hot-water bottles?' Emma asked him. 'It would be good to put them in Ben's and Tilly's beds.

And put some of their toys there too, so it'll feel more like home.'

The men didn't get the distribution of stuffed toys quite right but it was easy enough to fix as the children climbed into the twin beds that were side by side in one of the smallest bedrooms. It was James who agreed to read a bedtime story to his grandchildren while Pirate lay outside the bedroom door. Max was learning how to bath Alice and get her ready for bed. At six months old she was nothing like as fragile as a newborn, of course, but she still felt very small in Max's hands and it was fiddly enough to get her into her nappy and her stretchy sleepsuit to make him break out in a bit of a sweat.

'So you've put her cot in your room?' Emma asked.

'Well…the room I use when I'm staying, yes. It might be a good one for the nanny to use when she gets here.'

'Have you plugged in the baby monitor?'

'Yes. And, if I leave the door open, I should be able to hear if Ben or Tilly wakes up too. You don't think they'll sleepwalk or anything, do you? What would I do if they did?'

'If they do get up, they'll just be looking for comfort,' Emma told him. 'Cuddles. You could stay with them until they go back to sleep. Or let them share your bed.'

There was a hint of mischief in Emma's eyes as she made that suggestion. As if she knew perfectly well that sharing a bed in order to comfort small children was a totally alien concept for Max. As if she was trying to lighten the atmosphere a little too, to defuse some of the tension of the evening. The idea that Emma might be at all concerned for his own wellbeing did make him feel rather a lot better, in fact.

'Are you hungry?' she asked. 'There's plenty of pie and chips left.'

'And red sauce?'

The smile he received from Emma felt like a reward for what seemed like a major achievement in caring for the children for the first time. Glancing at his watch, Max was astonished at how much time had gone by. 'It's late,' he said. 'No wonder I'm starving.'

'Let's see if we can get Alice settled properly. Your dad should be back from taking Pirate for a walk by then and we can all have something to eat.'

James came back with the news that, while the snow had settled in places, it seemed to have stopped and the roads were still clear enough to be safe for Emma to drive back into Cheltenham in the morning.

'And they're very good about getting the snow ploughs out on our road first,' he told her as they ate dinner together at the old table in the huge kitchen. 'One of the perks of being the only local doctor.'

'Do you do nights as well?' Emma asked.

It was Max who shook his head. 'Theoretically, that's covered by an afterhours service from town,' he told her. 'In reality, though, Dad often gets called.'

'I don't mind,' James said. 'I've known these families for a long time. They trust me. Thanks for taking care of Terry today, Emma. Jenny's still overanxious about his angina.'

'It was a pleasure.' Emma sounded as though she meant it.

James stood up to take his plate to the sink. 'Might turn in,' he said. 'It's been a big day.' He snapped his fingers and Pirate jumped out of his basket near the Aga. 'Can you look after the fire, Max?'

'Of course. Sleep well, Dad.'

The huff of sound was doubtful and the words were an under-the-breath mutter as James left the room. 'Let's hope we all get some sleep.'

Emma stacked the dishes into the dishwasher but Max wouldn't let her do anything else in the kitchen.

'Maggie will be back in the morning. Being used as a housekeeper or a nanny is not part of your locum contract, you know.'

Emma shrugged. 'They say that variety is the spice of life. To tell you the truth, I've never been in a house like this before and it's amazing.' Which it was. Every room she had seen in this old house was beautiful but her favourite so far had to be the kitchen, with its old range and the dresser with the antique china and an ancient scrubbed table that reminded her of outside terraces in Italy because it made her think of generations of extended family gathering to eat together. The time had flown, as well. They'd been so busy with dinner and baths and getting everybody settled into bed that Emma hadn't had time to worry about how it could potentially be messing with her head and, in fact, now that she did have the time to think about it, she was confident that she could deal with it.

'The children really haven't been much trouble, have they?' she said aloud. 'And the way Ben tries so hard to help look after Tilly is just gorgeous.'

'Mmm...'

The tone in that sound gave Emma's heart a squeeze as she pushed the door of the dishwasher closed. It was a note of trepidation. Fear, almost.

She caught his gaze. 'It's going to be okay, Max,' she

said softly. 'You'll work things out. I know it feels huge and scary at the moment but just take it a day at a time. An hour at a time, if you need to.'

'Is that your strategy for when you find yourself in totally unfamiliar surroundings in your locum work?'

Emma smiled. 'Sometimes I'm taking it a second at a time. Oh…did you want some dessert? Ice cream, like the kids had, maybe?'

Max made another huff of sound. 'I think I need something a bit stronger than ice cream. Do you fancy a small whisky?'

Emma wrinkled her nose. 'I don't do whisky. A glass of wine would be nice, though. White, if you have any.'

'There's usually something in the fridge. Or there's rather a large wine cellar downstairs and it's cold enough at this time of year to be perfectly drinkable.'

The thought of being in a house that had a large wine cellar was as surreal as every other surprise this day had thrown at her. 'Just a small glass,' she warned. 'I've got a very early start tomorrow. I'll need to leave at least an hour to get into Cheltenham in case there's more snow in the night. More, if I need to put the chains on my tyres. And my shift starts at seven a.m., yes?'

'You're onto it.' Max was heading towards a large fridge. 'You sound like you could cope with anything, in fact.'

'It's part of what I like about locum work. You never quite know what's round the next corner. I've been out to remote islands off Scotland in a boat. I did a stint with an air rescue service in Canada once too, and our agency specialises in insurance company work when an injured or ill traveller needs to get brought back home. I went out to an oil rig in a helicopter once.'

'Sounds exciting.'

'I love it. But it can be daunting as well. That's how I know that sometimes you need to focus on just the next step in front of you and block out the big picture.'

'I think I'd rather be on the way out to an oil rig than wondering what I'm going to do with unhappy children in the middle of the night.'

Emma took the glass of wine Max had poured for her. Her smile was one of both appreciation and, hopefully, some reassurance. The softening of his features and that hint of a smile told her that it seemed to have helped.

'Come in by the fire for a minute. I need to make that safe for the night and the whisky's in there too.'

And maybe he needed a bit more reassurance? Emma could provide that. For the sake of Max and his father. And those beautiful children. She'd been perfectly genuine when she'd told Max that the children hadn't been any trouble to look after and she was quite hopeful that she wasn't going to be kept awake tonight by ghosts from the past. Even when she had been helping Max bathe and dress the baby she had been able to keep that door in her own heart firmly closed. These children were like patients. Helping them was just an unexpected—and temporary—twist in her professional life.

It was no great hardship to take a few minutes to sit and sip an excellent wine in front of the fireplace, either. Despite the size of this impressive room, the flames created a flickering light and warmth that made the area directly in front of it seem homely. Almost intimate.

'So how long have you been working as a locum?' Max asked when they had chosen to sit at either end of the big couch rather than use the wing chairs.

'A bit over four years, now.' She had been offered bereavement leave but Emma had found she needed to get back to the job she loved so much, even though she'd been conscious of how hard it was going to be to work amongst young children and babies for a while. She'd learned to cope faster than she'd expected, however. She'd built those walls and kept going but some of the joy had gone and, as the months wore on, she'd known that if she wanted to move forward with her life and re-claim that joy, she needed to make some big changes. Hearing about someone's exciting career as a locum had happened at just the right time.

'If I'd ever thought about it, I would have said you'd be a consultant paediatrician by now.'

Emma tilted her head but didn't say anything. She could have agreed with him and said that was exactly what she'd been planning on being but, if she told him that, she'd have to tell him why it hadn't happened and she didn't want to go there. It was easier to focus on what else he'd just said that implied he'd never given her another thought after the time they'd worked together.

It was inevitable that that took her mind back to their kiss. The one *she'd* never forgotten…

Max broke the silence. 'I guess none of us know what twists and turns life has in store for us. We just know that they're going to happen—usually at what seems to be the worst possible time.'

'Mmm.' Emma could certainly agree with that. For a long moment, they both sipped their drinks and the si-lence was companionable. She knew she might be tak-ing a risk that could destroy this pleasant ambience but Emma was curious. There was so much about Max that she'd never known. Would never have guessed.

'How old were you when your mum died, Max?' she asked gently.

His glance was swift. Intense. 'So Jenny did tell you? Or was it Maggie?'

'They both told me a little. Not much. Maggie told me about your brother. Jenny said something about your mother.'

'Something about the "Curse of the Cunninghams", perhaps?'

Embarrassed, Emma dropped her gaze. She'd hate Max to think she'd been gossiping about his family.

'It's okay,' he said with a sigh. 'I know people like to talk and it's no wonder it's all resurfacing now. Here it is, Christmas again, and tragedy number three strikes the Cunningham family.'

'That should be it, then.'

'Sorry?'

'Bad things are supposed to come in threes.' Emma bit her lip. The tragedies that had befallen this family were nothing to make light of but all she wanted to do was offer…something. Comfort wasn't possible but perhaps some hope? 'Christmas will be different this year.' She offered a smile this time. 'I'm sure the tree will just be the first of all the rules that Ben knows about.'

Max snorted. 'Christmas rules are just part of the commercial hype that's all this season is all about. Reasons to make you spend more and more money.'

'You think?'

'I don't imagine this is the first Christmas you've worked so you know about the effects of the kind of stress it creates. People drink too much. Domestic violence goes through the roof. It's marketed as a promise for peace and love for everyone who bothers to follow all those "rules" but anyone who stands back far enough can see it for what it is.'

There was a defensiveness in his tone that made Emma think he was protesting too much. Because he'd had to—to protect himself? Because it was so much harder if you let yourself sink into what was missing from a celebration of family? She, of all people, could understand that.

'I don't believe that,' she said quietly. 'I'm not saying it's not a particularly difficult time for a lot of people but, if you're lucky, it's an opportunity to hit pause for a day. To celebrate the things that are really important—like family and friends. And, yes, we do that by buying stuff and eating special food but that's okay too, because it's all part of what makes it special. And they're not "rules". They're traditions and every family makes their own. I expect Ben is holding onto the ones he knows about as tightly as he can because he's lost just about everything else.'

Emma had to stop talking then, so that she could swallow the lump in her throat. She could feel Max's gaze resting on her.

'So…why aren't you with *your* family, then? You do have one, don't you?'

Emma nodded. 'In Italy. We have quite different traditions there. Like the feast of the seven fishes on Christmas Eve—the *Festa dei Sette Pesci*. And there's always a nativity scene in the house and someone gets chosen to put the baby Jesus in the crib on Christmas Eve.' She let her breath out in a sigh. 'I haven't been back home for a few years, though.'

'Why not?'

'As a locum, it can be one of the busiest times of the year because so many people want time off to be with their families.' Emma closed her eyes for a heartbeat, ignoring the faint alarm bell in her head. She had, albeit unintentionally, stepped into a private part of Max Cunningham's life. It was only fair if he knew a little more about her, wasn't it? 'Plus, I had a pretty rough Christmas a few years back and I needed some time out. Especially from my family, who would have insisted on talking about it endlessly.'

'What happened?'

'Um…well, it started a bit before Christmas, I guess, when the guy I thought I was going to marry walked out on me. But then…someone special died…'

'At Christmas time?'

'On Christmas Day.' Emma gulped in some air. 'I knew it was coming but that doesn't necessarily make it any easier at the time, you know?'

'Oh, yeah…' Max's tone was heartfelt. 'I know.' It was his turn to take a deeper breath. 'I didn't answer your question before. I was eleven when my mum died. My brother Andy was only eight. Not much older than Ben.'

'Oh, Max… I'm so sorry. That must have been so hard for you all.'

'I think we were too shocked to think about Christmas that year. It was the next one that was the hardest. Andy wanted it to be like it had been, but it was too hard on Dad. I found him crying and that shocked me so much. I had no idea what to do.'

'Of course you didn't. You were a child.'

'I'm not proud of what I did do.'

Emma watched the way Max's face creased into lines of regret. 'I'm sure it wasn't that bad.'

'I told Andy that Father Christmas wasn't real. That it had been Mum who'd put all the decorations up and all those presents under the tree and in our stockings and that, now she wasn't here, it couldn't happen any more because it would make Dad too sad.'

Oh... Emma could just imagine the serious conversation between two small boys. A fragmented family trying to find a way to be together without it causing too much pain for anyone. It was heartbreaking.

'So it didn't happen that year. Or the next. And then we just got used to it. We'd give each other a gift but we never put up a Christmas tree again or did any of the other decorations that Mum used to love—like winding long ropes of artificial leafy stuff like ivy and holly with its red berries between the bannisters on the staircase and hanging little bunches of golden bells on every door so that they jingled whenever they were opened and closed. Andy started doing it all again once he had children of his own, mind you.' Max drained his glass. 'Me, I just got more cynical about it all but then, it only really matters for the kids, doesn't it?'

'I'm not sure about that,' Emma said slowly. 'But it's certainly a very special time of the year for children. Exciting...and magical, until you know the truth about Father Christmas.'

Max grimaced. 'Don't worry. I'm not about to burst the bubble for Ben or Tilly. They've got more than enough of real life to get their heads around at the moment.'

'But...' Again, Emma bit her lip. This really wasn't any of her business.

'But, what?'

'It's just that...well...putting up a Christmas tree is only a part of it. And it's only a decoration if you don't really believe...'

'In Father Christmas?'

Emma shook her head. 'No. In family. In celebrating the bond. Or, in your case this year, perhaps it's about creating a bond. The new one that's going to be the foundation for Ben and Tilly and Alice to feel like they belong.'

Max was staring at her. 'I can't do that.'

'You can. You and your dad. All you have to do is love these children and I'm sure you do already.'

'Yes, but...we don't know how to do Christmas. It's been more than twenty years since we even had a piece of tinsel in the house. Dad wouldn't want it.'

'Are you sure? It's been a long time, Max. Sometimes it takes a gentle push to get people past something that's holding them back. This new family of yours is a gift. It could turn out to be the best thing that could have happened.'

'The breaking of the curse?'

'If you like. The start of something new, anyway. Something very special.'

Emma's tone had softened as she thought about these two bachelor men of different generations sharing their lives with three small children. About the amount of love that would be available within the thick stone walls of this ancient house. She was smiling at Max as she finished speaking. He was holding her gaze with that kind of intensity she had felt before—when it had seemed like he was really seeing her for the first time.

'You're right,' he said softly. 'This could be the most important Christmas these kids will ever have. It *has* to be special.' He still hadn't broken the eye contact and Emma was starting to feel an odd tingle spreading through her body.

'You have to help me, Emma. Please...' The plea in

Max's tone was so heartfelt. 'I don't know how to do this by myself. I... I need you...'

The tingle had just reached Emma's toes.

'We *all* need you,' Max added, as if summoning every power of persuasion he could find. 'Me and Dad. Ben and Tilly and Alice. Probably Pirate too. Just to be here when you're not at the hospital. Just to be...well...just to be *you*... And...and you did promise to show Ben and Tilly how to make stars and we didn't get time to do that tonight, did we?'

Emma nodded. 'I did say I'd show them how to make stars.'

But to stay here in this house?

To spend Christmas with a family?

It was terrifying and compelling at the same time. Emma knew she should run a mile but there was something in her way.

Maybe it was a small boy with solemn eyes. A little girl with a bunny that had chewed ears or a baby that had been watching her as if she was the most important person on earth as she'd sucked her bottle. Perhaps it was a man of her father's generation who loved his little dog but had lost the joy of this season so long ago. Or... maybe it was this man who was looking lost but was so determined to do his best for the entire little family that had just turned up on his doorstep. A man who wanted her to be here. Who *needed* her...

Christmas... With children. And a baby. How could she possibly cope with saying yes?

But Max needed her. Perhaps everybody needed her because she was outside the tragedy that had brought them together so maybe she could see what needed to happen more clearly. How could she possibly say no?

CHAPTER FOUR

WHO WOULD HAVE THOUGHT?

Max had certainly never expected to be here, in the Christmas grotto of Cheltenham's largest department store. Or to be in sole charge of three small children, for that matter, but it seemed that things were going well on this outing. They had been going surprisingly well for the whole day, so far, in fact. He had wrangled the three different sizes of safety seats into his vehicle, figured out how to operate the three-wheeled mountain buggy for Alice and had taken the children on a drive to find a service station that hadn't run out of Christmas trees yet, after deciding that taking the children into the patch of forest on their property and trying to saw off large branches probably wasn't the most sensible idea. It was only after he had tied the tree securely to the roof rack of his Jeep and was planning to head back home to Upper Barnsley that Ben had informed him of the next Christmas 'rule', which was a visit to tell Father Christmas what they hoped would be their special gift this year.

So, here they were. Father Christmas, resplendent in red suit with white faux fur edging to match his luxuriant beard and the trimmings on his hat, was sitting on a large red velvet-covered chair with a golden edging.

Christmas carols were playing softly in the background and the store staff were wearing red hats or headbands with glowing yellow stars. There were Christmas trees with twinkling lights and fake snow on either side of the chair, giant teddy bears, burlap sacks with the corners of pretend gifts peeping out and a life-sized reindeer that had a round red nose and a mouth curved into a rather unlikely smile. It was everything that Max had dismissed about Christmas for as long as he could remember.

Commercial hype. Children begged their parents to bring them here and there would be plenty of other shopping that needed to be done at the same time. Max could see the stoic expressions on some of the parents' faces already as they kept their places in the queue of over-excited children who were waiting their turn to whisper their secret Christmas wishes into the ear of the man who could make it happen. The children standing close to Max weren't over-excited, however. Ben and Tilly were standing very quietly, holding hands, beside the buggy in which Alice was soundly asleep for the moment. Too quietly, Max decided, looking around at the shining faces of other children and the way they were bouncing on their toes, barely able to contain themselves, when it was nearly their turn.

'What are you going to ask Father Christmas for?' he asked Ben.

Ben gave him a patient look. 'It's secret,' he said. 'It's—'

'—a rule,' Max said at the same time. He smiled at Ben. 'I get it.' He wondered if there was any way he could manage to stand close enough to overhear the request, however. Because how else was he going to know what he could get as Christmas gifts for his nephew and nieces?

They moved up the queue a little and Max let his gaze roam away from the grotto towards the strategically placed aisles of every kind of decoration you might want for your house or tree. During a breakfast that was still chaotic even though Maggie had arrived not long after Emma had left for the hospital, he'd told James about his decision to buy a Christmas tree and he'd been on the point of suggesting that they already had all the decorations they could possibly need, boxed up and stored in the attic. It was instantly obvious that his dad knew exactly what he was thinking about and it was just as clear that he wanted to avoid that discussion at all costs. The haunted look in his eyes was swiftly followed by excusing himself to go into the clinic rooms to get ready for a morning surgery followed by house calls.

'You know what?' Max said to Ben.

'What?'

'I think we're going to have a new Christmas rule this year. One that's just for us.'

The deep crease that appeared on Ben's forehead made his glance even more suspicious.

'Only if you think it's a good one,' Max added gravely. 'I reckon you know more about the rules than me.'

Ben considered this and then nodded his agreement. 'What is it?' he asked.

'Well…we've bought a new Christmas tree, haven't we?'

'Yes.'

'And we need to put things on it to look pretty, yes?'

'Stars…' Tilly was listening to the conversation. 'Emma said we can make stars and I can help.'

'I know.' Max had the sudden thought that maybe he might have a word in the ear of Father Christmas himself when they got close enough. So that he could put in a request that Emma would stay in the house for the next week at least. She hadn't exactly said yes when he'd asked her last night. But she hadn't said no either, so he hadn't given up hope. 'I'm sure she will,' he reassured Tilly. 'Emma is not the kind of person who would break a promise. But I was thinking that we might need something else to go with the stars. Something special that you guys can choose all by yourselves. After you've had your photo with Father Christmas.'

Ben was still frowning. 'But why is that a new rule?'

'Because we'll do it every Christmas,' Max told him quietly. 'And that means we'll always have special decorations to go on the tree that you know are yours because you chose them.'

Would the message beneath his words that Max only recognised himself as he was saying them be understood on some level by the children? That he was trying to make a promise that they were safe now and that he would do everything in his power to ensure that there weren't going to be any more huge and traumatic changes in their lives? It seemed to have helped a little, because Tilly's face was starting to look like the other little girls in this line. Her eyes were almost shining.

'Fairies,' she whispered. 'I like fairies.'

'I'll help you find a fairy,' Max said. 'Maybe one that can go right on the tippy top of the tree?'

They were getting closer to the front of the queue now and they were all watching as a small girl was lifted onto Father Christmas's knee. He tilted his head and she cupped her hands around her mouth to keep her wish secret and then beamed at her mother, who was standing beside the photographer. Noticing that the mother's purse was already open so that she could purchase the image should have scored another point for the commercialism that Max detested but, oddly, it didn't. What he could see was the love in this mother's face, her pleasure in having brought her daughter to the Christmas grotto and the sheer joy in the little girl's face.

And he remembered something else then. From the time before he had learned to dismiss everything about Christmas. He remembered being taken to see Father Christmas when he wouldn't have been much older than Ben. With Andy, who would have been about Tilly's age. And their mother had been watching them with love written all over *her* face and…and…

And he could remember the magic. The belief that the man in the red suit could make something special happen. He could also remember that belief becoming something even bigger when he'd come downstairs on Christmas morning to find the gift he'd set his heart on underneath the tree—his first two-wheeler bike with red tinsel wrapped all over it. His wish had come true and it was the best thing *ever*.

Look at that… His mother had the biggest smile on her face as she stood there wrapped in his father's arms. *I wonder how Father Christmas got that down the chimney?*

Max had known. By magic. And even though he knew perfectly well now that it had been his parents who'd put the bike there, he also knew that there had been magic involved. The kind of magic that Emma had been talking about in the bonds within a family. About the sharing and celebration and joy. And she had been right about something else too. These particular children needed to find new bonds that they could trust enough to feel safe and they needed a particularly special Christmas this year.

But he needed help to make that happen. From someone who knew far more about children than he did. Someone who knew more about families than he did and who was warm and caring enough to be able to encourage the connections that would lead to bonds that could form and then get stronger and stronger.

'Do you want to go and visit Emma after we're finished here?' he asked Ben and Tilly. 'It's not far away to where she's working in my hospital. If we find out what she needs to help you make stars, we could pick that up on the way home.'

Emma's first thought when she came out of a curtained cubicle and saw Max Cunningham coming into the emergency department of the Royal with the three children in tow was that something was wrong. Her heart skipped a beat as she imagined one of the children was ill or injured and that must have shown in her face as she walked towards them because Max was smiling reassuringly.

More than reassuringly, actually. He was smiling at Emma as if she was the person he most wanted to see in the world and her body was responding with that glow of warmth and funny tingling thing that went down to her toes. It was impossible not to smile back. Or to hold the gaze of those amazingly blue eyes. He'd always been a very good-looking man but ageing ten years had added a maturity that was even more appealing. It wasn't hard to stamp on her body's response, though, and tell herself how stupid it would be to entertain any ideas of Max being aware of any physical reactions to *her* proximity. She only had to remember how he'd laughed after that kiss. How quick he'd been to reassure her.

'Don't worry, Emma, you're completely safe. We both know you're so not my type and I'm certainly not yours...'

She'd laughed along with him, albeit a heartbeat later. He was right. What woman in her right mind would willingly go near someone who was guaranteed to break their heart if they were silly enough to fall for him?

Her smile was fading as the memory flashed through the back of her mind but Max was still beaming at her.

'We just came in to say hullo,' he said. 'I wondered how things were going?'

'Everything's great,' Emma assured him. 'It was quiet enough first thing for me to get to know my way around and meet most of the staff. Miriam's been amazingly helpful.'

The senior nurse was making a beeline for the group as she was speaking.

'Emma's a complete pro,' she told Max. 'I doubt there's anything she couldn't cope with.' But Miriam's attention was on the children and she automatically reached into the buggy to unclip and pick up the baby as Alice began to whimper. 'May I?'

'Please do,' Max said. 'But she's due for a nappy change and a bottle. We've been busy visiting Father Christmas in Derby's department store.'

'Just the sort of thing a grandma is expert in,' Miriam responded, as she gathered Alice into her arms. 'Is everything in that bag there?'

'She's hungry,' Ben told Miriam.

'I think you're right, lovey. And what about you? We've got some lovely Christmas cookies in our staff-room that look like snowmen. Would you like to come and have some?'

Ben nodded solemnly and Emma had to smile as she saw Tilly's hand slide into his. If her big brother was going to get cookies, she wanted to go too.

Max was still smiling as he watched Miriam take Ben's hand to lead both the older children towards the staffroom.

'You look like you're having a good day,' she said.

'So far, so good.' Max nodded. 'I did want to get close enough to hear what Ben and Tilly were asking Father Christmas for but it didn't work.' He raised an eyebrow at Emma. 'Maybe you could find out? I'd really like to put something special under the tree for them both.'

Was he expecting her to be heading back to the Cunningham house after work? It was only then that Emma realised she hadn't made any effort to look for alternative accommodation yet. She'd been far too focused on her work in this new emergency department. She could find out, she thought. She could help the children write a letter to Father Christmas, maybe, to put into the fire so it went up the chimney. If she promised to keep their secrets, they might tell her exactly what to write.

'Oh, we got a tree too,' Max continued. 'And they both chose some decorations to go on it. Ben got a box of tin soldiers and Tilly chose an angel to go on top of the tree—although she thinks it's a fairy.' His gaze was roaming around his department over Emma's shoulder. 'So...have you had any excitement?'

'Not really. We've only used a resuscitation room once, for a serious stroke that came in early this morning. Apart from that, it's been the usual range of problems like chest pain and asthma and some diabetes complications. There was an interesting tib/fib fracture, though…it—'

But Max obviously wasn't listening. His gaze was fixed behind Emma. About where the first set of automatic doors to the ambulance bay were.

'Something's happening,' he interrupted her.

Emma turned swiftly to see someone standing outside the outer doors that needed a code to open. It was a man who had a child in his arms and, even from this distance, Emma could see that the child was bleeding heavily. One of the two paramedics who were using the space between the sets of doors to finish some paperwork and clean a stretcher moved to press the button that would open the doors at the same time as both Emma and Max had moved close enough for the inner doors to slide open.

'There's more.' The man carrying the injured child was out of breath and sounded panicked. 'Out on the main road. A truck just smashed into about three parked cars. They need help…'

Another ED consultant was right behind Max and Emma.

'I'll take him,' she said. 'Do you want me to activate the trauma team as well?'

'Yes.'

Both Emma and Max spoke at the same time and she had the immediate thought that perhaps she should let Max take charge of this emergency, even though, technically, she was here to do his job. He must have felt her swift glance because he caught her gaze and he clearly wasn't thinking about whether or not he was even supposed to be there.

'We'd better get out there,' he said. 'We're needed.'

Emma hadn't been waiting for his direction. She was already heading for the outer doors despite being in her scrubs, with nothing more than a long-sleeved tee shirt underneath the tunic.

'I'll get our kit,' one of the paramedics said. He turned to his partner. 'You bring the truck so we can transport more quickly.'

Glancing back into the department as the child was carried inside for assessment and treatment, Emma saw Max hesitating for a brief moment before he followed her and he too was looking back into the department. Towards the staffroom where Miriam had taken the children to give them cookies? Emma could sense that he was struggling with something different this time. Not who should take charge of this incident but with his new responsibilities as a father figure clashing with what he was programmed to respond to as an emergency physician. Was this another reminder of just how much his life was changing? His next words confirmed her line of thought.

'Tell Miriam where I am,' he called after his colleague. 'Ask her to keep an eye on the children for me?'

And then they were outside and running towards the scene that lay just out of the hospital grounds, in the direction that Emma had taken only yesterday when she'd walked with Max to see his apartment. The same intersection where they'd waited for the traffic lights to change and she'd noticed the impressive overhead decorations of icicle lights. Any thought of pretty things to do with Christmas was totally incongruous at this moment, however. It looked as though a large truck had failed to notice the line of stationary cars waiting at a red light and had smashed into the end of the line, in a nose-to-tail concertina of at least three vehicles that suggested a great deal of speed had been involved. The truck had tipped sideways with the impact and there was another vehicle almost hidden beneath the body of the truck.

Emma had seen plenty of road traffic accidents over the years but nothing quite like this. There was a crowd gathering, with people trying to get into vehicles where doors had been crushed and couldn't open. They must have come from the lines of traffic now building up in a traffic jam on all sides of the intersection because many of them looked deserted, with doors hanging open. There were flashing lights and sirens coming from all directions as emergency service vehicles rushed to the scene but, even over all that noise, Emma could hear the cries of frightened people. Her steps slowed as she got closer to the carnage and—although Max had been a step or two ahead of her the whole time they'd been running—he seemed to sense the distance between them increasing and he also slowed, turning back to catch her gaze.

'You okay, Em?'

She nodded, sucking in a deep, deep breath. She knew she had the skills to tackle a scene like this but, for this moment, it was overwhelming. The temptation to hang back and allow Max to take the lead was strong but there was something equally strong and that was a hard-won determination to face up to the most difficult things life could throw at her and Emma wasn't about to throw away any part of her confidence in being able to do that successfully.

Max was still holding her gaze and it felt as if he

could sense that momentary doubt. As if he was having a similar one of his own, even, and wondering if he should take the lead.

'We're right beside the hospital,' she said, turning her head now to survey the scene and assess the dangers and where they might be needed as a priority. 'All we need to do at this point is to make sure they're stable enough to get them inside. Basics. Airway, breathing, circulation. Look after the cervical spine. We've got lots of help. The firies will cut into the vehicles for us if it's needed. The paramedics can direct the extrication and transfer.'

'Here...' A paramedic was coming towards them. 'Put these on.'

'These' were fluorescent vests with the word 'Doctor' on the back on a reflective strip.

'No...hang on...' A female paramedic was pulling off her jacket, which she handed to Emma. 'You're going to freeze in scrubs. Put this on first.'

'But what about you?'

'I've got something else I can wear.'

'Has anybody started triage?' Max asked.

'We've only just got here. That's our MCI command vehicle arriving now, behind the fire truck.'

Emma knew that MCI stood for Mass Casualty Incident. She looked at the line of crushed vehicles. Should they start at the front and work back? One of the cars was sandwiched between one in front and one behind and it looked as though the damage in that case was worse than the others. But what about the vehicle beneath the overturned truck?

Max clearly wanted to start the work that urgently needed to be done here. Emma shoved her arms into the warm jacket.

'Have you got triage labels?'

The paramedic who'd opened the ambulance bay doors of the Royal to let in the man with the injured child was beside Emma now. 'I've got them,' he said. 'Can you come with me? We'll do a first sweep and if you're both with me, I can leave you to start treating any red labels and move on. We still don't know what we're dealing with in terms of numbers or severity of injuries.'

Emma had worked with the triage labelling system as well. A red label meant that the victim could only survive with immediate treatment. They might have an obstructed airway or rate of respiration that was far too slow or fast, a very rapid heart rate or an absent radial pulse indicating low blood pressure, potentially from severe blood loss.

The first car in the line had been shunted well into the intersection. There were bystanders clustered around the driver's side of the car. The window was broken and Emma could see the deflated airbag hanging from the steering wheel.

'She's awake,' someone told them. 'She says her neck hurts and she doesn't want to try moving.'

She was conscious, breathing and talking so this driver wasn't going to get a red label indicating the need for urgent intervention to save a life. A potential neck injury could still be serious but it could wait.

'Tell her to keep as still as possible,' the paramedic instructed. 'Someone will be with her very soon.'

They moved swiftly to the next vehicle. The paramedic was using his radio to relay information to the person who was taking charge of the scene and would use the available resources of people and equipment according to information coming in and any changes during the operation. Police officers were on scene now, as well, moving bystanders out of the way and trying to clear the blocked traffic.

There were two people inside the second vehicle, both conscious.

'It's my leg,' the front seat passenger groaned. 'I think it's broken.'

The driver was only semi-conscious. 'Where am I?' she mumbled. 'What's happened?'

More paramedics had arrived on scene and were immediately dispatched to manage these patients.

It was the third car in the line that was the most seriously damaged, apart from the one beneath the truck, and it was rapidly, sadly clear that there was nothing they could do for this woman. Her black triage label was a sombre confirmation that the rescue teams were not needed.

'Maybe if we'd got here a bit faster?' Emma said.

But Max shook his head. 'Unsurvivable injuries. I suspect the force from behind and the weight of obstruction in front was enough to just snap her neck.'

A fire crew was close and had a tarpaulin to put over the car containing the fatality.

'Truck driver seems uninjured,' they told Emma and Max. 'Got himself out of the cab. The cops are having a word with him.'

'I'll go and check him out.' The paramedic's tone was carefully neutral. It was obvious that the truck driver was responsible for this horrific crash that had killed at least one person but they couldn't make judgements about the driver involved. It was possible that it was a medical event or mechanical failure that had caused him to hit a line of stationary vehicles at high speed.

The fire crew was also making decisions about how to get to the car trapped beneath the truck and Emma heard someone talking about stabilising the truck until they could get the machinery they needed to lift it clear. Looking at how crushed the car was, with its roof almost down past the level of the steering wheel, she fully expected that the driver would be another fatality. She bent to try and look through the front window on the passenger's side.

'Careful, there, Doc,' one of the fire officers shouted. 'We're not sure how stable it is.'

The call was enough to have Max by her side instantly and it felt as though he was there to try and protect her. He was certainly ready to assist. Or did he want to take over?

'What can you see?'

'Facial injuries. I can't see any chest wall movement…' Emma had her bottom lip caught between her teeth as she scanned the driver's body as best she could. The seat had been flattened by the roof being crushed so he was lying almost flat, still wearing his seat belt. She couldn't see any major bleeding other than the injury to his face but… 'Oh…' Emma felt her heart skip a beat. 'I *can* see chest wall movement. He's breathing. Or trying to…'

Max had his head right beside hers now, as he tried to get a visual assessment of the crash victim. He was so close she could feel the warmth of his skin and, like the way he'd looked at her when they'd first arrived on this scene, it seemed that just being close to him was empowering Emma with more confidence than she'd ever known she had.

She turned to the fire crew. 'I have to get in here,' she said. 'It's urgent.'

'We're still assessing how stable this truck is. We can't start cutting the car up for access until we've got jacks in place or lifted the chassis clear.'

'There's no time for that.' Emma shook her head. 'Can you break this back window? I reckon I could get in there.'

'There's hardly any space in there.' The paramedic had come back. 'There's no way we could get a spinal board in and get him out.'

Both the paramedic and Max were tall, broad-shouldered men. They wouldn't even be able to get through a window space. But Emma could—if she was brave enough. Again, as she had when first arriving on this scene, she had a moment of wondering if she might be about to tackle something that might defeat her. And, again, she found herself catching Max's gaze. This time, it felt different. He wasn't considering taking over because he couldn't do what Emma could attempt, thanks to her size. This time, it felt as if he was offering her encouragement. Bolstering her confidence by letting her know that he believed she could do this. And it felt...great. It was exactly what she needed to vanquish any beat of fear.

'I can get in,' she told them. 'I need to secure his airway. I can work in a tight space. You could pass me in the gear I need.' She had to try and save this man. He'd been simply sitting in his car, stopped at a red traffic light, and his world had just been overturned in a split second and it just...well, it wasn't fair...

The chief fire officer looked undecided but Emma held his gaze to give him the silent message if he wasn't going to help her, she was going to try by herself.

He finally nodded. 'Okay. Stand back and I'll get the window out.'

* * *

He should go back to his emergency department, Max thought. It wasn't just that he'd left all the children in the care of a staff member. He was automatically focusing on how the department was going to cope with a sudden influx of trauma patients. He knew that his staff would be managing the first of these patients from the crash scene perfectly well, but the more seriously injured, like the semi-conscious driver of the second vehicle, might be stretching immediate resources and they needed to plan for someone who could need major resuscitation—if they could get him into the department alive. Or maybe it should be Emma who went back to manage the department, seeing as she was officially doing his job today.

But right now she was wriggling herself through an empty window space of a crashed car and somehow contorting her body so that she could touch and assess the unconscious driver. She was inside a partially crushed car and there was a heavy truck still lying across the vehicle. It looked difficult and bloody dangerous and…and there was no way Max was going to leave until he knew that Emma was okay. He couldn't believe the courage she'd shown even crawling into that vehicle. The fact that she now sounded calm and in control of the situation was, well…it was seriously impressive.

'He's got multiple fractures in his face and his airway's obstructed.' Emma put down the bag mask she had been trying to use to assist the man's breathing. 'There's no way I'm going to be able to do an orotracheal or nasotracheal intubation. How far away are we from being able to get him out?'

Max signalled one of the fire officers and repeated Emma's query.

'We're getting some jacks in place. It should be safe enough to cut the side out of the car in about ten minutes.'

Emma had heard the response. 'Too long,' she said. She was almost lying down beside her patient in the narrow space left in the crushed car but she twisted her head to look directly at Max.

'Surgical cricothyroidotomy?' she suggested.

'It's what I'd do in ED.' He nodded. 'But have you got enough space in there?'

'It'll have to be enough,' Emma said. 'His pulse is dropping. We're going to lose him if I don't do something right now. I need some fresh gloves, a number ten or eleven scalpel, a bougie and a size six endotracheal tube, please.'

It was Max who handed everything that Emma required in through the empty window space, reaching in so that he could place things in her hands without her having to try and move. With her new gloves on, he watched her find her landmarks on the man's neck, stabilising the larynx with one hand and then locating the space between the thyroid and cricoid cartilages. He was ready to hand her the scalpel as soon as she was ready to make her first incision.

'I'm through the cricoid membrane,' she said, seconds later. 'I'm going to make the horizontal incisions now.'

Max knew this was where things could get messy and enough blood could not only obscure the field but undermine the confidence of anyone who might not be very familiar with this emergency procedure. He knew that Emma was going to be working purely by feel from now on and when there was movement of the crushed vehicle from what the firies were doing to stabilise the truck above them, he held his breath to see whether that might give Emma enough of a fright to interfere with what was the critical moment of her attempt to save this man's life.

It didn't seem to rattle her at all. She slid the bougie guide into the hole she'd made in his neck, slipped the endotracheal tube over the top of the bougie and managed to make it look easy to secure the tube, despite the awkwardness of the space she was working in and gloved hands that were slippery with blood.

'Can you see where the bag mask is?' she asked Max.

'It's right behind you.'

'I can't reach...'

'I've got it.' Max leaned further into the car and picked it up. He pulled off the plastic face mask and the paramedic beside him had the attachment needed so that Emma could clip it to the endotracheal tube.

'Equal chest movement,' she said a moment later. 'Can we get some oxygen on? I'd like to get an IV in, as well.'

Max could see the firies setting up their hydraulic cutting gear right beside him. As he looked at the officer in charge he received a nod in response.

'They're ready to start cutting,' he told Emma. 'Is he breathing well enough to wait a couple of minutes until we can get him out? The sooner we can get him into the department the better, yes?'

'Of course.' Emma had one hand on the man's abdomen, feeling for his efforts at respiration. She had her other hand on his wrist, feeling for his pulse. 'Okay... yes...let's get him out of here.'

She stayed with her patient for as long as possible as the firies cut through twisted metal and lifted a door and the central pillar out of the way. Then she had to move and the paramedics took over, being the experts in getting the victim onto a spinal board and then out of the vehicle and onto the waiting stretcher. It took only a few minutes but, for that period of time, Max had Emma standing right beside him and he could sense her focus on what was happening for her patient and a tension that suggested that a successful outcome to this case was very, very important to her.

He was looking at her face as the badly injured man was finally lifted from the car and, as if sensing his gaze, she looked up at him and he could see what he had suspected in her eyes. Emma was determined to win this fight for life. She not only had a bucket of courage, this woman, but she loved her job as much as Max loved his and she truly cared about doing the absolute best she could for anyone under her care. It was a moment of connection that was as powerful as it was brief.

Their patient had been freed but needed more intervention and then a high level of monitoring even for the few minutes it would take to get him inside the hospital walls. The other victims of this incident had already been transported into the Royal's emergency department and that was where Emma and Max both headed back to now. There was still a lot of work to be done and Max wanted to be working alongside Emma to make sure the department could handle everything that needed to be done for everybody involved.

It was then he realised that, during the tense minutes of assisting Emma in the amazing job she'd just done in saving a man's life, he'd actually forgotten that he had other responsibilities as well. That there were three small children waiting for him, probably in the staffroom of his emergency department. He felt completely torn in that moment—in two very different directions—and it was overwhelming.

Had Emma sensed that it was almost too much? Was that why she chose to look up from her patient for a heartbeat and catch his gaze? There was a softness to her mouth that hinted at a smile and there was a confidence in her eyes that told him she thought they were winning. That they had a very good chance of winning this challenge they had just tackled together.

Max chose to take something more from that look as well. That he might well be facing the biggest challenge of his own life but he had a very good chance of winning that too. Especially if he could persuade Emma to hang around, even if was only for a short time. And then he remembered that was why he had dropped by the hospital in the first place—to try and persuade her not to find alternative accommodation.

He'd have to wait before he could find an appropriate moment to do that so he hoped the children were happy to stay for a bit longer. That would also give him time to think up an approach that Emma couldn't refuse.

He could remind her of her promise to help Ben and Tilly make stars.

Or he could remind her of what she believed about Christmas. About the magic that could happen when a family came together to celebrate the bonds they had. The love. He could tell her what he believed—that they all needed Emma to make that happen.

CHAPTER FIVE

THIS FELT AS if it could be a mistake.

As if Emma was doing something that meant she was stepping over a line and it might be impossible to step back again even if she really needed to. But here she was, doing it. Driving back to Upper Barnsley. And it was Max Cunningham's fault.

He had made it impossible for her not to return to the manor house after her shift had ended. He had stayed on at the Royal, allowing staff members to take care of his nieces and nephew, until they had stabilised all the victims of the major accident and their patients had been transferred either to Theatre under the care of surgical teams or admitted to various wards for further treatment.

And then he'd brought the children in from the staff-room or the relatives' room or wherever someone had been caring for them and Ben had pinned Emma with that gaze that was far too serious for a six-year-old boy to have mastered.

'Is it time for you to go home now, Emma?' he'd asked.

'I guess it is,' she'd admitted, checking her watch. But just where it was that she would be heading as her temporary home was totally unknown. She hadn't found a single moment today to go online and check for the availability of hotel rooms within a manageable distance.

'Are we going to make stars?' Tilly's gaze was almost as sombre as her brother's—as if she was still processing her new knowledge that life didn't always deliver what it was supposed to. 'I like stars and...and you said I could help.'

Ben still had her pinned. 'You promised...'

Technically, Emma had offered rather than promised to show the children how to make stars but the semantics were irrelevant because she couldn't let Ben and Tilly down.

Or Max...

If he'd brought these children in to see her as a form of emotional blackmail to get another night of her assistance with their care, he had certainly achieved his goal but that wasn't what Emma was thinking about as her gaze touched, and then held, his.

To be honest, she wasn't thinking of anything very coherent at all. It was more of a feeling. A warmth. They had worked together this afternoon. They had saved a life and the connection that gave them was more than simply professional. They had shared a goal and they'd needed each other in order to achieve it and they had succeeded and...trust between them had been born. It was that trust that was creating a warmth that started in Emma's chest and unfurled and grew to reach right to the tips of her fingers and toes.

Or maybe the connection had already been there from years ago and had been rediscovered.

And maybe a new depth to that connection had been established between them yesterday when Emma had been present while Max was struggling to get his head around the enormous changes that had just overturned his world. She had helped because she was there and she couldn't *not* help but then he'd asked her to stay. He'd said that he *needed* her...

Whatever it was, it was powerful. And it was touching something very deep in Emma's heart. Not in the space that was still locked away because she didn't quite recognise this new part of her heart. It felt like no-man's land, halfway between caring so much that something could tear your heart apart when you lost it and caring only because you knew that it was temporary so the loss was already built in—the now very familiar space that her locum work had given her in her professional life and the avoidance of any long-term relationships had provided in her private life.

For a moment, Emma had to shake off a longing that came completely from left field—that she was over being in this space and ready to put roots down and create a life that wasn't going to keep changing. As always, the best way to deal with a doubt like that was to think of a positive point to balance it and there was one that sprang to mind instantly. It almost felt as if she could allow herself to enjoy the sensations that came from unwrapping an old attraction that didn't seem to have faded at all because this was as temporary as her new position being the stand-in HOD of the Royal's emergency department. She knew that when this locum position ended she would walk out of the job and away from Max Cunningham and his now very complicated life would be none of her business. Perhaps she could even allow herself to enjoy the company of young children—away from her professional environment—

which was something she knew she had instinctively kept herself away from.

It was all temporary. Keeping her word to show Ben and Tilly how to make stars committed her to no more than spending one more night at the manor house. She could find the time to search for a hotel room tomorrow.

Pulling her car to a halt beside Max's, outside his family home, Emma sat still for a moment, watching Max get out of the driver's seat and move to open the back door to lift his small passengers from their car seats. He paused for a heartbeat, however, and looked over the Christmas tree strapped to the roof of the vehicle to catch Emma's gaze, his lips curling into a smile.

Emma's breath came out in a sigh that held the edge of an unexpected sound.

Oh, yeah...that attraction hadn't faded at all. It seemed to have matured into something that had rather a lot more bite to it and she recognised the tiny sound that had escaped with her breath for what it was—an expression of physical desire.

Lust, even...

It had been a weird thing to think about as he unclipped Tilly's safety belt and lifted her from her car seat but there was no way that Max could have stopped the memory filling his head.

That time he'd kissed Emma Moretti under the mistletoe at the paediatric ward's staff Christmas party. He hadn't given it any more thought after it had happened because, no matter how soft her lips had been and how delicious the curves of her body were and how astonishingly powerful the urge to do a lot more than kiss Emma had been, it was never going to happen.

Emma was the earth mother type. The type who was destined to marry and have a family as soon as possible. A huge family, probably, seeing as she had adored children and babies so much and, because that was something Max wanted to avoid at all costs, it had been easy to dismiss the attraction that had both led to and been inflamed by that kiss.

Dismissing it hadn't made it go away, though, had it? Judging by the kick in his gut that Max recognised all too easily as a reaction to a very healthy physical attraction, it was actually stronger than it had ever been.

Was that because there were things about Emma that were familiar but other things that were so very different? She was just as gorgeous as she'd been ten years ago, even though she was less curvy and she had cut off those glorious long waves of her hair and she seemed... what was it, exactly? More contained, perhaps? Less ready to laugh or even smile. Yes, she was definitely different but that gave the attraction an edge of mystery that added surprisingly to its power.

Emma wasn't the only one who was different, either. Who could have predicted that he'd be the one who'd end up with what seemed a huge family and the earth mother would still be alone?

He set Tilly down on her feet beside Ben, who immediately took hold of his sister's hand, and then he unclipped the bucket seat that Alice was strapped into.

'Okay, guys. Let's go inside and say hullo to Grandpa and then I'll bring the Christmas tree inside.'

But James Cunningham was nowhere to be seen. Neither was their housekeeper, Maggie, though she'd left a note in the kitchen with a list of food she had prepared for both the children and adults.

'Dad's probably in the clinic. Or on a house call. Or he might have taken Pirate for a walk.'

Or he might be avoiding spending time with his grandchildren because, like Max, he was still grappling with how to cope with his new responsibilities.

Alice had begun to cry as they'd come inside. Max had a brief but fierce yearning for the old days in the paediatric ward when he'd been working with Emma and how he had been able to hand a baby back to its mother or a nurse when it needed changing or feeding, but he wasn't about to repeat his actions of the previous evening of shoving Alice into Emma's arms.

Not when he had been quite aware of that flash of something like panic he'd seen in her eyes, even as her arms had gathered the baby close. Besides, he had to learn how to cope and this was as good a time as any. He pulled wipes and a clean nappy from the bag of supplies he had taken into town earlier and set about making Alice comfortable. It was a mission to deal with all those fiddly little fasteners on her stretchy suit and clean that tiny bottom when she was kicking her legs so energetically and by the time he carried the baby into the kitchen to get on with his next task of preparing a bottle of formula he found Emma sitting at the long table with an array of materials in front of her that included all the cardboard boxes she had gathered at the hospital before coming home.

She was cutting a shape from the cardboard as Max held Alice with one arm and used his free hand to measure scoops of formula into a bottle the way Maggie had shown him yesterday.

'So this will be a big star,' Emma told Ben and Tilly. 'And I'll make a shape for a small star, as well. You can trace around them on other pieces of cardboard and then I can help you cut them out.'

'I can cut things out all by myself,' Ben said.

'Me too,' said Tilly.

Emma's nod was apologetic. 'Of course you can,' she said. 'But I can help if you want me to. And when we've cut some out, I'll show you how to cover them with the silver foil. And then we need to make a hole in one of the pointy bits.'

'Why?'

'So we can tie the stars to the tree. I'm sure we can find some string somewhere.'

Ben looked up at Max as he shook the bottle to dissolve the formula in the cooled boiled water. 'Did you bring the tree inside, Uncle Max?'

'Not yet, Ben. But I will, just as soon as I give Alice her dinner.' He tested the temperature of the milk against his wrist and hoped that how confident he'd just sounded was justified. He still hadn't managed to get Alice to accept a bottle from him yet. Last night he'd needed Emma to rescue him. Maggie had been on hand this morning and Miriam, along with other staff members, had been only too happy to take over when he'd taken the children into work.

Max was holding his breath as he took a seat at the far end of the kitchen table, tipped Alice back into the crook of his elbow and offered her the teat of the bottle as her hungry whimpers became more frantic. He saw the startled expression on her face as she looked up at this new person trying to feed her but she had already tasted the milk and hunger seemed to win the battle with any lack of trust. Her lips closed around the teat and her tiny hands came up to help Max hold the bottle as she began to suck.

He knew he was smiling as he looked up to see if Emma had witnessed this triumph. Max felt absurdly proud of himself. So much so, he actually had a bit of a lump in his throat. He could do this. He *was* doing it.

Emma had a rather oddly shaped cardboard star in her hands and she was showing the children how to wrap it in silver foil but she must have been watching Max's efforts with Alice from the corner of her eye because she caught his gaze as the contented silence of the baby continued and her smile only made him feel even prouder.

Emma was impressed.

And then something weird happened.

It was like one of those photographs where the image had been captured from multiple cameras surrounding the group or one that had been created during that mannequin challenge that had gone viral where everybody froze in the middle of doing something. The effect was that Max was suddenly and acutely aware of so many tiny things, all at once.

There was the weight and warmth of the baby in his arms and the feather-light touch of those miniature fingers against his own hands. He could smell the combination of the milk she was drinking and the baby smell that was partly shampoo and lotion but something else that was just unique to babies, or maybe to this particular baby. He could also see the older children. Ben was standing beside Emma, leaning on her arm as he watched what she was doing with absolute concentration. Tilly had somehow wriggled onto Emma's lap to get closer to the action but she wasn't watching the foil being folded around the points of the cardboard star—she was looking up at Emma.

And Emma, well, she was looking at Max and, while the scene couldn't actually be any more different to the drama of the rescue scene this afternoon when Emma was folded inside that wreck of a car and he was assisting her with that life-saving intervention, there was something similar in this connection. They were a team and, in this moment of time, they were succeeding in what they were trying to achieve.

But there was more to it than that. A whole lot more.

This... Max had to swallow the lump in his throat that had just become oddly uncomfortable. This was a *family* moment and it took him back in time. To when he still had his younger brother in his life. And the mother he had adored so much. A time when they might well have been doing something together, in this very kitchen. A time when this house had been such a happy place. A real home...

Suddenly—shockingly—Max could see right through that barrier he'd started creating as a young boy. The barrier that made him believe that he never really wanted what he'd once had as part of a loving family. That life would be far less painful and much more fun if he just skated across the surface when it came to relationships with other people. If he could turn away from things that were so big they were terrifying and he could simply shut them away in a place he never really needed to visit.

He became the son who loved his father very much but never strayed into the private, sad space that James Cunningham had retreated to after his beloved wife's death.

A big brother who thought he was being kind by telling Andy that Father Christmas didn't exist and that they needed to grow up and look after themselves so that they didn't make things worse for their father.

An uncle who was quite happy to play with the members of a new generation of the Cunningham family but was never tempted by the idea of having children of his own.

A lover who could recognise the moment a woman was falling in love with him and wanted more and took the first opportunity to end things as kindly, but finally, as possible.

And, in this rather shocking moment, he could see that behind those barriers was someone who actually, desperately wanted precisely the things he had spent a lifetime protecting himself from. He wanted the kind of committed, loving relationship his parents had had. He wanted to watch his children grow up. To protect and guide them.

To love them. To have a partner by his side who would also love his children. Who would love *him* and choose to be with him for the rest of her life.

Someone like… Emma…?

As if she had sensed that astonishing thought, Emma broke the eye contact with Max.

'It's your turn now, Ben,' she said. 'You can put the silver foil on the star you cut out.'

Max could have smiled at the wonky star with rather round points that Ben had made but he didn't. It was partly because he wouldn't have wanted to hurt Ben's feelings but it was more to do with the shock of that insight and the idea that he might have got things terribly wrong all those years ago. Thankfully, he could sense those barriers becoming rapidly cloudy again so that he was losing the impression of what he'd seen behind them. He had taught himself well to push those things that were emotionally too big to deal with into the space where they could be locked away.

He might be being forced to have the family he'd never imagined he'd ever have, but that didn't mean he had to take the risk of including anyone else in his life. Good grief…he only had to remember Andy's anguish when his marriage had failed to know that trusting the romantic kind of love was even more of a risk than opening your heart to being a loving father figure. He'd never know whether driving into that tree at high speed had really been accidental but the grief from his brother's death had been devastating enough anyway. He'd lost half his family now. A bit more than that, perhaps, because his father had never been the same since his mother had died so he'd lost a part of him as well.

It was too much loss for anyone.

Max let his breath out in a sigh of relief as Alice finished the last drops of her milk. He set the bottle on the table and moved Alice so that she was upright against his shoulder and he could rub her back to encourage a burp. That barrier was solid again, he realised. He was safe. Maybe it was partly that relief that made him turn his head so that he could press a soft kiss to that silky baby hair. Okay, the barrier had clearly shifted a little and he knew he could make space for these children in his heart. But that was all. His father had never recovered from losing the woman he'd given his heart to and Max knew that the failure of Andy's marriage had been the cause of his death, whether it had been deliberate or simply the fact that he'd been so devastated it had been enough to make him do something he'd never have normally done and get behind the wheel of a car when he was drunk. Marriage—or any kind of long-term commitment to a partner—was still well off Max's radar.

Emma was as safe as he was from anything more than a professional relationship and/or friendship.

James Cunningham didn't approve of the Christmas tree in the drawing room.

Not that he'd said anything, but Emma could sense his shock when he'd walked in when she was helping Ben tie his homemade stars to the branches of the tree that Max had brought inside and set up on one side of the fireplace under Ben's direction.

'It has to be close to the chimney,' he'd told them. 'So that Father Christmas doesn't have to go looking for it. He doesn't have time to do that when he's got so many chimneys he has to go down.'

When James came into the room, Max was holding Tilly up to put her fairy/angel on the top of the tree and Emma had her arms around Ben, gently guiding his small fingers as he tried to tie a bow in the string that they had threaded through the hole in one point of his star.

Max's father had frozen—just for a heartbeat—and, for Emma, it felt as if the world stopped turning for that instant in time as well. She could see what James was seeing. A man with a small girl in his arms, smiling as he watched her stretch out to put the skirt of the angel over the uppermost branch of the tree. A woman almost cradling an older child and a baby asleep in a pram to one side. The fire was crackling softly beside them and it didn't matter that the small number of homemade silver stars, even with the tin soldiers Ben had chosen and the angel for the top of the tree that had been Tilly's choice, still left the tree looking virtually devoid of decorations—this was a snapshot of a family Christmas and all it needed now was the grandfather looking on from the comfort of his leather chair, with his cute dog at his feet.

And Emma could feel something expanding inside her chest. She knew it wasn't physically possible that her heart could be changing size but that was what it felt like. It was getting rapidly bigger. Too big, because it was starting to crack. And bleed...

This... This feeling of family and Christmas. Of having different generations coming together to celebrate something special. Of having children dependent on her for as much love and protection that she could offer and having a partner that she could share the journey with...

She still wanted this. She wanted it so badly it was making her heart ache as much as if it had really split open.

And, maybe, Max's father was aware of a similar sense of yearning. Or loss, perhaps. Because, after that single heartbeat of time, he turned on his heel, snapping his fingers for Pirate to follow him out of the room and his spoken words were only for his dog.

'Sorry,' he muttered. 'I forgot. It's time for your walk, boy.'

Pirate hesitated for a moment, as if he was also contemplating the scene in front of him and would rather stay, but then turned and followed his master out of the room.

Emma had to take her hands away from where they were touching Ben's because she knew that he would notice they were shaking. She needed to gulp in a breath of air as well, because it might have only been an instant in time but it felt like she hadn't taken a breath in quite a while.

This was exactly what she had feared might happen if she became any more involved with the Cunningham men and these children. That she would be reminded that she still didn't have what she'd wanted most in life for almost as long as she could remember—to have a family of her own. She'd taught herself to live without it. To be okay with the idea that it might never happen, in fact, because the walls she had built around her heart and her new lifestyle of never being in one place for a long time had been how she'd coped so well for so long. But she was safe, because that wasn't about to change. Or not yet, anyway. Not when she would be leaving this part of the world in a matter of days. Not for children who belonged to another family or a man who'd never been interested in her.

Except…that wasn't quite true, was it?

He'd been interested enough to kiss her that one time.

And Emma was almost sure he remembered that kiss as well as she did. She also knew they'd both changed enough for curiosity to be part of a feeling of connection between them and…after the intense way Max had been looking at her over the top of the Christmas tree strapped to his car this afternoon, she had a sense that the increased attraction she was so aware of could very well be mutual.

She let out the breath she had taken slowly. A sexual attraction was completely different to the minefield of emotions that came with the notions of family and forever. That was something she could cope with, even if it wasn't something she'd included in her life for a very long time. And she didn't have to think about it right now because there were more important things to focus on. 'Good job, Ben,' she said aloud. 'That's a beautiful star.'

CHAPTER SIX

THE WALK WITH Pirate seemed to have given James whatever inner strength he needed to get back on track with coping and he helped with getting the children fed, bathed and into bed. He excused himself as he stood up from the kitchen table after dinner, however, to retire to his room instead of sitting by the fire.

'It's been a long day,' he said.

'You sure you don't want a nightcap?' Max asked. 'I'm going to have one. Emma? Would you like a glass of wine?'

'I would,' Emma said. 'Thank you.'

'You deserve a chance to wind down properly,' Max said as he went to the fridge to collect the bottle he'd opened the night before. 'You've had a pretty big day as well.'

They had told James about the horrific accident outside the hospital and how they'd worked together at the scene. Emma had wondered if the topic of conversation had been of such interest to James due to professional reasons or because it was a relief to stop talking or even thinking about the three young children under his roof. He was looking so tired now that it was clear he was struggling with the changes in his life as much, if not more than his son and Emma's heart went out to him. It was no surprise that he needed some time on his own and refused the offer of a drink or further company.

Max was silent until he'd put a glass of wine into Emma's hand and then poured himself a small glass of whisky in the drawing room.

'It's this tree,' he told her. 'I can understand why it's upsetting Dad so much. We haven't had a Christmas tree in this house since Mum died.'

'It can't be easy,' Emma agreed quietly. 'But it's important, isn't it? For the children. And...' She stepped closer to the sparsely decorated tree to touch one of the crooked stars, looking up at the angel/fairy who was listing badly to one side at the top. 'And it's a beautiful tree.'

Max sounded as if he was suppressing a snort of laughter as he put his glass down and reached up to straighten the angel.

'It's a bit sad compared to what I remember our Christmas trees being like. Mum was a true fan. She loved fairy lights and candles and had so many boxes of decorations her trees were works of art. It was always a special evening when Andy and I were allowed to help decorate the tree.'

'I think Ben will remember making that star and tying it onto this tree. His first Christmas with the new part of his family.'

Max was silent for a moment and then cleared his throat as if he was intending to change the subject. 'The last time I remember seeing you was at Christmas time,' he said, as if an amusing memory had just surfaced. 'Must be ten years ago? It was at that party...'

Oh...*help*...

Emma could feel spots of bright colour appear on

her cheeks and she couldn't meet his glance. He *did* remember their kiss. For a heartbeat, she couldn't think of anything else. The distance of time had vanished and it might have been only seconds since he'd lifted his lips from hers. That tingle was back, dancing through her body before settling into a tight, hot knot somewhere deep in her gut. To try and cool it down Emma made herself remember what had happened next. That Max had laughed that kiss off as meaning nothing at all and she had followed his example a heartbeat later.

Max's tone was a little more hesitant when he broke the silence again. 'Do you know why I kissed you that night, Emma?'

It was her turn to suppress a sound of laughter. She turned away, heading for one end of the couch. 'You were carrying mistletoe,' she reminded him. 'You were kissing every woman at the party.'

'But you were the first. You were the reason I picked up that silly plastic mistletoe so I had an excuse.' He had picked up his glass again. 'Have you got any idea why I might have wanted to do that?'

Emma sat down on the soft leather cushion.

Did she want to know?

No. She didn't want to know that Max might have been as attracted to her as she had been to him. Because that might put a match to any residual attraction that might be there and…and something might happen…

Which actually meant—if she was really honest with herself—the answer to her silent question was yes. In fact, Emma wanted to know so badly she lifted her gaze when Max remained silent for a long moment, her eyebrows raised to encourage him to tell her.

'Tell me,' she said.

'I saw you crying.'

Shocked, Emma remained silent as Max came to sit down in his father's chair, between her end of the couch and the odd-looking Christmas tree.

'You didn't see me,' he continued quietly. 'And I wanted to try and make you smile again because I knew why you had been crying.'

Emma swallowed hard. 'Did you?'

'It was the day that little boy died. I've forgotten his name. The one who had such a severe case of hypoplastic left ventricle syndrome that the only way to save him would have been a heart transplant. We had just put a PICC line in a few days earlier to give him medication for his heart failure but it hadn't been enough and you'd been there when he—'

'Tyler,' Emma interrupted. 'His name was Tyler.'

'He was special to you.'

More than special. Emma had been totally in love with that ten-month-old baby who had a smile that lit up the room, despite how sick he was.

'He changed my life,' she whispered. 'More than you would believe.'

Max was giving her that look again. The one that made her feel as if he was seeing her properly for the first time. The one that made her feel as if she was the only person in the world that mattered at this very moment in time.

'I knew something big had changed the moment I saw you again in the Royal.' Max hadn't even blinked as he held her gaze. 'It took a while to recognise you. But what did it have to do with Tyler?'

Emma took a sip of her wine. And then another. This wasn't something she talked about. Or even thought about very much if she could help it. It was well in the past now and she was moving on as best she could. But Max's life had just changed as monumentally as Emma's had all those years ago and that gave them a new connection. That fragile new trust was still there as well, and trust always deserved a chance to be nurtured. She would be trusting him with an important part of her own heart if she did tell him her story but there was something in those astonishingly blue eyes that made her feel safe. That said she mattered enough to make her story important. Vital, even…

'I got pregnant,' she admitted. 'A few years after we worked together on that paediatric rotation.'

That didn't seem to surprise Max. 'We all knew you were destined for motherhood,' he said. 'You just loved being with those babies on the paediatric ward so much. Did you get married, then?'

'No. But I was with the person I believed I was going to marry. A paediatric surgeon called Richard. The pregnancy killed our relationship completely.'

'He didn't want children?'

'Oh, he wanted children. That baby wasn't going to be one of them, though. It became obvious during my second trimester scan that she wasn't going to survive. She was anencephalic.'

'Oh, my God…' Max drained his glass. 'I'm so sorry. That must have been so hard to have had to choose a termination at a late stage like that.'

'But I didn't.' Emma's voice was little more than a whisper. 'That was the problem. Richard wanted to get rid of the problem as fast as possible but I chose to carry my baby until she was due to be born. Because of Tyler.'

The pain was still there, wasn't it? The sense of betrayal. That someone who'd said they loved her wasn't prepared to support her in a challenge that was always going to be heartbreaking but felt important enough to be something she had to do in order to be true to herself.

Max was still staring at her so she could see the moment that comprehension dawned. His jaw visibly dropped. 'You carried a baby that you knew could never survive so that she could be a donor for babies like Tyler?'

Emma nodded, blinking hard to make sure she didn't let any tears escape. 'I thought I knew what I was doing. That it wouldn't be as hard as it turned out to be. Losing my relationship because of my choice made it harder, but, in a way, that was probably a good thing because it became obvious that we were too different to ever be happy together.' Emma drew in a shaky breath. 'What broke my heart even more was that she was born on Christmas Day. She only lived for a few hours.' Emma had to swipe away a tear that she hadn't fought off. 'I called her Holly.'

Max said nothing. He got up and went to the sideboard to pour himself another drink from the cut glass decanter. He stood there looking down at the amber liquid as he swirled it in his glass for a long time before he looked up at Emma. It was a look that went straight to her heart and she could feel its intensity in every cell of her body. This wasn't sexual in any way. It was respect. Admiration. Something that felt as if it was wrapping the threads of the connection they already had in a material that was strong enough to be impermeable.

'You're amazing, Em,' he told her. 'You know that, don't you?'

Emma shrugged off what seemed to be an over-the-top compliment, even if it was one that made her feel truly proud of the choice she had made. 'If I hadn't known Tyler maybe I would have made different choices. I might still be a paediatrician instead of a locum. I might be married to Richard and have had three more children and be spending my Christmases in Italy so that they could play with all their cousins...'

But Max was shaking his head. 'I'm glad you didn't,' he said. 'If this Richard couldn't support your choice to do such an incredibly brave and selfless thing then he wasn't someone you would have wanted to spend the rest of your life with, believe me.'

Emma blinked. He thought she was brave? Selfless? Amazing, even...? Would *he* have supported that choice? She had the feeling that he would have and that sparked something that was even more powerful than any physical attraction she was aware of for Max Cunningham. Stronger than friendship, in fact. You could fall in love with a man who could support you to do the really difficult things in life.

More than a little shocked by the thought, Emma had to break any eye contact with Max. Fortunately, she had an excuse to move because she'd just noticed that the bow in the string of the star Ben had tried so hard to attach to the tree had come undone and the star was on the floor. She stooped to pick it up and reattach it.

'I can't imagine how hard that Christmas Day must have been for you,' Max said, moments later. 'I'm really sorry you had to go through that alone.'

His voice was unexpectedly close as Emma straightened up from tying the string, so she wasn't really surprised to find that Max had moved to come and stand beside her. Her body seemed to be startled, however, because it was waking up with an acute awareness of his proximity that was so powerful it was actually painful. More like a stabbing sensation than any pleasant tingle.

'I knew it was coming. I knew I'd be able to cope even though it was hard. And...there was a kind of joy to be found there, as well, knowing that other babies were going to get to go home because of what Holly could give them. One like Tyler, even, who got a heart that was going to work. And, later, I heard that her kidneys had been used...and her liver...'

Emma's voice trailed away. It was still such a bittersweet balance to think about, let alone say aloud. She cleared her throat. 'You've had Christmas Days that were just as tough,' she added. 'Losing your brother last year. Losing your mum when you were so young. That must have cast a shadow over every Christmas since then.'

'We just didn't do Christmas,' Max agreed. 'And that's why this is so hard for my dad.'

It wasn't just hard for James, though. This was just as hard for Max. A part of him had to be missing his mother all over again as he watched Ben and Tilly and Alice struggle to adapt to their new family. And was this year the first he'd ever put up a Christmas tree? Given the way he'd dismissed the whole seasonal celebration as 'commercial hype', she suspected that he had always avoided anything to do with trees or decorations. She also suspected that his avoidance had far more to do with grief than anything else. It gave them another connection but it felt different to her own experience of grief. Max's had started so long ago, when he was no more than a boy and, looking at it from the point of view of an outsider, Emma could see how sad it was. That a father and his sons had been so lost and there clearly hadn't been anyone to help them through their grief. They probably believed they could never change how they felt about Christmas, but how sad would it be if their aversion to celebrating was transferred to yet another generation?

Emma wished there was something she could do to help because this was a lot bigger than her own sadness that was associated with Christmas. This was all to do with three innocent children.

'Do you think he can cope?' she asked. She was referring to James but she held Max's gaze in the hope that he would realise she was asking about his own ability to manage an emotionally difficult situation.

'He'll have to,' Max said—and he could have been speaking for both his father and himself. 'The children are here to stay and…well…it would appear that there are rules when it comes to Christmas.'

Emma smiled. 'There are rules,' she said. 'And I expect Ben knows them all.'

Max was smiling back at her. A small smile that grew. And then grew a bit more.

'What?' she asked. 'What's funny?'

'Nothing,' Max said. 'I'm just pleased to see you smile. The last time I wanted to make that happen for you I had to kiss you.'

Emma could feel her own smile fading. The mention of that kiss again made the intense subject of their recent conversation start to fade instantly into the background and then it hung in the air between them.

Like a suggestion. As if they were both wondering what it would be like to do it again. As if they were both realising that perhaps they really *wanted* to do it again. They were standing so close together it wouldn't take much for one of them to move and if they held this eye contact any longer, that was what was going to happen.

One of them would move and then Max would bend his head or Emma would stand on her tiptoes and they wouldn't need any mistletoe because they didn't need any reason to kiss other than that they were two single adults who happened to be attracted to each other. Possibly seriously attracted...

In that split second of time, however, as the ghost of their first kiss pulled them together like the most powerful magnet imaginable, a sound broke the moment. A crackle of sound that was coming from the handset of the baby monitor as Alice woke and began to cry.

'I'd better go and get her.' But Max seemed reluctant to move.

Emma opened her mouth to offer to help but no words came out because her thoughts were moving so fast they were getting tangled. Warning bells were ringing very loudly as she remembered the moment earlier this evening when that old longing for her own family had resurfaced. She couldn't afford—and didn't want—to get any closer to these children herself than she already was. And what about that moment when she'd realised how easy it would be to fall in love with Max? That should be enough to send her running all on its own because what she remembered most about this man was that he was a playboy. He'd never had the slightest interest in a relationship that was anything more than fun. Short term fun.

But it wasn't just the three bereaved children upstairs that Emma was thinking about right now. It was the two small boys who had lost their own mother decades ago and whose father must have been too wrapped up in his own grief to be able to know what to do and the end result was that they didn't know how to 'do Christmas' any more. Somehow, they needed to get past the ghosts of past Christmas tragedies, but that might not be possible without help from someone who hadn't been a part of that past.

Someone like Emma, who could understand how difficult it was but could also see how important it was for the sake of the children. She could do that if she was brave enough. The safe thing to do would be to remove herself from this house—to stay away from any more reminders of what was missing from her own life and away from the increasing pull she was feeling towards Max, but if she didn't run away—if she stayed here and helped both the Cunningham men and the children—it could be the foundation for a new family to form and bond. For a new life to be possible.

That would be a real gift, wouldn't it?

Not totally dissimilar to the choice she'd made more than five years ago, to do something hard in order to make new life possible for others. Max thought she was amazing for doing that.

Maybe she wanted him to think she was still amazing?

Emma took a deep breath. 'You go and get Alice,' she told Max. 'I'll get a bottle ready for you but then I really need to have a shower and get some sleep. I've got another early start tomorrow.'

Max still hadn't quite moved. 'And tomorrow?' he asked quietly. 'Will you come back here after work and help us put some more decorations on our tree?'

Oh…the warmth in those eyes. A mix of the new trust between them that had grown considerably this evening, shared memories of the past and the remnants of a kiss that hadn't quite happened. And behind what was there between herself and Max, Emma was aware of the needs of others. Of three children who badly needed something special to make them feel safe. Of a sad older man who was still suffering because his memories of Christmas were too painful. What James needed, as well as Max, was to be able to trust in family enough to open their hearts again. Emma could understand exactly why they had shut themselves off but she could also see how much better life would be if they could let go of the past and embrace a new future. And, if she could help them do that, she would be helping herself at the same time. She hadn't actually celebrated Christmas in any meaningful way herself since the day Holly had been born and died.

Maybe fate had brought her here because it was time for a new start. For all of them. It hadn't really been a mistake to come back here today. The mistake would be to leave before they had all taken that new step forwards.

Emma didn't trust herself to say anything aloud, though. All she could manage was to nod before she headed for the kitchen to make up the bottle of formula for Alice, but it was a definitive answer to Max's question nonetheless.

She would be here again tomorrow. And the next day. And Christmas Day.

This was definitely getting a little easier.

Yesterday, in this very room, Max had been trying to feed a baby who wanted nothing to do with him. Now, he was sitting in his father's favourite chair, holding a baby who was almost asleep again before she'd got halfway through her bottle of milk. He should probably take her back upstairs and put her in her cot but he didn't want to move again just yet.

The shape of Alice in his arms was already becoming familiar. The smell of her, as well, as Max bowed his head to get closer to that small head cradled in the crook of his elbow. Imagine holding a baby like this, he thought—your own baby that you'd just given birth to—knowing that, in a blink of time, she would be taken away from you for ever. Max had been totally blown away by hearing Emma's story and his respect for her had gone completely off the scale. He'd never met a woman like her. He'd never met *anyone* like Emma Moretti, in fact.

He could understand now that it really had been fear he'd seen in her eyes the other night when Emma had come into the room to see him holding a miserable, hungry baby that he couldn't cope with. And what had he done? Simply shoved Alice into her arms, that was what, and he felt awful about that now. He wanted to gather Emma into his arms and tell her how sorry he was. Not just for forcing her to take Alice but for everything that had happened to her in the years since they'd gone on separate paths. For the grief she must have gone through. For the broken relationship, although he was quite confident that that Richard had not been good enough for Emma.

She was someone incredibly special. Astonishingly attractive, for that matter. He'd almost *kissed* her again, for heaven's sake. How had that happened in the wake of listening to her tragic story? And why had he longed to do it even more than the first time when all he'd wanted to do was to see that gorgeous smile appear again?

The reminder of that Christmas party made Max wonder if dealing with the aftermath of the grief of losing her baby Holly had contributed to her walking away from the career she had chosen because she loved children and babies so much? She was clearly very good at her locum work, fitting in instantly to new environments and being able to function brilliantly, but it didn't feel like the right fit for someone like Emma. In some ways, she reminded Max of his own mother—someone so clever and capable, with so much love to give the people lucky enough to be within her immediate circle.

It was weird that, even after decades, it was possible to feel a beat of that loss all over again, but it was muted enough that Max could easily refocus his thoughts. Emma was flitting from one job to another now, avoiding commitment to anything. To anyone? Did Christmas Day bring her any joy or was it only filled with unbearably sad memories?

He could understand that.

But...she'd said she was going to come back after work tomorrow and help with some more decorations. That she would stay until Christmas day, in fact. What if...?

Max gently removed the teat from Alice's now slack little rosebud of a mouth but he paused for a long moment before putting the bottle on the table beside him.

What if he could somehow make this Christmas something joyous for Emma? A time when she could smile and enjoy being with children and babies—a family, even? That might help her to take a step forward into a future that she really deserved, where grief could be outweighed by joy. Where sadness could be dimmed by the kind of light that laughter and love could create.

It wouldn't just help Emma. How good would it be for his father? For himself, perhaps, as well. It might not be easy but look at the way he and Emma had worked together today. If he could get her on board, by making it all about the children—or perhaps his father—they could help each other get past any personal issues. He could bury his distaste for the commercial hype of the season and hopefully Emma would get a glimpse of a future where she could see herself celebrating the family bonds that she believed Christmas was all about. A future that she could embrace with no restrictions or fear.

Not being at work meant that Max would have plenty of time to remember the way his mother had made the house come alive at Christmas time. He could go shopping— online, if necessary—to find gifts he could wrap up to go under the tree. He could ask Maggie to do a bit of Christmas baking so that the house would be filled with those delicious aromas he had a faint memory of. He could go up into the dusty attics of this house and drag out those dozens of boxes that contained miles of fairy lights and candles and every kind of decoration you could imagine.

Max looked down at the baby in his arms. He touched her cheek with his forefinger with the softest stroke.

'That's what I'm going to do,' he told Alice. 'For your big brother and sister. For my dad. For Emma. And don't worry, we'll take lots of photos so that it won't matter that you're not old enough to remember your first Christmas and it might be a good thing. This will be kind of a practice run and we'll be really good at it by the time you are old enough to remember.'

He got slowly to his feet, so as not to wake Alice, and carried her upstairs to her cot. It felt good that she was comforted enough to sleep again. It felt good to pass the door of the room not so far from his where he knew Emma would be tucked up in her bed and possibly also asleep.

And it felt really good that he had a mission for the next few days that might help Emma. And his father. Max had always worked hard and played hard. This mission was neither work nor play but the effort he was going to put into it was going to be a hundred and one per cent.

Because it mattered to everybody in this house and Max wanted to protect them all and give them the gift of joy. It might be focused only on one special day for now but it was a beginning and he was determined to make it the best one possible. For everyone, including Emma.

Maybe—given what he'd learned about her today—*especially* for Emma.

CHAPTER SEVEN

LOOPING HER STETHOSCOPE around her neck as she walked into the emergency department of the Royal early the next morning, Emma's steps slowed and almost stopped. Okay, it was Christmas Eve tomorrow, but what the heck were so many people doing in here wearing Santa suits? There had to be about ten of them—a sea of red and white in the cubicle area for injured or ill patients that weren't serious enough to need to be in one of the resuscitation rooms.

Senior nurse Miriam was trying to keep a straight face. 'Seems like it was rather a good Christmas party,' she told Emma. 'There were too many people dancing on the table and a leg broke.'

Emma's eyebrows rose. 'A table leg or a person's leg?'

Miriam's smile escaped. 'The table, but there is a guy with an ankle injury, a woman with a possibly fractured wrist and quite a few bumps and bruises. The others are their partners or colleagues so we couldn't tell them to go away.'

'Who needs to be seen first?'

'Ankle Santa, I think. He's the boss. He's also rather drunk so he might be injured more than he realises.'

The middle-aged man was still wearing his red hat

with white fur trim. Having glanced at the chart on the
end of his bed that told her his vital signs were all within
normal limits, Emma introduced herself and then asked
how he was feeling.

'Never better,' he told her. 'It was the best party ever.
Gonna need a new table in the boardroom, though.'

Several Santas, including one that called from the
next cubicle, seemed to be in agreement that it had been
a memorable party.

'It must have been good,' Emma agreed, 'if it went
on till nearly dawn.'

'Oh, I don't think it's finished yet.' A woman wearing
a red dress with white trimming and a headband with a
small red hat in the middle was holding her arm cradled
against her chest, which suggested she was the patient
with the wrist injury. 'There was a new case of prosecco
being opened when our taxis arrived to bring us here.'

'Hmm…' Emma was already assessing the ankle injury of the man lying on the bed. It was certainly swollen
enough to be either a serious sprain or a fracture but his
toes were a good colour and she could feel a peripheral
pulse on the top of the foot. 'Can you try and wriggle
your toes for me, please?'

She watched the movement and heard the groan that
told her it was causing pain but Emma was not quite
as focused as she would normally have been. It wasn't
just being surrounded by an unusual number of people
dressed like Father Christmas who were all inebriated
to some extent. It was more the mention of the Italian
bubbly they'd been drinking, in combination with knowing that it had been a Christmas party. Because it immediately made her think of *that* particular party. That
particular kiss.

The kiss that had very nearly happened again last night.

How much she had wanted it to happen had been the reason she'd left Max to cope alone with feeding Alice and why she'd slipped out of the house early this morning before anyone else was up. Things were complicated enough in the Cunningham household without letting a sexual attraction get out of hand. Emma wanted to help weld the new family of James, Max and the children together but, at some point in her almost sleepless night, she had decided that even the casual type of relationship that Max Cunningham was famous for would only be a distraction from what he needed to be focused on—the children—so her mission needed to be to keep him on task. If that wasn't exactly what she wanted, she was prepared to deal with it for the sake of everybody else involved.

She needed to keep herself on task as well.

'Have you ever injured this ankle before?'

'Nope. Mind you, I've never done the floss dance before, either.'

'You were really good at it.' A much younger Santa poked his head around the curtain. 'I'm still trying to figure it out.' He straightened his arms and held them out, staring at them as if he was trying to decide which one to move.

'Move your hips first,' someone called. 'Get the rhythm.'

'Uh-uh…' The firm voice belonged to Miriam. 'No dancing in here, folks. If you're well enough to dance, you need to go out to the waiting room. We've got sick people in here.' She tilted her head in Emma's direction. 'You need any help, Dr Moretti?'

Emma shook her head. 'But call me if anything major comes in.'

'I'm major,' her patient told her. 'Don't leave me, darlin'.'

'Do you have any medical conditions I should be aware of? Heart disease or high blood pressure? Diabetes or lung problems?'

'Nah. I'm as fit as a fiddle. Or I will be. I've asked Santa for a gym subscription this year. In fact, I think I asked several Santas.'

A ripple of laughter came from adjoining cubicles. 'Wasn't me,' someone called.

'I don't remember being asked,' someone else shouted. 'But I can't remember much at all right now, come to think of it.'

Emma was examining the ankle more closely. She put her hand under the foot near the toes. 'Can you push your foot against my hand, please?' She shifted her hand to the top of the foot next. 'Pull up against it, now?'

'Ouch.'

'I don't think it's broken,' Emma told him a short time later. 'But we'll send you off for an X-ray just to be on the safe side.'

The woman with the wrist injury was also sent to X-ray, but the other injuries were deemed minor and the crowd of red and white patients gradually dispersed, some beginning to complain of headaches and feeling rather unwell.

'Christmas parties,' Miriam muttered, shaking her head. 'More trouble than they're worth most of the time.'

'Mmm.' Emma needed to stop thinking about Christmas parties.

About Max and being thoroughly kissed by him.

Her next patient, coming in by ambulance already intubated and being ventilated after what appeared to be a serious stroke, was more than enough to give Emma complete focus on her job and that continued for the rest of her shift, with one case after another that required rapid assessment and treatment to stabilise them. There was an elderly man with septic shock, a drug overdose, pulmonary embolism, two heart attacks and a ten-year-old child with a severe asthma attack who needed transferring to the intensive care unit for close monitoring when she was finally out of immediate danger.

Emma was still thinking about that last case as she drove back to Upper Barnsley. The child's mother had burst into tears when told that the worst seemed to be over.

'She'd just been writing a reminder list for Father Christmas,' she sobbed. 'And I was feeling so smug because I've already got everything hidden away but...but I've just had an hour to wonder what it would have been like if they'd never been unwrapped...'

Those gifts would get unwrapped and that made it a good note on which to have finished her day. It had also reminded Emma that Max had asked her to find out what Ben and Tilly might have asked to receive for a special Christmas gift. Maybe when she got home she could help them write a list to put up the chimney. She was all ready to suggest this to Max the minute she walked through the door, but she didn't get a chance to say anything.

'Come with me.' It looked as if he'd been waiting for her to get home. 'We haven't got long.'

He grabbed Emma by the hand and started to head upstairs. Towards the bedrooms? Emma thought about tugging her hand free and trying to find out what was going on, but the warmth of Max's hand around hers and the determination of his forward movement was irresistible and all Emma could actually think about was that she'd probably go anywhere with this man if he wanted her to—even to a totally unknown destination. It was exciting. Thrilling, even. Especially the feeling of his skin against hers as they hurried upstairs. Her resolution to stay away from any intimate involvement with him seemed to be fading rapidly as the heat and feeling of strength in the hand holding hers made her curl her fingers tighter to make sure the connection wouldn't be lost.

They went past the bedrooms, into another hallway Emma hadn't seen before, with old portraits hanging on the walls, and then up a smaller staircase.

'The servants' quarters were up here long before my family moved in,' Max told her. 'It's where we used to hide when we were kids, Andy and me.'

'Is that what we're doing? Playing hide and seek with Ben and Tilly?'

'No.' They were up the small staircase now and leaving footprints on dust-covered floorboards. 'They're in the kitchen with Maggie and her daughter Ruth. Ruth's just gone on maternity leave from her job as an infant school teacher and she's brilliant with the kids. They're icing Christmas cookies at the moment. Alice is asleep. Dad's out on a house call. It's the first chance I've had all day to do this.' He stopped to peer up yet another staircase that was steep and narrow enough to be more like a ladder. Then he grinned at Emma. 'The main attic's up here,' he added, letting go of her hand as he started to climb. 'And there should be enough Christmas decorations to sink a battleship, if they haven't been eaten by

mice or something. I need some help getting them downstairs but I didn't want Ben trying to get up and down
these stairs. And I didn't want Dad to know what I was
doing because he would have tried to stop me. He won't
like it but if we can start putting them up I figured he
would see how much fun it is for the kids and…and…'

'He won't want to disappoint them.' Emma nodded
as she followed Max up the narrow stairs. 'A bit of emotional blackmail, huh? Well, it certainly worked on me.'

'What? When?' Max sounded appalled.

'When you reminded me about telling the children
I'd show them how to make stars. Or getting them to
remind me…'

'Oh…' Max disappeared through the hole in the ceiling and then turned to offer his hand to help Emma as
she reached the final stairs. Having been holding it so
recently, it felt completely natural to take it again, allowing him to pull her into the attic space. He was still
smiling as he tugged her forward.

'Do you forgive me?' he asked. 'For emotionally
blackmailing you?'

'It was for a good cause.' Emma realised that if she
kept that forward momentum going she would end up
bumping into Max's body. He'd probably put his hands
on her shoulders to steady her and it might very well be
an opportunity to pick up where they'd left off last night.
To step back into that 'pre-kiss' moment if she wanted to.

She did want to. Very much. But, at the same time, it
was making her nervous. Emma put the brakes on that
forward movement unconsciously and, for a heartbeat,
she stood completely still. She was now aware of the
faint light coming from dormer windows in this highest
level of the house. It was crowded with boxes and fur-

niture and any amount of objects and it smelled musty and secretive. Even without kissing Max, it was still exciting because she'd never been in a real, storybook kind of attic before and they were here together and… and, well…

It was fun. And how long was it since Emma had done anything just for the sheer enjoyment of it?

'Look…there's one.' Max let go of Emma's hand to open a box. 'It's the fake greenery,' he exclaimed, moments later. 'I remember that Mum used to wind it through the bannister posts on the main stairs. And this one…' He pulled open another box. 'It's fairy lights. We need fairy lights on our tree, don't we?'

'Absolutely.' Emma was reaching for another box on the stack. This one was full of objects wrapped in tissue paper. 'Decorations,' she exclaimed. 'Oh, look… it's fruit. Little silver and gold apples and pears. And red cherries.'

'Don't open them yet.' Max caught her hand as she delved further into the box. 'Let's take them downstairs and the kids can help us.'

The touch of his hand, yet again, was more than enough to stop Emma. Turning her head, she found she was just as close to Max as they'd been last night beside the Christmas tree when she had been sure they would have ended up kissing if Alice's cry hadn't interrupted the moment. There was no baby's cry happening right now and they were possibly in the most secret part of this huge old house but, as Emma's gaze locked with Max's, she knew that they weren't about to steal a kiss. It felt as if they were making a kind of silent pact in this moment. That this was about the children and they were equal partners on the same team. Which was pretty much the conclusion Emma had reached last night, however tempting it might be to explore this unexpected revival of a seemingly mutual attraction between herself and Max. And it would appear that Max had decided the same thing.

She shouldn't be disappointed, Emma told herself firmly. She wasn't. Not really...

If she told herself that often enough, maybe she would actually believe it.

Oh, man...

He wanted to kiss Emma so much. Had she noticed that he couldn't seem to stop himself touching her? She'd been perfectly capable of climbing those stairs or getting up into the attic all by herself and here he was, holding her hand again, under the pretext of stopping her unwrapping any more decorations.

And the way she was looking at him. As if she wanted him to kiss her?

Well, he couldn't and that was all there was to it. Giving in to the temptation was the way the old Max would have responded. The one who was happy to play with any number of beautiful women. To love them and leave them and give himself a reputation that he was, finally, rather ashamed of. He had far more important responsibilities now and, besides, he respected Emma far too much to think that she might be happy to indulge in a casual affair.

She seemed perfectly happy to play Christmas decorations with him, however. Together, they ferried box after box downstairs and, as Max had been hoping, Ben and Tilly were so excited about what was inside all the boxes that they were almost unrecognisable compared to the silent, scared children who'd been sitting on the couch in the drawing room only a few evenings ago.

Maggie and her pregnant daughter Ruth were staying on to help—as curious as the children about what was being unearthed from decades of storage. Alice lay, still sleeping, in her pram near the couch as they spread out the boxes and opened them all.

'Look at these cute bunches of bells.' Ruth held up a trio of tiny golden bells, tied together with a loop of red ribbon.

'They went on the doors,' Max told her. 'So they would jingle every time someone went in or out of a room. And that really big wreath? That's for the front door.'

'There are so many candles.' Maggie had opened another box. 'And what's this? A tablecloth? And Christmas serviettes?'

'I don't think we'll need them,' Max said. 'I'm not sure I'd know where to start making a Christmas dinner.'

Maggie and her daughter shared a glance. 'Perhaps we could help,' she said. 'It was only going to be me and Ruth at our house and we've got a turkey that's far too big for just the two of us. We could come here and do dinner for everybody if you like.'

'What do you think, Ben?' Max asked. 'Are there rules about Christmas dinner?'

Ben nodded. 'Pigs in blankets,' he said. 'And red jelly for pudding.'

Maggie laughed. 'I think we could manage that.' She looked at Emma. 'You'll be here for dinner, I hope?'

'It sounds great,' Emma said. 'I'm covering a night shift on Christmas Eve so I'll definitely be back in time for dinner.'

Max wound a long string of fairy lights all over the tree in the drawing room but told Ben and Tilly to stand back while he plugged them in and turned the switch on. 'I'm not quite sure what's going to happen,' he told them. 'These lights haven't been used for a very long time.'

'Why not?' Ben asked.

'Because they were my mum's—your grandma's—special Christmas things and…well, she died and we were very sad so we never used them again.'

'Why not?' Ben was frowning. 'You've got to have lights on your Christmas tree. It's a—'

'—rule. I know.' Max flicked the switch and the lights came to life, making the tree sparkle as they flashed on and off sequentially. Instead of having bulbs that didn't work any more, or wires that caught fire because they had deteriorated over the years, it looked as if these decorative lights were as good as new. Max decided he was going to take that as a good omen. That everything was going to work and sparkle with a bit of Christmas magic.

'My mummy's died too.' Tilly's bottom lip was wobbling. 'And *I'm* sad.'

'I know, sweetheart.' From the corner of his eye, Max saw Emma start to reach out to Tilly but then he saw the way she stopped herself—the way her hands curled into soft fists—as if she was just too afraid to let herself follow her natural instinct to comfort this small girl. So he was the one who went to Tilly to scoop her up and cuddle her. He resisted the urge to draw Emma into the hug as well. If he tried to force her to open her heart to these children she might change her mind about staying to share Christmas with them and run away. He could only hope that some of that sparkly Christmas magic would wrap itself around Emma and she could find the courage to step past the perfectly understandable fear she had and that, by doing so, she would see what a new future could offer her.

'Can you help me?' he asked Tilly. 'You could unwrap all the ornaments in that box and then we can all hang them on the tree.'

'There's this green stuff too,' Emma said, pulling at loops of the long, thin length of artificial foliage of ivy, mistletoe and holly with red berries. 'I could go and put that on the bannisters, perhaps? And hang the bells on the doors?'

If it was time away from the children that she needed, it wasn't going to work. Ben's eyes widened as he saw the impressive amount of greenery appearing.

'I want to help,' he said.

'Me too.' Tilly wriggled out of Max's arms. 'I like bells *and* stars.'

She was almost running in her haste to get closer to Emma when it happened. The doorframe of the drawing room was filled with the tall figure of James Cunningham and the furious vibe radiated from him with the speed of light.

'What the *hell* is going on here?' he roared. 'Where did you get those boxes?'

'From the attic, Dad.' Max kept his tone carefully neutral. 'We needed more decorations for the tree.'

But his words could barely be heard over the sound of children crying. The angry roar had made Ben cower behind Emma's legs, still holding one end of a garland of greenery. Tilly had burst into tears and even Alice had woken in her pram and started howling. Maggie and Ruth both moved towards the baby. He saw the way Emma instinctively stretched out her arms as if creating a safe circle for the two children close to her. She was glaring at his father, as well, looking both horrified and angry that he was scaring everybody.

Max was angry too, even though part of his heart was breaking for his dad. He'd known his father would be upset at having his wife's precious decorations appear again with no prior warning but it wasn't fair to take it out on the children like this. Even Pirate was looking worried, slinking away from James to hide beneath one of the chairs.

'You've got no right.' James's voice was still loud enough to qualify as shouting. 'Put them back. Ben... put that down. Right now.'

The garland slid instantly from Ben's hands.

Max cleared his throat. 'If Mum was here, this is exactly what she'd be doing,' he told his father.

'I want *my* mummy,' Tilly sobbed, sinking into a puddle of miserable child on the floor. Ben came out from behind Emma and crouched to put his arms around his little sister. Pirate came out from beneath the chair and went slowly towards the children. He sat down close to Tilly and pressed his nose to the hands covering her eyes. Perhaps it was the surprise of seeing the little dog as she opened her eyes that made her stop crying.

Maggie was rocking baby Alice and successfully soothing her. Ruth had her hands protectively on the impressive bump of her belly and was staring nervously at her mother's employer. Max shifted his gaze to Emma to find she was staring straight back at him. If he'd had any doubts at all about her level of commitment to help him make this Christmas special for the children, they evaporated instantly. In the face of opposition she had just become as determined as he was to make this work.

She was going to do whatever it took to protect these children, even if she had to do it alone, but she wanted his help. She needed him to be by her side and that made him feel remarkably fierce.

He would do whatever it took to protect Emma, as well as the children.

'It's what Mum would have wanted us to do, Dad,' he said firmly. 'You know that. You know how much she loved Christmas. How much she wanted everyone to be happy. I know it's been a very long time but we are going to have a proper Christmas in this house this year.'

James was staring at the boxes. At the huge wreath that Maggie had put to one side to take out to the front door. At the bunches of bells and the tissue-wrapped decorations.

'Oh…do what you want, then,' he snapped. 'You're obviously going to, anyway. I'm going out.' He snapped his fingers. 'Pirate…come with me…'

But Pirate didn't move. If anything, the little dog pressed itself closer to Tilly and Ben's hand moved to rest on the small white head. For a horrified moment, Max wondered if his father was about to march further into the room and drag his dog away from the children but James just stared for a moment longer, made a sound that was a frustrated growl and then turned on his heel and marched out of the room.

For a long, long moment, there was silence in the drawing room. It was broken by Ben's small voice.

'I don't think Grandpa likes Christmas,' he said.

Max walked over to his nephew and crouched down beside him. 'He used to,' he told Ben. 'It was the best day of the year for all of us when I was a little boy like you. He's just forgotten, that's all. But we can help him remember. He's not cross with you. He's just...'

'Sad.' Ben nodded. 'Because his mummy died.'

Max didn't bother trying to correct his interpretation of a former generation's relationships. 'It's always sad when someone you love dies,' he agreed. 'And it's okay to be sad but it's okay to have fun too. Why don't we all have fun now and see how pretty we can make everything with all these decorations? Do you think you and Tilly can pull that long rope of leaves and berries all the way up the stairs?'

Max caught Emma's anxious glance as the children headed for the door.

'It's all right,' he said. 'Dad will have gone out for a walk or something. He just needs time to get his head around this.'

Emma didn't look convinced.

'It's been a very long time,' Max added. 'I suspect he's healed far more than he even realises but he's never going to find out if that plaster doesn't get ripped off. Having a proper Christmas with his grandchildren might be the best thing that could ever happen for him.'

Emma was still frowning. 'As long as he doesn't hurt the children. Don't you think Ben's going to be a bit scared of him after that outburst?'

'Maybe.' Max was holding Emma's gaze. 'But I think he's going to be fine. Even the scary stuff isn't too bad as long as you've got someone on your side and Ben's got me. He's always going to have me.'

Would Emma pick up on the silent message that he was there for her as well? That she had him by her side as she faced what was probably her first real celebration of Christmas for a long time?

Maybe she had. There was a sparkle in her eyes that looked as if a tear or two was gathering.

'He's a lucky little boy,' she said quietly. 'And I think you're right. He's going to be fine.'

'He'll need help with that green stuff. Why don't I come and show you how Mum used to do it and then we can all do the decorations for the tree?'

It was much later that evening that Emma went down the stairs, admiring the greenery woven through the bannister railings, heading for the kitchen to get a glass of water. To her surprise, she found Max sitting at the kitchen table with his laptop open in front of him and the handset from the baby monitor to one side. James was also there, an empty plate in front of him that told Emma he'd eaten the meal they'd left in the oven when he hadn't come home in time for dinner.

'I owe you an apology too,' he said gruffly.

Emma nodded her acceptance. 'The children missed you at bedtime,' she told him. 'They wanted you to read them a story. Ben said that it might make you feel better because stories always make *him* feel better.'

James stared at her for a long moment. 'You always know the right thing to say, don't you, love? You're like my Hannah was, like that.' He got to his feet. 'I'm off to bed,' he said. 'But I'd better take Pirate out first. It's starting to snow and he doesn't like it when it gets too deep on the grass. Do you know where he is?'

'Lying beside Ben's bed,' Emma told him. 'I think he's decided it's his job to protect the children.'

'He's not the only one, is he?' James put his plate in the sink. 'It's okay… Now that I'm over the shock, I know I was wrong and I'll tell the children that tomorrow. It's time for Christmas to happen again here. Time for a new beginning.' He smiled at Emma. 'Maybe I should write my Christmas wish on a bit of paper too, and you could put it up the chimney. Max told me about you doing that for the children this evening.'

'It's what I'm working on now,' Max put in. 'Seeing if I can find exactly what they want online and get it delivered secretly tomorrow.'

'Didn't Ben say he wanted a blue bicycle?' Emma reminded him. 'That might be a bit hard to keep secret.'

'There's some rooms that aren't being used above the clinic. Extra bedrooms and a bathroom or two. It could make a good suite for live-in help for a housekeeper or nanny later, maybe. In the meantime, it'll be easy to get things delivered out of sight and hide them in there, wrap them up tomorrow night and put them under the tree for Christmas morning.'

James was heading for the door. 'Don't forget the stockings.' His voice was a growl. 'The ones your mum always hung up above the fireplace. They must be in one of those boxes.'

Max waited until his father had left the room. 'He's trying hard,' he said quietly. 'It's not easy.'

'I know. For you too.' Emma had been watching Max as they'd decorated the tree earlier. She'd seen the way he'd held some of those decorations so reverently—like the gorgeous glass angels and wooden gingerbread men—as if he was remembering the last time he'd done this, when his mother had been there as well, and her heart had ached for that little boy who must have dreaded Christmas for so many years afterwards.

She pulled up a chair to sit close beside him so that

she could see the screen of his laptop. 'How are you going on finding things?'

'Not bad. Derby's has a great toy department. I've found a bicycle for Ben and a football and a tent.'

'A tent?'

'It was something that Andy and I used to do—put a tent up in the woods and pretend we were miles from anywhere. I thought Ben might like to try that.'

'It's a great idea.'

'I'm not sure what Tilly meant by "fairy stuff", though.'

'Oh... I can help with that.' Emma leaned closer so that she could use the mouse and scroll through the available items. 'Look...a tutu, wand, tiara and wings all in a set. There's even a pot of fairy dust, which is probably glitter and will make an awful mess. That's what "fairy stuff" is all about.'

Emma looked up, her smile full of the delight of imagining the look on Tilly's face when she discovered exactly what Emma had helped her write on her scrap of paper that had gone up the chimney. She hadn't realised just how close she'd got to Max as she leaned over the laptop, however. And she hadn't expected him to be grinning down at her, as pleased as she was to have found the perfect gift.

And there it was.

That moment again, as their gazes locked and their smiles faded as they both found they couldn't look away from each other. That the magnetic pull was simply too powerful to resist.

'Thanks.' Max's voice was a little hoarse. A deep, sexy growl. 'I wouldn't be managing this if I didn't have you to help.'

'Oh…it's my pleasure.' Emma's voice was more like a whisper and her last word was the one that tipped the balance of control. *Pleasure*… It hung there between them and she knew that Max was thinking exactly the same as what was going through her own head. That real pleasure was also hanging there, just waiting for one of them to make the first move.

Maybe both of them did, because a split second later their lips were touching. So softly at first that Emma had to close her eyes so that she could feel it properly. And then she felt the movement of Max's lips on hers and her own lips parting. The kiss wasn't so soft now but it was when she was aware of the touch of his tongue on her lip before meeting the tip of her own tongue that Emma stopped even thinking about what was happening and fell into a forgotten sensation.

Sheer pleasure, that was for sure. So intense that nothing else existed. This was nothing like that public kiss under the mistletoe at that long-ago Christmas party. This was nothing like any kiss Emma had ever had in her life. She didn't want it to stop but the need for oxygen made it a necessity and her first breath was a gasp. She opened her eyes to find Max staring at her, looking as stunned as she was feeling.

Oh…*help*…

This wasn't supposed to have happened.

Emma braced herself for what was about to happen next. Laughter, perhaps, to dismiss the kiss as no big deal? The reassurance that she had nothing to worry about because she was 'so not' Max's type?

As he opened his mouth to say something, Emma closed her eyes so that she could hide her reaction to whatever he might be about to say.

CHAPTER EIGHT

MAX HAD NO idea what to say but felt the need to express appreciation for what had to have been the most memorable kiss of his lifetime and that was saying something, given how much practice he'd had.

There was something very different about Emma Moretti. It wasn't just the softness of her lips, or the incredible taste of her mouth, or the way she responded to him as if they were having a conversation in a language they were the only two people in the world who could speak. It was bigger than that. Because he'd come to realise that Emma was the most extraordinary woman he'd ever met and he had huge respect for her, professionally but even more on a personal level.

That she had chosen to go through such a traumatic experience as carrying a baby for months that was never going to survive only to help others was something he felt put Emma way out of his league in terms of humanity and kindness and the kind of virtues that nobody would associate with someone who had his kind of reputation with women. It made him feel curiously shy to even think that she might be interested in him but that kiss had just revealed that she was possibly just as attracted to him as he was to her. That she might, in fact, be just as desperate to take it a lot further than just a kiss.

Just a kiss?

Ha! The words that finally escaped Max's lips were not ones he normally used in public but he needed something very succinct and powerful to sum up his reaction. His words certainly startled Emma. Her eyes flew open and then widened in shock.

'I thought you were going to laugh,' she said. 'Not say…*that*…'

'Why on earth would I laugh?'

'That's what you did the last time you kissed me.'

'Did I?' Max searched his memory. 'No… I think it was *you* that laughed and I was pleased that you were looking happier again because that was what I wanted to happen.'

'You laughed first,' Emma insisted. 'And then you told me not to worry because I was so not your type.'

Oh…that was true. But not true at the same time. Even then he'd known precisely how attractive Emma Moretti was but she definitely wasn't his 'type' because she was dangerous. Or he was dangerous as far as she was concerned. She wanted such different things out of life and he would have ended up hurting her if he'd acted on that attraction. How ironic was it that he was the one who'd ended up with a bunch of kids and Emma was footloose and fancy free, roaming the world and perfectly entitled to work and play wherever and with whomever she chose.

Another thought that was a little disturbing was that if Emma had remembered his exact words after all this time, was it because he'd managed to hurt her anyway when he'd been trying to make sure he didn't? Max held Emma's gaze.

'No man in his right mind wouldn't have fancied you, Emma. I said that because I knew I wasn't *your* type. Maybe I wanted to say it before you did.'

'You weren't my type,' Emma agreed. There was a tiny smile tugging at one corner of her mouth. 'You were the "love 'em and leave 'em" bad boy of that group of registrars. But no woman in her right mind wouldn't have fancied you.'

Max found it suddenly rather difficult to swallow. Was she saying what he thought she might be saying? That she had fancied him? That she still did? He could find that out, he thought, if he kissed her again. If Emma wanted him to kiss her again. And, if she did, then he could scoop her up into his arms and take her...where... to his bedroom?

Where Alice lay sleeping in her cot?

His head turned to where the baby monitor handset was sitting beside his laptop. Emma had followed the direction of his gaze and he heard the sigh as she let her breath go. The reminder of the close proximity of three children was creating enough of a problem even theoretically. The small voice they both heard at the kitchen door a second later made it even more of a reality.

'Uncle Max?'

He turned swiftly. 'What is it, Ben?'

'I woke up.'

'I can see that, mate.' Max shut the lid of his laptop before Ben could see that he'd been surfing the toy department of Derby's. 'Did you have a bad dream?'

'Pirate's run away.'

'No, he hasn't.' Emma was smiling reassuringly at

Ben. 'Your grandpa just took him outside for a little walk. He'll be back any minute.'

Her gaze snagged Max's and it was another reminder of how difficult it was going to be to find time to be alone in the near future, if ever. It wasn't as if Emma was even going to be here for very long, either. Was he crazy to think that getting to know this amazing woman on a more intimate level was possible, let alone a sensible idea? It felt like Emma was thinking along the same lines. It also felt like she was reaching the same conclusions.

That it was no more crazy than this set of totally un-expected circumstances they had found themselves in, temporarily living together in this old house with or-phaned children, their grandfather and his dog and with a Christmas celebration to orchestrate when they'd both been avoiding doing something like that for many years. That they were both single adults and, if they wanted to, they could choose to indulge in a sexual attraction that wasn't going to hurt anybody else. And that the attrac-tion between them wasn't about to vanish any time soon and perhaps they both needed to find out if it could live up to its promise of being one of those experiences that you might only find once in a lifetime.

Not that they were about to get the chance to find that out right now. Max needed to get Ben settled back into his bed but, as he led his nephew out of the kitchen, the front door of the house opened and his father and Pirate came inside. He felt Ben's hand clutch his fingers more tightly but the brave little boy straightened as he stood beside Max, as if he was getting ready to be growled at again by his grandfather.

Emma had come out of the kitchen as well so, for a moment, they all stood there holding their breath. It was Pirate who broke the tension, trotting towards Ben with his tail wagging. Ben let go of his uncle's hand and dropped to cuddle the small white dog.

'I think Pirate wants to go back to bed,' James said into the silence that followed. 'Shall I come and tuck you both in?'

This silence was even more tense and Max let his breath out in a silent but very relieved sigh as, after staring at his grandfather for a long moment, Ben nodded solemnly and started walking towards him. He had almost reached him when there was a loud thumping on the door behind James.

'What the—?' James opened the door. *'Jenny...?'*

'Oh, Dr Cunningham—I'm so sorry to disturb you at this time of night but I saw you walking past. It's Terry. I think he really is having a heart attack this time...'

Both Max and Emma were moving towards the distressed woman. Emma reached for her coat on the rack near the door. 'I'll come,' she told Jenny. 'Have you called an ambulance?'

'Yes, but it's really snowing hard now and I'm not sure if they'll get through.'

Max didn't bother finding his coat. 'I'll get our first-aid pack from the clinic,' he told Emma. 'And the defibrillator. I'll meet you there in a minute.'

He turned back to find that his father was holding Ben's hand. 'Don't worry,' he told Max. 'I've got this. You go with Emma. I'll look after the children.'

'You sure?'

'Yes. Take your phone. I'll call if I need you. Go...'

Max must have run very fast, both to collect the equipment and then get down the long driveway, up the road and into the neighbouring property so quickly. Emma had only had minutes to start assessing Terry.

'The pain came on about twenty minutes ago,' she told Max. 'Central chest pain, radiating to his left arm. Ten out of ten, with vomiting and profuse sweating. Unrelieved by his spray. Radial pulse palpable but faint.'

They were classic symptoms of a heart attack and nothing like the pain he had presented with after his muscle strain the other day. He also had other symptoms that made it far less likely to be anything muscular. Max opened pouches on the defibrillator pack and began unrolling wires and snapping electrodes onto their ends.

'There's an IV roll in the pack,' he told Emma. 'And a small oxygen tank in the side pocket.'

'Onto it.' Emma put a reassuring hand on Terry's shoulder. 'Max is going to do what I did the other day and put the electrodes on your chest so we can see what's going on with your heart. I'm going to give you some oxygen and put a small cannula in a vein on your arm so that we can give you something for the pain. We're going to give you some fluid through that line as well, to help your blood pressure. Is that all okay with you?'

Terry nodded. He was looking terrified. So was his wife.

'Do whatever you need to,' Jenny whispered. 'Please...'

Emma opened the IV roll and found everything she needed to put an IV line in. There was a separate pouch that contained drugs in both ampoules and packets. She popped a tablet from its foil strip.

'I'll get you to chew this up for me first,' she told Terry. 'It's an aspirin tablet. Jenny, maybe you could get a sip of water to help it go down?'

Jenny looked relieved to be given a helpful task.

Emma focused on gaining access to a vein on the back of Terry's hand with a needle and then sliding the plastic cannula into place and taping it down securely. Max was working around her, sticking electrodes to Terry's shoulders and each side of his abdomen and then in a pattern across his chest and around his heart. They were working together, as smoothly as they had the day they had been treating the victims of that multi-car pile-up outside the Royal, but it felt different now. The professional trust they already had was coloured by a far more personal connection. Not that either of them would have been giving that kiss a moment's head space but it was there, somewhere in the background, and it had brought them a whole lot closer.

'Are you allergic to any medications?' Emma asked.

'No…' Terry's voice was slightly muffled behind the oxygen mask that was now in place.

'Is the pain still ten out of ten?'

Terry closed his eyes as he nodded. Jenny was hunched over the back of the chair her husband was slumped in, one hand pressed against her mouth, the other stroking Terry's head.

'I'm going to give you some morphine,' Emma told him. 'As well as something else to stop you feeling sick. You should notice a difference in the pain very soon.'

'And I need you to keep as still as possible, Terry,' Max said. 'I'm going to take a recording of your heart now.'

He looked up to catch Emma's gaze as the graph paper began to spill out of the monitor. He knew she had seen the big picture of what was going on already on the screen and that Terry was, indeed, having a heart attack.

'ST elevation leads two, three and aVF,' Max confirmed as he showed Emma the printout. 'T wave changes starting.'

'Inferior infarct,' Emma agreed quietly. Heart attacks in this region had a better prognosis than other regions but it was still time critical to get Terry to hospital for the definitive treatment that would reopen his coronary arteries.

'I'll ring the hospital,' Max offered. 'They can get the catheter lab team on standby for angioplasty.'

'Can you find out how far away the ambulance is?' Emma asked. 'And do they have transmission ability so we can send the twelve-lead ECG through first?'

Max nodded. 'Yes, and yes.'

Emma turned back to their patient. 'How's the pain now, Terry?'

'Better.'

'On the scale of zero to ten?'

'Maybe five.'

'That's great. I'm going to take your blood pressure and a few other measurements now. Try and relax. We're going to get you to hospital very soon.'

'So he is really having a heart attack this time?'

'It looks like it, Jenny. But try not to worry too much, okay? The treatment of angioplasty will stop the damage that's happening. You did exactly the right thing in calling the ambulance and then coming to find us so quickly, which meant we could start the treatment faster.'

'Ambulance is only a few minutes away,' Max reported as Emma wrote down the set of vital signs she had just taken. 'Apparently the road's not too bad with the snow yet and the call's gone out to the cath lab. They're expecting Terry in Emergency as well.'

'Jenny? Could you go and pack a bag for Terry? Just

his pyjamas and toothbrush and things he might need for a day or two in hospital?'

Again, Jenny seemed grateful for something useful she could do and she had accomplished her task by the time the paramedics arrived with a dusting of snow on their shoulders and a cheerful ambience that was immediately reassuring.

'How lucky are you to have doctors living next door?' they said to Terry. 'Looks like they've done all the hard work for us too. We just need to put you on our comfy stretcher, change you over to our monitor and oxygen and we'll be at the hospital in no time at all.'

'Can I come with him?' Jenny asked anxiously.

'Of course you can, love.'

'I can come as well.' Emma picked up her coat from where it had been thrown over the back of a couch.

'No need, Doc. You've done everything already and all we need to do is keep a close eye on Terry here until we get him into the Royal.'

They both knew that the only real danger was that Terry could go into a cardiac arrest en route but it seemed unlikely given how stable his cardiac rhythm was looking despite the changes happening with the heart attack and they were going to get Terry into the safety of the emergency department as soon as possible. They were already rolling the stretcher towards the door. These paramedics were just as capable as Emma of dealing with a cardiac arrest and, if she went in with the ambulance, how would she get home again?

Max was winding up the wires for the defibrillator. 'You go with Terry,' he told Jenny. 'We'll tidy up the mess we've made and then lock up. I'll leave the key in the usual place, yes?'

'Oh…thank you, Max. I can't tell you how grateful we are… You and your dad… Well, we're just blessed to have you in Upper Barnsley, that's what…'

'I'll call the hospital in a bit to find out what's happening.' Max had paused in his task to smile at Jenny. 'He's going to exactly where he needs to be,' he said gently. 'Try not to worry.'

Emma went with Jenny to see her climb into the front passenger seat of the ambulance, which had its lights flashing in the drift of snowflakes as it drove away. She went back inside to help Max tidy up, picking up packaging from the IV supplies and the plastic squares that had come off the ECG electrodes. He was rolling up the IV kit and slotting it back into place in the first-aid pack.

It was only then that Emma realised they were alone again for the first time since they had shared that astonishing kiss.

Since Max had pretty much admitted that he'd always fancied her. Since she had told him pretty much the same thing.

The silence was suddenly a little awkward.

'It's really snowing out there,' Emma finally said. 'I might have to put chains on my car to get into work in the morning.'

'They'll clear the roads fast.' Max zipped up the pocket that held the small oxygen tank in the kit.

'Should I have gone in with Terry, do you think?'

'He didn't need you.' Max's tone was reassuring. 'I know those paramedics and they're great. He'll be safely in the cath lab within an hour and I reckon he's going to be fine. It might muck up their Christmas plans but Terry will probably end up being a lot healthier than he's been for a long time.' He stood up. 'Besides… I need you.' He offered her the ghost of a wink. 'There's too much gear to carry.'

Emma's heart skipped a beat but her mouth was suddenly too dry to supply the obvious comment that he had managed to carry everything here by himself not so long ago. The look he was giving her was intense enough to make her quite sure that Max was not referring to any help with returning the clinic's gear. No... That look had made it feel as if Max was thinking about that kiss again. About what it might be like to do it again. To take it wherever it might lead—and they both knew exactly where that was. They were also about to head to a part of that huge house that was well away from the children and any threat of interruption. If Emma wanted to reinstate her resolution not to distract Max from his new responsibilities as a father figure by making herself available, this was quite probably her last chance.

But would it be such a bad thing if they both gave in to the simmering attraction that was on the point of boiling over? It wasn't as if it was going to change anything. In less than a couple of weeks, Emma could be almost anywhere in the world taking up a new locum position. She might never see Max again. How weird was this, that she was talking herself into being with a man she had steered well clear of years ago because he lived his life thinking along those same lines—that it was perfectly acceptable to give in to physical desire with no intention of it ever being anything more than that?

And if she didn't, Emma might never know if what she was imagining was true. That Max Cunningham could give her a night that she would remember for the rest of her life.

'I'll take the kit,' she said, turning away because if

she kept eye contact with Max it might make her so nervous she would change her mind. 'It looks lighter than the defibrillator.'

They walked past the front door of the main part of the house.

'Looks like it's all quiet on the western front,' Max said.

It was a bit of a relief for Emma to find something new to talk about. They had already exhausted how thickly the snow was falling and whether Terry might already be out of the emergency department at the Royal and on his way to the catheter laboratory.

'I thought the clinic rooms were in the west wing. And they're around the corner.'

'True. But it wouldn't sound right saying it looks like it's all quiet on the southern front, would it?'

They turned the corner of the house. There were downstairs lights still on so it was easy enough to see where they were going. Emma could also see snow gathering on the ivy that scrambled over the old stones and even a curl of smoke coming from one of the many chimneys.

'It's a gorgeous house,' she said aloud. 'What a magic place to have grown up in.'

'It was,' Max agreed. 'But it was never the same after Mum died. I was glad to get away when I went to med school, to tell the truth. There were sad shadows everywhere and I don't think any of us knew how to shine a light to get rid of them. Andy got the closest. He set out to create a family of his own. To celebrate Christmas again.' Max shook his head as he opened the door of Upper Barnsley's general practice. 'That gave us a whole new level of sad stuff, what with the failure of his marriage and then his death and now three kids who are going to grow up without any parents.'

'They've got you.' Emma put the first-aid pack down in a corner of the waiting room. 'And I think they've got their grandpa now, as well. Did you see the way he was holding hands with Ben when we left the house? The way Pirate was right beside them? He's given them a bond, that little dog.'

'I think you might be right.' Max put the defibrillator back where it belonged on the bench. 'I hope so, anyway. I was old enough to help take care of Andy when Mum died but these kids really need him and that might well be enough to bring him out of his shell. He's been hiding for far too long.'

Emma opened her mouth. She had been about to say that James wasn't the only one who'd been hiding. That maybe Max himself needed to learn to trust in love again—enough to be able to commit to making that love a significant part of his life. That loving his nieces and nephew would be a very good place to start.

But that was something he needed to discover for himself, wasn't it?

'It's not easy,' she said, instead. 'Letting anybody into your heart when you know how hard it is to lose a person you care about that much. I think your mum must have been a wonderful person. She certainly loved Christmas. I can't believe how many decorations we've put out today.'

'You know what?' Max was smiling at Emma. 'I love seeing them out again. There are happy memories to be found now and they're even stronger than the sad ones. We kept the smallest decorations that we could find and put them on that little tree that Ben was carrying with him when he arrived. I put it in their bedroom.'

Emma's smile was meant to be encouraging but she knew it was wobbling a bit. 'That was a sweet thing to do. That tree was special.'

'I want to remember what Christmas used to be like when I was a kid,' Max added. 'I want Ben and Tilly to feel like that too. And Alice, when she's old enough. I want to get that blue bike for Ben and have it waiting under the Christmas tree for him so that he comes down and just knows that the magic is real. That Father Christmas is real and got his letter—the way I did when I got my first bike.'

Emma's smile felt even more wobbly, now. Maybe Max was already well on the way to opening his heart again. It was quite possible that he didn't trust the idea of marriage after his father was so devastated by his wife's death and then his brother by his broken marriage, but if he changed his mind he wouldn't have any trouble finding someone who would want to love him back. Someone who could end up being a mother to those three children and give him the kind of family he'd once had himself? He deserved that.

'I know he'll find out the truth one day but that can wait, can't it? He can have a bit of time to believe in magic?'

Max had stepped closer to Emma as he was speaking and now he was close enough to touch her face. To let his fingers and thumb slide so gently down her cheeks and then to cup her chin softly as he bent his head ready to cover her lips with his own.

'This is magic I can still believe in...' he said softly.

Emma's weight was on her toes and she tilted her

body to touch his as she returned that kiss and felt his hands move to trace the shape of her shoulders and slip between them to touch her breasts. Emma could only gasp at the spear of sensation that coursed through her body and the movement of Max's hands stilled instantly, as though he was afraid she didn't want this.

Which couldn't be further from the truth. Emma had never wanted anything in her life as much as she wanted the escape of sinking into a timeless bliss that would make anything else in the world irrelevant. She wanted that magic…

'Don't stop,' she whispered, lifting her face to kiss Max again. 'Please don't stop…'

CHAPTER NINE

HAD SHE REALLY believed that giving in to this over-whelmingly powerful attraction between herself and Max Cunningham meant nothing would actually change?

How wrong had Emma been?

Everything had changed.

She couldn't stop thinking about it. About every touch of his hands. Every kiss, from those so tender they could bring tears to her eyes to ones so passionate they made the world tilt on its axis. Almost falling asleep cradled in his arms in the aftermath of their lovemaking, feeling the steady thump of his heartbeat beneath her cheek, until he'd reminded her gently that they needed to leave this secret room above the practice clinic. He had to be in the main part of the house in case the children needed him during the night.

She'd lain awake in her own room for a long time, reliving every moment of their time together. She'd been absolutely right about one thing—she'd experienced something she would never, ever forget. Something which had made her feel as if she was stepping out of ordinary life into a place that felt very different. A bright place where colours were more intense, where food tasted better and something as simple as the scent

of a pine tree in the house was special. A place where
laughter was the most beautiful sound in the world, the
excitement of watching snow falling thickly was so
strong it took her back to her own childhood and even
the chore of getting the chains onto her tyres so that she
could get to work this afternoon was not nearly as tire-
some as it could have been.

It was a place that Emma finally recognised, even
though she'd never experienced it to this kind of level.

At first, it was a surprise to be getting frequent text
messages from Max as she attended to one task after
another during a busy Christmas Eve shift in an emergency department. She received images of Ben and Tilly
standing in the snow in their gumboots, with carrots in
their hands that they were going to leave out for the reindeer, when she snatched a few minutes to go and visit
Terry on the cardiology ward and catch up with the great
news that he'd received several stents in his coronary
arteries, fast enough for the damage from his heart attack to be minimal.

There was one of Pirate with some tinsel tied to his
collar, being cuddled by Ben, that arrived in the minute or two between Emma sending an eighty-year-old
woman off to X-ray, knowing that she'd broken her hip
when she'd slipped in the snow on her front step, and
going to stitch up a nasty laceration on a young man
whose Christmas party had gone seriously awry.

The best thing about that image was that the small
boy was sitting on his grandfather's knee when the picture had been taken and Emma had to blink away a tear,
knowing that at least one of the barriers in the Cunningham household was beginning to crumble.

The one Max had sent much later, when the children

must have been settled in bed and he'd been able to sneak back to the rooms above the clinic where the gifts had been hidden had broken her focus quite noticeably.

Was Max remembering what had happened in that room last night in as much detail as she was? His attempt to wrap Ben's bicycle in Christmas paper did make her laugh, though, and that eased the emotional tension that she could feel building.

She texted back.

Great effort. Just leave it like that with the pedals and handlebars sticking out. It's not as if Ben's not going to recognise it instantly—he asked Father Christmas for it, didn't he?

Things got really busy in the department as it got closer to midnight. A stabbing victim from a pub brawl meant that Emma was tied up in Resus for a long, difficult time. When they'd finally sent the critically ill patient up to Theatre, finding the selfie Max had taken wearing the sparkly tiara that was part of Tilly's fairy supplies had made her smile rather than laugh.

She'd spent long seconds just staring at the face that filled her screen and remembering what it had been like to have those beautiful, dark blue eyes staring into her own when they'd been as physically close as it was possible for two people to be.

She texted back again.

Wish I was there. Looks much more fun than being here.

Max's text came instantly.

Wish you were here too. More than you can imagine.

Oh…she could actually imagine it only too well if it was anything like she was feeling and it was when the physical tingling in her body morphed into a longing that was intense enough to steal her breath that Emma finally recognised what was going on.

She was in love with Max Cunningham.

It wasn't just that he'd given her the best sex she'd ever experienced in her life. The sex could only have been that amazing thanks to the connection that had already been there. Because the trust had already been there between them—a mix of familiarity from knowing each other long ago, respecting each other in both professional and personal capacities and shared experiences of dealing with tough things in life. Because there was a possibility that she'd always been a little bit in love with Max, she'd just never let herself go there because she didn't belong in his kind of world.

She still didn't belong here with a new family just trying to glue themselves together, so being in love with this man was only ever going to be a problem—especially when it made her feel as if she wanted to stay in exactly this part of the world and not move on to a new position in the very near future. When it made her feel as if she could quite easily open her heart to the generations of Cunninghams on either side of Max and have an instant family of a size that her Italian relatives would approve of heartily.

Even if Max wasn't taking the first steps to try and piece together a new lifestyle when his old one had exploded around him, he had never wanted the same things in life as Emma. She could understand why he'd thrown around that catchphrase of being here for a good time not a long time, given the early tragedy in his life, but the truth of the matter was that Max was never going to give his heart away. Not in the way that Emma could with the person she might want to choose to spend the rest of her life with.

Oh, he would love the children who had unexpectedly come to share his life—he already did—and he would take the best care of them and of his father, but that was far more responsibility than he'd ever planned to take on and, eventually, he would sort out the current chaos around him. He would employ a full-time housekeeper and nanny and be able to come back to his job in the Royal's emergency department in the very near future. He would get his apartment repaired and most likely keep it on, despite living in the manor house, because it would be the perfect place to find private time with the women who would always be eager to be chosen even though they knew—like Emma did—that it might only be a one-off night to treasure. He might be even less likely to consider a long-term relationship— not only because he'd seen his brother's marriage end in misery—but because it wouldn't be fair on three children who'd already experienced far too much disruption in their lives.

Being in love with Max was her problem, Emma realised, and it would be far better if nobody else knew anything about it. Max probably wouldn't notice, especially tomorrow when it was Christmas Day and would be all about the children. Or make that today, she thought, as she checked her watch to find midnight had come and gone a while back. That meant she was closer to being able to escape before Max had the chance to notice anything different about her. She'd only ever promised to stay long enough to help create a magical Christmas Day for Ben and Tilly and Alice. Only one more day and that had started already. She had a day off rostered for Boxing Day and Emma could use that to find somewhere else to stay. There was only one more week after that until New Year's Day and that was when Max had told her the new nanny was due to arrive.

So that would be that. Maybe they'd stay in touch and Max would send a Christmas card every year with photos tracking the changes as the children grew up. It was just as well you could send digital cards now because goodness only knew where in the world Emma was likely to be.

She tapped the screen to enlarge the photo of Max in the tiara again. To soak in the expression in his eyes and that smile.

'Dr Moretti? We've got a Status One patient arriving by ambulance. Electrocution from faulty Christmas tree lights but someone had started CPR before the paramedics got there and they've got a perfusing rhythm again. ETA two minutes…'

'Resus One clear?'

'Yes.'

'Activate the trauma team, please. And get whoever's on call in Cardiology down here stat.'

Her phone slipped back into the pocket of her scrub suit. Goodness also only knew when she'd get the next chance to check on the progress of the gift wrapping and that was a good thing.

Emma needed to try and step back.

To keep things under control so that nobody got hurt, including herself. It was Christmas Day and she was going to play her part to make it as perfect as possible for the Cunningham family and as little as possible about herself. It was a strategy that had worked for years now.

She was good at it.

She was also good at her job and right now she had the challenge of dealing with a post-cardiac arrest due to electrocution. This person wasn't going to die in the early hours of Christmas Day. Not if Emma Moretti could do anything to change that.

Max was the first person awake in the Cunningham household on Christmas Day which surprised him, not only because he'd been up in the night with Alice and should have been tired enough to sleep through all but a major disturbance but because he remembered the way he and Andy would get up while it was still dark and tiptoe past their parents' bedroom to go downstairs and see if the Christmas magic had happened again this year.

He could hear soft snuffles coming from the cot in the corner of his room but that wasn't the sound which had woken him. It was the light tapping that was coming from the hallway beyond his open door—the sound of a small dog's toenails on the wooden floorboards on either side of the carpet runner. So he wasn't really the first person awake, after all. He had to smile when he heard Ben's whisper that was even more audible than Pirate's toenails.

'Shh, Pirate… Don't wake up Uncle Max. Let's find Grandpa first because we have to have a Christmas cuddle… It's one of the rules…'

Oh… Max knew who he'd like to be having a Christmas cuddle with right now. How horrified would Emma be if she knew just how much she'd been on his mind since they'd made love in the early hours of Christmas Eve? He wanted to do that again. As soon as possible.

As often as possible.

For the rest of his life…

Good grief… Max was properly awake now, that was for sure. How on earth had that thought surfaced again? He'd already sorted things out in his head after he'd had that disturbing glimpse through his personal barriers and thought, for a heartbeat, that he wanted the kind of partnership his parents had had when they'd created their family. That Andy had thought he'd found with the woman he'd fallen so deeply in love with.

Was that what was happening here?

Was Max falling in love with Emma?

No. He didn't do 'falling in love'. Never had, never would allow himself to take that kind of risk. It was what women did with him and it had always been enough to make him end things rapidly. Falling in love was a magic you only believed in until you learned that the truth could be very different and he'd learned that at a very young age. It was like Christmas magic, until you discovered Father Christmas didn't actually exist. Ben still believed. And Max wanted to be there when the little boy went downstairs and saw his bike under the Christmas tree because he wanted to remember what it had been like for himself all those years ago. He wanted to feel *that* magic, just for a heartbeat.

Max pushed the bedclothes away and reached for his clothes. A pair of jeans and a tee shirt and an extra warm woollen jersey because he could feel that the central heating was already struggling this morning. There was also that odd feeling of silence that only came when the world was blanketed thickly enough by snow. Would Emma make it home safely after her shift ended this morning?

And there she was again. In his head.

In his heart, as well, judging by the squeezing sensation he was aware of in his chest even though he knew that the heart was not an organ that was capable of either thinking or feeling. That was disturbing too. A kind of magic all of its own.

He had to get a handle on this. He wanted this Christmas Day to be special for Emma so that she could get on with her life and find joy again. He wanted it to be special for Ben and Tilly and Alice. For his father as well, because it might be a struggle for him to cope today. How had he reacted to a small boy and a dog climbing into his bed for a pre-dawn Christmas cuddle? Taking the handset of the baby monitor with him, Max left his room to go and find out.

'I got a *bike*, Emma. A blue bike—just like I asked for...'

'Oh...that's amazing, Ben.' It was impossible not to return the happy smile that Emma had received full blast when she'd finally arrived back after a shift that had gone overtime.

'Did he make it?' Max came out of the drawing room a few seconds after Ben had run to meet Emma at the front door. He had Tilly perched on one hip and she was in her full fairy outfit with the tutu and wings and tiara. 'The Christmas lights guy?'

'He was sitting up and talking by the time I left. He's not going to get home for his Christmas dinner but I don't think his family's too bothered.'

'I'm sure they're just delighted he's still alive.' Max nodded. He was holding Emma's gaze and he looked delighted as well, she thought. Because of a successful case in his department, or was he as pleased to see her as she was to see him again? The warmth that was coursing through her body made it urgent to get her coat and hat and scarf off and hang them on the hooks.

'I'm a fairy,' Tilly told her.

'I can see that, sweetheart. You're the prettiest fairy I've ever seen.' Emma pulled in a deep breath. 'Something smells gorgeous,' she added.

'That'll be what Maggie and Ruth are cooking up. Turkey and bread sauce and Brussels sprouts and roasted potatoes—the whole nine yards. Pigs in blankets for Ben too. They got here before it started snowing again, which is lucky. How did you find the roads?'

'A bit dodgy around here. They must have cleared them this morning but it was just as well I had chains on. It's still snowing hard.'

'But I want to ride my bike,' Ben said sadly.

'How 'bout we make a snowman instead?' Max suggested. 'After we've had our dinner? It might have stopped snowing by then. Otherwise, we might be stuck inside for a while yet.' He gave Emma just the ghost of a wink. 'We'll have to think of other ways to entertain ourselves if that happens.'

Emma had to drag her gaze away from Max. That gleam in his eyes told her exactly what kind of entertainment he had in mind and it felt wrong to be thinking about that in the presence of two small children.

'I'll go and see if Maggie and Ruth need my help in the kitchen,' she said.

'Come in by the fire for a minute first. Dad insisted on opening some champagne,' Max told her. 'There's a glass with your name on it.'

'It's a rule,' Ben told her. 'Grandpa said it was one of Nana's rules but it's only for grown-ups. Come on, Emma. Come and see our new toys. And there's new stories too…'

'Yes…' Max was smiling. 'Come on, Emma. We're having a very special Christmas but we've all been waiting for you to come and share it.'

The floor of the drawing room was littered with crumpled wrapping paper. Alice was asleep in her pram near James's chair and Pirate was lying at his feet chewing happily on a dog treat bone. The lights on the Christmas tree were sparkling and the fire was glowing. Emma watched Tilly slide to the floor from her uncle's arms so he could pour the champagne and then she went to climb onto her grandfather's lap as if it was the most natural thing in the world to do. Ben picked up a picture book from a pile and handed it to James, curling up on the floor beside Pirate as the most senior member of the Cunningham family started reading the story.

She was already a little spaced out from working a night shift and it felt as if she had stepped into a Christmas card scene so she sipped her celebratory drink cautiously as Max came to stand beside her near the fire. This was exactly what she'd imagined when she'd told Max how important this Christmas was to these children and the opportunity it was providing for them to bond as a family. This was perfect and it was a pleasure to be a part of it and to be watching it happening. And, according to Max, even better news was waiting in the wings.

'Do you remember that I told you that Maggie's daughter Ruth is an infant school teacher?'

Emma nodded. 'You said she was wonderful with the children.'

She'd been looking after them when Max had taken Emma up to the attic to find the boxes of decorations. It seemed a long time ago already that James had been so upset to see them being used again. He had a grand-child on his lap right now and another one leaning on his leg and he looked like a man who'd had his heart well and truly stolen.

'She is. And Maggie says she wants to come and live in Upper Barnsley so that her mum can help after the baby's born. They've cooked up a plan between them that Ruth could be our nanny and Maggie can stay on as housekeeper as well as helping to look after Ruth's baby. It sounds like a good plan, doesn't it?'

Emma's head was definitely spinning now. 'It sounds perfect,' she agreed. 'You'll be able to go back to work. You might not even need to wait until the New Year?'

Which meant that Emma wouldn't be needed as a locum any longer. If she left the manor house tomor-row, she might never see it again. Or see James or the children or Max again and that simply felt...wrong...

Very wrong...

'Dr Cunningham?'

'What is it, Maggie?' Both Max and James turned to-wards the anxious voice at the door, where their house-keeper was wiping her hands on her apron.

'Would one of you have a minute? Ruth isn't feeling terribly well.'

Emma put her glass on the mantelpiece, turning back swiftly, but Max was well ahead of her as she left the room. Glancing over her shoulder just before she pulled the door closed behind her, Emma could see that Ben was climbing up to join his grandad and Tilly in the roomy leather chair and that James was nodding, quite prepared to take responsibility for the children.

A short time later Emma wished she had stayed where she was and sent James in to assist his son. It had taken Max only minutes to find out why Ruth had started feeling so awful she had gone to lie down on the old couch at one end of the huge kitchen.

'You're in labour,' he told her. 'You're far enough along for it to be safe for the baby but it looks as though you might already be close to the end of the first stage and that means that it's happening very fast. I'm not happy to try driving you to hospital and risk you having your baby on the side of the road. I'll call for an ambulance but there's no guarantee it'll get here in time with the amount of snow on the road.'

The way Emma's head was spinning now had nothing to do with fatigue or the sip of champagne she'd had. This was more like an adrenaline overload. A fight or flight response and all she wanted to do was flee.

Another baby was about to be born on Christmas Day?

No…no, no, no…

She couldn't do this.

But now Max was standing in front of her and his gaze was telling her that she *could* do this. That she had to because he needed her to.

'You know where the kit is in the clinic,' he said. 'Could you go and get it, please? There's an obstetric pack right beside the drug cupboard too. Maggie's got a key. She'll go with you to get what we need, but we need it fast.'

Getting out of this room was good. Getting out fast was even better.

Emma turned and ran.

CHAPTER TEN

THIS HAD TO be the most unusual management of an emergency that Max had ever been in charge of. Here he was, in the kitchen of his childhood home, the aromas of a traditional Christmas dinner beginning to fill the room, and he was about to help a new baby into the world.

An ambulance was on its way to the house but he was pretty sure it was not going to arrive in time for the crew to be present at the birth of this baby. He hoped that was the case, anyway, because a long delay at this stage of a delivery could mean there were complications so a smooth transition and fast birth were preferable.

Ruth must have been having contractions for some time. She'd told Max that she'd put her discomfort down to an increase in the backache she'd been aware of for a couple of days, due to being on her feet since early this morning helping her mother cook the Christmas dinner they'd all been planning to share. By the time Emma and Maggie had come back into the room with the kit and Max had pulled gloves on, he could feel the bulge in Ruth's perineum that meant that crowning of the baby's head was imminent.

Ruth wasn't his only patient here. There was a baby

that was about to come into the world a lot faster than usual, and that was a worry due to increased risks of haemorrhage or tearing for the mother and aspiration of amniotic fluid for the baby, or infection due to a less than sterile environment for the birth.

'Grab some clean towels, Maggie. We'll put some under Ruth right away. I'm surprised her waters haven't broken already.'

Maggie was pale but composed. 'I'll be right back... Oh, my...that's the bread sauce boiling over. I thought I could smell something burning...'

Max wasn't the only doctor here either. Emma had opened the kit. She had also put gloves on and she was unrolling the IV pack. She knew that IV access was a priority. Not for intravenous pain relief because it was probably already too late for that, but they might need to be able to give fluids if Ruth started losing too much blood.

But Emma was even paler than Maggie. She was doing what she needed to do but Max could feel how difficult this was for her. He could almost see the pressure that she was fighting against.

And he understood completely just how hard this had to be for Emma.

Her own baby had been born on Christmas Day and, while Holly had been born alive, it had only been a short time later that Emma had lost her daughter. This had to be taking her back to the pain, both physical and emotional, and Max could feel a piece of his own heart tearing.

It was unbearable to see Emma in such pain. He wished he could have protected her from this but he hadn't been able to. The urge to offer comfort now was so strong it had the potential to interfere with what he needed to focus on, and it was in that split second that Max realised just how important Emma was to him.

He wasn't in danger of falling in love with this woman.

It had already happened. In the space of only a few days, with his world as he knew it crumbling into chaos around him, he had found a human rock who had anchored him. Who had shown him a future that he could embrace. Someone who had touched him on levels he'd never experienced before and he knew he could never find with anyone else. Max was a better man for having had Emma Moretti in his life for only a matter of days. Already, he couldn't imagine his life without her in it.

So he was feeling her pain but he knew that, somehow, she had to face it or she would never be able to move on and embrace a future of her own—whether it was with him or not. And, because he loved her, he had to help her.

The thoughts flashed through his brain as more of an awareness than any conscious analysis. His focus had to be fully on his patients and, as Maggie arrived with soft, clean towels that were put in place merely seconds before Ruth's waters broke, Max only had a heartbeat to catch Emma's gaze. To try and let her know that he understood. That he was going to do whatever it took to make sure that Emma could cope. That everything was going to be okay.

You've got this...

His message was silent but he knew that it had been received because he could sense the contact. As if she had accepted an outstretched hand. As if his strength was welcome.

* * *

It seemed as if every new situation that Emma saw Max dealing with increased her respect for this man and filled her heart with a mix of emotions that felt limitless.

Like how proud she was of his abilities. Like how much she loved how gentle he was trying to be but how uncompromising he was in doing what needed to be done, like cradling the back of the baby's head as it appeared and putting pressure on it to prevent an explosive delivery. His hand looked huge as he supported the tiny head as the forehead and then the face and finally the chin and neck were delivered and then helping to deliver each shoulder by careful downward pressure for the first and upward for the second.

'You're doing great, Ruth. Almost there...'

Dear Lord, it was hard to try and keep a totally professional focus, here. Emma could feel the pain of every contraction Ruth was having and she could remember exactly what it felt like to have the rest of a baby's body slither out after the shoulders were delivered. That moment, suspended in time, when you were listening for the first cry of your child. That moment had been so much worse for Emma, because she'd known there was a very good chance she might never hear a first cry but oh...she could have wished to have had Max present at the birth of her own baby.

The way he'd looked at her, only minutes ago, when she'd returned to try and assist him in this unexpected and precipitous birth. As if he understood exactly how hard this might be for her but he had complete confidence that his admiration for how she could cope with difficult things was not misplaced. It felt like the way he'd looked at her when she'd first told him the tragic story of Holly's birth. As though the threads of connection between them were becoming so strong they could be trusted to take any amount of weight.

But perhaps he was wrong...

It was that first cry of Ruth's baby that tipped the balance. It took Emma straight back to that delivery room five years ago. To the mindset that she could cope because she'd known what was going to happen but...but then *she'd* been wrong. It might have looked to others as if she'd coped and carried on coping but that was only because she'd been hiding. She'd run away emotionally and built protective walls that had just come crashing down with the single warbling cry of a newborn baby.

'I'm...sorry...' The words came out as a whisper as Emma pushed herself to her feet. 'I... I have to go...'

Where was she?

It was nearly an hour later that Max could finally focus on what had been an increasingly urgent concern. Emma hadn't been seen since she'd fled the kitchen after the birth of Ruth's baby. He hadn't been able to go after her then, of course. His responsibilities lay with caring for his patients, even though it appeared that everything had gone as well as he could have hoped it would. The baby's Apgar score was good at one minute and perfect at ten minutes. Ruth experienced only minor blood loss and her placenta was delivered without any problem. When the ambulance arrived, along with a police escort and a snow plough waiting at the end of the driveway, Ruth's tiny son was already nursing well and a proud grandmother was ready to accompany them to hospital.

'Just to be on the safe side,' Max told Maggie. 'I'm sure they'll have you all back home by this afternoon.'

'I can't thank you enough.' Maggie brushed back tears. 'I've just helped Dr Cunningham to change Alice's nappy and given him a bottle for her but I think your Christmas dinner might be a bit ruined. The turkey and potatoes have been in the oven a bit too long and that bread sauce is inedible.'

'It doesn't matter.' Max was smiling. 'It was your Christmas dinner as well and I'm sure you're not worried about missing it.'

'You could heat up the pigs in blankets for Ben. And there's red jelly in the fridge. I'm sorry, Max. I wanted to help make this Christmas perfect for all of you.'

'We'll be fine. You go and take care of your family, Maggie. I can take care of mine.'

'But where's Emma?'

'That's what I'm about to find out.'

He checked the drawing room but hadn't expected to find her with his father and the children. That heartbreaking look in her eyes when she'd heard Ruth's baby cry for the first time had told him that she was facing a ghost she thought she had to grapple with alone.

But she was wrong.

She needed him. Or maybe it was that Max needed to be with her.

He checked her room but it was empty.

He went outside into a world that was silent and white, with a fresh burst of fat snowflakes drifting slowly down to cover the tyre tracks of the emergency vehicles that were now long gone. The biting cold nipped at his skin and Max stared towards the woods on either side of the driveway but then he shook his head. Emma was far from stupid and she hadn't been dressed for being outdoors. Besides, there were no footprints in the snow leading towards the woods.

There were, however, footprints that led around the corner of the house. A lot of prints, but was that because they'd been made when Maggie and Emma had gone to fetch the medical gear he'd asked for? With the new snow falling, it was hard to tell whether there were any more recent tracks but Max kept following them.

Because he was remembering walking this way with Emma when they'd brought the emergency kit back from the neighbours' house and where they'd ended up, later that night. He was remembering not the mind-blowing sexual encounter but what it had been like afterwards. When he'd held Emma in his arms, skin to skin. Heartbeat to heartbeat. How it had felt like the most perfect place in the world to ever be.

If he was in pain, or scared, or he simply needed comfort, that would be the place he would want to be, wouldn't it? In Emma's arms. But, if that hadn't been possible, he might well have chosen the next best thing— to be in the place that he *had* once been in Emma's arms, so that he could imagine that comfort and wrap himself in it like the warmest blanket on a day exactly like today.

Max let himself into the clinic and then headed for the stairs to the room above.

Those agonised tears had finally stopped a while back.

Emma had curled herself into the smallest ball and pulled the old eiderdown that had been rolled up on the end of this antique brass bed over herself. She'd heard someone coming up the stairs from the clinic rooms and she'd known that it would be Max, because he was the only person who would know that she knew about the existence of this room, but she was too exhausted to move. So utterly drained she thought she might never be able to move again.

He didn't say anything when he came into this room. What he did do was to lie down on the other side of the bed, beneath the eiderdown and behind Emma, to not only take her into his arms but to wrap his whole body around hers. His warmth seeped into her skin with far more effect than the feather-filled cover over them both and she could feel his heartbeat against her back. A steady ticking that was an affirmation of life.

Of caring…

It felt like love…

His words, when they came, were soft against her ear. 'I know it hurts. I've got you. It's going to be okay…'

Emma's words were shaky. 'But it's not. I thought it was. I want it to be but… I'm scared. I thought I had it sorted but I didn't really. I've been hiding—all this time. It broke me, Max, hearing that cry. I would give anything to hear another baby of mine cry, but how could I ever go through that again when I know how much it can hurt?'

'You can't hide for ever.' Max was stroking Emma's hair. 'Well, you can, but I hope you don't. You have so much love to give, Em. So much love that others will want to give you. If you keep hiding, they won't be able to find you and you'll miss out on both giving and receiving that love, and how sad would that be?'

Emma turned in his arms so that she could press her face against the reassuring beat of his heart.

'Nobody's trying to find me,' she said quietly. 'I've made sure I never stay in one place long enough for that to happen.'

'It doesn't always take a long time.' Emma felt Max's

lips press against the top of her head. 'I've found you—and I wasn't even looking.'

Emma's breath caught.

'I didn't want to look,' he continued softly. 'Because I guess I was hiding too. Even when it was right in front of my eyes I couldn't see it properly. Like that night when you were making stars with Ben and Tilly and I was feeding Alice and I felt like...like we were...'

'A family?' Emma whispered into the silence. 'I know. I felt like that too, when we were decorating the tree. Until your dad got so upset. Until I remembered how much safer it was to step back. To hide...'

'I didn't believe in Christmas,' Max said. 'I knew the magic wasn't real. That it had died when Mum had gone but, you know what?'

Emma pulled back just far enough to be able to see Max's face. 'What?'

'You've made me believe in a different sort of Christmas. And a different sort of magic. Not the sort when you believe someone comes down the chimney and gives you the bike you've wanted for so long, but it's still magic. The family kind. My dad's probably still sitting in front of the fire, playing with his grandkids or reading them another story. Maybe he's gone into the kitchen to heat up those pigs in blankets for Ben or maybe they've just gone straight for the red jelly. But what he's really doing is letting those kids into his heart and that means he's going to start living again. Really living...and that's magic, isn't it?'

Emma could feel her eyes filling. A single tear escaping to trickle down her cheek. 'It is... It's real magic. Like love...'

'I tried to make you stay with us because I knew that

couldn't have happened without you. We need you, Em. We all need you but I need you most of all. I love you, Emma Moretti. I'm *in* love with you and I never thought I'd ever say that to anyone because I didn't believe in that magic either and I know that you're the only woman in the world that could make me believe in it. I want you to stay for the rest of this Christmas. And next Christmas. For every Christmas to come for as long as I live.'

Tears were falling freely now. Max had come out of the place he'd been hiding in for most of his life. He was risking his heart. For the children who had come into his life but for *her* as well.

Could Emma be that brave?

'I love you too, Max. I need you. I want to stop hiding but I can only do that because you make me feel a lot braver than I really am. I want to be here for every one of those Christmases and...'

And then Emma had to stop talking because Max was kissing her. There were tears mixed into that kiss. A bit of laughter too and a great deal of love. And then, with their arms wrapped tightly around each other, they went back into the house.

To the family that was waiting for them both.

EPILOGUE

Two years later...

IT WAS JUST as well that the Cunninghams' manor house had so many bedrooms because it seemed like the house had to cater for more visitors every year.

'Sorry, Maggie...' Emma eyed the huge pile of tiny sausages that were having strips of bacon wrapped around them and secured with toothpicks. 'I'll have to start limiting how many of my relatives come over here from Italy for Christmas before it gets to be way too much work.' She went to the sink to wash her hands so that she could start helping with the preparations. 'I wonder what they'll think of these pigs in blankets? I tried translating the idea but my *nonna* looked very dubious.'

Maggie laughed. 'I'm sure she'll love them. And I love how full the house is and how many children we've got running around. I loved that we had the feast of the seven fishes last night too. And that your mum brought your family's gorgeous nativity scene. Ruth's loving it all as well. She was so impressed with your star making class yesterday.'

It was Emma's turn to laugh. 'We've got so many wonky stars now, I think I'll have to make a string to put across the ceiling next year or we won't have room for all the other decorations on our tree.'

'Ruth will help with that. She says her job is like she's running her own little school and the best bit is that she gets to take her wee Joseph to work with her.'

Emma peered out of the window as she dried her hands. Ruth's two-year-old son was as much a part of the crowd of excited children outside as her Italian nieces and nephews.

'Ben's got him in the wheelbarrow,' she said. 'Along with Alice. I hope he can cope with both of them. They're a bit like twins, aren't they? There's six months between them but they're inseparable.'

'Maybe it's because we celebrate Joe's half-birthday so it doesn't get lost in Christmas. Tilly is convinced they're both the same age.' Maggie started a new row of the wrapped sausages on the oven tray. 'Is Ruth out there supervising?'

'Ruth *and* Max.' Emma was still looking out of the window. 'They look like they've got everything under control for the moment. Pirate's out there too but he's probably as eager as everyone to get back inside. What made us decide that the kids could only open their stockings before breakfast and we'd do the gifts under the tree before dinner?'

'Oh…that reminds me. Ben was worried about where his little tree was. You know, the one he brought with him when he first arrived and that we save all the tiniest decorations for?'

'I put it up high to keep it safe,' Emma said. 'The toddlers were getting into everything. It's a circus around here at the moment.'

But she was loving it. Every moment of it. Because

every day brought so much love, along with something new and special into her life. Today one of the special things was that this was the first Christmas for the newest member of the Cunningham clan. Emma forgot that she was about to help Maggie create the army of pigs in blankets. Instead, she walked towards the pram parked on the other side of the Aga stove, to gaze at her four-month-old daughter. Hannah had been named after her paternal grandmother and was currently dressed in the cutest stretchy suit ever—a tiny green elf outfit, right down to booties with curly toes and a green and red hat. She was awake in her pram but not crying and when she saw her mother her little face lit up with the widest smile and she held out her arms to be picked up.

The kitchen door opened as Emma gathered her baby into her arms. Max's face lit up with the same kind of joy as Hannah's and he went straight to his wife and daughter to wrap his arms around both of them.

'Where's Dad?' he asked Maggie.

Maggie's face softened with a smile that made Max and Emma share a knowing glance. They suspected that something might be going on there and this looked like another clue.

'He's upstairs, putting on that Santa suit so he can distribute the presents. Shall I go and see if he's ready?'

'Good idea.' Max nodded. 'I'm not sure how long Ruth will manage to keep the troops out of the way. I don't think we'll be getting any kind of white Christmas this year but it's pretty cold out there.'

He waited until Maggie had gone out of the kitchen before he bent his head to kiss Emma—a slow, tender kiss that tapped into everything she loved so much about her husband and about their life together which was only getting better with every passing month. How had they not known, when they'd first met all those years ago, that they were so perfect for each other? That they could meet every challenge in life as long as they faced it together?

'Champagne?' he asked. 'I do believe it's one of those Christmas rules.'

'After the presents.' She smiled. 'As the other half of Upper Barnsley's general practice, I think I have a duty to cover any calls until your dad has changed out of his Santa suit.'

'I guess I'll wait too, then—so we can share that first toast to a happy Christmas.'

'It's already happy.' Emma smiled up at Max. 'I don't think it could be any happier.'

Except it could.

The kitchen door opened again and a stream of small children came rushing in.

'Mummy... Daddy...' Six-year-old Tilly was bursting with excitement. 'You've got to come... *Father Christmas* is here...'

Ben was by her side. He and Max exchanged a grin and Emma knew what that was about. As the oldest child, Ben was now in on the secret—that it was the family that made the magic happen at Christmas time but that was fine by him. He knew how important a part of this family he was and he was going to help make that magic happen from now on.

This Christmas was going to be the best yet.

Until next time, of course...

* * * * *

MISTLETOE KISS WITH THE HEART DOCTOR

MARION LENNOX

CHAPTER ONE

HE'D MISS HIS plane if he didn't hurry.

Dr Marcus Pierce was on Gannet Island under pressure. Three weeks before she'd died, his mother had gripped his hand and pleaded, 'Marc, please scatter my ashes from Lightning Peak. It's the most beautiful place in the world, the place where I found comfort when I knew I had to leave your father. You were at boarding school, so I knew you were old enough to cope, but it was hard on me. That first Christmas I hiked up there to watch the sunset and I knew I'd done the right thing. Can I die knowing I'll be resting back there this Christmas?'

Despite the strains on their relationship—sometimes he'd even thought, *What relationship?* because surely he'd learned independence when he was a child—there was no way he could refuse such a plea. But his mother might have found an easier peak, Marc decided as he fought his way along the little used bush path. There were plenty of scenic spots near Sydney. Spots that didn't involve a long flight in a small plane, a rugged hike up an overgrown path he wasn't too sure of, and then another rush to catch the plane home again.

But as he watched his mother's ashes settle in the bushland around him, as he soaked in the salt-filled sea breeze and gazed down at the tiny town beneath him and the ocean beyond, he had to acknowledge this place was breathtakingly lovely.

Lightning Peak was almost at the top of the mountain. Moisture was slipping from above, forming a waterfall dropping to a pool of crystal-clear water. The only sound was the splash of water as it hit the pool and then found its way into some unknown underground stream.

He was sitting on a rock looking out at seemingly the whole world. Behind him was a haven for animals, a waterhole in this most unexpected of places.

Gannet was the largest of a group of six gorgeous, semitropical islands—the Birding Isles—set far out in the Pacific Ocean. This island in particular had been a healing place for his mountain climbing mother. Louise had been a doctor, an academic researcher. She was highly intelligent but, apart from her disastrous attempt at marriage and motherhood, she was intensely solitary. He could see why Louise had loved it.

There was, however, little time for reflection. His return flight to Sydney left in three hours. Today was Tuesday, and on Thursday he was due to fly to Switzerland. He needed to tie up loose ends at the hospital tomorrow, and pay a couple of cursory Christmas visits to elderly aunts. He needed to get down this mountain now.

He turned—but then he hesitated.

There were three paths leading from the rock platform where he stood.

Actually, they weren't proper paths—they looked more like desire lines for the animals that drank from this rock pool. He hadn't come up the main mountain path, but a side track his mother knew.

'The main lookout's gorgeous but my favourite place is where the water is, on the other side of the mountain,' his mother had told him. 'The path's overgrown—hardly anyone knows about it—but I'll draw you a map. You can't miss it.'

He'd taken care, following her shaky instructions and hand-drawn map to the letter.

When you reach the massive lightning-hit split rock, walk around it and you'll find the path continues. Then there's a Norfolk pine half a kilometre along where the path diverges. Keep left...

He'd reached the rocky platform he was now standing on with a feeling of relief. Turning now though... Which trace of a path had he used when he'd arrived? He'd been so relieved to make it he hadn't noticed.

He glanced again at Louise's map. Close though she'd been to death, her mind had still been sharp, and her instructions to climb to the peak were brilliant.

Her instructions to descend...not so much. She'd have expected him to notice.

He should have noticed. The omission annoyed him. Dr Marcus Pierce was a cardiac surgeon at the top of his field, and his normal setting was one of intelligence, incisiveness and surety.

He wasn't sure now—and he didn't have time to miss his plane.

So think. All the paths had to go down, he reasoned. If he chose the middle one then surely it'd join with the main track somewhere below.

He checked his phone, and even though he was now officially on leave he saw he'd been contacted. He and his friends had booked to fly to Switzerland on Thursday night. The plan was to arrive on Christmas Eve—Saturday—for two weeks of skiing at St Moritz. He was therefore off-duty but, no matter where he was, the medical calls didn't stop.

In honour of his mother he'd switched his phone to silent, so now he had scores of queued messages. The sight was normal, grounding. It reminded him that he was a surgeon who didn't have time for indecision.

But still he stood with his phone in his hand, fighting unusual qualms. He had an urge to ring Kayla. Kayla was a radiologist, a colleague, part of his friendship group about to head to Switzerland. For the last few months they'd been intermittently dating.

But their relationship was fun more than deep, and Kayla was practical. She'd have thought he was overly sentimental if he'd told her what he was doing. Maybe she was right. His isolated childhood had taught him emotion only got in the way of calm good sense, and there was no use phoning her now when calm good sense was all that was needed.

He was wasting time. The middle path seemed more used than the other two.

Go.

Lightning Peak was Dr Elsa McCrae's happy place. Her place of peace. Her place where she could say to patients, *'Sorry, I'm up on Lightning Peak, you'll have to contact Grandpa.'*

She couldn't say it too often these days. At seventy-eight, her grandpa was slowing down. Robert McCrae was unable to cope with the demands of being a doctor on his own, and she tried to spare him as much as she could, but every so often a woman just needed 'me' time.

For once her afternoon clinic had finished early. It was Wednesday, only four days until Christmas. From now on her life would be packed, with patients thinking every last niggle had to be sorted before Christmas Day itself. Then there was Boxing Day, with the usual influx of patients with injuries from new toys, or islanders who'd eaten far too much the day before. She had a queue of things she should be doing right now—there were always things—but her need to get away had been overwhelming. This would be her only chance to regroup before the rush.

She reached the peak after a solitary two-hour climb, checked her phone to make sure there were no catastrophes back in town, then sat on the massive rock platform, looking out to sea. And let her mind drift.

The other five islands that formed the Birding Isles were dots in the distance. Five hundred kilometres away—well out of sight—lay Australia, Sydney, where the evac team came from, where her patients went when she couldn't help them here. There were no doctors on the other islands. Fishing boats took patients back and forth at need—or took Elsa to them—but, apart from her grandfather, Sydney was her closest medical backup.

Last week a visiting tourist had had a major heart attack. She'd somehow hauled him back from cardiac arrest, but he'd arrested again and died before the medevac team had arrived. If he'd been closer to a major cardiac unit… If she'd had colleagues to help…

'Stop it,' she told herself. If she wasn't here there'd be no one at all. Grandpa was failing, and there were no bright young doctors hammering on the door to take up such a remote and scattered practice. What was needed was some sort of integrated medical facility, with means to transfer patients easily between the islands, but the cost of that would be prohibitive. Money was a huge problem.

An hour's boat ride across to an outer island, a couple of hours treating a patient and organising evacuation, an hour's boat ride back—how could she charge islanders anywhere near what that was worth? She couldn't. Her medical practice was therefore perpetually starved for funds, with no financial incentive for any other doctor to join her.

She loved this island. She loved its people and there'd never been a time she'd thought of leaving. It'd break her grandpa's heart and it'd break her heart, but sometimes—like now—she wouldn't mind time away. Christmas shopping in the big department stores. Crowds of shoppers where no one knew her. Bustle, chaos, fun.

A boyfriend who wasn't Tony?

Tony definitely wasn't the one. After just one date he'd

explained the very sensible reasons why they should marry, and he'd been proprietary ever since. He made no secret of his intentions and the islanders had jokingly egged him on. Of course she'd said no, and she'd keep saying no, but the pool of eligible guys on the island was depressingly small.

Sometimes she even found herself thinking she could— should?—end up with Tony. Or someone like Tony.

'You have to be kidding. No one I've dated in the whole time I've been here makes my toes curl,' she told the view, and her dopey beagle, Sherlock, came sniffing back to make sure she was okay.

'I'm fine,' she told the little dog, but she lifted him up and hugged him, because for some reason she really needed a hug. Last week's death had shattered her, maybe even more so because she knew her grandfather had heart problems. Plus he had renal problems. She was just…alone.

'But I'm not alone,' she told Sherlock fiercely, releasing him again to head into his sniffy places in the undergrowth. 'I have Grandpa. I have you. Even if I'm not going to marry Tony, I have the whole of the Birding Isles.'

'Who all depend on me,' she added.

'Yeah, so why are you here staring into space when they need you back in town?' she demanded of herself. 'What dramas am I missing now?'

She rose reluctantly and took a last long look at the view, soaking in the silence, the serenity, the peace. And then she turned to leave.

'Sherlock?' she called and got a sudden frenzied barking in return.

He was well into the bushes, investigating one of the myriad animal tracks that led from this point. He'd have some poor animal cornered, she thought—a wombat, a goanna. A snake?

She wasn't too fussed. Sherlock might be dumb, but he knew enough to stay out of darting distance from a snake, and he never hurt anything he'd cornered. Her dog was all nose and no follow through, but once he'd found the source of a scent he wouldn't leave it. Sighing, she reached into her pocket for his lead and headed into the bush after him.

But she went carefully. This was cave country. The water from the falls had undercut the limestone, and crevices and underground river routes made a trap for the unwary. Her grandpa had taught her the safe routes as a kid, and Sherlock's barking was well off the path she usually followed.

But by the sound of his frenzied barking he wasn't too far, and she knew the risks. She trod carefully, stepping on large rocks rather than loose undergrowth, testing the ground carefully before she put her weight on it.

Sherlock's yapping was reaching a crescendo—whatever he'd found had to be unusual. Not a 'roo then, or a wombat or koala. She wondered what it could be.

'Sherlock?' she yelled again in a useless attempt to divert him.

But the response left her stunned. It was a deep male voice, muffled, desperate.

'Help. Please help.'

He was stuck. Uselessly stuck. Hurting. Helpless.

He'd broken his leg and dislocated his shoulder. The pain was searing, but his predicament almost overrode the pain.

He was maybe fifteen feet down from the chink of light that showed the entrance to the underground chamber into which he'd fallen. The hole must have been covered with twigs and leaf litter, enough to cover it, enough for small animals to cross. Enough to think he was following a proper path.

He'd been moving fast. There'd been a sickening lurch as his boot had stepped through the fragile cover, and an unbelievable sensation as the entire ground seemed to give way. Then the freefall. The agony of his leg buckling underneath him. A searing pain in his shoulder.

And then fear.

He was on rock and dirt, on an almost level floor. He could see little except the light from the hole he'd made above him. The rest of the cave was gloomy, fading to blackness where the light from the hole above cut out.

He'd dropped his phone. He'd had it in his hand, but had let it go to clutch for a hold as he'd fallen. Maybe it was down here but he couldn't find it, and whenever he moved the pain in his leg and shoulder almost made him pass out. He could contact no one.

No phone. No light. Just pain.

According to his watch he'd been underground for twenty-seven hours. He'd dozed fretfully during the night but the pain was always with him. Today had stretched endlessly as he'd fought pain, exhaustion, panic.

He was unbelievably thirsty.

He was finding it hard to stay awake.

He was going nuts.

He'd been calling but he did it intermittently, knowing the chances of being heard in such a place were remote. The effort of calling was making him feel dizzy and sick. He knew he had to harness his resources, but what resources? He had nothing left.

And when could he expect help?

First rule of bushwalking—advise friends of dates and routes. He'd told Kayla he had family business to sort from his mother's death and he was turning his phone off for twenty-four hours. He hadn't told anyone he was flying all the way to Gannet Island.

Panic was so close…

And then, through the mist of pain and exhaustion, he heard a dog. The dog must have sensed he was down here—it was going crazy above him.

And then, even more unbelievably, he heard a woman calling, 'Sherlock!'

Don't go to her.

It was a silent plea to the dog, said over and over in his head as he yelled with every ounce of strength he possessed and tried to drag himself closer to the hole.

'Help... Don't come close—the ground's unsafe—but please get help.'

Elsa froze.

She knew at once what must have happened. Someone had fallen into one of the underground caverns.

Instinct would have had her shoving her way through the undergrowth to reach whoever it was, but triage had been drilled into her almost from the first day in med school.

First ensure your own safety.

Sherlock was barking in a place that was inherently unsafe. Her little beagle was light on his feet, used to following animal tracks. Elsa, not so much. She'd be dumb to charge off the path to investigate.

She stood still and called, as loud as she could, 'Hey! I'm here. Where are you?'

Sherlock stopped barking at that, seeming to sense the import of her words, and here came the voice again.

'I've fallen underground. Be careful. It looks...it looks like a path but it's not. The ground's unstable.'

'I'm careful,' she called, making her words prosaic and reassuring as possible. 'I'm a local. A doctor. Are you hurt?'

'Yes.' She could hear pain and exhaustion in his tone, and his words were cracking with strain. 'Broken leg and... I think...dislocated shoulder. I fell...through yesterday.'

Yesterday. To lie wounded in the dark for so long...this was the stuff of nightmares.

Next step? Reassurance.

'Okay, we're on it. I'll call for backup and we'll get you out of there,' she called back. 'It might take a while but help's coming.'

'Thank...thank you.'

But his words faded badly, and she wondered how much effort it had cost him to call out.

'Is your breathing okay?' she shouted. 'Are you bleeding? Do you have water?'

No answer.

'Hello?'

Silence.

Had he drifted into unconsciousness? Collapsed? Was he dying while she stood helplessly above?

Triage, she told herself fiercely. She was no use to anyone if she panicked.

She flipped open her satellite phone, dependable wherever she went, either here or on the outer islands. Her call went straight through to Macka, Gannet Island's only policeman.

'Elsa. What's up?' Macka was in his sixties, big, solid, dependable. He'd been a cop here for as long as Elsa could remember, and the sound of his voice grounded her.

'I'm up on Lightning Peak, following the back path around to the east, almost to the top,' she told him. 'Sherlock's just found someone who's fallen into an underground cavern.'

There was a moment's pause. Macka would know straight away the gravity of the situation.

'Alive?'

'I heard him call but he's been stuck since yesterday.'

'You're safe yourself?'

'Yeah, but I need to go down. He's stopped answering and his breathing sounded laboured. I have basic stuff in my backpack.'

'Elsa…'

'It's okay. I have a decent rope and it was you who taught me to rappel.'

'Wait for us.'

'I can't. It'll take you a couple of hours to reach us. The light'll fail before you get here and I don't know how bad he is. Macka, I'll turn on location sharing on my phone. Can you take a screenshot now so you know exactly where I am? I'm not sure if this phone will work underground.'

'It should, but Elsa…'

'I can't see that I have any other choice,' Elsa said, hearing his deep concern. 'But I'll stay safe, you know I will. And Sherlock will be up top—he'll bark when he hears you.'

'Elsa, please wait for us.'

'But it sounds like he's lost consciousness,' she said, almost gently. Macka's first concern was always to protect her—there was still a part of him that thought of her as the kid who'd landed on the island as a neglected seven-year-old. But she was all grown up now, and triage told her what she was doing was sensible. 'I need to go down and see what's going on, but I'll take every care. Can you let Grandpa know what's happening? Tell him it's under control, though. Don't scare him.'

'I wouldn't dare,' Macka said, and she heard the hint of a rueful smile. 'Anything you say, Elsa.'

'Hey, I'm not that bossy.'

'Reckon you are,' he said, and she heard another smile. Then, in a different tone, 'Reckon you've had to be. But be careful.'

'Same to you,' she told him. 'Don't come up here alone; bring a couple of the guys from the fire station.'

She heard the trace of a chuckle at that. 'Hey, you know Tony's a volunteer. He'll want to come.'

'Yeah, like that'll help,' she said wryly, thinking of staid, solid Tony who'd been acting more and more possessive without any encouragement. 'Macka, do me a favour and don't tell him.'

'This is Gannet, love. This news'll be all over the island before you even disconnect.'

'Fine,' she said wearily. 'Bring the cavalry then. Only Macka, be careful yourselves. This place is dangerous.'

'Don't I know it,' he said grimly. 'Okay, love, let's make sure I have this screenshot with co-ordinates so I know exactly where you are, and get this rescue underway.'

CHAPTER TWO

ELSA HAD BEEN back on the island, working as a doctor, for five years now, and in that time she'd learned to be self-sufficient. The Birding Isles were a speck of six islands in the middle of the Pacific Ocean. They formed a tourist paradise, and tourists sometimes did stupid things. The permanent population of Gannet was seven hundred, but the numbers swelled dramatically over the summer months, and both tourists and locals quickly learned who Elsa was.

She was Doc, and she was fair game. Always. Her latest heart sink had happened only this morning in the general store, in a tiny sliver of time she'd managed between seeing patients. She'd been choosing rolls of Christmas wrapping paper when one of the local fishermen had approached her, hauled off his boot, stood on one leg and held up a grubby foot.

'Reckon me toe's rotten, Doc,' he'd told her, swaying on one leg as the other shoppers had backed away in disgust. 'Pus's been coming out for two days now.'

It was indeed infected. She'd told him to replace his boot and meet her at the surgery. Thankfully, Mae, the owner of the shop, had yelled after her, 'How many of these rolls do you want, Doc?' and a dozen rolls of garish crimson paper had landed on her desk an hour later.

The locals were great, but this type of interruption happened to her all the time. She'd try to go for a swim and someone would yell, 'Doc, the lady over here's got a fish hook stuck in her arm...' Or, 'Doc, a kid's just done a header into a sandbank. Hurt his neck...'

The nurses at the tiny Gannet hospital and on the outer islands were skilled and professional. Her grandfather still did what he could, but she was always first on call.

Like now. She'd slipped away for a last break before the Christmas rush, and she had to rescue someone down a hole.

But she was always prepared. The advantage of being accustomed to urgent calls wherever she went was that she always carried a basic backpack. Small things but vital. A satellite phone. A water bottle. Bandages, antiseptic, adrenaline, antihistamine, glucagon, morphine. She'd almost forgotten what it felt like to walk around without her gear, and she blessed it now.

If she got down the hole, she had supplies that might help.

And she had rope too. This island was a climber's paradise. Most climbers knew their stuff, but it was also a fabulous place for a family holiday. She'd had emergency calls before. 'Doc, there's a kid stuck on a ledge ten feet down with a split knee...'

During her island childhood she'd learned to climb well, and it was often safer and faster to climb to whatever drama was playing out rather than wait for Macka's team.

So she had what she needed, a light, strong rope that looped permanently around the sides of her backpack.

She formed an arrow of stones on the path, backup to show rescuers where she was. Then she headed into the bush, towards the sound of Sherlock's barking, moving from rock to rock, testing each one before she shifted her weight. When the rocks ran out, ten feet before the spot where Sherlock was peering down, she looped the cord around a solid eucalypt. Then she inched further, testing and retesting, until she reached the break in the ground.

It was easy enough to see what had happened. This looked like part of an animal path. Trodden leaf litter lay on either side of a gaping hole where someone had obviously slipped, clutched in vain, then fallen. The surface of leaf litter had obviously held up for light-footed native animals. For a man, not so much.

As she neared the hole she lay on her stomach and inched forward, testing all the way. Using her phone's torch she peered down into the darkness, but she could see nothing. She had another stronger torch, attached to her belt with a carabiner. She fumbled it free and peered again.

She could make out the floor of the cave, maybe fifteen feet down. She couldn't see the man who'd called out.

'Hello?'

Nothing.

Sherlock was on his stomach as well, quivering with excitement, trying to lick her face as she peered down.

'You found him. Well done, boy,' she told him, 'but you're going to have to stay up top and wait for the cavalry.'

She'd have to rappel. Rappelling without a harness was not her favourite thing—for a start the cord would hurt like hell as she'd need to form a makeshift 'seat'. It'd cut into her waist and groin, but there was no avoiding it. With luck, the guys up top would provide her with a decent harness to haul her back up again.

But that was for later. For now she headed back to the tree, fastening her cord as she needed, taking both ends, tying them around her waist, then looping the cord between her legs to form a system where she could safely control her descent.

To Sherlock's disgust she attached him to the same tree. 'Stay,' she told him, and he looked at her with disbelief.

What? I found him and you won't let me come?

One swift pat and she left him, returning to the hole, moving backwards, then leaning back, testing the strength of her rope, testing her control.

Sherlock was staring after her in concern.

'Needs must,' she told him, with a forced attempt at cheer. 'You do dumb things because you're a dog. Me, I'm a doctor, and that means I get to do things that are even dumber.'

And on that note she backed carefully over the lip of the hole and started her descent.

Rappelling on thick flax rope was relatively easy. Rappelling on thin cord was entirely different. The cord did indeed dig into her pelvis and her waist, and her hands struggled to keep their grip. But she managed.

She'd checked out all sides of the hole and figured the side she was on looked the most stable—the last thing she wanted was for the hole to suddenly enlarge, throwing dirt and rock onto the man below. She moved with infinite care, inching her way. It would have been less painful to move faster, but losing control could mean disaster.

She edged into the hole, catching a last glimpse of a concerned Sherlock before she was in the darkness of the cavern.

She had no hands free to hold her phone, and she'd had to reattach her mini torch to her belt. The light from the torch swung in all the wrong directions. What she needed was a headlamp. Her legs sought for a foothold and found none.

Five feet. Ten.

And at fifteen she finally felt solid rock.

Still she kept the strain on her rope rather than putting her weight on the ground.

She hung in her makeshift harness, fighting back pain as she grabbed her torch again.

There was a mound of leaf litter under her—that must have fallen from above—but the cave stretched out into darkness. The floor was strewn with rocks, dusty grey. At least it seemed solid.

And there he was. The man lay slumped, seemingly lifeless, slightly to the side of where she hung. Her heart hit her boots as she saw him, but as the torchlight hit his face he stirred, winced, then raised his hand to hide his eyes from the beam.

He was a big guy, tall, lean, muscled, built like many of the rock climbers who loved this place.

He didn't look like a rock climber, though. He was wearing fawn chinos and a short-sleeved shirt that wouldn't be out of place in an informal business meeting. His face was framed with short dark hair, dust and an impressive after-five shadow. A trickle of dried blood ran across his forehead and down to his cheek. Still she had the impression of inherent strength.

As he lowered his hand and looked at her, the impression of strength deepened. His piercing eyes surveyed her, as if she was the patient rather than him.

But he *was* the patient and he'd obviously just surfaced from unconsciousness.

She'd done a fast assessment of the cave now. The ground seemed safe enough. She undid her makeshift harness, looped it, tied it to her belt—the last thing she wanted was to lose it, leaving her stuck here—and stooped to examine her patient.

He opened his mouth to speak, failed the first time and then tried again. 'You can't be real,' he managed. 'An... angel?'

'You guessed it. I'm an angel in scruffy jeans and a torn windcheater, with a daft dog barking his head off up top. An angel? Give me a minute while I figure where I put my wings.'

He managed a smile. Almost.

'Hey, I'm not a vision,' she told him, aware that, despite the piercing gaze, what this guy most needed was reassurance. 'I'm Elsa McCrae—Dr McCrae.' She reached for his wrist and was relieved to feel a steady heartbeat. Fast but not scary fast. 'And you?'

'Marcus Pierce,' he told her, struggling to get the words out. 'M... Marc.' His throat sounded thick, clogged. 'Also... I'm also a doctor.'

'Hey, how about that? A colleague?' Fat lot of good that'd be doing you down here, though, she thought. 'Does your neck hurt? Your back?'

'No. Just...my leg. And my shoulder.'

She'd already seen his leg. It lay twisted under him. And his shoulder? It was at the wrong angle. Dislocated? Ouch.

'Your head?' She was looking at the blood on his face.

'I hit it on the way down.' He winced. 'It's nothing. Didn't knock me out.'

'You fainted just now.'

'I never...faint.'

She fixed him with a look. If he was indeed a colleague, he'd know that was nonsense. 'You're lying. Everyone faints, given the right circumstances,' she told him. 'You certainly seem to have lost consciousness after you talked to me earlier.'

'I tried to drag myself under the hole so you'd see me,' he managed grimly. 'Stupid.'

'Yes, because if you'd succeeded I could have landed on you when I climbed down.' She was making her voice deliberately cheerful, deliberately matter-of-fact. 'So passing out was a good thing. It seems your body is more sensible than your head. So lie still now while I see what's what.'

He closed his eyes. Just how much pain are you in? she wondered.

But first things first. Carefully she checked his neck, his movement, his vision. She tested his hands. 'Squeeze please.' She checked his good leg. 'Wriggle your toes?' His good arm. 'Squeeze my fingers.'

He squeezed and held for longer than he needed. She got that. He must have been lying here terrified.

But what she was finding was reassuring. No obvious head injury. No spinal damage as far as she could see. Just the leg and shoulder. And the fact that he was trapped underground.

Next?

She took her water bottle from her backpack and gently raised his head. His eyes flew open.

'Water,' she said, and got a flash of gratitude so great it almost overwhelmed her.

She held the bottle to his mouth. Half the bottle went down before he paused, wiping his mouth, sinking back with a grunt of thanks.

'If you knew how good that tasted…'

'I guess I do. You fell down yesterday? You've had nothing to drink since then?'

'I had a bottle in my bag,' he told her. 'I think…my bag fell with me but I can't see where it is. I tried to search…'

He didn't have to explain further. To drag himself around this rock-filled cavern in the dark with a broken leg… His face was etched with pain; his voice didn't disguise it.

'If it's down here then I'll find it,' she told him, still with that careful cheerfulness. 'But let's get you something for the pain first. Any allergies? If you're a doctor you'll know the drill. Anything I should know about?'

'You don't have morphine?' he asked, incredulous, and she gave him a modest smile, which was probably wasted given that she was working only with the beam of her torch and she was shining the torch on him. To him she must merely be a shadow.

But that was her job, to be a professional, reassuring shadow. 'I'm a Girl Scout from way back,' she told him. 'I was raised to Be Prepared. Brown Owl would be proud of me.'

'I'm proud of you,' he murmured, sinking back on the

hard ground. 'No allergies. Feel free to give me as much as you have.'

She didn't. She'd been stuck before, on a ledge where she'd abseiled down, waiting for a helicopter to take an injured kid off. There'd been a five-hour wait and the kid had needed a top-up. She'd needed to keep some in reserve then, and she might need to do the same now. They might well be stuck here for hours. Or longer.

Her mind was racing now but, wherever it raced, she couldn't see a safe way out of here until morning. They'd need a stretcher and they'd need secure fastenings up top. The closest stable land was thirty feet from the hole. They'd increase the risk of ground collapsing if they weren't working in daylight. She'd definitely need her reserves of morphine.

She didn't say any of that, though. She swabbed his thigh, injected the drug, then carefully sliced away the torn leg of his jeans so she could see what she was dealing with.

That the leg was broken was obvious. She'd seen the rough stones under the entrance hole and thought he must have landed on those. The impact and falling awkwardly would have been enough to snap the bones.

But it wasn't all bad. She touched his ankle and was relieved to feel warmth, plus a pulse. 'Great news, your foot's still breathing,' she told him, taking him at his word that he was a doctor. It didn't take much medical training to know that a break could cut blood supply, and twenty-four hours without would mean dire consequences. 'But the leg does look broken.'

'Of course it's broken,' he growled. 'I couldn't have this degree of pain without a break. How badly?'

'I'm not sure,' she confessed. 'It doesn't look too bad from where I'm standing. When the morphine kicks in I'll check your toes.'

'Check 'em now.'

'No.' She wasn't having him passing out again. 'If you

can bear it, just lie back and see if you can relax until that pain relief kicks in. Then I'll cut off your boot and check your shoulder. It looks dislocated—maybe fractured...'

'I think dislocated,' he told her.

'You might be right, but let's not investigate until the morphine's had time to work. Meanwhile I need to summon the troops. Lie back and think of England while I organise me a posse.'

There was silence at that, and she could almost see his mind sifting her words.

'A posse?' he said at last, sounding cautious. 'You mean...you're on your own?'

'I have my dog. Me and Sherlock.'

'But you've climbed down here without backup.'

'I'm not an idiot,' she told him, hearing alarm. He'd gone straight to the scenario of two people stuck down here rather than one. 'First, I've used a secure rappelling loop, so I can get out again whenever I want. Carrying you with me, not so much, but I've covered that too, because secondly I've already let people know where I am and what I'm doing. Which I'm guessing you haven't?'

'No,' he said ruefully. 'I know, it was incredibly stupid of me, but it's too late to do anything about it now.'

'Don't worry about it,' she told him, thinking though that he was right to feel dumb. Didn't he realise just how close to total disaster he'd been? But she guessed he already knew that. He'd had more than twenty-four hours to think about it. 'Our lovely Sergeant of Police and his troops will probably already be on their way,' she told him, keeping her voice brisk and cheerful. 'I just need to update them on what's needed.'

'So...' He looked as if he was struggling to get his head around what was happening. 'You're not part of a search party already looking for me?'

'Afraid not. Will anyone be wondering where you are?'

'No.' Blunt. Harsh.

'Then that's what you get for not letting anyone know you're here. Downside—no one knows you're here.'

'You think I'm an idiot.'

'Mine's not to judge,' she said primly. Talking was a good way to distract him from pain. 'I just deal with stuff as I find it.'

'And I'm…stuff.'

'I'm sure you're very nice stuff,' she reassured him.

'But idiotic stuff.'

She smiled, hearing the mortification behind his words, but she didn't say anything. It certainly wasn't her place to judge, but he needed to accept that his actions had indeed been foolish.

'So…' he said at last. 'You and your dog were just scouring the mountains looking for any injured…stuff?'

'Sherlock and I found an orphaned wallaby last week,' she told him. 'So yeah, I guess that's us. Like St Bernards in the snow.' She wrinkled her nose. 'And that needs an apology. I forgot to attach the brandy keg around Sherlock's neck. The wallaby didn't need it, but here… Total fail. We'll be crossed off the Worldwide Beagle Rescue Association forthwith.'

He was looking dazed, struggling to follow the flippancy she was using to distract him until the morphine kicked in. 'So Sherlock's…a beagle?'

'Yes he is, and he found you. You owe him a month's supply of dog treats.'

'Who the hell are you?' It was almost a snap.

'Ooh, that's supposed to be my question.' She thought she wasn't doing such a bad job of distracting him. 'Drat, I have a whole questionnaire for new patients back at the surgery. Where's my form when I need it? But I already told you I'm a doctor. Elsa McCrae. FRACGP. General Practitioner. And you?'

'Marcus Pierce,' he responded. 'FRACS. FRACP. Cardiologist.'

FRACS—College of Surgeons. FRACP—College of Physicians. 'A heart surgeon,' she said, imbuing her voice with deferential awe. Thinking, though, that it was so often the intelligent ones that got themselves into dire trouble on the island. Smart didn't always equate to sensible, but she kept her voice neutral. 'That's great,' she told him. 'As soon as the morphine kicks in I'll get you to keep track of your pulse while I check your shoulder and take your boot off. Marcus, will anyone be out looking for you?'

'No.' A flat veto.

'You don't have friends on the island?'

'I came here to scatter my mother's ashes,' he said tightly. 'Privately.'

'I'm sorry,' she said, more gently. 'Did your mother live here?'

'She visited frequently. She loved this peak.'

She sat back on her heels, frowning. Thinking of his name. Pierce. Making associations.

Remembering a little lady with a fierce determination to climb every peak on the island. A lady who'd had to come to see her the last time she was on the island because she couldn't stop coughing. 'I know what's wrong with me, girl,' she'd said when Elsa had listened to her chest. 'I'm a doctor myself. There's nothing you can do to cure me. I just want something to alleviate the symptoms so I can climb Lightning Peak one last time.'

'Louise Pierce?' she said now, even more gentle. 'Was Louise your mum?'

'I...yes.'

'I knew her. She spent a lot of time here, at the Misses Harnett's guesthouse, and we were so sorry when we heard she'd died.' She sighed. 'I know it's easy to be wise after the event, but Rhonda and Marg Harnett were your mother's friends. They would have come up here with you in a heartbeat.'

'I didn't want complications,' he growled. 'I came on

yesterday morning's plane and I was intending to be out on the evening plane.'

'And now you have more complications than you could have imagined.' She sighed again. 'I'm so sorry. But I need you to shush now while I try my phone and see if I can get reception from down here.'

She phoned and the satellite did her proud. The line crackled and broke but Macka heard her. 'It's up to you,' she told him. 'But I can't think it'll be safe to bring him up until dawn. Can you bring us a decent lamp, pillows, rugs and maybe a couple of air mattresses? I have a rappelling loop set up so we can lower stuff. Oh, and can you bring some dog food for Sherlock?' Her dog had ceased barking but she knew he'd be waiting patiently above ground and wanting his dinner.

She disconnected and turned to find Marcus looking mortified. 'Morning?'

'Sorry, but I don't think it's safe to bring you up until we have decent light.'

'Hell,' he said. And then, 'There's no need for you to stay down here too.'

'You know there is,' she said matter-of-factly. 'You've done the medical training. You know the rules.'

'I won't have blood clots. I won't pass out again.'

'Yeah, but I didn't bring the indemnity forms,' she told him. 'And it's no problem. Because of the remoteness of this island I did extra training as an emergency doctor. Rappelling into caves and being stuck underground will add enormous credit to my CV.'

She was swinging her torch beam around the floor as she talked. She found his phone first. Smashed in the fall. Thank God for Sherlock's hunting instincts, she thought. Without his phone he could have lain here until...

No. It didn't bear thinking about.

She also found a good-looking leather slouch bag, which

held a wallet and, wonderfully, another bottle of water. On the strength of it she offered Marcus more.

He drank with gratitude. Despite the greyness of his face as she'd shown him his smashed phone—he must realise what he'd been facing even more acutely than she did—he was looking less rigid. The morphine must be taking effect.

'Right,' she said briskly as he settled again—or settled as much as anyone could on dirt and rocks— 'let's get you to work. Cardiac surgeon? I don't need the surgeon part so much, but can you keep track of your pulse while I get this boot off?'

He even managed a chuckle at that, a deep, nice chuckle, another great sign that the morphine was working.

Leg first. The shoulder needed attention but blood supply to the foot had to be her first concern.

She headed for his boot, blessing the sharp little everything tool she always carried. Yes, his ankle had a pulse, but she wanted to see pink toes. His foot was swollen—she'd expect nothing else with the damage to his leg—and the boot alone could now be constricting supply.

'So, your job...' he said, and she could hear the strain in his voice as she took her time to slice the thick, good quality leather. 'You're on permanent patrol up here? Is that how you make a living? Donations from the grateful lost? How many hikers do you find?'

'More than you might think,' she told him, remembering previous island walks interrupted as she'd come across lacerations, sprained ankles, insect bites—and, more recently and more dreadfully, the full-blown cardiac arrest.

She could have used a cardiac surgeon then, she thought bleakly. She'd never felt so alone, so helpless. Specialist help could have saved a life, but it was an ocean away.

'And the rest of the time?' he asked.

'I have a surgery down near the jetty,' she managed, hauling herself from just one of the memories of failure that haunted her. 'We have a hospital too. It serves all the islands. It's mostly used for our elderly—six of our ten beds are classified nursing home. The rest are simple problems—minor infections, patients waiting for evacuation to Sydney or continuing their recovery after being transported home. It's a very basic medical service but it's all we can manage.' She had his sock off now and was examining toes. 'Marcus, this is looking good. There can be no blood supply constriction at all.'

'Just the matter of a broken leg and twisted shoulder.'

'There is that,' she said, looking again at the damage. Thinking of possible movement. Possible consequences. 'Marcus...'

'My friends call me Marc.'

'You might not want to call me a friend when I tell you what I want to do,' she told him. 'That leg's definitely broken and I need to splint it to make sure circulation stays secure. You have lacerations and bruising where it must have struck rock, but nothing's piercing the skin. If I up the morphine and you manage to grit your teeth, I reckon it'll be safer to straighten it a little and brace it. It'll need to be braced before we move you tomorrow anyway, so I might as well do it now. Plus I might as well see if I can get that shoulder into a more comfortable position.' She tried to smile. 'It'll save you lying awake all night worrying about surgery in the morning.'

'You're all heart.' She saw him close his eyes, accept the inevitable. 'How are you at fixing dislocated shoulders?'

'Without an X-ray? I'd normally not even go there.'

'But in an emergency situation? Given the low risk? I've felt it. There's no suspicion of fracture.'

'You can't know that.'

'I felt it as I fell. It twisted hard but not hard enough to break. I'm sure this is a simple dislocation. Elsa, it's agony and I'm done with agony. I tried to put it back myself.'

'Yeah?' Like that was easy to do. 'With what results?'

'I did actually faint,' he admitted. 'So then I stopped.'

'Very wise.'

'But you could do it.'

'I might not be able to.'

'You could try. You're sensible enough to stop if it doesn't click into place fast.'

She sat back and considered. 'You'd accept the risk?'

'Yes, I would.'

There was a level of trust. He'd accepted her as competent enough to do no harm.

'I guess,' she said doubtfully. 'With the morphine on board... I could give you a muscle relaxant too.'

'Bless you,' he said simply and then moved on, almost colleague to colleague. 'The leg. What'll you brace it with?'

'That's the good side about you falling,' she told him, making her voice brisk, as professional as she could. 'We have a selection of bush litter around us. I can see at least three sticks I can whittle with my neat little knife to make a nice smooth brace. You'd have to agree with me though, Marc. You'd have to accept that I'll hurt you.'

He closed his eyes for a moment and then opened them, and his face had become resolute.

'Help me to sit up,' he asked her. 'I need to see my leg for myself first.'

'No.' She put her hands on his chest, firmly pressing him back. 'I know you've been trying to move but Marc, you must know there's the possibility of spinal damage. You fell hard. You know the rules. Let's get you safely X-rayed before you start shifting. We'll get you up on a stretcher and check you before you start doing fancy stuff like sitting up.'

'But...'

'No buts. You know what's sensible.'

He closed his eyes, looking grim. 'I'm supposed to be flying to St Moritz tomorrow, to be there over Christmas,' he muttered. 'For a couple of weeks' skiing.'

She raised her brows at that. 'Really?' She paused to

consider. 'I guess it could still happen. How are you at skiing on one leg?'

No answer.

She hadn't really expected one. She thought, tangentially, how amazing to live a life where you could pop over to St Moritz to ski when you felt like it.

He'd be a good skier, she thought. Okay, she didn't know for sure, but she could sense it. His body was solid, muscled, ripped in all the right places.

She was still holding him. She'd moved to stop him shifting and her arm had gone around his good shoulder as she'd tugged him back to a prone position and encouraged him to relax. She'd left her arm there for a moment. He was cold and she was warm. He needed contact.

Comfort?

But the comfort seemed to be working both ways. This underground dungeon was creepy. It was almost dark above them.

She had a phone light and a torch. She had a spare battery for her phone in her backpack. Help was on its way. There was no need for her to want comfort.

But still, as she held him and felt his inherent strength, she took it where she found it. She'd learned to do that. She had her grandpa's help when she needed it medically, but Grandpa was growing increasingly frail. She had Sherlock, but...

But there were still lots of times in Dr Elsa McCrae's medical life when she felt totally alone, and for just one brief moment now she let herself accept the feel of this man beside her. She let herself imagine that maybe she could depend on him.

Which was ridiculous. His mind was clearly focused on the next thing. Bracing his leg. Thinking about his shoulder.

'Okay,' he said briefly. 'Let's get it over with.'

She hesitated. She could—maybe she should—wait for more light. But it'd still be a couple of hours before help arrived. Macka was a great policeman but he wasn't the fittest bloke on the island. He'd have called on a couple of the fire brigade guys to help. They were fitter, faster than Macka but they didn't know the route.

Two hours. She released him and looked again at that leg and thought it did need to be fixed fast. If it was a compound fracture… She had no way of knowing for sure, and she had to work on the worst-case scenario.

'We do it now,' Marcus said, and she heard her own thoughts reflected in the tone of his voice. He'd know the risks as well as she did. 'And the shoulder if you can. Let's go.'

So she did.

CHAPTER THREE

SHE WAS NO orthopaedic surgeon and she wanted to be one. She had no X-ray equipment and she needed it. She had no help and she wanted that, too.

All she had were her instincts.

Do no harm. First rule in every situation. She had a leg that still had circulation. She could leave it exactly how it was. His shoulder needed to be X-rayed to make sure it wasn't broken. She should leave that in place too.

But a dislocated shoulder was too excruciatingly painful for him to sleep, even with the morphine, and in the morning he had to be moved regardless. The long night lay ahead of them and the shoulder would be agony. And if he moved during the night, if the leg twisted as they tried to get him up, if his circulation blocked… It didn't bear thinking about.

No X-ray machine would miraculously appear down here. No orthopaedic surgeon was on his way with Macka. She was on her own.

So what was new? She'd coped before, and she'd cope again.

She could have waited until Macka arrived with better light but what she was doing depended mainly on feel. Plus the cooperation of her patient. If she'd been back at the hospital she'd use general anaesthetic. She couldn't use it here but, blessedly, Marc's medical training would have him understanding the absolute imperative of keeping still.

Leg first. The shoulder was more painful, but the risk of blocked circulation to the foot meant it was triaged first.

She prepared one of the pieces of wood that had been shoved down the hole with the force of Marc's fall. She showed it to Marc, who made a crack about her whittling skills before falling silent again as she worked.

He was mentally preparing himself for what lay ahead, she thought. Morphine could only do so much.

Then, moving more slowly than she'd ever worked before, she inched the wood under his leg. With her hands feeling his leg, feeling for bone, she slowly, slowly straightened his knee, then straightened his leg, manoeuvring it onto her makeshift splint.

She cleaned and disinfected and bandaged and then fixed the leg as tightly as she dared to her whittled wood. Marc said nothing the entire time she worked, and she blessed him for it.

Finally she sat back and took a breath. It was cool and damp underground, but she found she was sweating.

'Well done,' Marc growled softly, and she caught herself. What was she doing sweating, when it was Marc who'd managed to hold himself rigid?

'Well…well done yourself,' she told him. 'I…' She caught herself, giving herself space to find the right words. To find a prosaic normalcy. 'The pulse in your lower leg is stronger. If I keep the morphine for during the night you should be able to sleep without worrying about shifting.'

'So now the shoulder.'

That was harder. She knew it'd mean more pain for him and she was less sure of herself. Heaven, she wanted an X-ray.

The simplest and safest technique for shoulder reduction was the Stimson technique, where the patient hung his or her arm down and weights were attached at the wrist.

This was normally her go-to method but here there was no bed, no raised surface. Scapular manipulation also had to be ruled out. Given the possibility of back injury, there was no way she was rolling him into the position required.

Which left external rotation as the next best option. That could at least be done with the patient lying on his back. She talked to Marc as she thought it through. 'You reckon?' she asked him. He was, after all, a colleague—and it was his shoulder.

'Go for it,' he urged.

So she did. With his arm tucked in as close to his body as possible, gently, slowly she rotated, letting gravity—and pain—limit the amount of movement. She watched his face every inch of the way, watching the greyness, the tight set of his mouth, the fierce determination to get this done. As his pain level increased his arm automatically tensed. She backed off, waited, then inched again.

And then, miraculously, wonderfully, came the moment when it slid back into place. She saw his face go slack with relief and knew her own face must reflect it.

'Thank you,' he said, his eyes closed, his whole body seeming to sag. 'Oh, my God, thank you.'

'Think nothing of it,' she managed, and to her disgust heard a tremor in her own voice. 'I'll strap it now. It needs to stay strapped until I get you to where we can check for rotator cuff injury. You must know the drill. Hopefully now though you'll be comfortable enough to get some sleep.'

'Sleep…' He grimaced. 'Look, now we have everything braced, surely I can be pulled up to the surface.'

'Not on my watch.' She had herself back under control now. 'You heard what I said to Macka. He'll bring stuff to make us more comfortable, but I'm not risking bringing you up until we have decent light.'

'But if my leg's braced…'

'I'm not thinking about you,' she told him, only partly truthfully. 'I'm thinking about the unstable ground and a team up there who aren't trained cavers. I'm thinking about that ground collapsing. I'm thinking about half the Gannet Island fire department landing on our heads.'

'Oh,' he said doubtfully.

'And I've used the last of my bandages,' she told him. 'If a team of burly firefighters fall down here, my emergency kit's going to look pretty darned empty. No. We wait until morning when Macka—he's our island cop and he's good—can do a thorough recce of the ground.'

'Right,' he said, clearly not liking it but reaching acceptance. 'But you could go up. There's no need for both of us to stay down here.'

'Yeah,' she told him, thinking of clots, thinking of delayed concussion, thinking of kinked blood vessels that still might block.

'I can do my own obs.'

That brought a wry smile. 'Really? A specialist cardiologist doing obs? When was the last time you did such a thing? Don't cardiologists have nursing staff for that?'

'You're not a nurse.'

'No, I'm a family doctor in a remote community, and as such I've even done hourly obs on a pregnant turtle. Mind, it was a special turtle and I had her in a sand tank on my veranda but there you go, needs must.'

'Did you have a good outcome?' he asked, distracted as she'd hoped he would be.

'An excellent outcome. Seventy-three babies that we hope went on to become seventy-three of Gannet Island's finest. Never doubt my skill, Dr Pierce. I can do your obs, no problem. There's no need to be scared at all.'

'Believe it or not, I'm not in the least scared,' he told her. 'Not from the moment you slid down your rope.'

'Then I've done my job until now,' she said cheerfully. 'And I'll keep doing it if you don't mind. So you settle down and see if you can sleep and I'll check the whereabouts of the team up top.'

'Elsa…'

'Yep?'

'If any of the team up top fall and break a leg…or if there's an emergency in town tonight…another turtle?'

'Then Grandpa will cope,' she told him, making her voice more sure than she felt.

'Grandpa?'

'He's our other doctor on the island. He's good.'

'How old is he?'

'Seventy-eight.'

'Then…'

'If you're going to be ageist I'll need to report you to the med board for discrimination. Grandpa can cope.'

'But apart from Grandpa…'

'His name's Robert.'

'Apart from Robert, you're the only doctor on the island?'

'I am,' she told him soundly. 'Plus vet and sometimes nurse and sometimes cook and sometimes janitor. General dogsbody, that's me. Grandpa and me and my beagle, Sherlock, together we practically run this island. Now, could you please shush because I need to ring Macka again.'

'Elsa…'

'Shush,' she told him severely. 'You get on with being a patient, Marcus Pierce, and let me get on with being Doctor in Charge.'

Macka's team arrived half an hour later. Sherlock announced their arrival with shrill excited barks—as well he might. These guys were friends and it was way past his dinnertime.

'Is that our rescue team?' Marc had been dozing under the effects of the morphine but the barking and yells above them had him opening his eyes.

'Doc?' Macka called down, strongly authoritative. 'Shut up, Sherlock.'

Amazingly, he did. Macka's word was law on this island.

'We are,' she called up. 'But stay back. The ground's unstable. Can you see where I've tethered my rope? Don't come any closer than that. I want Marc out of here, but not at the cost of another accident. Who's there?'

'Denise and Graham. We can call on more if we need them. How are things down there?'

'Stable,' she told him. 'No need for rush. Don't come any closer, guys. This ground is a trap for the unwary.'

'But you're safe?'

'We're both safe. Marc has a broken leg and an injured shoulder, but we can hold out until it's safe to pull us both up. Marc's going to need a stretcher.'

'We have the rescue stretcher.'

'That's great,' she told him, thinking thankfully of their newly acquired piece of kit, a collapsible stretcher with straps that could hold a patient completely immobile while being shifted. Or, in this case, lifted.

There was still the possibility of damage to Marc's back. First rule of medicine—do no harm. Shifting him before she could take an X-ray was the stuff of nightmares.

'Can you hold out until first light?' Macka called.

'I think we must.' She wanted a steady ascent, everything in their favour, and if it meant waiting then they had no choice. She was looking at Marc, meeting his gaze, calm and steady. He'd know the options.

'Then we'll hold off,' Macka said, sounding relieved. 'Tell us what's happened?'

She told him. There was silence as he thought things through.

'Right, then. We'll get the gear down to you and set up here. Your guy... Marc? Is there anyone we need to contact on his behalf?'

Marc shook his head, looking grim. 'No one will miss me until tomorrow.'

She frowned at that but Macka was waiting for a reply. 'He says not.'

'Fair enough,' Macka said.

'You want us to ring your grandpa? How about Tony?'

'I'll ring Grandpa,' she called back. 'And don't you dare ring Tony.'

There was a chuckle and then things turned businesslike.

'Okay, we'll use your rope as a pulley and lower enough gear to make you comfortable for the night,' Macka told her. 'We brought the medical supplies you need, plus a couple of air mattresses and blankets. You can set the air mattress below the stretcher so it won't need another shift in the morning. We'll stay up here in case the situation changes but, unless it does, at first light we'll organise a line across to keep us stable, get a stretcher down there and winch you both up.'

'Can you contact the mainland to stand by for an evac flight?' She wanted an orthopaedic surgeon to take over care of this leg, the sooner the better. 'We ought to be able to get him to the airport by late morning.'

'That might be harder,' Macka called back. 'There's bushfires on the mainland and the smoke's affecting all the major airports. Evac flights are detoured up north, but only if they're life or death—they have to come from Brisbane and the fires are keeping them flat-out. Normal commuter flights are already called off for tomorrow. Mae's going nuts because she has an order for forty Christmas turkeys. The way this is looking, they'll be lucky to arrive Boxing Day.'

'No! Five of those turkeys are for us.' She kept her voice deliberately light because the grim look on Marc's face had intensified. Had he still been hoping to make St Moritz?

It was sad about that, but it was tough for her, too. She'd have to take X-rays and set the leg herself. Grandpa would help, but doing such a procedure on someone who wasn't an islander and therefore couldn't be expected to accept the medical limits caused by their remoteness...

She'd worry about that tomorrow, she told herself.

There was a call from above them. A tightly wrapped bundle was descending, tied on her looped rappel rope. First delivery.

She caught it before it reached the ground. A lantern was attached to the side. She flicked it on and for the first time saw the extent of their cavern.

Or, rather, the enormity of it. It stretched downward on all sides. Marc had been so lucky that he'd landed on a site that was almost stable.

She didn't say anything though, just unfastened the bundle.

Two self-filling air mattresses.

'Hey, look at this,' she told him, holding the first up as it inflated. 'Who needs to go to St Moritz for luxury?' She shivered. 'Speaking of which, who needs to go to St Moritz for cold? Did you guys bring blankets?' she called.

'Coming down,' Macka told her, and ten minutes later they had everything they needed to keep themselves if not exactly comfortable, then not too cold and not too uncomfortable.

It took time and skill to move Marc onto the combined mattress and stretcher but at last he was where he needed to be.

'Done,' she called back up. 'All secure.'

'Then dinner,' Macka called and an insulated bag came down. 'Deirdre's chicken soup and bread rolls. It went in hot so it should still be warm. She figured your guy might be feeling a bit off, so chicken soup might be the ticket.'

'Wow, thank you,' she called back and guided the bag down and nestled it beside the now almost comfortable Marc.

Who was looking at her in disbelief.

'Hot food as well.'

'Gannet Island's all about service,' she told him, smiling. 'Do you think you can drink some? Let me help you. No, don't try and sit up. Just let me support your shoulders while you drink.'

'I can...'

'I'm very sure you can sit up,' she told him severely. 'But you know as well as I do that you risk your leg moving and I'm still worrying about your back. If there's spinal injury... And if that leg loses circulation...' She paused while they both thought of the consequences.

'So you're telling me to lie back, shut up and do what I'm told,' he said, still grim.

'That, Dr Pierce, is exactly what I'm doing, and if you knew how much I, as a family doctor, have longed to say that to a specialist then you'll know that this night is not all bad.'

'For who?'

'For me,' she told him and grinned. 'Now shut up and let's get this soup into you.'

CHAPTER FOUR

MARC LET HER support his shoulders while he drank the soup—for which he was pathetically grateful. For the last twenty-seven hours he'd been in agonising pain. Thirst had broken through, so practically all he'd thought of was fear, water and the pain in his leg and shoulder.

This magical woman had fixed the fear, given him water and made his leg and shoulder little more than dull aches. Now she was pretty much hand-feeding him the most delicious soup he'd ever tasted.

She'd wedged her body under his, sitting on the ground at his head, using her body to prop the pillow of his air mattress higher. There was canvas between them, but it felt as if there was nothing at all. His head seemed to be pillowed on a cushion of warmth and relief and gratitude.

She helped him hold the mug to his lips and he felt the warmth of her hand and he thought he'd never met someone so wonderful in all his life.

'Marry me,' he murmured as he finished the last of his soup and she chuckled.

'That's not even original. There's Tony, who asks me that once a week, plus I get proposals from whoever else is grateful right now. I was propositioned only yesterday when I lanced old Roger Havelock's abscess. He'd been putting up with it for a week so the relief from pressure was nothing less than sensational. I could have asked for half his kingdom. Not that that's saying anything,' she added reflectively. She shifted back, lowering his pillowed head gently, and he was aware of a sharp stab of loss as she shifted away. 'Roger owns fifteen sows, two boars and a handful of scraggy chickens. Are you offering anything better?'

'Anything better than Tony?'

'I'm not into comparisons.'

'Yet you counted sows as an alternative proposal. Surely that means you're available?'

'I'm always available,' she said, and he heard irony in the tone. 'How about you? I'm assuming your offer of marriage was something you make to every doctor who climbs down a hole to save your life, but seriously... Are you sure you don't have anyone who'll be out of their mind with worry right now?'

'I'm positive,' he said brusquely. 'I don't have any close family and I'm supposed to be on vacation. I'm due to fly to Switzerland tomorrow night with a group of fellow medics. That includes Kayla, a colleague. She'll worry if I don't turn up to the airport without letting her know, but a phone call tomorrow will fix that. Our relationship's only casual. She won't miss me until then, and she'll have a good time without me.'

'I suppose that's a good thing,' she said doubtfully. 'You want to sleep?'

'I guess. You must need to, too.'

'I do, and apart from checking you I might even get a whole night without interruptions.' She hauled her mattress to lie beside his and spread out blankets. 'Maybe I should try this more often—jumping down a hole to get a good night's sleep.'

'Is it so hard to get?'

'Yes, it is,' she said, tucking her blankets around her with care. 'You try being the only full-time doctor for a group of islands where every tourist seems intent on putting themselves in harm's way.'

'Like me.'

'You said it.' She checked out his blankets, twitched another over him and nodded. 'There. Tucked in and settled. Pain level?'

'About two.'

'That'll have to do.'

'It'll do me. Thank you, Elsa.'

'All my pleasure,' she told him. 'Wake me if it gets above three. There are no medals for being a martyr.'

'Are there any medals for being a lone doctor and a heroine to boot?'

'I'm not completely alone,' she said indignantly. 'There's Grandpa. He'd be full-time if I let him but there's the little matter of renal problems and a dicky heart.'

'Renal problems?'

'Diabetes. Not so bad.' Mostly.

'And a dicky heart?'

'That's the diagnosis,' she said lightly. 'I told you I'm a family doctor. Nothing fancy.'

'Surely he's been off the island to find out exactly what's wrong?'

'He has,' she said and lay down and tugged the blankets up to her chin. 'But he hates being off the island. That's the biggest reason I'm here, but I'm not about to discuss Grandpa's health in detail with another patient.'

'I'm a cardiologist.'

'Says you. For now you're my patient. You're suffering a broken leg and sore shoulder, plus a severe case of being stuck down a cave. I suggest you try and sleep, Dr Pierce, before that morphine wears off. Like I intend to.'

'You're going to sleep before my morphine wears off?'

'Exactly. I'm not stupid. If I wait any longer you'll start whinging and I need my beauty sleep.'

He dozed and then he woke and sleep wouldn't return.

He lay and thought of the complications one broken leg

entailed. He thought about his friends heading to St Moritz. He thought of Kayla. He'd told Elsa she'd go to St Moritz without him and of course she would. Their relationship was purely fun and casual. There was no need for her to stay and hold his hand.

This Christmas skiing vacation was an institution between a group of colleagues, something he'd done for six years now. Kayla was simply one of the group, and they'd started dating only recently. Their enjoyment of St Moritz had little to do with each other. They both enjoyed the hard physical challenge, the beauty of the slopes, the crowded bars, the excellent restaurants.

The avoidance of Christmas.

Though it wasn't totally avoided. The resort their small group stayed in took elegance to a whole new level, with sumptuous furnishings, exotic food, magnificent decorations and designer gifts for each guest. They'd arrive on Christmas Eve and the festivities would be in full swing. The setting was picture-perfect, a magical white Christmas full of people enjoying themselves.

As opposed to the Christmases he'd spent during his childhood, with his parents trying unsuccessfully to disguise mutual grievances. Stilted cheer in their harbourfront mansion. Gifts—something aspirational and educational and expensive from his father, something ecologically sound and expensive from his mother.

A part of him had almost been relieved the Christmas his mother had finally left. At ten he'd been old enough to realise that at least it had eased the sham of pretending not to hear the bitter fighting. Afterwards he could take his certificate from his mother saying he'd just donated a school to a village in Africa—surely what every kid wanted for Christmas—and thank her as if he meant it. He could accept his mind-bending educational challenge from his father and not have to figure how to negotiate the minefield of which gift he liked best.

Christmas when his parents were together had been a formal, rigid nightmare. Christmas as a teen when they'd been apart had been something he could almost get through.

Christmas in St Moritz?

Fun. Friendly. Busy.

Impersonal. Which was the way he liked his life.

The group congregating at the airport tomorrow would miss him, but only briefly. He was honest enough to suspect the short-term relationship he'd had with Kayla was pretty much already over. Kayla might even be secretly pleased she'd have a spare seat beside her on the long plane flight.

But then his tired mind drifted sideways. To the woman beside him.

Would a woman like this stay because her man had broken his leg?

She didn't have to tell him she was here on this island because of her commitment to the islanders and her grandfather—it was implied in almost every word she spoke. As for not talking about what was wrong with her grandfather... Patient confidentiality? Not so much. He was another doctor, a specialist, and the chance to talk to another professional about a worrying case would be grabbed by almost every colleague he knew.

Not by Elsa though. In that quick rejoinder about patient confidentiality he'd heard pain. Something grim in the background. Something she didn't need advice about.

Something she already knew? That staying here was putting her grandfather's life at risk?

She'd saved his life. Maybe he could help her in return. He needed to figure this out.

'You need more pain relief?' It was a sleepy murmur from beside him. She'd placed their air mattresses so close they were touching. He knew the reason for that too. He'd had a fall. She had no guarantee that it wasn't only his leg and shoulder that were damaged. If he was in hospital he'd be under constant observation for at least twenty-four hours.

'You know, this is the second night I've been stuck down here,' he told her. 'If I was going to die of internal bleeding I probably would have done it before this. There's no need for you to stay awake.'

'Which is why I'm sleeping.'

'You're awake.'

'So I'm dozing. You're a doctor. You know we can exist on dozes. So how's your pain?'

'Still okay.'

'Bladder?'

Hell, he was a surgeon at the top of his field. The physical dependencies this situation called for were humiliating.

'I'm fine,' he told her dourly and he heard her smile.

'Then drink more. Don't you dare stop drinking because you have too much pride to let me help you. You're a patient, remember.'

'I don't have to like it.'

'What's that quote about being given the serenity to accept things you can't change? I can't remember it exactly, but it's something like "*Grant me the serenity to accept the things I cannot change, courage to change the things I can and wisdom to know the difference.*" My grandpa has it on his wall and it's wise. So if you need the bottle, accept it with serenity.'

'Right,' he said wryly. 'But I don't need it.'

'And I'll accept that you're pig stubborn and we'll leave it at that,' she told him.

They lay in silence for a few moments. He thought she might have dozed off again but then her voice sounded cautiously into the dark.

'Tell me about St Moritz.'

'You've never been?'

'Hey, I've been to Sydney,' she said cheerfully. 'Is there a world past that?'

'Only Sydney?'

'No money to go further,' she told him, still upbeat. 'It took all Grandpa's resources to help me through med school. During vacations I came home and worked for my keep in the hospital. Actually,' she admitted, 'I've worked in the hospital since I was seven. One of my earliest memories is helping shell what seemed like a mountain of peas, but my official job was cheering patients up. Me and Loopy the Basset, then me and Peanut the Fox Terrier and finally me and Sherlock the Beagle—had to go in and find stuff to talk about. It was the best training for family medicine ever.'

'So what about your mum and dad?'

'Mum was your original hippie,' she said, almost curtly. 'My grandmother died when Mum was thirteen and Mum took it hard. She blamed Grandpa—"You're a doctor, why couldn't you save her?" Then she took up with the surf crowd who come here every summer. She ran away when she was seventeen, following her heart, only the guy her heart had chosen turned out to be a scumbag. Coming back here was never an option for her, though, and she died of an overdose when I was seven. Who knows where my Dad is now?—I certainly don't. After Mum died, Grandpa brought me to the island and, apart from the years in Sydney at med school, I've been here ever since. So I say again...tell me about St Moritz.'

He was silent for a moment, letting himself sink into the story behind the story. He was imagining a neglected child with a drug-addicted mother, a despairing grandfather, grief.

Hell, and he'd thought his childhood was hard.

'St Moritz,' she said again, and he gave himself a mental shake and tried to think of what she'd like to know.

'You've seen all those soppy Christmas cards with snow scenes and twinkling lights and carollers and reindeer...'

'Don't tell me there are reindeer!'

'I believe there are. Not on the ski slopes though, and that's where I mostly spend my time.'

'It's really white? Not just slush?'

'It can get slushy, but at this time of the year, especially when the snow's just fallen, it's beautiful.'

'I'd so love to see it. They say every snowflake is different. To stand in the snow...to taste snow on my tongue...'

'Would you let me give you a trip there—as payment for saving my life?'

It was the wrong thing to say. He knew it as soon as the words came out of his mouth. She was lying beside him, her arm just touching his. He wasn't close enough to really feel it, but he could sense the sudden rigidity in her. The withdrawal.

'Hey, you're just a patient and I don't need gifts from patients,' she told him, and her words were cool and stiff. 'Tourists have accidents on the island all the time, and it's my job to patch them up. You'll get a bill for services rendered.'

'What, standard consultation with medical procedure attached?'

'More than that,' she said with asperity. 'House call out of hours. Extended consultation. Minor surgery. You'll be slugged heaps.'

'Do you charge more than the government rebate?' he asked, knowing already what her answer would be.

'Even if I did it wouldn't equal a holiday in St Moritz,' she told him. 'Go to sleep.'

'I don't think I can.'

'Try,' she told him curtly and rolled over to face away from him.

And that was that.

Insensitive toe-rag.

A holiday in St Moritz! Grateful patients often gave her chocolates or wine, or nice handwritten cards. She never expected them, but when they came she appreciated them and shared them around with the receptionists and nursing staff. It seemed a thank you to all of them.

A holiday in St Moritz. As if.

But she lay in the dark, and for a little while she let herself imagine what it could be like. A plane ride to Sydney and then an overseas flight to Switzerland. A long flight. She wouldn't be the least surprised—given the insouciance of this guy's offer—if it'd be in business class, too. Then maybe a limo drive to the ski slopes.

Her receptionist had a passion for glossy lifestyle magazines, and they ended up in her waiting room. Occasionally, in the tiny spaces between patients, she let herself browse and dream.

There'd be a chalet—she'd seen the pictures. Luxurious resort suites. Views to die for. Maybe a sauna and a spa. Ski lessons with some gorgeous young Swiss, herself skimming down the ski slopes, then afterwards roaring fires, food and drink at expensive restaurants, laughter among friends…

And that was where the picture cut out. Friends.

She was so damned lonely.

Oh, for heaven's sake, what was she doing thinking she was lonely? She could count on almost every islander as her friend.

How many of them called her Elsa, though? From the time she'd returned to the island she'd been the doctor's kid. The islanders had taken her into their hearts, loved her, cared for her so her grandpa could keep up with his medicine. But mostly Grandpa had cared for her himself. She'd been his shadow and the locals had called her Little Doc. 'Here comes Doc and Little Doc,' they'd say, and if things got tricky then whoever was closest would spirit Little Doc away until she could resume her role as his helper.

So she'd been Little Doc until she'd come back from university, and then she'd been simply, proudly Doc. For

Grandpa had never been into money-making, and so the islanders had chipped in to help fund her studies, too.

Grandpa called her Matey. She was Grandpa's mate. Everyone else called her Doc.

Except recently Tony. Tony called her Elsa.

Dating Tony had been a disaster. She should never have agreed to that first date. He'd almost instantly become possessive, and his use of her first name was a claim all by itself.

He'd caught her at a weak moment.

Because she was lonely!

The guy beside her stirred, and she thought she should probably say something to cheer him up. She couldn't think of a single thing.

Instead she lay in the dark and for some unfathomable reason her future lay on her like a thick, heavy blanket.

St Moritz.

Why had one crazy offer disturbed her so much?

Or the way this guy had smiled at her?

He was just another patient. A tourist. He'd be out of here as soon as the smoke cleared enough for flights to resume.

More to distract herself than anything else, she let herself think of the situation on the mainland. What had seemed a series of small fires two days ago had merged into a much bigger front. If she'd been working on the mainland she'd be so busy—part of a team coping with burns, smoke inhalation, shock. Part of a team...

Oh, for heaven's sake, she was thinking longingly of a bushfire situation?

'What's the latest on the fires on the mainland?' Marc's deep growl cut through her thoughts, made her blink. Were his thoughts following hers?

He'd be worried about getting out of here, she thought. Nothing more.

'Latest report says there's light rain,' she told him

briefly. 'I guess that's why the smoke's so intense. Slow moisture on burning bushland. No lives lost, though.' She thought about it for a moment. 'If it was worse... Do cardiologists cope with fire trauma?'

'Everyone copes when it's major,' he said simply. 'But if it's settling now I won't be missed. Plus I'm now officially on vacation.'

'Lucky you.'

'You think I'd prefer to be on vacation rather than helping out?'

'Everyone needs a break sometimes,' she said flatly. 'Lucky you if you can get one. Go to sleep, Marc, or at least let me. I'm not on vacation and I need sleep even if you don't.'

CHAPTER FIVE

THE EVACUATION BEGAN the next morning and it nearly killed him that he had to play the victim. The idiot who'd got into such trouble.

He *was* the victim. He *was* the idiot.

So he lay strapped onto his stretcher while they worked around him.

The inflatable stretcher was amazing. The night before Elsa had simply—or not so simply—manoeuvred it so it was lying on top of the air mattress. At dawn, as the team above prepared the gear to lift him, she used its pump to inflate the sides. The air-filled bumpers would protect him as it was hauled to the surface.

It had head, neck and spine support. It had full body, pressure-point-free immobilisation. It had cross fix restraints and ten carry handles.

'It's also X-ray-transparent and it'll carry anyone up to two hundred and fifty kilograms,' Elsa told him proudly, as she adjusted the straps that held him fixed. 'Though if you'd weighed that much we might have had to raise a small army to haul you up.'

He didn't smile. He was now totally immobilised and he'd never felt so helpless.

Above ground the team was fixing cabling from one side of the unsafe ground to the other. What that meant was that team members could safely fix anchors above the hole, then abseil down if needed, or have someone stay safely above ground to guide him up.

Elsa was explaining things as she worked. She was upping his drug dose as well.

'It's a great stretcher and we're a good team,' she told him. 'But we can't stop it being bumpy while we carry you down the mountain. I'm sorry, Marc, but there'll need to be a bit of biting the bullet on your part.'

'You guys are saving me. I won't be whinging.'

That brought a wry smile.

'What, you don't believe me?'

'We'll see,' she said enigmatically. 'We hauled a tourist up a cliff face a few weeks back. He'd been trying to take a selfie, climbed the safety rail to get a better angle and leaned out a little too far over a fifty-foot drop to the sea below. He was super lucky to be caught on a ledge fifteen feet down, with only a fractured arm and bruises. It took our guys hours to pull him up, but do you think he was grateful? The first thing he did was abuse us because we hadn't brought up his camera. He shouted at us practically the whole time before we managed to get him airlifted out of here. The fact that his camera had fallen the whole way down and the team would have been risking their own lives to get it simply didn't register.'

'People do stupid things,' he managed, chagrined that he was in the same category.

'They do, and you did, but at least you've been grateful,' she told him, smiling down at him. 'Speaking of which, I've been thinking of that St Moritz offer. I should say no and leave it at that, but if you're serious...'

'I am.'

'Then could we swap St Moritz for a reclining lift chair for our nursing home patients?' she asked tentatively. 'Or maybe even two if you're feeling super generous. We have a couple of oldies who can't get out of chairs without help, and it makes them feel so dependent.'

'I know how that feels,' he said grimly, feeling the straps holding him immobile.

'Then it's a great time to ask,' she said, and grinned again. 'Damn, I didn't bring a pen and paper or I'd have you sign a promissory note—before we bring you to the surface and you get all St Moritzy again.'

'I won't get... St Moritzy. I've said goodbye to that fantasy.'

'You'll be back there next year,' she told him. 'While we enjoy two great lift chairs.'

'You won't enjoy two lift chairs.'

'You want to bet? Seeing Marigold Peterson get up from her chair and walk out to the veranda without having to wait for a nurse to help her... You take your St Moritz, Dr Pierce. I'll take Marigold's pleasure any day.'

He looked at her curiously, this competent, brisk young woman. With the dawn had come natural light, filtering down and angled so he could see her. The night before she'd been a shadow behind the lantern, or maybe he'd been too hazy, drug affected to see her clearly. Now he had a proper look.

She looked competent. Determined. Her jeans and windcheater were filthy, her hair dust-caked, but he could see more than just a general impression. She was only little, a package of efficiency about five feet two or three. Slight. Wiry? He'd have to say that—there was no trace of an idle life or an indulged lifestyle about her. Her hair seemed almost flame-red beneath the dust. It looked as if it could be amazing but right now her curls were tied back in a practical, businesslike ponytail.

Watching her as she adjusted his straps, he had a sudden irrational urge to reach out and release the ponytail. He wanted to see what those curls looked like floating free.

Yeah, like that was a good idea. Patient hitting on doctor? She was leaving the lower part of his good arm free—so he could scratch his nose if he wanted—but looking at that determined chin, feeling the brisk competence she was exuding, he thought she'd have his arms tied down in an instant if he tried it on.

He had the very strong impression that Dr Elsa McCrae was not a woman to mess with.

And she had principles. She'd just knocked back what to her, he suspected, might be the holiday of a lifetime, in order to barter for two chairs for her oldies. He'd seen the flash of amazement in her eyes as he'd made his offer. He'd also seen regret slam home. Common sense had taken over. With this woman, it probably always would.

'You like family medicine?' he asked curiously, watching her face as she worked.

'I like making people feel better.'

'Then you've made me feel better,' he said—and to his astonishment he saw a hint of a blush.

But she brushed it away, got efficient again fast. 'Then I've done my job,' she said lightly. 'Now...you want to say goodbye to your nice cosy bedroom before we hoist you up?'

'I thought I was going to die in this nice cosy bedroom. I hate this nice cosy bedroom.'

'Then let's get you out of here,' she said and glanced up. 'Righto, people, haul him up.'

She'd say this for him, the guy was stoic.

The trip down the mountain was tough on the carriers, but it'd be a whole lot tougher for the man on the stretcher. The path was rough, criss-crossed by tree roots. They were forced to detour round boulders the path makers had been unable to shift. With the dawn, five more of the islanders had come up to help, so there were two shifts of four to carry him down, but Marc had to endure the journey as best he could.

Elsa followed behind. She wasn't permitted to be a stretcher bearer.

'You slip and who do you think'll patch you up?' Macka had growled.

'Grandpa?'

'Yeah, and then he'd have this fella in one bed and you in another, and all the Christmas tourist influx to cope with on his own. You were a damned fool to go down that hole by yourself, Doc. We won't have you taking any more risks now.'

So she walked behind, watching her step, chatting to the guys on the alternate bearer shift, watching the man on the stretcher.

He was hurting—she could see that, but there was little she could do about it. She had his leg and arm firmly fixed but there was no way to stop the stretcher being jolted.

He'd said he wouldn't complain, and he didn't, but she could see the tension on his face.

And the mortification.

He was a cardiologist, a city surgeon. These guys were top of the tree in the medical profession. He'd offered her a holiday in St Moritz without blinking, and she'd heard in his voice that he was serious. He'd be earning big money. Huge.

He looked—what? Mid-thirties? He was lean, dark-haired, tanned beneath the dust. Even now, strapped to the stretcher and in pain, she could see an air of authority about him.

He was a guy who was used to being in charge of his world.

He wasn't in charge now. He was totally at the mercy of the people carrying his stretcher. Macka, a burly sixty-something policeman. Denise, the island mechanic, also in her sixties. Little, round, always grease-stained, she was the best square dancer on the island, tough as old boots. Graham, the local accountant, fiftyish, who wore prim three-piece suits for five days a week but as soon as he was out of the office he donned tartan lumberjack gear. Mike, a still pimply kid who'd just finished his schooling and would be off to university in the autumn, but who spent all his spare time climbing and abseiling.

The alternate shift consisted of just as motley a collection of characters, but every one of them was competent. They knew this island. They knew what they were doing.

Marc was forced to lie on his stretcher and trust them.

Elsa had once asked if she could have a go at being carried on the stretcher, just to see what it felt like. They'd strapped her down and taken her over a rough path and she'd felt almost claustrophobic, totally at the mercy of a team who could drop her at any minute. They wouldn't. She knew them and trusted them inherently, but Marc would have no such trust.

She watched his face and saw the strain and knew instinctively that this guy's life was all about control.

'Pain level?' she asked, coming alongside the stretcher. 'You want a top-up?'

'I'm fuzzy as it is,' he told her. 'I want my wits about me.'

'So if we drop you, you might be able to save yourself? It won't happen,' she told him. 'This team has never dropped a punter yet.'

He grunted and went back to staring straight upward. She fell back again and continued to watch him closely.

His control looked as if it was stretched to the limit. He didn't complain though. Not a whinge.

'He's a doctor, you say,' Macka said to her at the next change of shift.

'Yep.'

'You reckon we could organise a plane strike or something so we can set his leg and put him behind your grandpa's clinic desk for a week or six? Give your grandpa—and you—a bit of a break?'

'As if,' she said and then looked curiously up at Macka. 'Why do you say that?'

'It's only...well, I dropped in to pick up supplies before we came up to find you,' he told her. 'And I thought old Doc was looking a bit grey around the edges.'

'He's probably just worried about me.'

'Aye, that'd be it,' Macka said, but he sounded doubtful and Elsa winced and thought, *No, please, Grandpa, don't get sick.*

He had renal problems. He had heart problems.

He'd promised her he'd live for ever, and as a kid she'd depended on that promise. Now...not so much and the thought made her feel ill.

Her attention distracted, she stumbled on a tree root and Macka caught her arm and steadied her.

'Thanks,' she muttered to Macka, and then to herself she said, *Cut it out, focus on now.*

Finally they were down. Macka's police-van-cum-ambulance was parked near the start of the walking track. Elsa left them loading their patient on board and took her own car—and Sherlock—back to the hospital. Grandpa came out to greet her, and she had the opportunity to check him out as he bent to pat the exuberant Sherlock.

He did look tired, she conceded. Grey? Maybe. Robert McCrae had been the island's doctor for fifty years and he hated slowing down, but she was going to have to insist.

Though where did that leave her? When Robert had started here, the population of the island had been three hundred with practically no outsiders. Now it was a tourist mecca, its population of seven hundred exploding over the mainland holiday breaks. The outer islands had tourists flooding them too, and she and Robert were still the only doctors.

It wouldn't matter so much if tourists didn't insist on doing such risky things. Like Marcus Pierce, trekking up an unknown mountain trail by himself and letting no one know where he was going. If Sherlock hadn't found him...

She closed her eyes, unable to bear thinking of the consequences.

But he'd be thinking of the consequences, she thought. He'd have spent over twenty-four hours thinking the absolute worst. He'd probably need trauma counselling if he wasn't to cop PTSD. She needed a trauma counsellor on staff.

The trauma counsellor would have to be her.

But for now she was late for morning clinic and Grandpa looked as if he needed a good lie-down—he'd also have spent a wakeful night worrying about her. And then there was Christmas! Without turkeys? Even as she got out of the car she saw the hospital cook flapping in the background, waiting to talk to her. Waiting for Elsa to solve the turkey problem.

First things first. A shower. She felt disgusting and she guessed she smelled disgusting too. She had to move on, and she needed help. 'Grandpa, you know the situation?' she asked him. 'This guy needs fluids, intravenous antibiotics—he has a couple of decent lacerations—a bed bath to get most of the grime off before we can touch him. What's the situation with evacuation to the mainland?'

'Not possible,' Robert told her. 'There's still smoke haze drifting our way. Unless it's life or death we're on our own.'

'Then we ultrasound his shoulder and X-ray his leg and hope it's fixable here.' She grimaced. 'You know he's a doctor?'

'The worst kind of patient.'

'You'd know,' she said and managed a smile. 'Like me giving you orders to get eight hours' sleep no matter what? I'm betting you didn't sleep much last night.'

'I can sleep when I'm dead,' Robert said simply. 'Not when there's work to do. Go on and get yourself clean, girl, and worry about them who need it.'

* * *

The woman who appeared at his bedside an hour later stunned him.

In the gloom of the cave, layered in dust, wearing hiking gear, he'd thought she was good-looking.

Now though...she pushed back the curtain of the examination cubicle and he had to blink.

She was dressed in sky-blue trousers and a soft white shirt, both almost concealed by a white coat. Her shoes were sensible flats, but they were bright pink and she'd tied her hair back in a matching pink ribbon. The pink should clash with her hair, but it certainly didn't. She wore little if any make-up, but she didn't need it. She didn't need anything. With her flaming curls, her sparkling green eyes, the flash of colour in her clothing...she was enough to make a man feel better all on her own.

And he'd been feeling better anyway, soaking in the luxury of a decent mattress, pillows, warmth, no more bumping stretcher and enough painkiller to make him dozy.

'I think I've died and gone to heaven,' he managed. She smiled—and that made things even more confusing. It was a killer of a smile. A smile that made a man...

Get a grip. He needed to. It must be the drugs that were making him feel...woozy?

'Feeling better, then?' she asked.

'You'd better believe it. Did you ask for only two lift chairs? Try asking for a hundred. Half my kingdom if you like.'

'I'll believe it when I see it,' she said with a smile that robbed her words of offence. 'You have no idea of how many rescued tourists who've left the island promising largesse, never to be heard of again.'

'I keep my promises,' he told her, and her smile slipped. She looked at him for a long moment and then gave a determined little nod.

'I believe you will,' she said. 'Thank you. But mind, we

won't hold you to it. Do nothing until you're well, and then think about it. I had no business to ask.'

'As I had no business to expect you to save my life.'

'It's what we do,' she told him. 'Our whole team, including Sherlock. Do you need to let your people know what's happening?'

'One of the nurses lent me a phone.'

'And you got through? Great. I guess no one will be able to rush to your side before the mainland smoke clears, but I hope you stopped them being anxious. Tell them they can ring me if they want reassurance.'

He thought of Kayla's reaction to his call. Admittedly, he hadn't told her about being trapped—he'd just said he'd fallen while scattering his mother's ashes—but even so she'd been less than sympathetic. She'd asked incisive questions about his injuries but once she was reassured about their severity she'd moved on.

She'd go to St Moritz anyway, she'd decided. She'd let their friends know their party would be one person short, but she was busy. She had to pack. There'd been brief words of commiseration before she disconnected, and that was that.

'No one wants reassurance,' he said brusquely, and Elsa gave him a searching look and then flicked the overhead screen to blank, so it showed only white light.

'Okay, then. You want to see your X-rays? They're reassuring at least.'

'They're only reassuring if they show no break at all.'

'You still dreaming of St Moritz? Move on,' she told him and put up the X-ray.

It showed a clean break of both tibia and fibula. Slight dislocation but no splintering. It could have been much, much worse.

'I can set this,' she told him. 'Grandpa and I concur. We'd rather send you to the mainland to a decent orthopod, but you know the restrictions on flights at the moment. I did

specific training for remote medicine, including orthopaedics, before I came here, and so did Grandpa. We've both
set breaks like this, and so far we haven't managed to put
a single foot on backwards. Grandpa's competent with an-
aesthetics and I'll do the setting. The alternative is to leave
it as it is until evacuation, but even with strong splinting we
both know movement's possible. Which means circulation
could be blocked. So I'm asking you to trust us.'

'I trust you.'

She gave another of her brisk nods, a gesture he was
starting to know. And like.

'The good news is that your ultrasound shows little damage to your shoulder. No tears. It'll be sore for a while and
you'll have to protect it, but you seem to have done no
long-term damage.'

'Your grandfather told me that.'

'Right, then,' she said. 'You've had nothing to eat since
your muesli bars before we started the trek. We'll wait another couple of hours to make sure they're well down, and
then we'll set your leg. Meanwhile, I have a clinic queue
a mile long so you won't see me until Theatre. The nurses
will look after you.'

'They already have.' He looked into her face and behind
the smile, behind the briskness, he saw strain. She would
have slept badly last night, if at all. He knew enough of this
woman to accept that her first responsibility would have
been to check on him, probably hourly, so she wouldn't
have let herself fall into a deep sleep.

'You've had quite a night yourself. Your grandpa can't
run clinic while you have a rest?'

'I wish,' she said wryly. She was up-to-date with the
clinic news now. 'Grandpa was up during the night himself,
with a fisherman who decided at midnight that his finger
was infected. He hurt it last week. It was only when his
wife thought sweating in bed was a problem that they de-

cided to call for help. So it's Grandpa who needs the rest, not that he'll take it.'

'I wish I could help.'

'You can, by being sensible and compliant and not throwing out a single complication,' she told him. 'Focus, Dr Pierce. I want an exemplary patient.'

'I'll do my best.'

'And I'll do mine,' she told him. 'Now, you rest for all of us. See you in Theatre.'

And she was gone, her white coat a blur as she closed the door behind her.

He was left with the impression of capability and practicality. And more. An indefinable something.

He'd made a lot more work for this woman. She should be angry with him. She was just resigned, he thought. And capable and practical.

And that indefinable…something.

CHAPTER SIX

IN THE END Marc's surgery was straightforward. Her grandfather gave the general anaesthetic—this was the way they normally worked, and it worked well now. The leg was relatively easy to stabilise. She cleaned and debrided lacerations, put in stitches to the deepest and put a back slab on his leg. It'd eventually be a full cast, but not until the stitches were out and the swelling had gone down.

Despite the reassurance of the ultrasound, she still wanted to test shoulder rotation without the pain caused by the bruising. She found nothing to disturb her.

He'd got off lightly, Elsa thought as she left him in the care of the theatre staff.

Next.

Somehow she convinced Robert to take a nap—which was a worry all on its own. Yes, he'd had to work during the night but both of them were accustomed to doing that. Her grandfather hated conceding weakness, and his agreement to have an afternoon sleep surprised her. Now, not only did she have a queue a mile long at her clinic, she had the niggling fear that he wasn't telling all.

'Maybe I'm coming down with a cold,' he muttered when she pressed him. 'Or maybe it's just worrying about you, girl. Tell you what, you stop worrying about me and I'll stop worrying about you. Which means quitting with the diving down unknown caves.'

She grinned and asked no more questions, but as she sat in clinic and saw patient after patient, her sense of unease deepened.

And clinic was made worse by the fact that every patient wanted to discuss her night's adventures.

'They say he's a doctor. Louise Pierce's boy.' Marc's mother had been a member of the local climbing group, sometimes spending so much time here the islanders considered her almost one of them. 'Why didn't he take one of us up to the peak with him? Damned idiot, he could have killed you too.'

'No fear of that,' she told them. 'I had Sherlock and he has a nose for holes. He does the hunting. I stick to paths.'

'Except when you're rescuing tourists. What does he think he's doing, putting *our* doc at risk?'

And there was the nub, Elsa thought wearily as the day wore on. She was *their* doctor. She knew the islanders were fond of her, but they also depended on her.

She fielded a call from Tony, who put it more than bluntly. 'You had no right to put yourself at risk, Elsa. Don't you know what's at stake?'

'The whole island needs me. Yes, I know.'

'I need you.'

'No more than any other islander,' she said, trying to keep irritation out of her voice. One unwise date and he practically had her wedded, bedded and mother to half a dozen little Tonys. 'Tony, leave it. You know I had no choice.'

'If he's fool enough to have fallen…'

'I should have left him there, cold and hurting? I don't think so. Sorry, Tony, I need to run.'

'I want to see you. How about dinner?'

'No chance,' she said and cut him short. It was getting to the stage where hints weren't enough. 'Tony, stop it with the idea that we're a couple. We're not.'

And she did need to run. It was already Thursday.

Christmas Day was Sunday and how on earth was she going to get everything done by then? Dinner was a sandwich grabbed from the kitchen fridge, eaten while she typed up patient notes for the day with her spare hand—who knew that a five-fingered typist could be so efficient? Finally she headed over to the wards to check all was well before she could—hopefully—get some sleep.

She found Marc propped up on pillows, his leg in traction, scowling at a laptop. Actually...not a laptop. She recognised it as a generic tablet usually kept in the kids' ward.

'What, is Dorothy Dinosaur not co-operating?' she asked, smiling at the sight of one gorgeous guy, sparsely dressed in a white hospital gown, holding a pink, sparkly, dinosaur-decorated tablet.

He didn't smile back.

'One of your nurses kindly unlocked it from kid-safe mode,' he muttered, still glowering. 'So I managed to download my files from the ether and I'm trying to get some work done. But every time I try to save anything, it defaults back to Dorothy and locks me down. And the nurse won't give me the password. She comes in when she has time and unlocks it again like she's doing me a huge favour.'

She grinned at that. 'Maggie's old school,' she told him. 'She likes discipline in her hospital, and to her everyone under the age of forty is a kid.' She tugged up a chair, sat and took the tablet from him and typed in the password. 'There you go.'

'You're not going to give me the password either?'

'I'm with Maggie. We have two small boys in the kids' ward right now who'd barter their mother for the password. Who's to say you won't sell it on? Plus Maggie's knitting patterns are on this tablet.' She relented. 'You know you should be sleeping. Your body will demand sleep, even if your mind hasn't caught up yet. But I can lend you my spare laptop if you want. The med stuff is locked but I'll trust you not to try and break in.'

'Gee, thanks.'

'You're welcome.' She looked curiously at him. 'So you really came all this way without so much as a change of socks?'

'It was supposed to be a back and forth in a day trip,' he said, sighing and setting the tablet aside. 'Before she died, Mum told me it'd take three hours max to climb to the peak. The plane arrived at nine and was leaving at six, so getting here and back in a day seemed easy. I had a research paper to assess on the flight—a printout that's still sitting in a locker at the airport—so I didn't need my laptop. I can do urgent stuff on my phone, but that's now smashed.'

'So you're screenless.' She shook her head. 'That's truly horrible. But moving on…apart from your lack of screen, tell me what hurts?'

'Just about everything,' he admitted. 'But mostly my pride.' He pushed himself further up in the bed, grimacing with pain. He looked ruffled, she thought, and also… strangely defenceless? He was a big man, tall, lean, muscular. The dirt he'd been covered with was gone and he'd shaved, but his dark, wavy hair was ruffled as if he'd been raking it in frustration. Despite his immobilised leg, his arm in a sling and his loose hospital gown, his strongly boned face and what she could see of his ripped body combined to give the impression of barely contained strength. He looked powerful but confined, edgy to be gone.

His pride was hurting? Yeah, she could see it. For such a man to be in this position…

'I can't do much about your pride,' she told him, 'but I can do something about the aches and pain.'

'I'll make do with paracetamol.'

She grinned and motioned back to the tablet, where Dorothy and her dinosaurs were circling the perimeter of Marc's word document. 'I guess if you want to do battle with Dorothy you need to keep your wits about you, and the stronger painkillers might indeed make you feel a bit fuzzy,' she admitted. 'But there's no prizes for heroics, Dr Pierce. Your leg's a mass of bruises and lacerations, to say nothing of the break. Your shoulder must be giving you heaps. Plus your back… You can't see, but it's spectacularly black and blue.' Her voice grew serious. 'You were incredibly lucky not to break your spine.'

'I was incredibly lucky in more ways than one,' he said, and almost involuntarily he reached out with his good arm and took her hand in his. And held it tightly, as if reassuring himself she was real. 'I was lucky because of one Dr Elsa McCrae,' he said softly. 'Elsa, I'll never forget it.'

She stilled, looked down at their linked hands. It had been a casual gesture, an impulse, but their hands stayed locked.

She'd spent a long, scary night with this man. He must have been terrified when she'd found him, but he hadn't let on. He'd been matter-of-fact, uncomplaining, holding it together.

He was grateful. It was the only reason he was holding her hand.

Or maybe it was more than that. Maybe the terrors were still with him. Maybe he needed the contact.

She told herself that as she let her hand stay where it was. She'd had a hard night too. The work was piling up around her, but for just a moment she let herself be held. She felt the strength and comfort of his grip. She even let herself believe she wasn't alone.

But she was alone, and there was work a mile high to be waded through. She needed to get on.

She should tug her hand away.

But still she didn't. For his sake, she told herself. Not for hers.

'It'll be a darn sight easier to forget gratitude—forget anything else that's bothering you—if you let me give you some decent painkillers,' she managed, and was annoyed to find that her voice was unsteady. 'Have some now and I'll write you up more for the night. Just ask Maggie, she's on all night.'

'Maggie's scary,' he said, and she grinned.

'Better men than you are scared of Maggie. Wielding a bedpan, she's a force to be reckoned with, but she's a fine nurse.' Finally, reluctantly, she tugged back her hand and rose. Was it her imagination or had there been reluctance on his part to let her go? It was understandable, she told herself. He'd need human contact after feeling such fear.

And her reaction?

This was ridiculous. Moving on…

'Is…is there anything else you need?'

'A set of clean clothes?' he ventured, back to being practical. 'You cut off my pants. At least I didn't lose my wallet so I hope I can purchase something to wear.'

'I'd like to keep you in for a couple of days,' she warned him. 'I'm still worried about clots.'

'That's two of us,' he said grimly. 'I know the risks. So clothes can wait but I'd kill for decent pyjamas. Even more for a phone.'

'I can help there as well. Didn't you already use our ward phone? It has overseas capability—we cope with a lot of tourists and you'd be astonished at how many of them lose their phones. I'll tell Maggie to drop it in again.'

'I'd like my own,' he growled. Without his phone he felt stranded. Or even more stranded than he already was. 'Is there anyone on the island who could organise me one?'

'Jason,' she told him. 'He's a cray fisherman but he does a nice little sideline in technology. His boat's due in tonight so I'll ask him to come and see you tomorrow. Anything's possible if you're prepared to pay. In the meantime, Maggie will bring you my laptop. We'll even unlock the passwords for you.'

'Thank you,' he said stiffly, and she thought this was a

guy who hated being out of control. Not having his phone, not having the internet would be killing him. But his next question surprised her. 'What about you? Are you going to bed now?'

'Soon,' she lied.

'Soon, as in after you've seen what…another ten patients?'

'Only one,' she admitted and then decided maybe she needed to talk to this guy as a colleague. For some reason he had her unsettled and she couldn't figure it out. 'Mathew Hobson rang fifteen minutes ago and thinks he might have been bitten by a redback spider,' she told him. 'He's on his way in. He'll be fine, though. He met one once and never got over it—now every time he feels a prick from an ant or mosquito he thinks the worst.' She glanced at her watch. 'He should be arriving any minute.'

'And then you'll get to bed?'

'In time. I have the thirty-odd Christmas gifts to wrap over the next couple of days, and I'm already way behind.'

'Thirty!'

She smiled and shrugged. She should leave—she didn't have time to stay and gossip with patients—but those dark eyes of his were watching her with a hint of warmth, of humour, of understanding. He *was* a colleague, she thought. A real medical colleague who understood the pressure she was under.

Like a friend.

Whatever, the need to tell him was suddenly overwhelming.

'I do a thing,' she told him. 'On Christmas Day.'

'A thing?'

'Well, it's not all me,' she told him. 'But the gifts are me. I'm not sure what you know about this island.'

'Not much.'

'Yeah, well, it's been a quiet little backwater for years. We don't have decent educational facilities here—the kids have to go away for school if they want to do more than fish or farm. We now have a big tourist network, but local kids don't see that as an opportunity. Most of our local kids leave when they're old enough. Some come back but most don't. That means we're left with an ageing population and at Christmas a lot of lonely oldies.'

'Which is where you come in?'

'A lot of us come in,' she told him. 'The year I came back to the island I copped literally scores of calls on Christmas Day from oldies who really did feel ill. There's nothing like loneliness to make a slight niggle seem like something frightening. Then the next year Jonas Cruikshank, a local farmer, committed suicide on Christmas Day. His wife had died six months earlier, neither of his kids could make it back to the island and it must have been all too much for him.' She shrugged awkwardly. 'The local church ladies had put on a welfare-type dinner, but he hadn't put his name down for it. Why would he? Come and admit that he was one of the lonely? He had far too much pride. His death hit us all dreadfully, so after that we decided to change things up a bit. Make Christmas fun.'

'You mean *you* decided to make it fun.'

'I did,' she said a trifle defensively.

'How?'

What was she doing, sitting talking when she had so much to do? This guy was a patient. She'd written him up for the drugs he'd need for the night—if he'd take them. Her work here was done.

But this was Christmas.

Jonas Cruikshank had been a friend more than a patient. His wife had babysat her as a little girl. Jonas had given her her first dog, the predecessor of a long line leading to Sherlock. His death had cast a pall over the whole island, and the next year she'd overridden all objections and done it her way.

And this guy had asked. He should be sleeping but he

seemed wide awake and she wouldn't mind...just talking for a little while.

She shut her eyes for a moment, closing her mind to the to-do list still waiting for her. She tugged her chair back up to the bed and sat. And talked.

'For a start, I moved our communal Christmas dinner out of the church hall,' she told him.

'You're not religious?'

'I didn't say that. The churches on this island do a fabulous job, but the only one with a hall big enough to take us has walls covered in Easter images. They're beautiful but they're sad. I want fun at my Christmas celebration, Dr Pierce, not suffering. So I moved the whole thing to the footy ground training room. It's huge.'

'So let me guess,' he said, bemused. 'You now have portraits of sweaty, post grand final football teams, and rolls of past players?'

'They take 'em down for us,' she said smugly. 'They didn't want to, but three years back the whole team came down with norovirus two days before playing the grand final with one of the neighbouring islands. You have no idea how hard Grandpa and I worked to rehydrate those guys, and in the end we got them all match fit and they won. So the coach's speech included a public declaration that the footy club stood in our debt. Same as you. You're donating lift chairs, or I hope you are. They've donated a testosterone-free training room every Christmas, they take down their pictures and honour rolls and they even throw in a decorated tree for good measure.'

Marc chuckled. She met his eyes and saw a twinkle lurking in their depths. She chuckled too, and all at once she felt better. As if the weariness had lifted a little.

She should go now, she told herself.

She didn't.

'So you have a hall,' he prompted, sounding fascinated. 'What else?'

'I pull in favours wherever I can find 'em,' she told him. 'I also now have Douglas McCurdie's puddings, and that's really something.'

'Puddings?'

'Douglas is a local poultry farmer. His wife used to make a Christmas pudding which was a legend among her family, and when she died he found the recipe and started making them to sell. They're awesome but he's canny— he sells them for a ridiculous amount through a trendy Sydney outlet. But he was friends with Jonas, and when I twisted his arm he agreed to provide them—as long as he's on the guest list. He's lonely and it's a pride saver for him, too. And so it's spiralled. We have some of the best island cooks competing to have their food accepted. Grandpa and I have people we decree need to be invited, but the rest of the places are up for ballot, and that list's a mile long. But if you volunteer to help you become part of it. It's fabulous.'

'And the gifts?' he said cautiously, sounding entranced.

'They're just for the specials. If I did gifts for everyone I'd go nuts. But the islanders who don't have anyone waiting at home, or those too ill or elderly to have a decent Christmas themselves—they get a gift, and those gifts are personal. No handkerchiefs and socks from me.'

'Like what?'

'Little things,' she told him. 'You've already figured money on this island is tight so they can't be big. But I have spies in the welfare shop, with the fishermen, with the local tradies, with whoever I can think of to help, and I have a plan that lasts all year.'

He'd forgotten the pain in his leg. The pain all over his body. She had him fascinated.

'So tell me about your plan.'

'Well…like geraniums for Sandra Carter,' she told him. 'Sandra's been alone since her husband and her son drowned in a boating accident six years back. But she adores geraniums—she reckons she has every variety known to man. Six months ago we had an evacuation flight arrive without its usual doctor. They'd expected a routine problem, but it turned nasty so I had to go with them to Sydney. I needed to stay overnight and took a dusk walk and saw the most amazing geranium—I swear it was almost black. I knocked on the door and the lady gave me a cutting and it's actually grown. I reckon Sandra will be beside herself when she sees it. Not all my things hit the sweet spot, but I do my best. I have a "Beware, Vicious Dog" sign for May Trent with her ancient chihuahua. I have a perfect nautilus shell for Louise Addington whose grandson broke hers when he was here last holiday. I have a second-hand book on making artificial flies for Ron Nesbit—he spends his life fly-fishing. Oh, and I had another triumph—I found an ancient pottery wheel for Gay Ryan, who's always wanted to try throwing pots, and it goes with a promise of lessons from Chris Baker, who's an excellent local potter. That took me taking Chris's kid's appendix out to wheedle. So many things—and they all have to be wrapped.'

'Including the pottery wheel?' he said faintly.

'I'll use a long piece of string for that,' she told him. 'It'll lead to the janitor's room, where the wheel will be set up. I'll wrap a box with the end of the string in it to give to Gay. The trick is to make every gift look ordinary. It's become a bit of a thing—the islanders love it. I have people suggesting stuff now, but no one knows until Christmas Day what the gifts are. Actually, that's not true. Grandpa knows because he helps—he loves it too.' She paused and bit her lip. 'Or mostly he does. He's not even asking about it this year.'

And that was enough to haul her out of her story, to make her remember reality. 'Sorry,' she said contritely. 'That's far too much information about my hobby horse. You need to rest.'

'So do you.'

'I don't have a black and blue body. I'll send Maggie in with something.'

'You're worried about your grandpa?'

'Doesn't everyone worry about their grandpa? He should be...' She paused and managed a smile and shrugged. 'No. I was going to say he should be retired, but sitting in a rocker watching the world go by isn't his scene. He'll die in the traces. Except I don't want it to be...well, not for a very long time yet.'

This was personal. What was she doing, talking personal with a patient? Marc was watching her face—reading her astutely? The thought was unsettling.

If he was unsettling her then all the more reason for her to leave, but she didn't, and it was Marc who spoke up next.

'How sick is he?'

She sighed and spread her hands. Why not? She'd come this far. 'His renal problems aren't bad enough for dialysis or transplant yet, but they're worrying,' she told him. 'Plus there's his heart. He had a minor attack last year. We had to fly him to Sydney, where they put in a stent and gave him orders to slow down. Which he refuses to do. He should have gone back last month for a check-up but of course he won't. And don't you dare tell him I told you.'

'I won't. But you know I'm a cardiologist. Maybe I...'

'Could examine him before you leave? I'd like to see you try—I can only imagine what he'd say if he thought I was worrying a patient on his behalf.'

'I'm a colleague.'

'Says the man with his leg in plaster, an arm in a sling and bruises all over him.' She forced a smile back onto her face and decided she really did need to go now. The fact that this man was looking at her with empathy, with understanding, with concern...

She didn't need any of it. She didn't!

'Let me help you wrap your parcels,' he said, and she blinked.

'What, you?'

'That's hardly a gracious response.' He was sitting up in bed, smiling at her, and she thought he was bruised and battered, he was wearing a generic hospital gown and the man had no business to look as sexy as he did. Or have a smile that twisted something inside her that had no business being twisted.

'My arm's sore,' he told her, watching her with eyes that seemed to see far too much. 'But it's not terrible. My leg will stop me hiking for a while but neither of them preclude me from being useful. My friends have gone to St Moritz without me, and I'm at a loose end. So how about loading me up with lists, gifts, wrapping paper and sticky tape? My wrapping might be a bit off, but I can cover things.'

'I can't...'

'Ask me? You weren't forward in asking for lift chairs.'

'That's different. That's for the hospital.'

'And this is personal? I don't think so.'

'But it is,' she said seriously. 'If you knew the pleasure those gifts give me...'

'Because they're for other people,' he said gently. 'Who gives you a gift, Dr McCrae?'

'If you saw the selection of chocolates out at Reception...'

'I'm not talking of chocolates.'

'They're more appropriate than an offer to fly me to St Moritz,' she flung at him and then flushed. 'No. Sorry, I'm very grateful.'

'You shouldn't feel grateful.'

'I don't, because I have all the gifts I need.' He'd been watching her, their gazes almost locked, but now she deliberately lowered her eyes, staring blindly towards the chart at the end of the bed. 'I...if you really do mean it... about the wrapping...'

'I really do mean it.'

'Then I may well take you up on it,' she told him, still

not looking at him. 'You might still be running on adrenalin now, but I suspect you'll find you need to sleep tomorrow. Even if you don't think it, your injuries will take their toll. But if you're still here on Saturday... Maybe I could put a quarantine sign on your door and tell the nurses you're desperate for rest. A couple of them will be suspicious, but it'll give you privacy.'

'I'd barricade the door with my bed tray,' he told her solemnly. 'Secrets R Us. Speaking of which...'

'Marc, I really do need to go.' She did, too. This guy was making her feel more and more unsettled.

'Yeah, but I have a favour to ask,' he told her. 'My clothes are torn, filthy and bloodstained. And this gown...'

'It's a very nice gown,' she said and managed to smile. His gaze had met hers again and the twinkle in those dark eyes...

She had to get out of here!

'It's a great gown as far as gowns go,' he told her, the twinkle intensifying. 'But as far as secrets go... Every time I get out of bed I need to clutch my modesty around me and hope.'

'There's nothing under there the nurses haven't seen a hundred times before.'

'Dr McCrae...'

'Yes... Dr Pierce?'

'Could you please, please, please, see if you can find me some clothes. Some decent pyjamas.'

'I'm already on it,' she told him. 'Kylie—she's the lass who delivers your meals—has a sister who works in the charity store. I've sent her home with a list.'

'The welfare store!'

'There's not a great range on the island,' she told him. 'Mostly we buy online. It takes about a month to get here, but if you're prepared to wait...'

'So it's the welfare store or nothing.' He sounded re-volted and she chuckled.

'You never know. I saw Brenda Larsen drop off her husband's purple pyjamas only last week. Linus has gone up a size, from enormous to eye-popping. They're a bit stretched across the tummy but otherwise in perfect condition. If you're lucky they might still be there.'

'Elsa…'

She chuckled and threw up her hands. 'I know, every sense is offended. I'll send Maggie in with laptop, phone and drugs but you do need to sleep. I'm going.'

'Before I toss a pillow at you.'

'I'm gone,' she said, and was out of there, tugging the door firmly closed behind her.

He lay and stared at the closed door for a long time.

Maggie didn't bring the laptop or the phone or the drugs. She would soon, he thought. He'd shown her he'd been irritated, and she'd be making her point. Nurses were a bad breed to get offside. He knew that. As a cardiovascular surgeon he couldn't get by without the help of his extraordinary team, and he made a point of ensuring they weren't stressed.

Maggie had been busy, and he'd pushed her too hard to try and get the tablet password reset.

Was the password so important? Elsa had said there were two little boys in the kids' ward. Did he know what was wrong with them? Did he know how busy the nursing staff were?

He was getting the feeling he knew how busy Elsa was. Too damned busy. Plus she was tired.

Because she'd climbed down into unchartered territory to save him. She'd spent what must have been an almost sleepless night. She'd accompanied him back down the mountain this morning and then operated on his leg.

She had a grandpa with a bad heart, and a community dependent on her as its only full-time doctor.

And he'd been making a fuss about a password.

Because his work was so much more important?

He thought suddenly back to medical school, to the first of the numerous sessions where specialists outlined their roles, where students were expected to think seriously about which path they'd take.

The cardiovascular surgeon had been impressive. He remembered the talk clearly. 'We're at the cutting edge of technology, saving lives which even ten years ago would have been lost. We demand the highest level of intellectual and physical skill. I believe it's the peak of medical expertise—exciting, challenging and, yes, immensely lucrative. Only the best of you need think of applying and only the best of the best will make the grade.'

That was for him, he'd thought. Studying was a breeze. Cutting edge surgery excited him. As for lucrative...who didn't want lucrative? With the wealth he'd inherited from his parents he hardly needed it, but still...

But Elsa...

He thought back to that same lecture, the small, greying man who'd represented family doctors.

'We're not cutting edge,' he'd said quietly. 'In most cases I confess we're not all that lucrative, although most of us make a respectable living. But we do save lives. Not as dramatically as my compatriots on this panel, no life-saving heart or brain surgery for us. But we find and refer, and along the way we pick up the pieces of people's lives and we do our best to patch them together. We try to stop the dramas before they start. Most of us have a community we care for deeply, and we'll do anything for them. A mum with postnatal depression...a coal miner with a cough he thinks is nothing...that's who we're here for and it gives us just as much satisfaction as our more esteemed peers.'

Marc had hardly listened.

His father had been a neurologist. His mother had been a brilliant medical researcher. He was expected to be bright, and bright young doctors followed bright young professions.

They never saw mums with postnatal depression. They never saw a guy with a cold and pushed him to have a chest X-ray.

They never sat up late on the nights before Christmas and wrapped twenty or thirty parcels for needy locals.

He thought of his mother, who'd said she'd loved this island. Maybe she had, but she'd only come here to climb. She'd never have wrapped thirty gifts for people she hardly knew.

She'd been as selfish as he was.

Selfish? The thought made him wince. Was he? Dammit, he worked hard. He made a difference. Not everyone could be a hero.

Like Elsa.

There was a knock on the door and Maggie bustled in, her arms full of gear for him, her face set in prim disapproval.

'Dr McCrae's sent you the telephone and the laptop. You can use our phone tonight but she's organising Jason to see you tomorrow. There's also medication, but she says you don't want it. I dare say you'll try and sleep and then be asking me for it in a couple of hours when I'm busy with something else.'

'Are you busy?' he asked, but a sharp look was all he got for his pains.

'It's looking to be a big night.' She sniffed.

'Problems?'

'Nothing that need concern you.'

'I'm a doctor,' he said gently, probing to get past antagonism. 'If absolutely necessary I could get up and help.'

That produced a snort.

'I mean it.'

'You might well,' she snapped as she set her gear down on his tray. 'But a lot of help you'd be. One of our pregnant mums has just come in threatening to deliver, and she's only thirty-two weeks. The smoke on the mainland means she can't be evacuated, so Elsa has her hands full trying to keep that baby aboard. What use is a cardiologist with a broken leg?'

'No help at all,' he said humbly. 'Maggie...'

'Yes.' She tugged up the blood pressure machine and started taking his obs.

'Could you please give me the painkillers Elsa's written up?'

'She says you don't want them until later.'

'I didn't think I did,' he admitted. 'But it's true I'm hurting now, and if I take them then I'll go to sleep and won't need to disturb you later.'

She fixed him with a look of distrust. 'Why the change of heart?'

'Because I'm starting to realise that I need to lie here and be no trouble to you at all.'

'If you need us, we'll come,' she said shortly. 'Ignoring pain, ignoring any other worrying symptom might lead to more drama.'

'Then I won't ignore pain or any other worrying symptom,' he promised. 'But if it's humanly possible, for all our sakes I will cause no more drama.'

CHAPTER SEVEN

ON FRIDAY HE SLEPT. Which infuriated him. Every time he woke he found another two or three hours had drifted by. He'd stir when the nurses came to do his obs, or when his meals turned up. He was extraordinarily hungry, but meals simply seemed to make him sleepier. Jason arrived and set up his new phone and he managed to stay awake for that. Once he was back online he checked his hospital messages, but none of them seemed worth the effort of replying. He thought about opening his files on the borrowed laptop and doing some work, but that was as far as he got. Someone dropped in pyjamas. Getting rid of his hospital gown seemed important. He donned the boxer shorts but the T-shirt was too much trouble.

He slept.

Mid-afternoon he woke and found Elsa at the end of his bed, checking his chart. She smiled as she saw him stir.

'Excellent,' she told him. 'Your body's had a tough time. It needs sleep to recover and it's taking it. Told you so.'

'You don't need to sound so smug about it.'

'I'm enjoying the sensation of telling a specialist what's what,' she said, grinning. 'Allow me my small satisfaction, Dr Pierce. But all's good here. You can go back to sleep.'
And she was gone.

Confused, disconcerted, still half asleep, there seemed

little choice but to obey, but adding to his confusion was the way Elsa's smile stayed with him while he slept.

Some time in the long distant past, when he was little more than a toddler, he'd had a nanny he'd loved. He had fuzzy memories of being ill and his nanny bustling in and out of the room, sitting on his bed, reading to him, cuddling him.

For some strange reason, Elsa was providing the same comfort. For over twenty-four hours he'd been truly terrified, and the echoes of that terror were still with him. So he slept, but the vision of Elsa stayed with him—Elsa somewhere in the hospital, Elsa checking his obs, Elsa just…here.

It made him feel needy, and he was not needy.

But maybe he was.

He remembered the day that same nanny had left, how useless his tears had been. He'd long got over the idea of needing anyone, but at the moment he seemed to have no choice. He seemed to need to take comfort from her presence. He'd go back to being solitary—of course he would; nothing else made sense—but Elsa's smile stayed with him as he slept.

It helped.

Friday might have passed in a sleepy haze for Marc, but for Elsa it was far different. Her pregnant patient seemed to have settled for now, but she was still uneasy about her. She checked and checked, and worried and worried. She wanted her evacuated, but smoke haze was still a problem. Meanwhile she had so much work it seemed to be coming out of her ears.

Late at night she did a final round and found Marc awake, but she was too rushed to stay for more than a few moments.

'You're looking good,' she told him. 'Great. Sorry, Marc, but I need to go.'

'It's nine at night. Aren't you done yet?'

'I have a mum bringing in a kid with an ear infection. Why she waited until nine at night to call me... Okay, I know, she was hoping it'd clear by itself because she's so busy. I get it.'

'I wish I could help.'

'Just don't throw out a fever. Go back to sleep.'

'What about your Christmas gifts,' he demanded as she backed out of the door. 'Wrapping? Have you done them yet?'

No. She hadn't. She had to find time. Somehow.

'Bring them to me,' he ordered.

'Really?' She was astonished he'd even remembered.

'Please,' he told her. 'I've slept all day. By tomorrow I'll be bored to snores.'

'You're recuperating.'

'So I need therapy. Bring me what I need.'

She stared at him for a long moment. He was propped up in bed, rumpled with sleep. His arm was in a sling but he'd abandoned the hospital nightwear—he was now wearing decent boxers, but his chest was bare. He was wearing a five o'clock shadow. His dark eyes were smiling and he looked...

Like she had to back out of here now.

'Gifts,' he said, his voice becoming gentle, and she wondered if he knew what highly inappropriate thoughts had just slammed into her head.

'G...gifts,' she managed to echo. 'I'll bring them in the morning.'

She fled.

Saturday morning—Christmas Eve—she was up at five. By nine she felt as if she'd done a whole day's work, but there was more than a day's work still ahead of her.

Mid-morning she checked on Marc, to find him propped up in bed waiting for her and demanding his 'therapy'.

'Okay, you asked for it,' she managed and half an hour later his room was crowded with gifts, scissors, paper, cards, list and tape. She put the Do Not Disturb sign outside his door and left him staring in some bemusement at what he'd let himself in for.

At midday she snagged his lunch from the kitchen, plus sandwiches for herself, and went to see how he was getting on.

She found him surrounded by a sea of wrapping paper, with a pile of oddly wrapped gifts beside the bed.

He had a geranium on the bed beside him and he was glowering at it.

'Wow,' she said, surveying the chaos from the door. 'This is fantastic. How many have you done?'

'Twenty-six,' he said darkly. 'And *done* is a very loose word. Wrapping doesn't seem to be my forte.'

She grinned. 'So I'm guessing you always get your nurses to do your dressings?'

'Always.'

'No matter.' She perched on the foot of his bed and picked up his chart. 'I'm an appalling wrapper too, so the islanders won't notice any difference.' She took a moment while she read the chart, and then she beamed. 'Good boy, no surprises here.'

'Tell me about your pregnant patient?' he asked, and she screwed up her nose.

'The smoke's cleared so finally we can evacuate her,' she told him. 'Things look like they're settling but I still don't like it and I don't want a thirty-two-weeker delivered here. I've had it happen before when the family wouldn't accept advice.' She hesitated and he saw trauma, tightly held. Then she gave one of her characteristic nods and moved on. 'Well, my advice is stronger now, or maybe it's not even advice. Erica's out of here. The plane's due at three. That's what I needed to tell you. They'll take you too, if you want to go.'

And that took him aback. He could leave. He'd be back in Sydney tonight.

To what?

His mates were in St Moritz, or scattered for the Christmas holidays—either that or they'd be on duty, working their butts off. If he was evacuated he could be admitted into the hospital where he worked. There he'd suffer teasing by the staff, plus—heaven forbid—jovial visits by the elderly consultant who always played Santa. Or he could sit at home with his leg immobile and feel sorry for himself.

Oh, for heaven's sake, what was he thinking? He was involved in an immense international research project. There was always work to do.

But he still might feel sorry for himself, he conceded, and he glanced up and saw Elsa watching him with what looked like understanding.

'Conflicted, eh?' she asked. 'If you go home you'll realise how much you're missing St Moritz, and you still need bed rest. You know you're welcome to stay here. We can keep you as an inpatient for a couple more days and then you can take the regular flight home. Oh, and you needn't worry about being bored. If you finish these I have a hundred paper napkins I need folding into the shape of little bells. Origami at its finest.'

'Bells...' he said faintly.

'It's only fair to warn you,' she told him cheerfully, 'before you make a decision. So your choice is a nice quiet flight back to Sydney, with well-trained medics to keep you safe, or a hundred paper bells followed by total chaos on Christmas Day. Maybe I didn't mention that as a hospital patient you get to be first on the guest list at our Christmas dinner. We can organise you a wheelchair if you'd like to go.'

'A wheelchair?' he said, revolted.

'A wheelchair it is until that swelling goes down and we can replace that back slab,' she said, in a voice that brooked no argument. 'So, Dr Pierce, what shall it be? You want to share our island Christmas, or do you want to make a run for it? Make up your mind because the evac team needs to know.'

She was smiling down at him, her head cocked slightly to one side like an impertinent sparrow. He found himself smiling back.

Christmas here—or Christmas in Sydney.

Christmas alone—or Christmas with Elsa.

It wouldn't be Christmas with Elsa, he told himself. He was simply one of her many patients.

Still...

'I will help you with the napkin bells if you decide to stay,' she told him generously and he thought of her sitting beside him, that glorious head of fiery curls bent over origami bells. He thought of her smile.

The decision seemed to be made for him.

Christmas with Elsa it would be.

What was he thinking? He was shocked at the direction his errant thoughts were taking. Was this some type of Stockholm Syndrome, where the captive fell for the captor?

Um, that might possibly be overplaying a broken leg and a hospital bed, he conceded, and actually Elsa had freed him, not captured him.

So was it gratitude he was feeling?

Of course it was gratitude, he told himself with a certain amount of relief. It had nothing to do with the way Elsa was smiling at him now, with that inquisitive, intelligent sparrow look. The look that said whatever he decided would be okay by her.

The look that said that, regardless, if he got on that plane she'd fold all hundred napkins herself, and then see patients and take care of her grandpa and get up on Christmas morning and do a ward round and lug these crazily wrapped gifts across to the footy hall and have fun.

Fun. There was the hub of the matter. He looked down

at his pile of weird gifts and thought he wanted to be there when they were all opened.

'So what's your decision?' she asked gently, as if she guessed he was torn.

'I'll stay.'

'Wow, that's good of you.'

He grinned ruefully. 'Sorry. If it's okay with you, if you don't need my bed for someone else, if it's okay for me to join in your Christmas festivities...'

'Then you're very welcome. Now, about this geranium...'

'It's too...'

'Too big.' She smiled, a lovely, uncomplicated smile that said all was right with her world. 'The lady gave me a three-inch cutting and I had to carry it home in wet tissue and hope. And here it is, knee high and covered with flowers. When it started growing I had visions of it taking over the whole island—I had to check with our quarantine officer that it was okay to keep it. If we join two sheets together...you plonk it on the wrapping paper and hold it steady and I'll gather the paper together with a big ribbon at the top. What colour do you reckon? Red? Gold? How about rainbow?'

'Rainbow,' he said, slightly shocked as she hauled gaudy bows out of a box and laid them on his bed for his consideration. Memories stirred of elegant gifts in the past, mostly wrapped by the expensive stores they were purchased from. He didn't think he'd ever had a gift that looked so...so...

'How about that for Christmassy?' Elsa demanded as she finished attaching her bow and stood back to inspect their handwork. Scarlet Santa paper and a vast rainbow bow. The whole thing looked more like a scrunched ball of waste paper than elegant gift wrapping. 'Haven't we done well?'

'Very well,' he agreed faintly, and she grinned and touched his shoulder—a fleeting touch—doctor reassuring patient?

'You're doing good, Dr Pierce,' she told him. 'Grandpa will help me sneak these out later. Meanwhile you need to take a nap and gather strength for the bells.'

'Did you say a hundred?'

'Yep,' she said cheerfully, and then added, 'Nope, make that a hundred and one because we just added you to the guest list.'

CHAPTER EIGHT

Christmas Day

SHE REMEMBERED CHRISTMAS as a kid. There had been those first appalling ones with her dysfunctional mother—thankfully mostly a blur now. She did remember the last of those, waking to find her mother surfacing after yet another binge, with nothing planned, nothing to eat, nothing at all.

Her mother had simply forgotten it was Christmas—or hadn't thought of it in the first place.

And then somehow her mother had disappeared, and when her grandfather had swooped in to claim her Christmas had suddenly been magical. Yes, Grandpa had often been called out, but if she wasn't called on to 'help' in the hospital kitchen—she'd been chief taster—or if she didn't need to ride her brand-new scooter or play with her brand-new science kit, she'd go with him. And it seemed every single islander would be celebrating, welcoming her with hugs and mince pies and more sweets than one small kid could possibly consume.

Her island. Her people.

She did love this place, she conceded. Yes, sometimes she resented its demands, but she still remembered that first Christmas on the island, the feeling of being loved unconditionally, of being protected. Of belonging.

And today…

For a few indulgent moments after she woke she let herself stay where she was and just wallowed in the surge of excitement that was Christmas. The restlessness that had been with her for months seemed to have receded. Life was okay. It was Christmas and she was with the people she loved.

And Marc was here.

'But that has nothing to do with it,' she told herself out loud—or if it did it had no business doing so. This was Christmas excitement only. Marc would be gone tomorrow or the day after and she'd be left with...

Tony?

No, not Tony. She'd cleared that up—she hoped. One unwise date...

And that was the problem. The whole island seemed to be watching her, waiting for her to date. Plus all the rest. The islanders would like her to be even more wedded to the island than she was now. When eligible tourists rocked in—the male, single variety—she could almost see their collective nervousness. No one was to take away their Dr McCrae.

Which was fine with her, she conceded, because she had no intention of leaving. She owed the island too much. She loved the island too much.

However...

However, the pool of available islanders as life partners was limited, to say the least. Most of the young ones departed as soon as they could. There were maybe ten unmarried guys around her age on the whole island, and compared to most of them Tony looked good.

Wow, where were her thoughts going? There was a despondent thought to wake up to on Christmas morning. Did she need a reason to get up?

Of course she didn't. She struggled to retain the surge of excitement she'd woken with. She had a good life. A great life. She was the island doc. She didn't need to be anything more.

Except here was this gorgeous guy called Marcus, who'd fallen down a hole, who'd helped her wrap gifts and who'd smiled at her.

Get a grip, she told herself. She was indulging in a teenage fantasy, and she had no time for fantasies today. Grandpa would be heating panforte in the fire stove oven, waiting with a gift for her. Sherlock would be demanding a fast walk before she started work for the day. She needed to do a ward round. She needed to make sure of the final touches to the Christmas dinner.

And her fantasy?

'Marc's as real as Santa Claus,' she said out loud. 'Okay, he's flesh and blood and he'll be staying longer than a quick flit down the chimney, but not much longer. Put your sensible boots on, Dr McCrae, and get to work.'

Marc was accustomed to the extravagant Christmas décor of St Moritz at its glitziest, but the simple Gannet Island hall was a sight to take a man's breath away.
A giant gumtree stood behind the building, laced right to its tip with the island's delicate mistletoe. Who needed bought decorations with such crimson beauty at hand? Massive swathes of the brilliant clusters had been brought inside, creating an effect much more gorgeous than any commercial effort. The hall looked lovely and over a hundred people were set to enjoy themselves.

It seemed that what had begun years before as a Christmas party for hospital patients and for islanders who had no one to share with had grown. Elsa had told him that most island families organised their own Christmas dinner, but still almost all put their names in the ballot to attend this one. The ballot was for entire families, and if the family succeeded in the ballot then this party seemed to be the preferred option.

It meant the party wasn't just for the ill and the lonely. It was a true celebration.

The footy ground was right by the hospital. A couple of beefy footballers were in charge of patient transport, for anyone well enough to enjoy the day. Despite Marc's protests, they'd brought him in a wheelchair—'If you think I'm letting you use crutches before your shoulder's settled you can think again,' Elsa had told him sternly, so now he was seated at one of six vast trestle tables surrounded by...fun.

As everyone walked in they were presented with a hat. These weren't your typical novelty Christmas hats bought in bulk from a cheap supplier. These were knitted or crocheted beanies. Crazy beanies.

'They're an island project,' the guy sitting beside Marc told him. 'We no sooner finish one year's lot than we start another. It's called the Crazy Cap Club. We meet at the school hall every Thursday night and egg each other on to see who can crochet the craziest one.'

'You do it too?' Marc asked, fascinated. The guy he was talking to was an ex-fisherman who'd introduced himself as Wally, in a wheelchair that matched Marc's, in his eighties, a hospital patient with oxygen-dependent emphysema. Weathered from a life at sea, gruff, matter-of-fact, the thought of him with a crochet hook had Marc hornswoggled.

'Doc bullied me into it,' he told Marc. 'I was that tired of sitting on me bum all day, so she gave me a challenge. Do one with a fish on it,' she told me. 'So I did. First one was a bit wobbly but Martin Crosby got it and still wears it out on his boat. That was three years back. This year my one's over on Hazel Mitchell's head. See...the octopus with the tentacles made into braids that hang down her back looking like hair.'

Marc looked and looked again. He'd met Hazel—she was the prim hospital administrator who'd helped him fill in admission forms. She was wearing a very proper skirt and matching jacket—in prim pink. Sensible court shoes and stockings.

And an octopus hat with braids.

And then Elsa came swooping over to their table. He'd been watching her—of course he had. She seemed to be everywhere, hauling people into conversations, rearranging seating. He'd seen her take one old lady who was shrinking at the end of a noisy table and almost literally sweep her up and deposit her in the midst of another table, which seemed just as noisy but the people there seemed to know her. They shoved along to accommodate her and were currently in the midst of swapping hats to figure which hat best suited who. She was giggling and sipping champagne and Elsa had moved on.

'I think your hat's the best,' she told Wally now, stooping to give him a hug, careful, Marc noted, not to bump the oxygen tube that obviously kept the old man alive. 'An octopus with dreadlocks...where will you go from there?'

'I'm thinking of a fisherman with fishhooks and fish dangling,' Wally told her, grinning. 'I got the pattern just about worked out. It'll take me all year to make but it's worth it. You know Muriel Cuthbert got last year's mermaid and she's using it as a tea cosy. Pride of place on the kitchen table, she tells me, and everyone admires it.'

'And why wouldn't they?' Elsa demanded, looking at the hats on both their heads. Wally was wearing a Santa with seven elves stitched into the side. Marc was wearing a particularly mean-looking barracuda. 'Very fetching,' she said, grinning.

Elsa was wearing a pink confection, a crocheted merry-go-round, complete with little horses. It looked complex, weird, adorable.

Marc looked at Elsa's flushed, laughing face and thought he'd never seen anything more beautiful.

It must be the champagne, he thought. He imagined his friends, many of whom would be sipping their hugely expensive Christmas eggnogs in front of a roaring fire at the resort in St Moritz. They'd all be wearing après-ski wear, very chic.

Elsa was wearing a flouncy red skirt that looked as if it could well be homemade and a crisp, sleeveless blouse. She'd accessorised with a necklace of red tinsel and Santa Claus earrings. Plus her crazy hat. She'd braided her flaming curls and the two braids hung over her shoulders, tied at the ends with red and gold Christmas ribbon.

This was more Christmas cliché than he'd dreamed possible on one woman. Who knew it could look so great?

She was chuckling as she reached over and grabbed Wally's bon-bon. 'I can't believe you haven't pulled it yet!' Inside was a corny joke. She read it aloud to the table, and there was a roar of laughter.

'You guys take care of Marc,' she told everyone. 'He's had a very hard time so it's your responsibility to make him feel better.' And then she grinned. 'And don't be mean,' she added. 'Not one person is to mention hikers and satellite trackers and letting people know where you're going. Not one of you. It's Christmas. Cut the guy some slack.'

There was more laughter, all of it friendly, and Marc was seamlessly pulled into the general conversation.

Elsa hugged Wally and she moved on.

Marc wouldn't have minded a hug himself, he thought.

He was her patient. The way he was feeling was totally inappropriate.

Maybe it *is* Stockholm Syndrome, he thought.

But he didn't feel like a victim.

It was time to turn his attention to eating, and the food was magnificent. The turkeys had arrived—somehow they'd been organised to be delivered on the evacuation flight. That must have been down to Elsa, he thought. How many medics had to juggle the needs of patients with the need for turkeys?

He watched Elsa and thought that this wasn't about her patients or, if it was, her patients were the whole island.

Between main course and pudding there was entertainment. Christmas carols were sung in three-part harmony, led by the local choir, with everyone joining in. A weathered fisherman with a hat and a rabbit made corny magician jokes. A group of elderly ladies in twenties gear danced the Charleston with gusto. At the end of the dance each of the ladies grabbed an unsuspecting diner and dragged them up to join them. Elsa was one of the first to be grabbed, and she Charlestoned with the best of them. Of course she would, he thought, dazed. She was magnificent.

And then there were the gifts. He watched Sandra Carter gasp and flush with pleasure as she removed his dodgy wrapping from around her geranium. He watched the hall roar with laughter as little May Trent opened her 'Beware, Vicious Dog' sign. May giggled and showed the sign to the little dog under her chair, and he thought her Christmas had been made. It seemed the same for every gift recipient.

Thanks to Elsa.

She had him enthralled. When the meal was done and his footballer escorts decreed it was his turn to be wheeled back to the hospital, he looked for Elsa and saw she was already helping clear, chuckling with the locals as she worked. She looked busy and happy. And he thought that he really wanted to stay. Here. Now.

To do what? Help with the dishes? Ha.

He was a patient, an outsider, a visitor who'd already caused everyone massive inconvenience. He submitted meekly to being wheeled back to his ward, to his bed.

He'd missed a call from Kayla. It was early morning in St Moritz. He imagined how Christmas would play out over there—the magnificent, sophisticated Christmas he'd thought was perfect—and decided he hadn't missed it one bit.

'How's the leg?' Kayla's enquiry was perfunctory when

he returned the call, and he wondered if she really cared. Was this just a duty phone call?

'It's set and healing. I should be back in Sydney in the next couple of days.'

'That's good,' she told him and then proceeded to outline all her very exciting plans for the holiday.

'Kayla...' he said as she finished.

'Yes?' And he heard the reservation. Did she think he was going to ask her to do something different, mess with her plans?

'Kayla, this isn't working,' he said gently. 'I just thought...while you're over there having fun...please don't think you need to be loyal to me. I think we both know that shouldn't happen.'

There was a silence. He could almost see her sharp mind processing, considering ramifications.

'I guess that's logical,' she said at last. 'You and I...we have had fun.'

'We have.'

'But it was never serious.'

'It never was.' It never had been, he thought. He didn't do relationships, or not the type of relationship he'd seen some of his colleagues fall into. The type where there was co-dependence.

And Kayla was the same. He heard a sigh and he thought he detected relief. The sound of moving on.

'I'll admit I might have more fun here if everyone stops treating me as poor Kayla who's pining for her boyfriend,' she admitted.

'I can't imagine you pining over anyone.'

'It's not my style,' she agreed, and chuckled. She really was a friend. Just a colleague.

No longer an occasional lover.

'Okay, then, I'm off to enjoy Christmas,' she told him. 'I hope someone gives you pudding, though I can't imagine it'll come anywhere near what they'll give us here. Poor you. But take care of yourself, Marcus. Bye-ee.'

And she was gone.

What was gone with her?

The knowledge that he wanted to be part of that set? He might well want to, he thought, as soon as he got back to Sydney. As soon as he brushed off the dust of this island.

As soon as he stopped thinking of one gorgeous doctor, dancing through Christmas.

And, as if on cue, there was a knock on his door and the doctor in question appeared.

She was still wearing her gorgeous red skirt and her crazy hat. She had a white coat over the top.

'Good evening, Doctor,' he said, and she grinned.

'Thank you,' she told him. 'A bit of professional respect, that's what I like. Every single patient on my list tonight has greeted me with caution, like I might prescribe enemas instead of antibiotics. Even though I swear the only alcohol I had was in the brandy sauce.' It was said with indignation, followed by a chuckle and if he'd been entranced before he was more so now.

Enthralled, even?

She took his chart from the end of the bed and read it while he watched her. Her chuckle had faded but there was still a trace of a smile on her face. Or maybe that dimple was a permanent feature.

This chameleon doctor, who trekked with her beagle, who'd abseiled down a hole to rescue him, who operated with competence, who'd made Christmas happy for so many...

'This is great,' she said as she hung the chart up again. 'And you're the end of the line. Not a single spike in temperature for the whole hospital, not even an unexpected tummy ache. Christmas has been a success.'

'It's been a success for reasons other than lack of medical repercussions,' he told her. 'You've done great.'

'We've done great,' she corrected him. 'The whole island. Even you with your wrapping.'

'*Even* me?' He managed to sound wounded.

'I mean especially you,' she said and grinned. 'Of course.'

Wow, she was gorgeous. Dammit, why was he in this bed?

'Elsa, when this is all over, if we can organise it, can I see you again?' he asked before he knew he was going to say it. Certainly before he'd thought it through.

It was dumb and she reacted accordingly. There was no hesitation in her response. 'There's no way that's likely to happen,' she told him bluntly. Was he imagining it, or did he hear a note of regret in her voice? 'In a couple of days you'll be out of here.'

'I could stay.' He still had two weeks' leave.

That brought a rueful smile. 'What, and hike on that leg? Not a hope. You'd be stuck in the local guesthouse, bored to snores.'

'But I could take you out to dinner.'

'Which would lead where?' She shrugged and he saw her dredge up a smile from somewhere. Trying to keep it light. 'Marc, you and I both know the rules. Doctors don't hit on patients. Patients don't hit on doctors. Especially when both of them are full of Christmas punch.'

'Asking you out to dinner isn't exactly hitting on you.' He felt like swearing. He was at such a disadvantage, sitting in bed in his borrowed pyjamas. Thankfully, they weren't Linus Larsen's purple ones, but persuading this woman to go out with him could well take more finesse than even the finest pyjamas conveyed. Someone had found him a shirt and loose trousers to wear to dinner but he'd put his pyjama boxers and T-shirt back on when he'd returned to bed. Now he wished he hadn't, but he also knew it wouldn't have made a blind bit of difference what he wore.

'Dating is encompassed in the same rules,' she said firmly. 'Thanks, Marc, but no. I don't do casual dating.'

'Does it have to be casual?' Again it was said before he thought it through, and he winced even as the words came out. Was he talking about being serious? *Now?* He saw her withdraw a little and any last vestige of her smile vanished.

'You have a girlfriend.'

'I don't.' He needed to clear this up. 'Things between Kayla and me were pretty much over even before this happened. This accident's just made our split formal.'

'What, she dumped you because you couldn't go to St Moritz?' She sounded incensed.

'No, it was a mutual dumping,' he told her, 'of a tepid relationship. Maybe like the relationship the nurses tell me you have with Tony.'

She stared at him in astonishment. 'You've been gossiping.'

'I was encouraged to talk while my bed was made,' he said virtuously. 'And talking involves questions. The nurse was very pleased with my progress.'

That won a chuckle, but then her voice turned rueful. 'Well, I wish the dumping could be mutual. Tony's a local kelp farmer, dependable, stolid, and after one date he's utterly convinced that we can marry and raise a whole lot of little kelp farmers.' She sighed. 'But, moving on, your love life is nothing to do with me, and vice versa. Maybe if I'm over in Sydney on a case we can catch up, but you staying for two weeks just so we can date… It's not going to happen.'

'Why not?' He knew his approach was clumsy, but he was struggling here.

'Because at the end of the two weeks you'd go back to Sydney and I…' She hesitated and he saw a struggle to be honest. And honesty won. 'I could get even more unsettled than I am now.'

His gaze met hers and held it for a long moment. She tilted her chin and then dropped it.

'So tell me,' he said gently. 'Elsa, why are you unsettled?'

Maybe it was the brandy sauce. Or maybe it was because it was the end of a long day and she was still riding a wave of confidence.

Or maybe it was because it was Christmas and she was relaxed and he was just *there*.

Regardless, he saw her hesitate and then shrug and decide to go for it.

'Because this island has seven hundred residents and it's too darned small,' she told him, and then she closed her eyes and shook her head. 'No. That's not fair. Gannet Island is what it is. It's always been remote, and I knew what I was in for when I came back here.'

'You came back for your grandpa?'

'I came back because this is my home. Because the islanders are my family. Because they've loved and supported me from the moment I arrived here aged all of seven, so how could I possibly leave them now? I can't, and mostly it's okay except when I think maybe I wouldn't mind dating and having fun and being taken out to a restaurant where the proprietor doesn't skip the bill as long as I give him a consult on the way out as to how to manage his hormonal teenage daughter, or what to do with his infected toe.'

'That happens?' he asked, stunned, and she managed a wry smile.

'Of course. If you stayed, and if we did go out to dinner, it's just as likely to end that way. With you patiently waiting while I head out to the kitchen to watch someone take off his boot.'

'Elsa...'

'It's fine,' she said, and there was another of her wry shrugs. 'I'm over it. Though sometimes I wonder if it'd be nice to be…just normal. But that's my problem, Dr Pierce, not yours.'

'But…'

'No buts.' She hesitated and then forged on again, totally honest. 'You know, I do think you're lovely,' she told him. 'That's a totally unprofessional thing to even think, much less say…'

'The feeling's mutual.'

'Thank you.' Another of her brisk nods. 'That does my ego a whole lot of good, and I'll take it as another Christmas gift. But that's all. Your life's in Sydney and my life's here. There's not the faintest possibility, even if dating came to something…something more…that anything could come of it.'

'So you'll cut me off at the pass now?'

'I have no choice.' She met his gaze again, calm and direct. It was supposed to be a look of acceptance but behind that…he knew pain when he saw it. Almost involuntarily, he swung himself out of bed, steadying on his good leg.

'Elsa…'

'Don't you try and stand,' she said, alarmed. 'What if you fall? And I don't need this. Please. Back off, Marc.'

'Can you really say what you don't need? Or want?' He was balancing but only just. He took her hand and held on. One push and he'd be back on the bed.

But Elsa wasn't pushing. She stared down at their linked hands and he saw her lips quiver. There was an ache there, he thought. An ache that matched his?

'Don't,' she whispered.

'Do you really want me not to?'

'No. I mean…'

'Elsa, professional ethics or not, impossibility or not, I'd really like to kiss you.'

She closed her eyes for a moment and then looked up at him. Her gaze questioning. 'For Christmas?'

'If you need an excuse.'

'Marc, kissing you would be totally illogical.'

'Like any of the weird and wonderful gifts you've organised for everyone else this Christmas,' he told her. 'Where's your Christmas gift, Elsa?'

And that actually brought a smile. Her eyes suddenly danced with laughter. 'You're saying a kiss from you is equal to a black geranium?'

'Better.'

'Wow,' she said, and suddenly those dancing eyes met his and something changed.

'You'd have to prove it.' Her voice was suddenly decisive.

'Watch me try,' he told her and proceeded to do just that.

What she was doing broke every doctor-patient rule in the book.

Only it was Christmas and she didn't care. The moment his mouth touched hers she felt herself melting. She felt all sorts of things slipping away.

Mostly common sense.

She was standing in a patient's room. Her patient was in boxers and a T-shirt, balanced on one leg. He had a gammy shoulder. He should have his arm in a sling, but he had both hands on her waist. He'd tugged her close, so her breasts were moulding to his chest.

His mouth was on hers. Strong, warm, demanding. Totally, totally inappropriate.

Totally, totally delicious.

No.

It was more than delicious, she thought dazedly. It was wonderful. Magical.

She'd been kissed before—of course she had. Tony wasn't the only guy she'd dated.

It had never felt like this.

The way he held her…the strength of his hands on her

waist…the way he'd hesitated as his mouth found hers, as if checking that this was indeed what she wanted…

How could he doubt it? Her lips opened under his and she felt as if she'd been catapulted into another world.

A world where heat met heat. Where desire met desire.

Oh, she wanted him. She ached for him. Her whole body felt as if it was surrendering.

She was surrendering.

She was being kissed and she was kissing. He didn't need to balance on his bad leg because she was holding him.

Maybe it could count as therapy, she thought, almost hysterically. Helping patient stand. Maybe this *was* a medical tool designed to make him feel better.

It was surely making *her* feel better. Every sense seemed to have come alive. Every nerve-ending was tingling.

More. Every single part of her was screaming that she wanted this man, she needed this man, that she wouldn't mind in the least if they fell back on the bed and…

Um, not in a million years. Not!

Because she didn't want it?

Because this was a hospital ward and any minute the door could open as a nurse arrived for routine obs. This was a patient and she was a doctor and…

Shut up, Elsa, she told her inner self fiercely. Just let this moment be.

So she did. Her mind shut down and she let herself just kiss. And be kissed.

The kiss was deep and long and magical, and as it finally ended—as all kisses surely must—it was as much as she could do not to weep. But Marc was still holding her. He had her at arm's length now, smiling into her eyes with such tenderness that…

No! She made a herculean effort to haul herself together. This was way past unprofessional. She could just about get herself struck off the medical register for this.

Right now she was having trouble thinking that it mattered, whether she was struck off or not. For Marc was smiling at her, and that seemed to be the only thing that mattered in the whole world.

But this was still well out of order. This man's life was in Sydney. It could only ever be a casual fling with a guy who was bored.

Oh, but his smile…

'About that date…' he ventured, and she needed to shake her head but all she could do was look up into his dark eyes and sense went right out of the window.

But then reality suddenly slammed back with a vengeance. The hospital speaker system crackled into life and she heard Kim, one of the hospital's junior nurses. Even through the dodgy hospital intercom she heard the fear in Kim's tone. 'Code Blue. Nurses' station. Code Blue.'

Code Blue!

What was happening with Marc was pure fantasy. This was the reality of her life.

She was out of the door and she was gone.

CHAPTER NINE

WHAT WAS HE supposed to do—go back to bed?

Code Blue was hospital speak almost the world over for 'Get here fast because someone's dying'. Usually it meant cardiac infarct—heart failure.

He was a cardiologist. A heart surgeon.

He was a patient. He was wearing matching boxer and T-shirt pyjamas.

The wheelchair was still beside the bed, left there by the footballer who'd brought him back from lunch. 'No one seems to need this, mate. You might as well keep it; it'll let you get around a bit.' He glanced at it and discarded the idea almost instantly. It was too clumsy. It'd take too long.

He had no crutches but even if he did he'd be no use to anyone if his shoulder slipped out again. There were rails all along the corridor so ambulant patients could practise their walking. 'I'm ambulant,' he said out loud, and managed to hop to the door, grab the rail with his good hand and proceed to demonstrate just how ambulant he really was.

It wasn't hard to find the source of the Code Blue. Less than a minute's hobbling had him reaching a turn in the corridor to see a cluster of people outside the nurses' station.

He could see two nurses, one with a crash cart, another kneeling. Someone on the floor.

Elsa was also kneeling, her crimson skirt flared around her.

'Grandpa,' she breathed, and his world seemed to still.

He'd met Robert McCrae—of course he had. The elderly doctor had given him the anaesthetic while Elsa had set his leg, and he'd chatted to him a couple of times over the last couple of days. In his late seventies, he'd thought Robert looked a bit too thin, a bit too pale. Marc had had every intention of cornering him before he left and casually offering a full heart check. 'Just to reassure Elsa...' he'd planned to say.

It was too late now. Or was it? 'Grandpa...' Elsa murmured again, and there was a hoarse whisper in response.

'I'll be fine, girl. Don't fuss.'

Not dead. Marc had been present at so many cardiac deaths. Why did this seem so personal? Why was his relief so profound?

'You weren't breathing.' That was the nurse by the crash cart. She looked as if she was about to burst into tears.

'Let me up. Give me a hand, girl,' Robert attempted to snap at Elsa, but the snap was little more than a whisper and Elsa was having none of it. She had the portable defibrillator at hand, and before he could argue she'd ripped his shirt open.

The old guy could scarcely breathe but he was still indignation personified. 'This is my best shirt.'

'Ex shirt,' she told him. 'Kim doesn't make mistakes, and if she said you stopped breathing then you stopped breathing. And you were still unconscious when I got here.'

'I just got a bit dizzy, that's all.'

'I'm fitting the pads in case we need them,' she told him. 'You know you'd do the same for any patient with collapse and a history of cardiac problems.' She looked up. 'Kim,

contact Geoff and Ryan. Tell 'em we need to lift a prostrate patient...'

'Prostrate?' It must be hard to sound outraged when
there was clear difficulty in breathing, but Robert managed it.

'And you'll stay prostrate until I say otherwise,' Elsa
told him, bossiness underpinned with a definite shake in
her voice. 'You taught me to be bossy in a crisis, Grandpa,
so don't you fight me when I follow your orders.'

'It's not a crisis.' But he'd had enough. He'd been trying to lift his head. Now he slumped back and let his protests die to nothing.

'Elsa, would you let me help?'

She was fitting the pads of the defibrillator. Designed to
jerk the heart back into motion when it stopped, it wasn't
necessary now that Robert was conscious, but the elderly
doctor had clearly lost consciousness, had clearly fallen.
There was something else going on here. If there'd been a
blockage then it could block again at any minute, and seconds would be precious.

She finished fitting the pads and then turned to Marc.
'Go back to bed,' she said quietly.

'Elsa, I have a broken leg, not the plague. You have a
cardiologist on site, and I may well be what your grandfather needs right now. Make use of me.'

He saw her hesitate, torn. Every instinct would be to
protect her patient—him. Every desire would be to do what
was best for her grandfather.

'Please, then,' she said gruffly, and he could hear the
emotion in the two words. Then she turned back to Robert. 'Grandpa, you remember Marc's here—Dr Pierce? You
know he's a cardiologist from Sydney? He's offered to ignore his broken leg and give his opinion.'

'What's he charging?' Robert demanded, and there was
a hint of humour in his thready voice that further reassured
Marc. He might have lost consciousness for a moment, but

the blood supply hadn't been cut off for long enough to cause even minor mental impairment.

'Cut rate special,' he said as one of the nurses moved forward to help him hop from the support of the handrail to where Robert lay. 'You fixed my leg, so I'll have a shot at fixing your heart.'

'Might be a damned sight harder to fix,' Robert growled.

'It might,' Marc said quietly. Robert was still on the floor and he dropped to join him. It was hardly the usual medical scene—patient on floor, doctor dressed in pyjamas also on floor, his back slabbed leg stretched out before him.

He wedged himself around so he was side-on to Robert. Elsa was on the other side and a glance told him the strain she was under. Her face was almost as pale as her grandfather's.

And there was reason. Robert's breathing was fast, shallow, laboured. His skin was bluish, cool to the touch. Marc lifted his wrist and kept his face impassive as he noted the racing pulse. For all his fieriness, his attempt at humour, Robert was looking terrified.

'Pain?' Marc asked and watched him close his eyes for a moment and then decide to be honest.

'Bad,' he conceded. 'Chest. Shoulder. Another bloody heart attack. Must be a minor one this time, though. I'll be all right.'

'You'll have to go back to Sydney,' Elsa managed, and Marc could still hear the tremor. Finding her grandfather unconscious must have been horrific. 'We'll get you stabilised and call for evacuation.'

'Leave things for a moment,' Marc said softly. He was looking further, seeing things he didn't like.

The probability was that this was a heart attack, hopefully small, but there was no guarantee it wouldn't be a precursor to a bigger one. Yes, evacuation was called for, to a hospital with a state-of-the-art cardiac facility, with a team of trained medics on board the flight. But the look on Robert's face... And what was beneath...

He was seeing swollen, bulging neck veins and they were acting like flashing lights to Marc's trained eye. The heart was pumping blood out, but there was some impediment to its return.

'Can I have your stethoscope?' he asked Elsa, and she handed it wordlessly across. He listened to the muffled heart sounds, and his unease deepened.

'Blood pressure?' he asked, and the nurse fitted the cuff. Low.

'What are you thinking?' It was Robert himself who demanded to know. This was doctor to doctor. There'd be no sugar-coating what he was starting to suspect, and it'd be an insult to even try.

'I'm thinking we need to exclude cardiac tamponade,' he said briefly. 'Your veins are swollen. Low blood pressure. Muffled heart sounds. That's Beck's triad—the three symptoms that make me sound clever when I'm just fitting a pattern to what's happening.'

There was an expletive from Robert, and Marc gave him what he hoped was a reassuring grin.

'Exactly. No sweat though, Robert, because even if I'm right I've coped with cardiac tamponade before and I can cope with it now.'

He glanced up at Elsa then, and saw her face had bleached even whiter. She'd know the risks.

Cardiac tamponade was indeed frightening. Caused by trauma, by cancer or sometimes by a heart attack, fluid or blood built up between the heart and the pericardium, the sac surrounding the heart. The pericardium consisted of two layers of tissue, with a small amount of fluid preventing friction between the layers. If this fluid built up, it put pressure on the heart, affecting its ability to pump blood around the body.

Robert might have just suffered a heart attack, or he

might have suffered a minor attack weeks ago. The pressure might have built slowly, finally causing collapse. Or the leak could be recent, the pressure building fast.

Regardless, cardiac tamponade meant there was no time for evacuation. The pressure had to be removed now.

The two guys who worked as occasional orderlies, handymen or gardeners appeared and seamlessly went into action, helping Elsa transfer Robert to a stretcher and then lifting him onto a trolley. One of the nurses helped Marc to his feet. He was swearing inwardly. He wanted two good legs. He wanted to be dressed—at least in the soft shirt and loose gym pants he'd worn to lunch. He wanted to feel professional, fully functional—he *needed* to be at the top of his game. This was a situation he was trained for, and he wanted the capacity to move fast.

'Can you organise an echocardiograph and a chest X-ray?' he asked Elsa. Dammit, he felt helpless. 'And can someone help me get dressed?'

'Marc, you can't…' Elsa's voice trailed off. If the ECG and chest X-ray confirmed the diagnosis, there was no choice and she—and her grandfather—would know it.

'Robert,' Marc said, taking a moment to rest a hand on the shoulder of the elderly doctor, 'you know what's at stake here. If it is indeed tamponade then we need to get the pressure off fast. You'll need to go to the mainland to get any underlying problems with your heart sorted, but the tamponade has to be fixed now. I might be a cardiologist with a gammy leg and a sore shoulder, but that doesn't interfere with my skills. If the echocardiograph confirms my diagnosis you'll need percutaneous drainage and that's a skill I have. Will you let me and your granddaughter make you safe?'

And the old man's hand came up and gripped his, hard. Marc could feel the tremor. He could feel the fear.

'Do what you have to do, son,' Robert managed. 'You

seem a damned idiot at bushwalking, but I assume you're not the same in an operating theatre.'

'I'm very good,' Marc told him. This was no time for false modesty. 'I'm who you need right now, gammy leg or not. Trust me.'

'I trust you,' Robert said and the grip on his hand tightened.

'Marc...' It was Elsa, and there was fear in her voice, too.

'And so must you, girl,' Robert said, forcefully now, as he directed his attention to his granddaughter. 'We're lucky to have a cardiologist to hand, even if you did have to crawl underground and sleep with him for a full night to get him here.'

The echocardiograph reinforced Marc's diagnosis. The chest X-ray and ultrasound confirmed it. Elsa stared at the image on the ultrasound screen and felt ill.

If she'd been on her own here she couldn't have coped. She'd have had to evacuate her grandfather, and with the pressure building in the hours it would have taken to get him to Sydney... The outcome didn't bear thinking of.

And doing such a procedure herself? She knew the principles, but to perform the drainage, especially on someone who was probably compromised with heart damage anyway... When that someone was her grandfather... To insert a needle into such a risky place, to do no damage...

She didn't need to. She had a cardiologist right here. The knowledge made her feel dizzy.

Marc was scrubbing. The nurses had found a stool with wheels and height adjustment. At full stretch it made him tall enough to use the sinks, to operate, to be fully functional.

He looked across at her as Maggie helped him on with theatre gear, and he must have seen the tension.

'It's okay,' he told her gently. 'We have this in hand.

We'll try percutaneous drainage first. If that doesn't work then we'll move to the subxiphoid approach—taking away a slice of the pericardium. But I don't anticipate that. We'll give him the lightest possible general—I don't want any more risk to his breathing than he already has. While you monitor that, then I'll use the ultrasound to guide a nice fat needle into the cavity, set up a catheter and let it drain.'

Said like that it sounded simple. She knew it wasn't.

'Then we'll move him to Sydney and let the big boys deal with whatever the underlying cause is,' Marc told her, his voice calm, reassuring but firm. She wasn't the doctor here. She wasn't being asked to make decisions—she was being told the best course of action for her grandpa. 'Given his history, I'm almost sure this'll have been caused by another heart attack. Maybe a small one. There's no sign of neurological impairment. This seems straightforward. For me this is common or garden repair work, Dr McCrae, so you can take that fearful look off your face, accept that your grandpa's going to live and turn into the professional I know you are.'

His gaze was still on her face, his look steady, strong, sure. *You can do this,* his gaze said. And *I need a doctor, not a whimpering relative.*

Right. She could do this.

She must.

And half an hour later the thing was done. A light anaesthetic. An awful, breath-holding time while she watched as Marc used the ultrasound wand to guide the needle into position.

His approach was sure, unhesitating, skilled.

Using an eight-centimetre, eighteen-gauge angio-catheter—thank heaven for the comprehensive surgical kit the island possessed—watching the ultrasound every fraction of an inch of the way, he slowly, skilfully found what he was looking for. When the pericardial sac was entered there was a grunt of satisfaction as the ultrasound showed the needle where he needed it to be. Slowly he advanced the sheath and withdrew the needle. A guide wire was then advanced through the angiocatheter, followed by a dilator and a pigtail catheter.

'Yes!' he said with relief as the fluid started to flow, as the tamponade started to shrink, and that was the first time Elsa heard pressure in his voice. Even though he'd sounded sure, this was a procedure that took skill. Even now. Elsa was monitoring breathing, watching the heart monitor like a hawk, waiting for a reaction. Robert's heart was damaged. Any minute now…

'Not going to happen,' Marc said softly, glancing at the monitor and then her face. 'Fluid's coming off, and things are looking good.'

And so it was. Once the catheter was in place the pericardial fluid drained like a dream. The fluid would be submitted for culture and cytological analysis, checking for signs of something other than heart attack—trauma or cancer—but there seemed no sign of either.

She watched on, staring at the monitor as if she could will the heartbeat to strengthen. And it did.

'I'm only draining a thousand mil,' Marc told her. 'I don't want hypotensive shock. But I'm pretty sure it's enough to keep him safe.'

It maybe it was. Robert's heart had returned to a reassuringly normal rhythm. He was breathing on his own now, and when Elsa removed the oxygen his chest rose and fell normally. His colour was returning. He was safe.

For now. There was still the underlying cause to treat.

'I told one of the nurses to arrange evacuation,' Marc said briefly, once again watching her face. 'He'll need more aspirations, usually every four to six hours. We'll do another just as he leaves, and then the cardiac unit in Sydney can take over.' Robert was already stirring. The anaesthetic had been the lightest possible. 'Hey, Robert,' Marc said gently, and he took the old man's hand. 'All done. How do you feel?'

There was silence for a couple of moments while Robert got his bearings, while his world settled. They watched him take conscious breaths, watched him feel his chest expand, watched him realise the pressure was no longer there.

'Beautiful,' he murmured, and Elsa smiled and smiled and gripped Robert's hands and then decided she needed to wipe away a stupid tear that was tracking down her cheek. Only she couldn't because she was holding onto her grandpa.

And then Marc was leaning over the table and wiping it away for her, smiling at them both. 'Well done, Dr McCrae,' he told her.

'There was nothing well done about it,' she said gruffly. 'Marc operated, Grandpa, not me.'

'And your granddaughter held it together, acted professionally with a brilliant anaesthetic and didn't once behave like you'd scared her out of her wits,' Marc said, still smiling at her. 'But now she needs to act like a relative. Elsa, I want you to go pack for your grandpa and for yourself. Robert, we're evacuating you to Sydney. You know the underlying cause of the tamponade is most likely to have been another heart attack, or complications from the last one. There'll be an emergency physician on board the plane to keep you safe in transit. You'll be assessed fully in Sydney, so you need to be prepared to stay for a while. Hope for the best—maybe another stent—but prepare for a full bypass. That could mean a two-week stay before they let you fly home. Elsa, you know there's relative accommodation at the hospital. When we asked for the evac plane we asked for that to be organised as well.'

'But...' Elsa was staring at him in dismay '... I can't go. Two weeks...'

'You have no choice.'

'When Grandpa had his last attack and had the stent

inserted, I was away for two days,' she told him, almost stammering. 'There was no one here to take over. We got away without a disaster that time, but for the island to have no doctor...'

'Elsa'll stay here,' Robert growled. 'There's no need to come with me. It's a fuss over nothing.'

But there was every need. Elsa stared down at her grandpa and saw it in his eyes.

This latest episode would have terrified him. Not being able to breathe... Feeling the pressure build... Oh, thank God for Marc, but the old man wasn't out of the woods yet, and she could see by his face that he knew it.

Yes, there'd be an emergency physician on the plane, but Grandpa needed family beside him. He needed her. She *had* to be with him, but she could see the warring needs on her grandfather's face. He would know the risks. And for there to be no doctor on the island at all...

'You have to stay,' Robert muttered grimly. 'Don't be a fool, girl. You think we can get a locum at this short notice, at this time of year? You know after Christmas half of Australia goes to sleep and the other half goes to the beach until mid-January. Or they come here and break their necks doing damned silly things. You have no choice. I'll be fine, girl.'

But still she saw the fear—and she glanced up at Marc and realised that he'd seen it too.

'There's no need for a locum,' he said gently. 'Aren't you lucky that you already have a resident doctor?'

They both stared at him, their expressions suggesting he'd suddenly grown two heads. 'You?' Elsa stammered, as if such a thing was tantamount to suggesting a five-year-old took over the medical needs of the island.

'Don't look at me as if I'm an idiot,' he told them. 'I know I'm a cardiologist, but I have basic skills as well. I'm sure I can remember the treatment for nice normal things like the common cold. Isn't it to give the patient honey and lemon drinks and it'll cure itself? I can probably cope with that.' He grinned, his smile encouraging them to override their fear.

'Seriously,' he continued, 'you have a great nursing staff. My shoulder's sore but it's firmly back in place and I won't be needing to lift any weights. I know a slightly battered doctor is less than ideal, but it seems a darned sight better than no doctor at all. I have a bung leg but I'll not be running any races. We can organise someone to drive me if I need to go off site. I have the next two weeks off. I know I should be in St Moritz but as far as prestige points go when I finally head back to work, two weeks on Gannet Island with a climbing injury cuts it almost as well.'

'A climbing injury? More like a falling down a hole injury,' Elsa said before she could help herself, and his grin widened.

'Are you intending to mess with my hero image, Dr McCrae?'

'Let him be heroic if that's what's needed for him to stay here,' Robert said gruffly, and reached out and took Marc's hand. 'I'll even sign something to say you fell down the hole saving…what, a kitten? Would that do?'

'A kitten?' Elsa said, astounded.

'He was saving Sherlock then,' Robert said, and the elderly doctor even managed a chuckle. 'Sherlock won't mind sacrificing his pride for the greater good.'

'I'll even take care of Sherlock while you're away,' Marc offered. 'Or Sherlock might take care of me.'

But Elsa wasn't smiling. 'Grandpa, you know I can't leave. We can't ask this of Marc.'

'Let's get this down to basics,' Marc demanded. 'Robert, do you want your granddaughter to come with you?' He fixed Robert with a look that demanded honesty. And the elderly doctor looked from him to Elsa and back again.

He'd know the odds. An underlying heart attack had

probably caused the tamponade, and the damage wasn't yet diagnosed. He was still in peril and he knew it.

'I do,' he whispered, and Elsa's face twisted in fear and uncertainty.

'And Elsa, do you want your grandpa to go alone?'

'Of course not. But...'

'Then you have no choice,' Marc said gently.

'I know. But oh, Grandpa...'

'Now don't you make this into a big deal just because I said I need you,' Robert managed. He managed a smile, fighting to recover his pride. 'Love, you know I hate hospital coffee. I'll... I'll need someone to bring me a decent cup a couple of times a day.'

'So there you are,' Marc told her. 'You have two weeks of being personal barista for your grandfather, while a one-legged doctor takes over all your duties on the island. You might need to organise someone else to walk Sherlock, but for the rest... All sorted.'

'Marc...'

'Enough.' He put his hand out and cupped her chin, forcing her gaze to meet his, suddenly stern.

'As your grandpa says, don't make a fuss,' he said softly. 'Just do what you need to do. I suspect your grandpa's coffee needs won't be too extensive. You might even have time to see a bit of Sydney at the same time. You might even have time to have fun.'

Elsa disappeared to pack and probably to do a bit of panicking on the side.

Marc returned to his nice, quiet hospital bed and did a bit of panicking himself. What had he let himself in for? He'd offered to be the island doctor for up to two weeks. A family doctor.

He hadn't done any family medicine since a placement during internship. He remembered minor illnesses, minor injuries, stress, depression, teen pregnancies, the problems of the elderly with multiple health problems. He remembered being hit by an elderly patient because he couldn't justify signing a form saying the old guy could retain his car licence.

'You need to learn to care,' the family doctor he'd been working beside had told him. 'If you genuinely care for your patients, then everything else will follow. Empathy is everything—emotional connection.'

The experience had confirmed Marc's decision to specialise in heart surgery. He'd been raised to be emotionally distant. The idea of providing an emotional connection to his patients seemed impossible.

Elsa had the ability, he thought, remembering the faces of those who'd received her extraordinary gifts. She had it in spades. Which was why she was a family doctor and he wasn't.

Except now he was, for two weeks.

No one could expect emotional connection in two weeks, he told himself. He'd offered because it was the least he could do—after all, Elsa had saved his life. This would repay a debt. He could see patients in need and then walk away.

And then the door opened, tentatively. It was Maggie. Despite their initial conflict over the Dorothy the Dinosaur tablet, she'd helped care for him, she'd assisted in Robert's surgery with efficiency and he was aware that she was an excellent nurse.

'Are you ready to start work?' she asked.

'What, now?'

'Bradley Norfolk's just fallen off his Christmas trampoline,' she told him. 'It looks like a greenstick arm fracture. Are you up for it?' She eyed him, lying on his pillows, his bedding pulled up to his chin. 'You look like a new intern,' she said bluntly, and she grinned. 'Scared rigid.'

Maybe it was time to pull himself together. He pushed back his covers, sat up and swung his bad leg off the bed.

'We're setting you up with a permanent wheelchair,' she told him. 'With leg support so your leg's out straight.'

'I can manage without a wheelchair.'

'Elsa's orders. She says she doesn't want any more pressure on that arm, and if you're balancing then you're at risk.'

His first reaction was to reject the wheelchair out of hand—he needed to act like a doctor, not a patient. But his shoulder was still painful. Elsa's suggestion was sensible.

He needed to be sensible.

'For today and maybe for tomorrow,' he told Maggie. 'By then I should be able to manage with sticks.' Even that revolted him.

'Very wise,' Maggie said, and her smile widened. 'You know, the islanders have learned it's much easier to do what Doc Elsa says. She's pretty much always right. If you're standing in for her you have pretty big shoes to fill.'

'Just lucky my foot's already swollen then,' he said grimly. 'Maggie, I'm going to need more clothes.'

'Elsa's already given orders,' she told him. 'We're on it.'

'Then Maggie…'

'Yes?'

'It's time for Elsa to stop giving the orders,' he told her. 'From now on, you're stuck with me.'

The evacuation crew oozed medical competence. The doctor in charge listened to Elsa's stuttered explanation, spoke briefly to Robert—and then did a hand-over with Marc.

Marc was in his wheelchair, but his medical competence matched the medic in charge. They exchanged notes, films, cardiographs. Elsa was on the sidelines, holding Robert's hand.

Robert was the patient. Elsa was family.

'Takes a bit of getting used to,' Robert growled. He was on the transfer trolley, waiting to be lifted into the plane.

'Yeah.'

'He'll do good by us. The island's in good hands.' He was trying to reassure her. For heaven's sake...

'I'm sure he will,' she managed, and as she listened to the clipped professional handover between the two men she knew she was right. 'Except...'

'Except Dotty Morrison might have to forgo her placebo pills for a while,' Robert said with a forced chuckle, and Elsa thought of the pills she'd been prescribing for the old lady affected by Alzheimer's for the last few months and grimaced.

'I haven't even told him about that.'

'Told me what?' Finishing his handover, Marc had wheeled himself across to join them.

'Dotty Morrison,' Elsa told him, thinking of all the other things she hadn't told him. 'She has Alzheimer's and high blood pressure. She's struggling to stay at home and her medication's the biggest hurdle—she takes it too often or not at all, but she hates the thought of not being in charge. So now I give her placebos, telling her to take one every morning, one every night. Her daughter comes around twice a day with her 'extra' pills—the real ones—which she tells her are multivitamins. Dotty takes them to humour her, but she knows the ones I prescribe and she gets from the pharmacist are the important ones. She takes them whenever she thinks it might be morning or night and everyone's happy.'

'And they're what? Sugar pills?'

'Sugar pills?' Elsa asked incredulously. 'No such thing. I give her a nice formal script that says "Disaccharide C12H22O11, twice daily".'

'Which is sugar.'

'If you're going to be pedantic, then yes,' she said with asperity, 'but don't you dare tell Dotty. I tell her it's to improve cerebral function—she likes that because she knows she forgets things. She takes her script along to the pharmacy, Doug puts her pills in a bottle with her name on and everyone's happy. Except she tends to go through her bottle about once a week and sometimes more, and she loses her repeat scripts so I expect you'll see her soon. Marc, there's so much I haven't told you.'

'He'll be all right, girl,' Robert said, gripping Marc's hand as the crew prepared to lift him into the plane. 'If he's got his cardiology ticket he must have the brains to prescribe sugar pills and he can always phone you. Thank you, son,' he said and then he was lifted up and away.

The medic crew boarded the plane, busying themselves, fitting Robert with the equipment, the oxygen, the stabilisers he'd need for the journey. Marc and Elsa were finally left alone.

'I don't… I can't think what to say,' Elsa told him.

'Don't say anything. You're not going out of contact. If someone presents at the surgery demanding medication for their leprosy or whatever, I have your number.'

'I can't thank you…'

'And I can't thank you. So let's not.'

'Marc…'

'Just relax. Robert's in good hands. He'll be fine. You might even have a chance of a holiday yourself.'

'If he doesn't need me, I can come home.'

'He will need you. Hospital's a lonely place with no family.' Before she could stop him he'd pushed himself to his feet. Instinctively she reached forward to steady him, but afterwards she couldn't remember whether he'd gripped her hands before she'd gripped his.

Regardless, she gripped and he held, or vice versa.

He was her patient. No, he wasn't her patient now. He was the doctor who'd saved her grandfather's life.

He was Marc.

The three images were blurring. Boundaries weren't being crossed, they were dissolving.

'Your grandpa will be fine,' he said, strongly now. 'I've phoned my boss—he's head of cardiology at Sydney Central. He's promised to take on Robert's care himself and there's no one better. This guy here...' he motioned into the plane, to the medic in charge '...he's the best as well. The only extra Robert needs is family, and in you he has gold. Take care of yourself, Elsa. Come back with a patched-up grandpa but come back rested yourself. I can't think of anyone who deserves a break more.'

'Marc...'

'Just go,' he said softly, but his grip on her hands tightened. 'But I'll be in touch and thinking of you every step of the way.'

She looked up at him, feeling dazed. Too much was happening, too fast.

He was holding her. For support, she told herself frantically but as her gaze met his she knew it was no such thing. His eyes were dark, fathomless, compelling. There was a faint smile, a question—an answer? She couldn't look away.

The question? It was being asked of her and all she had to do was respond. Which was what she did. Almost of their own volition her feet tilted so she was on tiptoe. So lips could meet.

And kiss.

Warmth, heat, strength.

Or maybe it was the opposite of strength. Maybe it was loss of control, for how could she be in control when she was being kissed like this?

Twice in one day. Twice! But this was different.

Behind them were Geoff and Ryan, the hospital orderlies who'd helped load Robert into the ambulance for transport to the runway and were now waiting to take Marc back to the hospital. There were a couple of airport workers round the plane—locals.

News of this kiss would be all over the island before the plane even took off.

But right now she couldn't care less. How could she

care? All that mattered was the feel of Marc holding her. He'd saved her grandpa. He was holding her steady. He was her rock.

Her rock with a broken leg. Her rock who was here for only two weeks. He was her rock who was supposed to be in St Moritz right now with his glamorous ex-girlfriend.

She had no right to kiss him, and he had no right to kiss her. But still she clung for one last, long sweet moment. It was a moment of madness, a moment that she knew must mean nothing, but she took it, she savoured it, she loved it.

And then there was an apologetic cough from behind Marc's shoulder.

'Sorry miss, but we need to get going,' one of the medics called to Elsa. 'You need to board. Don't worry, sir, we'll take good care of them and bring them home safe.'

Home safe... Two lovely words.

But the medic was looking at her with sympathy. He thought he was tearing her away from...her partner? Her lover?

No such thing. She didn't want sympathy, and she didn't...couldn't...want complications.

'I'm ready to go,' she managed, struggling to sound professional, as if she hadn't just been kissed so thoroughly she felt dizzy. 'Thank you for your help, Dr Pierce. I'll see you soon.'

'I hope so,' he said, and lifted the back of his hand to brush her cheek. It was a gesture of farewell, an acknowledgement of times shared, of forced intimacy that was now over, and there was no reason for it to make her feel even more disoriented than she already was.

But disoriented was too simple a word to describe what she was feeling. She needed to join her grandfather in the plane, but turning and walking away from Marc felt wrong.

CHAPTER TEN

'I'VE RUN OUT of pills.'

'Already?' It was just as well he'd been warned. This was the first clinic on Boxing Day—'for urgent cases only'—but Dotty Morrison had insisted she was tacked onto the end of his list.

'I think I might have doubled up,' the little lady said doubtfully. 'What with Christmas and all. But an extra pill or two won't hurt me, will it, Doctor?'

He checked. Elsa's notes were comprehensive and, worded in case Dotty caught sight of them, carefully benign.

'Dr McCrae wrote you a script with five repeats only last week,' he said cautiously. 'Have you used them all?'

'Oh, no, Doctor. It was much longer than a week ago. The chemist says I should leave the script at the pharmacy, but they keep muddling them. I do like to keep an eye on my own medications. It's my body, isn't that right, Doctor? I have a responsibility to care for what goes into it.'

'You certainly do,' Marc said, suppressing a grin as he replaced her script.

She accepted it with grace and checked it with care. 'Thank you, dear,' she told him. 'But you're not as neat as our Dr Elsa.'

'I'm afraid I'm not. I'm not as fast either.' Dottie had

been kept waiting three-quarters of an hour for her appointment.

'Well, that's because you've broken your leg,' Dottie said reasonably.

It wasn't exactly that, he thought as he bade the elderly lady goodbye. It was because family medical practice required skills Marc had pretty much forgotten. He'd just had to cope with a teenager whose acne had flared up. She was hysterical because her family was heading to Sydney to meet friends—'and there's this boy...'

He'd had to excuse himself 'to take an urgent phone call' which involved hobbling out to Reception to check current meds for acne, correct dosages, contraindications.

There'd been many 'urgent phone calls' this morning. But finally he was done. He had house calls scheduled for later this afternoon—either Geoff or Ryan would drive him—but he had time to put his leg up for half an hour and field a call from Elsa.

'How's it going?' he asked.

Her voice sounded tense, distracted and he thought *uh-oh*.

'He's okay.'

Then he heard her pause and take a deep breath. 'No. More than okay. The tamponade's pretty much settled—they've stopped the draining.' That made sense. The pericardium had to retain a little fluid to protect the heart. 'But you were right. He's had another heart attack. When pressed, he admitted he'd had what he thought was an event during the night while I was on the mountain with you. It passed and he didn't want to worry me—he said he'd think about it after Christmas. Anyway, he's in the right hands now. He's scheduled for a quadruple bypass late this afternoon, but he's already worrying about the need to spend time here in cardio rehab. His biggest worry is me being here rather than back on the island.'

'And you? Are you worrying about being there rather than back on the island?'

'Of course,' she said simply. 'I can't help it. Have there been any problems?'

'No.'

'Not a one?'

'My biggest hurdle so far has been finding current treatment for teenage acne,' he admitted. 'I had Jess Lowan here, threatening suicide or worse. It seems she's in love with the son of family friends, and how can she face him with zits on her nose?'

'I hope you took it seriously,' she told him. 'Jess is… high strung to say the least.'

'I took it very seriously. The treatment's changed since I was in med school but, thanks to the internet, Jess has now been hit with a barrage of treatment that should effectively nuke every zit before it has a chance to interfere with the course of young love. I just hope he's worth it.'

'Oh, dear. You know she'll be in love with someone else next week.'

'Someone who prefers his women with zits? Then Houston, we have a problem. I see no chance of reversal.'

She chuckled but it sounded strained. 'Seriously though, Marc…'

'Seriously, I'm doing well.' He let himself sound serious too, still hearing the stress in her voice. 'There's been no pressure. I have two house calls to make this afternoon, then a simple ward round, and as long as everything stays quiet I'll be in bed with a book by eight-thirty.'

'When you should be drinking mulled wine with your mates in St Moritz.'

'I'm not missing it a bit.' And as he said it he realised it was true. The situation here was challenging—and he didn't mind this phone call with Elsa. There'd be more of them, he knew. The thought of working as he was doing, of helping her out for two weeks…it wasn't a penance.

'You know things will hot up from today?' Elsa warned. 'The holiday crowds start streaming in on Boxing Day, and they do really dumb things.'

'Like falling down holes.'

'Like falling down holes,' she agreed. 'Though the guys have hiked back up to where you fell and fenced off that whole area, with huge warning signs saying death and destruction for all who enter here. It's a pity we can't do that for every peril on the island. Like the sun. What's the betting you'll have half a dozen cases of sunstroke by this time tomorrow? Our work practically quadruples in the holiday period.'

He thought about that. Today had been relatively quiet— no dramas, a simple clinic and stable inpatients. Still, by the end of the day he'd have worked reasonably hard.

If it quadrupled…

'How do you cope?'

'I have Grandpa.'

'You won't have your grandpa for a few weeks. He's going to need decent rehab. Seriously.'

'Which is why I'll rest up before I come home. I know I need to stay. If I leave Grandpa here he'll be on the next plane after me. But Marc, I'm worrying about you coping.'

'I'll read up on sunstroke before I go to bed tonight.'

'It won't just be sunstroke. You don't have… I don't know…a friend who could help? Maybe your Kayla? Is she another doctor?'

'She is,' he told her. 'But she's not my Kayla and there's not a snowball's chance in a bushfire she'll cut her holiday short to come here.'

'Another colleague then?' She was clutching at straws. 'If I stay here for two full weeks you will need help.'

'And you'll need help long-term,' he told her. 'At his age and after two heart attacks, it's time for Robert to think of retiring.'

'You think I don't know that?'

'So you need to think about hiring a full-time partner.'

'Like that's going to happen.'

'Why not?'

'Because it's not viable,' she said shortly. 'An island with a population of seven hundred provides a meagre income. The six islands have far too much medical need for me to handle alone, but they're too far apart to service. In an ideal world, with more doctors and a fast ferry service, we could set up a central medical centre on Gannet. But a ferry service requires money the islanders don't have and, even if there was one, no island doctor could make the kind of money I bet you're making in Sydney. Why would anyone come here by choice?'

She caught herself, and he heard her pause and regroup. 'Sorry. That was uncalled for. The money thing's minor but I am facing the problem that without Grandpa's help...' Her voice trailed off.

'Without his help maybe you need to leave the island?' he said gently. 'It seems harsh but someone else will take your place.'

'I couldn't think of leaving.'

'You need to think about it. With your grandpa's medical needs he'd be much safer on the mainland. And you... You've already said you feel constricted here.'

'But it's *my* island,' she said, suddenly angry. '*My* home. You don't get that?'

'There are lots of other places in the world.'

'Like St Moritz. No, that was mean. But where could I work? In a city clinic so Grandpa could be within cooee of specialist help? We'd both hate that. Or a country practice where my problems would be the same—and I wouldn't be surrounded by family.'

'You'd have Robert.'

'He's only one small part of my family. My family's the whole island. It's home. You must see, Marc...' She broke off and sighed. 'Enough. My future's not your problem and you have your own problems. Acne to sort. A leg that needs resting.'

'The acne's sorted and my leg's resting as we speak.'

'Then rest some more,' she told him. 'I'll return as soon as possible.'

'As soon as the doctors say it's safe for your grandfather to be here?' He hesitated but it had to be said. 'Elsa, there'll always be underlying medical problems. It seems harsh to say it, but I won't be here to help next time.'

She faltered at that, but then gathered herself again. 'That has to be okay. We've managed to cope without you before. Go rest that leg, Marc. Goodbye.'

She abandoned her phone and walked out onto the balcony. The apartments designed for hospital relatives were spartan but the views were fantastic. At least they were fantastic if she stood at the very far end and leaned out. She could even see the Opera House and the harbour bridge, only her angle was a bit precarious.

She stopped leaning and stood and watched the traffic below. *So* much traffic. She could see the sea if she craned her neck, but she couldn't smell it. All she could smell was traffic fumes.

She was so homesick…

Oh, for heaven's sake, she liked visiting Sydney. She liked the shopping, the restaurants, the anonymity. It was only the fear of the last twenty-four hours that was making her feel bereft.

But it was also the thought of her conversation with Marc. The difficulties of continuing on the island as her grandpa grew older.

She thought of Robert's heart, the risks of returning long-term to the island, the difficulty of coping as the island's only doctor. Even if he wanted to, Robert could hardly continue—she knew that. She'd be on her own.

And with that came a wash of despair so profound that she found she was shaking.

'Oh, cut it out.' She said it out loud, scolding herself. 'You won't be on your own. You'll have all the islanders. And if things get really desperate you can always marry Tony and have a tribe of kids and never feel lonely again.'

Except...loneliness wasn't always about a lack of people. Loneliness was being without a person.

One special person.

Marc?

'Well, you can cut that out too,' she said, even louder. 'You've known the man for what, four days, and here you are fantasising about him...

'I kind of like fantasising about him.' She was arguing with herself now. 'If I moved to Sydney I might...we might...

'And ditto for that thought, too.' Her own two-way conversation was getting heated. 'He's a high-flying doctor with high-flying friends. If I moved to Sydney I'd be lucky to get a job in some outer suburban clinic, somewhere cheap enough for us to live, with an increasingly dependent grandpa. There's not the slightest chance there'd be anything between me and Marc.

'But he kissed me.' There it was, a solid fact. She tried to hug it to herself as a promise—and failed.

'So he's a good kisser,' her sane self argued. 'He only kissed me to make me feel better. It's probably quicker and easier for a guy like that to give a decent kiss than to say "I hope you feel better soon".'

Luckily her sense of humour stepped in there to make her grin at the suddenly ridiculous vision of Marc doing ward rounds, kissing everyone as he went.

Like he'd kissed her?

Her fingers moved almost involuntarily to her mouth, as if she could still feel the pressure of his lips. His warmth, his strength, his solid, comforting, sexy, amazing self.

Marc…

'You're behaving like a teenager with a crush,' she told herself harshly, and stared down at the traffic again. 'Me and Marc? You're dreaming. Like me and Grandpa moving to Sydney. No and no and no.'

The thought of Robert dragged her out of her pointless conversation with herself, back to reality. She needed to head back to Intensive Care to see him. He'd be nervous about the upcoming surgery—no, he'd be terrified. She'd need every resource she possessed to calm him.

'So stop thinking about Marc and think about Grandpa.'

'I am thinking about Grandpa,' she said out loud again. 'And I'm thinking about me and the island and a heart specialist with a broken leg who's so far out of my league that I need my head read to be thinking about him. I need to get Grandpa better and then go home. Maybe even to Tony.

'Are you out of your mind? Tony? No!

'Yeah, but five little Tonys might make you happy.

'Buy yourself five dogs,' she snapped to herself. 'Dogs are a much safer bet than people any day.'

CHAPTER ELEVEN

TWELVE DAYS LATER Elsa and Robert flew back to the island on the normal passenger flight. Elsa had told Marc they were coming. He'd had every intention of meeting the plane, but where medicine was concerned plans were made to be broken.

He'd been inundated with minor issues since Boxing Day—sunburn, sunstroke, lacerations, stomach upsets, a couple of kids with alcohol poisoning after drinking their father's high shelf spirits on New Year's Eve. The works.

When Elsa and Robert's plane touched down he was in Theatre, sewing up a lacerated thigh. Bob Cruikshank, the local realtor, had hired tradesmen to construct a cluster of holiday cottages, and progress was slow. In an attempt to hurry things up over the holiday period he'd bought himself a chainsaw to cut planking, with the aim of building the decks himself. It wasn't his brightest idea. That he hadn't bled to death was pure luck. A neighbour had heard his yell and knew enough to apply pressure while calling for help.

'I guess you need training to operate those things,' Bob had said feebly, as Macka's police van-cum-ambulance had brought him in.

'I imagine chainsaw operation doesn't get included in most realtor training manuals,' Marc agreed. The cut was deep and filthy. He was incredibly lucky he hadn't cut nerves.

Marc would have preferred to use local anaesthetic but Bob was deeply shocked and agitated. It had to be a general anaesthetic, using Maggie to monitor breathing.

It wasn't optimal but it was the only choice. Then, halfway through the procedure, Elsa walked in. 'Hi, guys,' she said as she stood in the doorway. 'Anything I can do to help?'

'Oh, thank heaven,' Maggie said vehemently.

Marc had his forceps on a sliver of wood that was dangerously close to the artery. He couldn't afford to look up. It didn't stop him reacting, though. Elsa was back. Maggie's 'thank heaven' didn't begin to describe the sensation he felt hearing her voice.

His reaction was disproportionate. Undeniable.

'Hooray, you're back,' Maggie was saying. 'Can you take over here? Doc Pierce has been talking me through it, but we're worried about his oxygen levels.' Then she amended the statement. 'No, *Dr Pierce* is worried about Bob's oxygen levels. My job's just to tell him what the monitors are saying and doing what he tells me.'

'They told me out front what's been happening,' Elsa said briefly. 'I've already scrubbed.'

'Then I'm back to being nurse assistant.' Maggie handed over to Elsa, and Marc's stress level dropped about tenfold. He'd been operating at the same time as watching and instructing Maggie. Bob was a big man with background health issues, and the anaesthetic was as fraught as the surgery itself.

The question slammed back, as it had hit him over and over for the past few days. How the hell could Elsa work here alone?

The splinter of wood finally came free. He gave a grunt of satisfaction and glanced up.

'Welcome back,' he said, and smiled. She looked strained, he thought, but she still looked great. Fantastic.

Something deep in his gut seemed to clench. It was all he could do not to abandon Bob and go hug her.

'Thank you,' she said primly. 'How's the needlework?'

'Basic.' Somehow he made his voice prosaic. Professional. As if she was a colleague and nothing else. 'If I'd realised how grubby this injury was internally, I'd have had him evacuated. I'm just lucky we didn't try this under local.'

'Bob would never had cooperated under local,' she told him. 'He'd have been demanding to take pictures for his Facebook page and probably fainting in the process.' She hesitated. 'You know he has emphysema?'

'I read his file.' He was starting a final clear and swab before stitching. 'That's why we've gone for the lightest anaesthesia possible. How's your grandpa?'

'Okay. Resting.'

'He should have stayed another week.'

'You try telling him that. He's pig-stubborn.'

'Too pig-stubborn to accept he needs to back right off, workwise?'

'I guess…' She sighed. 'He accepts that.'

'Excellent.' And then he threw out the question which had become a constant drumming in his head as the load of tourist patients had escalated. 'Elsa, how the hell are you going to manage here on your own?'

There was a moment's silence. Too long a silence.

'I'll manage,' she said at last. 'Did I tell you I spent a year's surgery rotation before I came back to the island?' She sounded as if she was struggling for lightness.

'Yeah, but *I* didn't do a year's anaesthetic training.' That was Maggie, entering the conversation with force. She handed Marc a threaded needle and glanced at Elsa with concern. 'Marc's been great, talking me through anaesthetising while he worked, but it's given us both heebie-jeebies. Is Robert going to be well enough to keep this up?'

'I guess. If…if that's all he does.'

'That's not viable and you know it,' Marc growled, thinking of the massive mix of human needs he'd been called on to fill over the past days. 'And you know I'm not just talking about this incident. Elsa, you need help.'

'No other doctor will want to work here with what we can offer.' She said it lightly, as if it didn't matter so much, but he knew it did. 'I need a full-time income, and there's not enough work during non-holiday periods to support two full-time doctors. Not unless we could somehow join the outer islands to form a bigger service, and where would we get the money to do that? We've approached the government before and it's not possible.'

'Then you need to leave,' he said bluntly. 'Maybe offer the job to a couple who might be happy to work here as one and a half doctors.'

'And where would that leave Grandpa and me?' She tilted her chin and met his look head-on. 'It's not your problem, Dr Pierce, so butt out. Right... Are you ready for reverse? You won't want to keep him under for any longer than you need to.'

'Go teach your grandmother to suck eggs,' Marc said, casting her a smile but seeing the strain behind her eyes.

'Sorry... Doctor,' she muttered.

'That's quite all right... Doctor,' he said and tried for another smile. 'And of course you're right to advise me. If you've done a year's surgery rotation and you know the patient you're equipped to give me advice.'

'I'm not sure what I'm equipped for any more,' she said heavily. 'But I suspect I'm about to find out.'

With surgery finished, and with Bob surfacing to hear his wife informing him she'd tossed his chainsaw off a cliff and if he ever lifted so much as a pair of scissors from now on she'd do the same with them, Marc was left with a gap until afternoon clinic. He escaped the escalating row in Bob's room—'Geez, Marjorie, do you know how much that chainsaw cost?'—and limped out to the hospital veranda. He needed to think.

The raised voices of the Cruikshanks followed him. There was little escape on this island, he thought, and then wondered how could Elsa stand it. But she'd been bred into it, he thought. She'd been inculcated with a sense of obligation to the islanders since she was seven. Plus she had her obligation to her grandfather.

But she loved her grandfather. Of course she did. He knew that, but he was on shaky ground here. There wasn't a lot of emotion in his background.

He didn't get the love thing, but somehow that was where his thoughts were heading. The sensation that had overwhelmed him when she'd walked into Theatre had almost blown him away. Was that love? It didn't make sense, and Marc Pierce was a man who liked to make sense of his world.

So make sense of the quandary Elsa has found herself in, he told himself. It was the least he could do.

The least he could do...

Elsa McCrae.

The two collections of words didn't seem to go together.

Elsa was a colleague. She'd saved his life. It made sense to feel gratitude, admiration, obligation. But none of those sentiments accounted for the wave of sensation he'd felt when she'd walked into the theatre just now, and that was troubling him. The way he'd felt then... The way he still felt...

'It's nonsense.' He said the words out loud and Ryan, who tended the hospital garden in between acting as an orderly, raised his head from where he'd been cutting back ferns and looked a query.

'What makes no sense, Doc?'

This dratted island! Was nowhere private? He hadn't realised Ryan was there. He'd been so caught up in his thoughts.

So say nothing, he told himself. This was his business, not the business of the whole island. Tell Ryan to mind his own.

What came out instead was, 'It makes no sense how two weeks can change your life.'

Ryan rose and scratched filthy fingers on his hat. 'Mate, you can drop dead in two weeks,' he said cheerfully. 'Hey, you might have starved to death in that cave and that wouldn't have even taken two weeks. That would have changed your life and then some.'

'I meant emotionally.' For heaven's sake, what was he doing? He was confessing all to a guy he hardly knew?

But Ryan seemed unperturbed—and also, to Marc's bewilderment, he seemed completely understanding. 'I'm guessing you've fallen for Doc Elsa,' he said simply, as though it was no big deal. 'Well, good luck with that, mate. Every young buck on the island seems to do it at some time. You'll get over it. They all do.'

'Thanks,' he managed weakly, and Ryan gave him a cheery wave and headed off to the compost bin with his wheelbarrow of fern clippings. Leaving his advice behind.

You'll get over it.

It was a sensible statement, the only problem being that Marc didn't exactly know what *it* was. This thing he was feeling.

It was temporary, he told himself. It was the result of shock and relief and gratitude.

Be practical.

'What you need to do is help her see her way forward,' he said, only this time he said it under his breath because the walls had ears around here.

But that brought another thought. If she did leave the island, if she and Robert moved to Sydney... 'Then maybe we'd have time to...'

And that was where he stopped, because when it came

to time to do *what*, he couldn't begin to imagine what that might be.

He should go find a cold shower, he told himself. He should at least talk sense into himself. Instead his thoughts kept drifting to a place that didn't seem at all sensible.

The way he felt about Elsa... The feeling in his gut as she'd walked into Theatre... It seemed a chasm he hadn't even noticed approaching.

So step back. Find solid ground. Accept the way you're feeling and work around it.

'Whatever happens, it'd have to be on my terms,' he said, and this time he said it out loud. He needed to reassure himself there was still room for him to be sensible.

He thought of his gorgeous harbourside house, inherited from his father, who'd died a few years ago. He thought of the space, the garden, the room for people to live pretty much separately.

'Even if we...' he started to say, but then he paused. He hadn't the least idea where his thoughts were headed.

Even as a child he'd known emotional ties were transitory and he'd never really considered the idea of a permanent relationship. When his friends fell in love he always felt as if he was looking at something totally foreign to him. But with Elsa suddenly his mind was going there whether he willed it or not.

'But my life wouldn't have to change all that much.'

Something at the back of his mind was suddenly flabbergasted. He almost felt dizzy.

'What the hell are you thinking?' he demanded, out loud again, and quickly looked around to make sure Ryan hadn't returned.

He hadn't. He was free to argue with himself.

'I have no idea,' he confessed to the sensible part of his brain, but sensible wasn't winning right now.

Nothing was winning. He kept sitting there. He needed to get his head clear. He needed a plan.

It didn't happen. The dizziness stayed.

Finally he shook his head and limped back into the hospital. He needed something to do. Something medical. Something that had nothing to do with the weird infighting that was going on in his head.

Elsa stayed busy for the rest of the day. Marc had insisted on continuing with the afternoon clinic so she wasn't needed there. She bossed her grandfather into settling down to rest, starting what she hoped would be the new norm. Then she did a round of the hospital patients. Maggie filled her in as she went.

'Marc's been pretty much over everything,' she told her. 'The islanders think he's great. Dotty Morrison has run out of scripts four times—I think she's fallen in love with him.'

'Who wouldn't?' Elsa said absently. She was reading a patient file as she spoke, and was aware of a sudden silence. She glanced up to see that Maggie was skewering her with a look.

'Yeah?' Maggie said softly. 'Really?'

'I just meant…' Elsa flushed. 'Oh, Maggie, cut it out. He's tall, dark and dishy, he saved Grandpa's life, he's taken over my workload and I'm incredibly grateful. What's not to like?'

'The word though,' Maggie said thoughtfully, 'was love.'

'As if that's going to happen.' She let the clip on the file she was reading close with a snap. 'I imagine he'll be leaving tomorrow now I'm back.'

'But you…'

'Oh, for heaven's sake, Maggie, please don't.' To her horror she found she was suddenly close to tears. She closed her eyes and her friend was right there, giving her a hug.

'Hey, Elsa, sweetheart…'

'It's okay.' She let herself savour her friend's hug for a moment and then pulled away, gathering herself together.

'This is just a reaction. From homecoming. From worry about Grandpa.'

'Nothing at all to do with Marc?'

'Maybe,' she admitted. 'But surely I'm allowed to have the same sort of crush that Dottie has? It's been a long couple of weeks and I'm overwrought. Marc's been great and I've let myself fantasise a little. There's nothing else to it.'

'No,' Maggie said thoughtfully. 'Of course there's nothing else. That'd require you putting yourself before the island, maybe even before your grandpa. As if that'd ever happen.'

'And it'd require interest on his part.' It was a snap, and she caught herself. She'd spent twelve stressful days in Sydney trying to figure out her future. What she didn't need now was her friend imagining a non-existent romantic interest to complicate things even further.

'You know, Tony's started to go out with Kylie from the bakery,' Maggie told her, still thoughtful. 'He's obviously given up on you.'

'Bully for Tony.'

'So who else is in the offing?'

'There's no one,' she replied before she could help herself.

'Then why not do a little more than fantasising? Marc's here and he's lovely and he's not attached. He's just split up with his girlfriend and…'

'Have you been grilling him?'

'Of course,' Maggie said, grinning. 'Why not? So the field is clear. Why not go for it?'

'Because he's going back to Sydney and my life is here.'

'Your life might not be able to be here much longer. You need to face facts, love.'

'But not now,' Elsa said with a weary sigh. 'Leave it, Maggie. There are so many complications in my life anyway. Where would I find time for romance?'

'What's wrong with tonight? He's here. He's available. If I was twenty years younger I'd go for it.'

'Maggie!'

'Chicken.'

'I'd rather be a chicken than a dead hen.'

'And I'd rather have a wild fling with a gorgeous doctor than be a chicken,' Maggie said, and chuckled and headed back to the wards.

Elsa was left floundering. A wild fling? She'd never had such a thing. He'd be gone in the next couple of days. How could she possibly expose her heart like that?

She headed through to her house, adjoining the hospital. The locals had been in as soon as they'd learned she and Robert were home, and casseroles and cakes were lined up on the bench.

The islanders had helped her for ever, she thought as she sorted them. They'd supported her grandpa in raising her. They'd helped cover the cost of her medical training.

A wild fling? She thought of Maggie's words and rejected them. A fling and then what? It'd leave her unhappy, unsettled, ungrateful for the life she needed to live.

'At least I'll never go hungry *if* I stay here,' she told Sherlock—who was already looking tubbier after two weeks of islander care—and heard the *if* that she'd just said.

Ouch.

Robert was asleep. She roused him. They ate one of the casseroles together but he was silent throughout, and then he headed straight back to bed. The last few days seemed to have aged him ten years or more.

She washed and wiped, then let Sherlock out. There was a brief bark and she thought there must be a possum on the veranda. She should chase it off to protect her grapevines and then she thought, *Who cares about grapevines?*

She felt totally, absolutely discombobulated. Then she walked outside, and if it was possible to feel even more discombobulated, she did.

Marc was sitting on the back step, under the outside light. Just sitting.

'Marc!'

'Hey,' he said, rising and backing away a little. 'It's only me. I know this looks like stalking, but I didn't want to interrupt you and your grandpa. We need to talk, so I thought—what would I do if I'd been off this island for twelve days? I'd want to soak it up, that's what. So I decided to come here and wait.'

She eyed him with suspicion that was definitely justified. 'So you just guessed where I might be?' she ventured. 'It wasn't Maggie who told you I mostly drink a glass of wine out on my back step after dinner?'

'Okay, it might have been,' he confessed, and he sent her a lopsided smile that did something to her heart that she somehow had to ignore. He motioned to a bottle and two glasses set out on the top step. 'I brought these. Just in case.'

She harrumphed her indignation at her scheming friend. 'I don't believe Maggie.'

'She's great.'

'She's incorrigible.'

'But she's still great.'

'Yeah,' she said, casting him another suspicious glare, but then she succumbed. This was her porch after all, and there was wine. She plonked herself down on the top step and filled a glass and then filled one for him. 'Everyone's great. I have seventeen casseroles jammed into the freezer, that's how great everyone is. I won't have to cook for a month.'

'Lucky you.' He sat down beside her. Not too close. Still giving her space. Sherlock, glorying in having his mistress back, but also extremely pleased to see his new friend, wriggled in between them.

Silence. The warmth of the night closed over them. The surf below the house provided the faint hush of waves. The moon had flung a ribbon of silver out over the water. A bush turkey was scratching somewhere in the bushes—she could hear its faint rustle.

This man had her so off-balance. The concerns that had been building over the last twelve days were still with her.

Marc's presence here tonight wasn't helping a bit.

It was Marc who finally broke the silence. 'Elsa, I've been thinking,' he told her. 'I came to tell you I can take another two weeks off before I need to return to Sydney. You don't need to jump back into work straight away. Give yourself some space. Your grandpa needs you.'

'Everyone needs me.' It was said flatly, an inescapable fact.

There was another moment's silence. And then, 'You know,' Marc said softly into the stillness, 'I could get to need you, too.'

And with that, all the complications of the islanders' needs, her grandfather's needs, fell away. There was so much in Marc's statement it took her breath away.

She sat with her wine glass in her hand, but she could well have dropped it. She was looking out to sea but seeing nothing. There was some sort of fog in her mind. Some dense mist that meant she couldn't make sense of what he'd just said.

She didn't want to make sense of it?

'I… That's not very helpful,' she said at last because, for some stupid reason, the first thing that came into her head wasn't rejection. It was simply impossibility.

In answer he lifted the glass from her suddenly limp hand and set it aside. Then he took her hand in his. He didn't tug her to face him, though. He simply intertwined their fingers and let the silence envelop them again.

His hand was strong. Warm. Compelling.

Impossible.

The word was slamming round and round her head, like a metal ball bashing against the sides as it bounced. It hurt.

'Elsa, you can't continue to do this alone,' he said softly

at last. 'You know you can't. I've been talking to Maggie. She says you were barely managing before Robert had this attack. She said the walk you went on when you found me was the first time you'd taken time off for weeks.'

'What's that got to do…'

'With you and me? Nothing,' he told her. 'Except everything.'

'You're not offering to come here and help, are you?'

'I'd love to say I would, but no. I'm a cardiologist, not a family doctor. I need to go where my skills are most needed. In two weeks we have new interns starting rotation at the hospital, so I need to be back in Sydney.'

'Two weeks' medical help would be great,' she told him, struggling desperately to sound practical. 'But where does that fit with what you're saying about need?'

'I'm talking of possibilities in the future.' He spread his hands. 'Elsa, I come from a background that's emotionally barren, to say the least. My parents were rich and dysfunctional, and they used money as a substitute for affection. The way I feel about you has me confused. Blindsided, if you like. You and me…'

'There is no you and me.'

'There might be. I have no idea, but the way I'm feeling…isn't it worth exploring?'

She was well out of her comfort zone now, feeling as if she were swimming in uncharted waters, towards what seemed like a whirlpool.

'The way you're feeling?' She intended her voice to sound mocking, but she was mocking herself as well as him. There was no choice but to mock the impossibility of what he was saying. 'You've known me for what, four days?'

'We've talked every day while you were in Sydney.'

They had. Every night after Robert slept she'd rung him, ostensibly to check if there were any medical problems on the island. Which she knew there weren't. Or he'd rung to consult on something she knew he didn't really need to consult with her about. In the end they'd abandoned reasons and simply talked. She'd sat on her balcony in her anonymous hospital relatives' apartment and she'd talked to him as a friend.

Only now he felt like more than a friend.

When had that line been crossed?

It hadn't, she told herself frantically. It couldn't.

She needed to get a grip.

'Marc, what we're both feeling… It's just that we've both been thrown into fraught situations,' she managed. 'I've been frightened and stressed, and you've been a godsend. You came here for hours, with plans to head off for a glamorous holiday, with glamorous friends…a glamorous girlfriend.'

'And found a friend who's maybe not so glamorous,' he said seriously. 'But a friend who's beautiful. Who's caring, brave, funny, devoted…'

'To my island. To my people.'

'There's a complication.'

'You think?' She almost snapped it at him. 'If this really was…a thing…'

'It's interesting, this thing,' he said, and his eyes were smiling. Oh, that smile… 'We can't define it. To be honest, I'm all at sea with what I'm feeling, yet maybe I know what it might be.'

'Well, it can't be,' she said. 'And if it is…' She struggled to find a way to say what she had no words for. 'If this… thing…turns out to be, I don't know, more than just a passing thing, then where would we go from there?'

'Anywhere you like.'

'Like that's possible.' Anger came to her aid then, and it helped. 'You work in one of the most prestigious coronary care units in the world. I work on this island.'

'But you need to leave.' His words were gentle enough, but behind them she heard a note of implacability. 'Elsa, you know this island needs more than one doctor, and your grandpa can't keep working. I know the island will hardly support another doctor who needs a full wage, but there are medical couples who might well jump at the lifestyle. Couples who'd like the opportunity for one to work part-time. For the island's sake, Elsa, you need to open up that opportunity.'

'By leaving?'

'By leaving.' It was said flatly. A truth that hurt.

'But how do I know any other doctor would give my islanders the care they deserve?' She'd thought this through—of course she had. She'd spent a long time in Sydney contemplating her future. 'What if some nine-to-fiver takes over? Where would my island be then? So what's the choice? If I leave here and make Grandpa safer, the islanders would be at risk and Grandpa would be deeply unhappy. If I stay here I need to accept that Grandpa will probably die earlier. But Grandpa and I have discussed it and it's no choice at all. He wants to stay.'

'So where does that leave you personally? Or...us?' His eyes were still on hers, serious, questioning. 'Maybe that's what we need to find out.'

'I don't understand.'

'I think you do. This thing we're feeling...'

'I don't want...' But her voice trailed off. She didn't want what? A nebulous something. A problem that had no solution?

This man?

All of him was compelling, she thought. He was drawing her into some sweet web she had no hope of escaping. But it was a web she had to escape, because her grandfather's happiness, the security of the islanders, depended on it.

'Marc...'

'You know, I don't understand it either,' he said, and there was a note of uncertainty in his voice that told her he was speaking the truth. 'Honestly, Elsa, I didn't expect to feel like this about someone so...'

'Unsuitable,' she finished for him, but he shook his head.

'You know that's not true. But different, yes. I've been brought up without family ties. My father was indifferent to his family, committed to his work. My mother was loyal in her own way—sort of—but her work and the mountains always came first. I was essentially raised by servants. But the way you feel about your grandpa...'

'It's normal.'

'It's great.'

'It's no big deal. It's just called love.'

'I get that. It's just... I didn't think I could feel...'

'Well, don't feel,' she said, breathless now but angry again. What was he doing, sitting on her back step looking like he was offering her the world when she knew very well that the world wasn't his to offer? Her tiny part of the world was prescribed, definite, and there was no escape clause.

'I don't think this thing is something that can be turned off at will,' he was saying.

'Then put a plug in it. Take your wine and go back to your side of the hospital.' While she was away he'd shifted out of his hospital bed and was staying in an apartment used for the occasional patient relative who needed to stay overnight.

'I will—in a moment. Elsa, I'm not threatening you.'

'But you are. My life can't change. I have no choice.'

'You have no choice but to change.'

'But not with you.'

'Elsa.' He reached out and caught both her hands, compelling now, assured. 'You sound terrified but there's no need. I'm not threatening,' he repeated.

'You are.'

'Is it me you're frightened of or the situation?'

There was no answer to that. She tried to sort it in her head, but her head was struggling to co-operate. Was she frightened of her situation? Being forced to leave the island to make her living somewhere else? Was she terrified of breaking her grandfather's heart by insisting he leave the island, too? Yes, she was.

Was she frightened of Marc? No, but she was frightened of the way she was feeling.

He was being practical whereas she...

She was totally, absolutely terrified, because falling for this man, exposing what she wanted most in all the world seemed unthinkable.

'Elsa, relax,' Marc said, gently now, as he watched her face. 'Stop it with the convolutions. Just feel.'

Just feel. So easy for him to say. But his hands were holding hers. His eyes were holding hers too, and what she saw there... She managed to fight back panic just for a moment, and in that moment something else surged in. Something sweet and sure and right. Something strong enough to drive everything else from her tired mind.

Love? Who knew? All she knew was that suddenly she was over trying to understand what she felt. He was sitting beside her in the moonlight, turned towards her. His eyes were gentle, kind and he was tugging her close.

She should protest. She should pull away. She should do a million things.

She didn't. The night seemed to dissolve. Everything melted away as his hands tugged her closer. As he released her for a nanosecond so that instead of holding her hands he was cupping her face. Tilting her chin. Looking into her eyes, searching for a truth she didn't understand.

The fight, the logic had simply disappeared.

Almost of their own volition, her arms moved to hold him, and with that hold came surety, strength, power. In the last few days her world had been tilting so much that at times she'd felt in danger of falling off.

This man was no long-term safe anchorage—she knew

that—but for now he was here, he was Marc, and he was holding her.

He wanted her and she wanted him. Nothing more, nothing less.

He was holding her, but he'd paused, a fraction of a breath away from kissing her. This was no practised seduction. The final decision was being left to her.

And with that knowledge came a longing so strong, so fierce that any reservations disappeared into the night.

He was giving her space but she wanted no space.

'Yes,' she murmured. She hardly knew whether the word was said out loud or not, but there was room for no other.

His mouth claimed hers, and the way she was feeling there'd be no need for words for ever.

What was he doing?

He knew damned well what he was doing. He was kissing a woman he wanted in a way he'd never wanted a woman before.

To have and to hold... He'd heard those lines before, in the marriage ceremonies of countless friends, but until now they'd simply been a formality.

They weren't a formality. *To have and to hold*. That was what he wanted, what he was melting into—a sense of rightness...desire. Possession?

She was in his arms and she felt as if she belonged. She did belong there. This was his woman and as his mouth claimed her, so did his head.

Elsa. *His woman*.

She was letting him kiss her, and unbelievably she was kissing him back. The desire between them was white-hot, a fire that felt all-consuming.

The porch light was on. They could probably be seen by half the island—and indeed Sherlock had backed away and was watching them, his head cocked to one side as if this was a moment he should take note of. It was merely a kiss, but it felt like much, much more.

It felt like a joining. A claiming. It was a sensation of being where he belonged. Home? Who knew what such a word meant, but it suddenly seemed like a siren song.

And when they finally pulled apart, as pull apart they were forced to do because Sherlock finally decided what they were doing seemed interesting and he might just join in, Marc knew his world had changed.

'Elsa...' The word was a caress. She was looking at him in confusion. Her hands were cupping her cheeks and a blush of rose had spread across her face.

'I don't...'

'Don't understand? Neither do I.' He went to take her hands again, but she pulled back. As he watched he saw her confusion turning to fear.

'Marc, don't.'

'You don't want this?'

'Yes. No! I can't.'

'Why not, my love?' Was this the first time he'd ever used such an endearment? No matter, it felt right.

But the look of fear was still there. 'Marc, I can't afford to fall in love with you.'

'Hey, I'm cheap to run,' he told her, trying to take the fear from her face. Trying to make light of what seemed so important. 'In fact, I might even run in the black rather than the red. I make a decent income as a cardiologist, you know, and I'm wealthy in my own right.'

She tried to laugh but it didn't happen. It turned into a choke that seemed perilously close to a sob.

'As if that matters. Marc, this can't happen. It's far too soon.'

'Well, *too soon* is something we can do something about,' he told her. 'We have all the time in the world to sort out *too soon*.'

'You're going back to Sydney.'

'Which is where I think you should go, too. I have friends, influence... Love, there'll be a score of jobs for a doctor with your skills. You'll find work in a minute. My house is huge and you're welcome to stay there, but if it's indeed *too soon* then we can find you and Robert a decent apartment while we figure how long is soon enough.' Then he glanced at Sherlock who was looking at him in confusion. 'Or,' he added practically, 'a house with a backyard.'

'So Sherlock can stay in the backyard all day and Grandpa can stay in the house?'

'Your grandpa will die if he stays on the island,' he said bluntly. 'You've seen the cardiology reports and the reports from the renal physician. He needs constant monitoring. That heart of his is no longer strong enough to cope with anything worse than a bad cold.'

'You don't know that.'

'I can guess it, and so can you.'

'Then it's Grandpa's choice.' Her hands were still holding her cheeks. She looked stressed, frightened—but also angry. 'Marc, why are you saying this? It has to be our decision, mine and Grandpa's, where we live, and our choice is here.'

'Then we'll never see how our relationship might work.'

'That's blackmail!'

'It's only blackmail if you want what I think we both want. To see if you and I...'

'There is no you and I.' The anger was still there. 'There can't be a *you and I* unless you decide that being an islander is part of your life plan. But people don't come here to live. They're born here, and some of them stay and some of them don't. Apart from half a dozen hippies who live at the far end of the island where the surf's best, no one's migrated here for decades.'

'I know that, which is why...'

'Which is why I have to leave if I want a life with anyone other than another islander. But that's okay because my other islander is my grandpa.'

'He won't live for ever.'

'So you're threatening me as well as blackmailing me?'

'Elsa...'

'Leave it.' She closed her eyes for a moment and when she opened them again he saw a wash of weariness so deep it was all he could do not to reach out and support her. But she was holding out her hands in a gesture that said she was warding him off, not wanting him to come closer.

He'd stuffed it.

He'd totally, absolutely stuffed it.

He'd only spoken the truth.

But it hadn't worked. She was tipping the untouched wine from her glass onto the garden. She was done.

'Go back to your quarters, Marc,' she said quietly. 'I have enough to think about tonight without a proposal that has so many impossible conditions that it makes me feel ill.'

'It wasn't a proposal,' he denied automatically.

Or was it? The way he'd framed it...

'Then I'm glad,' she said, and sighed and clicked her fingers. Sherlock sidled to her side, cocking his head to one side as if he was trying to figure what was wrong. Then he nuzzled next to her leg and pressed his body against her knee. It was an unmistakable gesture of comfort, and Marc looked down at the dog and thought that Sherlock had got it right.

And he'd got it impossibly wrong.

'I'll still stay for two weeks anyway,' he told her, searching for anything to allay the pain he could feel washing over her in waves. 'That should take care of the worst of the tourist season.'

'Thank you,' she said simply. 'We'll pay you full time clinician rates.'

'There's no need...'

'There's every need,' she said, suddenly angry again. 'From now on… Well, we'll start as we mean to go on, Dr Pierce. As medical colleagues and nothing more.'

CHAPTER TWELVE

MARC HAD TWO weeks to repair the mistakes of that night. He had two weeks to find a way to undo the damage.

In two weeks he found not a single solution.

She was pig stubborn, he told himself as it neared the time he had to leave. She had to face a future off the island.

And yet, as he saw Robert gradually regain health, as he watched the elderly doctor sitting on the veranda with Sherlock at his feet, with his islander mates sitting beside him, as he saw Robert's devotion to the islanders and the islanders' devotion to Robert, he had to concede that it'd be extremely hard to drag him to a new life in Sydney.

Yet it meant that Elsa could have no new life. Until...

Yeah, that was a good thing to think—not. Wait until her grandfather died to move away? How bleak was that? But meanwhile, for Elsa to work herself into the ground holding this practice together while she waited for her grandfather's health to fail, as it surely must without specialist care...

It made him feel ill to imagine it, but there was nothing he could do.

He worked beside her, taking clinics while she did house calls and took care of the patients in the hospital. That had been pretty much the set-up before Robert fell ill, and it worked. The island could function on one and a half doctors, but that doctor couldn't be Robert.

Nor could it be Marc. He'd thought of staying on the island—of course he had—but he wasn't so deeply thrown by these new emotions that he failed to see the impossibility of such a plan. He was a cardiologist and there was little here for him to do. He'd worked hard to achieve his skill set. Managing the occasional imperative heart problem on Gannet with no support staff... No.

But the more he saw of Elsa, the more he knew how much he wanted her. He also knew how badly he'd messed up his proposal. Blackmail and threats? It honestly hadn't seemed like that to him—surely he'd only been laying out the truth—but he knew he'd hurt her.

And that hurt him. As he saw her flinch whenever she caught sight of him in the distance, as he saw each flash of pain in her eyes, as he watched her quickly turn away, he knew his clumsy attempts to get her to accept a future off the island had done nothing but cause her distress. He felt gutted.

So what to do?

There was little he could do. He worked on. Elsa paid him and he couldn't refuse—she said she'd lock the clinic doors on him if he didn't accept it. He funnelled the payments via Maggie into funds for a new incubator, something the hospital desperately needed.

'I'll tell Elsa it's from an anonymous donor,' Maggie said when he proposed it. 'She might suspect it's from you, but she doesn't need to know for sure. If she did...well, she's already grateful to you for the lift chairs and this might stress her more.'

'Because?'

'You know very well why,' she said, irritated. But then she softened. 'I know it's an impossible situation and I'm desperately sorry that the pair of you can't take this further, but this is our Elsa we're talking about. Ours.'

Ours. The island's.

That line wormed its way back into his head. *To have and to hold.*

The island had staked its claim and it was holding on. Elsa was staying, and the bottom line was that he had to leave.

So he worked on, but as he did he racked his brain as to how he could help her. Half a doctor—that was what she needed. That was what Gannet Island needed. It couldn't be him, not long-term, but she had to have help.

None of his colleagues would be even vaguely interested. They were all high-flying achievers.

So where to find half a doctor?

And then, a week before he was due to leave, he found himself thinking of his mother, mixing medicine with mountain climbing.

Half a doctor...

He started making phone calls. Half a doctor couldn't be him, but at least this could help Elsa.

It wasn't nearly enough, he thought as his departure date loomed closer, but at least it was something.

It seemed *something* was all he had left to offer.

Saturday. The day of his flight home. He'd asked Elsa to have dinner with him on Friday night and she'd agreed— 'But at our kitchen table with Grandpa. We still have a mountain of casseroles.'

What followed was a stilted dinner where he and Robert talked medicine and island history, and Elsa said little at all. She saw him to the door afterwards and he wanted to kiss her—no, he was desperate to kiss her—but she backed away. The closed look on her face said there was no compromise. Ryan drove him to the airport the next morning, and that was that.

But then, just as the incoming plane landed, he saw Elsa's car pull into the car park. He watched and waited, saw her hesitate as if she was regretting coming and wasn't too sure she was doing the right thing, but then she came right in.

This was a tiny airport. There weren't such things as separate arrival and departure lounges. She walked through the swing doors and saw him straight away.

'Hey,' he said as she reached him. Her eyes were troubled. Sad. He desperately wanted to hug her, but somehow he stopped himself and managed to smile. 'Going somewhere?'

She tried to smile back. 'You must know that I wish I could.'

He did know that. It was breaking something inside him, but he understood.

'I just… I couldn't let you go before I thanked you again,' she told him. 'Last night was too formal. Too… unhappy. I didn't say it, just how grateful Grandpa and I are for all you've done.'

'You don't need to say it,' he told her. 'The thanks on both sides just about balance themselves out. And I've brought you trouble. I'm so sorry, Elsa, that I've made you feel…'

'Trapped?' she told him and managed a smile. 'That's not your call. I felt trapped long before you arrived.'

'But you still won't come to Sydney.'

'Don't go there again, Marc. You know it's impossible. I'd still be trapped in Sydney, only it'd be worse. I'd have an unhappy Grandpa and I'd have the islanders on my mind for the rest of my life.'

You'd have me. He wanted to say it, but he couldn't. The time for that was over.

'So I just need to say goodbye,' she told him, and she reached out and took his hands. Around them a small group of his fellow travellers were doing much the same, hugging goodbye, shaking hands, shedding tears.

That was how he felt. Like shedding tears. How could he feel like this about a woman he'd known for such a short time?

How could he feel like this about any woman?

No woman but Elsa.

'Goodbye, Marc,' she told him and the tug on his hands was suddenly urgent. She pulled him close and then reached up and kissed him.

It was a light kiss, a feather touch. A friends' farewell. Good friends. Friends who could never be more.

His instinct was to kiss her back, tug her arms around him... *To have and to hold.*

He couldn't. He didn't. She stepped back and he let her go.

'Marc!' It was a booming yell from the far side of the lounge, where a cluster of incoming passengers were collecting their baggage.

He turned and saw a woman, middle-aged, small and dumpy, dressed for what looked like a two-week hike. She'd just gathered a gigantic pack from the pile of baggage and was hitching it onto her back as she yelled.

'Stella,' he said and then grinned. Of course it was Stella. He'd thought she wouldn't get here for days, yet here she was.

She was stumping her way towards him. With the pack she was carrying she was almost as wide as she was high.

'I'll go,' Elsa said quickly but he caught her hand.

'No. I'm glad this has happened. This is someone I'd like you to meet.'

'Marc,' the woman said again as she reached them and she gripped his hand with a ferocity that made him wince. 'Excellent,' she boomed. 'A handover. How long do we have before the plane leaves?'

'Only minutes,' he told her, 'but Elsa can fill you in.' He turned to Elsa, who was looking faintly stunned. 'Elsa, this is Stella Harbour—Dr Harbour. Stella, this is Dr McCrae. Elsa, Stella's a hiking friend of my mother's. She retired from family medicine a couple of years ago and has been hiking the world since.'

'And starting to get bored doing it,' Stella said bluntly.

'Not that I haven't seen some amazing places, but Marc's call seemed a godsend. I'm missing my medicine. Not that it's a sure thing,' she said hastily, seeing Elsa's look of incomprehension. 'I'm here to hike all over this island, and while I'm doing it I'll be seeing if there might be a place here for me. A work place, I mean.'

'What…?' Elsa managed.

'He didn't tell you? No, he said he'd leave it up to me to explain. Now, you don't have to have me if you don't want me. Marc was clear on that. He said there might be the possibility of work that'd fluctuate according to need. Not much in the quiet times, but full-on in the peak of the tourist season. Which pretty much suits me beautifully. I don't depend on work to provide an income. I love this island—Marc's mum and I hiked here together a couple of times. Peak tourist times are the times when I hate being on the trails anyway and I'd far rather be sewing up cuts and being busy. Anyway, no decision needed yet, my dear. Marc just put it forward as an option, so I thought I'd come over, do a couple of hikes and maybe see if you could make use of me.'

Elsa stared at her as if she couldn't believe what she was seeing—and then she turned to Marc. 'How…?'

'I thought laterally,' he said, smiling at the confusion—and hope—he saw on her face. 'I remembered the host of lady bushwalkers my mother collected around her, thought of their demographic—pretty much all nearing retiring age—so I rang Mum's best friend.'

'And Lucy rang round all of us with a medical background—there were a few because you know Marc's mum was a medical researcher? And when Lucy rang me… Well, it sounds perfect. To live and work here…'

'I need to go now,' Marc said apologetically. The boarding call for his flight was getting insistent. 'Elsa, Stella knows this is an idea only. If you don't like it then…'

'Then I get a walking holiday here, and no one's the

worse off,' Stella added cheerfully. 'Of you go, dear,' she told Marc and gave him a gentle push. 'Back to your cardiology and leave the nuts and bolts of general medicine to us. Byee.'

'Marc...' Elsa said helplessly.

'Do what's best for you,' Marc told her. He hoisted his bag over his shoulder, found his balance on his still-plastered leg and looked at her for one last time. 'Goodbye, Elsa.'

'Marc,' she said again, and then, before he could anticipate what she intended, she reached up and cupped his face and tugged it down to hers.

And kissed him. Fiercely. Possessively.

And then she let him go with a gasp that turned into something that was suspiciously like a sob.

But it was cut off. She put a hand to her face as if to hide her emotions, and when her hand dropped again she had herself under control.

'Goodbye, Marc,' she said and somehow she managed it without so much as a tremor. 'Thank you and farewell.'

He sat on the plane, looking out on the island receding in the distance below and felt blank. Empty. Done.

His leg ached. Everything ached.

Work was piling up in Sydney. He had interns starting on Monday. He had a paper to present at a conference in New York at the beginning of next month. He had a meeting this week with researchers investigating a new drug that promised to reduce blood pressure without the current side-effects.

His diary also showed a party next Saturday that sounded amazing—Grant Thurgood's fortieth would surely be the social event of the season. Grant was a cardiologist at the top of his game, his wife was a socialite extraordinaire and the money and effort they'd thrown at this event would take their guests' collective breath away.

He tried to imagine Elsa throwing such a party, and couldn't. He tried to imagine Elsa living in that milieu, and couldn't.

Unbidden, his hands moved to his face. To his mouth. As if he could still taste her.

Elsa.

He glanced down at the island beneath him. Somewhere down there Elsa would be talking to Stella, planning a future. Without him.

That was okay. It had to be. Solitude had been pretty much drilled into him from childhood, and it was the easy retreat now.

Life would move on, he told himself. No matter what Elsa decided, it was hardly his business now. He'd thought of marriage when he'd suggested she move to Sydney, but honestly...would he be any good at it?

Elsa would be good at it, he thought. Loving was her specialty, but she surely deserved better than him.

But the pressure from that kiss was still with him and it wouldn't leave. Maybe solitude wasn't so appealing.

But maybe... nothing. Was he still thinking about marriage? If she couldn't leave the island it was impossible to go down that road unless he joined her, abandoned his career, became a part-time generalist.

But that thought was rejected almost before it was formed. He didn't have the empathy, the skills, to be a really good family doctor. A month of such medicine had left him in awe of what Elsa did, but he'd also accepted she had a skill set that was just as important as any cardiology techniques he'd learned. He'd go crazy, watching Elsa seamlessly do what he couldn't. He had to have a challenge.

A challenge... The word seemed to hang.

From up here he could see all the islands, the six that made up the Birding group. He'd seen patients from the outer isles while he'd been at Gannet. He'd even visited a couple, with their remote medical clinics run by capable nurses.

Six islands.

They were Elsa's responsibility. Not his.

Why did it seem as if they were his?

He'd booked a double seat so he could stretch his leg. That meant he was undisturbed, so now he sat back and closed his eyes. Forcing his mind to go blank was a technique he used when he was struggling to find a solution to a fraught medical dilemma—clear all preconceived ideas and start from scratch.

This was surely a dilemma. He needed his technique now.

And suddenly it worked. His mind switched into overdrive and fragments were shooting at him like brightly lit arrows from all sides.

Six islands.

A career that was challenging.

Stella and her mountain climbing and part-time medicine.

Part-time doctors.

A jigsaw that could be put together?

Maybe.

The jumble was coalescing into a whole that was making him feel dizzy.

'It'll never work,' he said out loud, and the flight attendant was suddenly at his side, looking concerned. She was being super helpful to someone she obviously saw as disabled.

'Sir? Is there something wrong?'

She was middle-aged, friendly, reminding him of Maggie. She smiled encouragingly, and amazingly he found himself talking.

'Just a problem I'm trying to solve.'

'Is there anything I can do to help?' The plane was half empty. Clearly she had time to chat.

'I don't think anything's wrong,' he said slowly. 'Except... I might just need to toss my job.'

'Oh, but surely your leg will get better.' She still sounded worried. 'This is the only plane that services Gannet so we know all about you. You were trapped underground. That must have been an awful experience, but surely your life can get back to normal now.'

'But maybe it wasn't being trapped that stopped me feeling normal.' He was feeling as confused as she was looking. 'Maybe it was being rescued.'

'I gather it was Dr McCrae who found you,' the woman said, and smiled encouragingly. 'She has quite a reputation among the islanders. She'd have kept you safe if anyone could. The islanders think she's wonderful.'

'She is indeed,' Marc said softly.

'Well, take care of yourself, sir.' Duty done, she left to check on the other passengers and Marc was left with his circling thoughts. Which centred now around Elsa.

He let his mind drift back to that time of being trapped with Elsa. Her warmth. Her humour. The feeling that he was safe with her.

And then later... The way she'd melted into him as he'd kissed her. The feeling that he'd found his way home.

Home?

Home was Sydney. Home was a demanding clinical life, his research, cutting-edge medicine, friends who felt the same as he did.

As a lone kid of wealthy but dysfunctional parents, his studies and his career had become his refuge. They were still his pole stars. His career and his research were the most important thing, and everything else fitted around the edges.

What if home was the pole star?

'You need two pole stars,' he said out loud. He'd read that in an astronomy encyclopaedia his father had given him when he was seven.

Earth's pole stars are Polaris, a magnitude two star aligned approximately with its northern axis, and Polaris Australis, a much dimmer star...

The book had been a birthday gift when he was seven. His parents had been shouting at each other before he'd even unwrapped it, and afterwards they'd been rigidly formal, bidding him goodnight with their anger still obvious.

He'd buried himself in the pole stars. Two pole stars used for navigation for thousands of years.

Pole stars guiding him home. There was that word again. *Home.*

Elsa.

He was thinking laterally now. His father's gift of the astronomy book made him think of Elsa's gifts. Her carefully nurtured geraniums. Gifts given with love.

And now he was remembering again the line that had come into his head as he'd held her and kissed her.

To have and to hold.

He couldn't hold her. What sort of arrogance had made him demand that? He wanted to hold Elsa, but she wouldn't be held just because that was what he wanted.

He wanted to have, but Elsa needed to have as well. She wanted her island. She needed her island.

And there suddenly was his idea, his light bulb moment. His astounding plan.

He thought of his salary. His inherited wealth. His skills, his contacts, his resources. If he couldn't do it, no one could.

It might be impossible, but his light bulb plan was coalescing by the second.

'I won't know unless I try,' he said out loud. He saw the passenger across the aisle eye him with caution, and he grinned. Maybe the guy thought he was nuts and maybe he was. What he was hoping for probably made no sense at all.

'It's politics and funding and feet on the ground,' he

muttered. 'And realistically… It'll take at least a year to organise, if it's even possible.'

A year without Elsa? He wanted to turn the plane around now, share his idea with her, tug her into his arms.

To have and to hold? No. Because if it failed, or if he failed… It wasn't fair to either of them.

'A year,' he told himself. A year to change. A whole dammed year.

'You can contact her. Phone her. Go visit her. Be a friend.'

A friend. Friend with benefits?

'As if that's likely to happen. What if she meets someone else? What if she hooks up with that Tony guy?

'It's a risk.' He struggled with the thought, but common sense had to prevail. 'If this is real, if she feels like I do…' He sighed. 'Back off, Pierce, and get your ducks in order first. She's worth fighting for. She's worth risking all. Prove to yourself that you love her enough to wait.'

Love… There was the biggie. Could he really love?

'If you love her then you'll do what it takes,' he told himself. 'Fight for what *she* wants, not for what *you* want. Starting now.'

But still he hesitated, staring out of the window as if he could still see the islands. The urge to turn around and head back to her was overwhelming. Maybe he could do this from Gannet?

He knew he couldn't. He needed to be in Sydney. He needed to be networking, politicking, fighting for something more important than both of them.

'And if I tell her my plan and it fails, then I'll break her heart,' he said out loud. 'But by next Christmas…'

Eleven months. Was it possible?

He turned from the window and flicked open the memo function on his phone to write the first hopeful outline. He was suddenly a man with a purpose. A man with a woman worth fighting for.

'If Elsa can produce a black geranium then surely I can produce a dream,' he vowed. 'But dreams aren't real...

'And neither's Santa Claus,' he told himself. 'But by next Christmas... It's the season of miracles after all, so at least I can try.'

CHAPTER THIRTEEN

Christmas Day, eleven months later:

MARC STARED DOWN at the mountainous Birding Isles, set in a ring against the sparkling sapphire sea, and felt an overwhelming sense of peace.

Last time he'd come here he'd brought a simple day pack. Today he had three bags of gear in the cargo hold. Most of it was medical equipment which would stay here regardless of today's outcome. Some of it was personal.

Some of it was the baggage of a man who hoped he was coming home.

Nothing was settled. He should be apprehensive and part of him was, but there was also a core within him that felt complete.

These last eleven months had been long and fraught. He'd worked desperately hard to achieve what he'd be presenting to the islanders today. It had been an enormous challenge, and there were challenges yet to come.

But underneath... As the months had worn on, as the 'friendship' calls to Elsa had grown longer, as he'd had to summon an almost superhuman effort to hold his emotions in check during her one visit to Sydney in July... As he'd fought with his desire to drop everything he was working for and go to her, any doubt of how he felt had fallen away.

He loved this woman with all his heart, and he'd do

whatever it took to win her. He hoped today that he was providing enough, but if it didn't succeed...

'Then I'll figure some other way to be with her,' he said to himself. 'On her terms. I'll do whatever it takes.'

They were circling now, coming in to land. The landing gear settled into place with a gentle thump. The runway loomed ahead, and then they were down.

He was back on Gannet Island.

And the last barriers to his carefully guarded heart seemed to fall away right there and then. Years of solitude, of isolation, of carefully constructed independence faded to nothing.

His heart was in the hands of one slip of a red-haired doctor.

It had to be right.

He was home.

It was a great Christmas Day—as far as Christmas Days went. There'd been no emergencies, no unexpected illnesses. The hospital was quiet. Grandpa was looking good. Elsa had planned her Christmas gifts with love and care. The island's cooks had cooked up a storm. The hall was looked great, the decorations superb. It was crowded, full of laughter, friendship and Christmas cheer.

Then why was she so flat?

So sad.

It was Ghosts of Christmas Past, she told herself, and struggled to act happy, even if something inside her felt like lead. She watched Eileen O'Hara unwrap dozens of balls of leftover wool collected from knitters all around the island during the year, squirreled away for just this moment. Eileen's crocheted rugs were legendary but she struggled to afford wool. As her parcel opened she burst into tears and then beamed her happiness. Around her the islanders whooped at her delight and Elsa thought that this was the most important thing in the world. Community.

Not self.

Not Elsa, who still felt as if a gaping hole had been ripped open inside her and would never be filled.

Except by Marc. And that could never happen.

She'd been in contact with him during the year. He'd phoned, often, but only as a friend.

In July, Robert had needed a check-up and Elsa had gone with him to the mainland. To Sydney Central. They'd stayed for only one night, but Robert had gone to sleep early and Elsa had had dinner with Marc.

She'd felt almost light-headed, jubilant with the all-clear her grandfather's check-up had produced, but totally thrown by the Marc who'd picked her up at their hotel and taken her to a gorgeous restaurant overlooking Sydney Harbour.

It had been a different Marc. This was where he was meant to be, she'd thought. He'd looked a million dollars, a surgeon at the top of his game.

And he was her friend. He was only her friend.

'How's it going, working with Stella?' he'd asked.

'It's so good, Marc,' she'd told him. 'I still don't know how you conjured her up, but we work brilliantly together. Plus she plays chess with Grandpa almost every night and sometimes she even beats him. We're so happy, thanks to you.'

'But you? Are you happy?'

'I have everything I want,' she'd said, a little too firmly. 'A healthy Grandpa. A colleague I adore. A fantastic medical set-up for the island. I can't ask for more. Now, tell me about you. I read one of your research papers in *Cutting-Edge Medical* last month. Wow...'

And that was as personal as she'd got. She'd shaken hands formally at the end of the evening and that was it.

Back to the occasional phone call. Back to being friends.

Back to the rest of her life.

They were almost at the end of their gift list now. There

was a bundle of new fishing sinkers for Tom Hammond, a dozen assorted envelopes of different poppy seeds for Chrissie Harding and they'd be done.

And then there was a stir at the doorway. She looked up to see a group of strangers gathered at the glass doors. A mix of maybe twenty people? It included young couples, a few older folk, a smattering of kids. A woman holding a baby.

They were all dressed in Santa hats, even the baby.

This must be the group who'd booked out Bob Cruikshank's cottages, she thought. The cottages had only been three-quarters done when, in September, a team of builders had arrived from the mainland and completed the job in weeks. Bob had been going around looking like the cat that got the cream ever since, but he wouldn't say where the money had come from to bring in the builders, nor would he say who the first occupants would be.

A family group? Who?

It was Maggie who opened the door, but she put her body in the way of anyone entering. 'I'm sorry,' she said, kindly but firmly. 'This is a private function.'

And then there was a stir in the group. It parted and someone from the back made their way through.

A man. Tall, dark, lean. Wearing a Santa hat.

Marc.

Elsa had been standing by the Christmas tree, handing presents to Bob Cruikshank, who'd been playing Father Christmas. Bob, the realtor whose thigh had healed beautifully after his argument with the chainsaw, held out his arms in welcome.

'Ho-ho-ho!' he boomed. 'These people are welcome, Maggie. These people are a gift to all the island.'

She couldn't make any sense of what Bob was saying but it didn't seem to matter anyway.

Marc was here.

Maggie stood aside, stunned, and they trooped in, a

weird assorted bunch. Robert rose stiffly from his seat, beamed and shook Marc's hand. As if he'd expected him? Then Marc led them up to the front of the hall, leaping lightly up onto the stage to where Elsa stood beside the Christmas tree.

He smiled at her, a huge enveloping smile that made her heart turn over. He took her hands and for a moment she thought he meant to kiss her.

He didn't. His gaze was a kiss all on its own, but they were in front of a hall full of people. She was totally confused, and maybe he sensed that a kiss would send her right over the edge.

'Happy Christmas, love,' he said gently, and she felt as if she was over the edge already.

But then he released one of her hands and tugged her around so they were both facing the audience. Who'd fallen silent, stunned. Expectant?

Bob Cruikshank was still beaming and so was her grandfather. What the...?

'We have a gift for you all,' Marc said, his words falling into a void of hushed bewilderment. 'And that gift might be us. If you want us.' And then he smiled and motioned to the two gifts left under the tree. 'But we've interrupted. Can Santa give these out first?'

'No!' It was a roar of dissent from the confused guests, but when it finished there were two faces reflecting dismay.

Tom and Chrissie.

'Yes,' Elsa managed, and Tom received his sinkers and Chrissie beamed over her poppies, and then everyone looked at Marc as if he was a genie about to produce...who knew? Nobody knew.

'Can I introduce the new residents of Bob Cruikshank's cottages,' Marc told the gathered audience, and proceeded to do just that.

'This couple are Ellen and Graham Parkes,' he told everyone. 'Ellen's an obstetrician, Graham's a renal physician, and these are their three kids, Hamish, Archie and Kim. Next is Angus Knox, a family doctor, and his little son Noah. Then we have Arthur and Lois Campbell. Lois is a gerontologist, Arthur's a general surgeon. David Wyndham behind them is an orthopaedic surgeon. Next is Cathy Graham, a theatre nurse. Then Nic Scott, a paediatrician...'

A host of supremely qualified medics. Here on holiday? Apparently not.

'We're here to see if we can make Gannet Island the centre of the best regional health service in the world,' Marc said, and Elsa thought her legs might give way.

'No pressure,' Marc continued, still speaking to the stunned and silent islanders. 'This is a try-it-and-see. Some are here for quick visit, to see if they like it. Some are here on a month's vacation, hoping to talk to you all, plus the residents on the outlying islands. We're all specialists, and all of us would like to back off from our city practices. Our thought is to build up a medical base on Gannet that's second to none and, in doing so, provide a comprehensive medical service to the outer islands.'

She stared. She tried to think of something to say.

She couldn't.

'We have tentative plans—and funds—to build a helicopter pad and purchase a decent chopper,' Marc continued, smiling at her before he turned back to the audience. 'Plus we can afford a decent fast boat, capable of transfers between the islands. We'll need to extend your hospital. That'll need your cooperation—everything will need your cooperation—but our approach to the government for funding has already met with unqualified approval. Your Dr McCrae—Robert—has been assisting us from this end. The government funds your health care, either here or in Sydney. It'll cost the government a whole lot less if every major case doesn't need to be evacuated.'

What…? How…? Her jaw had dropped to her ankles.

'This is impossible,' she breathed, staring from Marc out to the group of newcomers—who were all smiling and laughing—and looking really, really hopeful. 'How can it possibly work?'

'Your grandfather thinks it can work,' Marc told her, and Elsa turned to look at Robert. He was grinning as if all his Christmases had come at once.

'These people might just have consulted me,' he told her happily. 'I am, after all, Gannet Island's senior doctor. I had the first call last February, and we've been working on the plans ever since.'

'Hey, does this mean I won't have to go to Sydney for my hip replacement?' someone at the back of the hall called, and Marc nodded.

'If you can wait a couple of months, mate. It'll take time to get things in place but surgery such as hip replacements will be our bread and butter. Also obstetrics. Mums shouldn't have to fly to Sydney to have their babies. If everyone supports us there'll be far fewer evacuations. But, as I said, there's no pressure. We're all here for a try-it-and-see vacation, with no compulsion to commit on either side.'

There was another moment's silence while everyone in the hall took this on board. And then another.

And finally it was the redoubtable Maggie who broke it. She lifted her amazing crocheted hat off her head and walked forward and stuck it on Marc's head, replacing his Santa hat. And then, as of one accord, there was a rush as every islander tried to put their island caps on the newcomers. The silence was more than broken—the noise in the hall was unbelievable as the incoming medics were welcomed into the celebration with jubilant enthusiasm.

Elsa stood on the stage and stared out at the melee and thought the ground beneath her was giving way.

Before a hand took hers and drew her away. Out through a side door, out behind the hall. Out to stand underneath the giant eucalypt, with its towering canopy laced with glorious crimson mistletoe.

Out to where she could be thoroughly, ruthlessly kissed.

She was being kissed by a guy in a crocheted elf hat with a tail and a pompom. She was being kissed by someone who'd just offered her the world.

She didn't believe it.

But she didn't struggle. She couldn't. This was Christmas Day, the time of miracles, and why not let herself believe for this short, sweet time? Why not let herself be kissed and kiss back as if miracles truly could happen? As if she had any choice?

And he felt so good. So right.

His elf hat was drooping forward. The pompom had swung round and was hitting her nose.

There was nothing like a drooping pompom to mess with the Christmas spirit, she thought dazedly, deciding—deep into a magnificently prolonged kiss—that sense had to surface soon. But not yet.

Just another few minutes. Minutes of holding him close, feeling herself surrender to his touch, wanting, aching to believe…

And in the end it was Marc who pulled away, who held her at arm's length and smiled and smiled.

And said, 'You don't believe me, do you?'

'I don't have a clue what's going on,' she managed, and her voice sounded…bruised? She felt bruised…or was it winded? She didn't have a clue. 'Is it…? It has to be some kind of a joke?'

'No joke, my love,' he told her and pulled her in to hug her against him again to kiss the top of her hair. 'I'm hoping to put everything I own and then some into this venture, so it'd better not be a joke.'

She let herself sink against him while she tried to make sense of his words. Finally she tugged away. He tried to catch her hands but she was having none of it. She held her hands up as if to ward him off and he accepted it.

Inside there was the sound of celebration, of shouts of laughter, of welcome. Someone had put the carols back on the sound system. *We wish you a merry Christmas, We wish you a merry Christmas...*

A sudden soft wind sent a shower of mistletoe flowers floating to the ground.

Her head was spinning.

'You know I'm wealthy,' Marc told her.

'Medical specialists are always wealthy,' she managed. 'You gave us two great lift chairs. Plus the incubator. I know that was you.'

'But didn't I tell you my parents were independently wealthy? Very wealthy. I've often thought I ought to do something with the family trust rather than keep it mouldering, ready to pass to the next generation, but indecision has left it in the too hard basket. This Christmas...thinking of the impossibility of black geraniums...and thinking of you... I decided why not?'

'The black geranium isn't doing so well now,' she told him, searching for something solid to hold onto. 'We think it's the sea air... Sandra's had to put it in a hot house and hope for the best.'

'I guess there's a bit of hoping for the best in what I plan to do too,' he told her. 'So many things are yet to be decided. But I put feelers out for medics who weren't focused on income, who put working on an island like this right on top of their list of priorities. Amazingly, one column in the *Gazette* had them coming out of my ears. These medics aren't in it for the money. Yes, we have a restricted patient base, but every one of these people value the lifestyle these islands can offer as much as the medicine they can provide.'

'I still can't believe it,' she stammered.

'Then watch this space,' he told her, and he reached out and cupped her face with his lovely hands. 'This is your own Christmas gift, Elsa. Your generosity to me and to this island has made it possible. Happy Christmas, love.'

She stared up at him, speechless, and his gaze met hers. There was no smile. His look was deep and sure and steady. His gaze said that he meant every word.

'And I have another gift for you,' he told her. 'Or maybe not. Maybe it's a gift on hold.'

Releasing her for a moment, he fished in his pocket, then brought out a tiny box, flicking it open to reveal a ring so exquisite she could only gasp. It was a twisted plait of ancient gold with tiny rubies set into each twist, rounding to one magnificent diamond front and centre. It glittered in the sunlight, a siren song, a temptation so great...

'But not for now,' Marc said softly, and her gaze flew up to his. He was smiling with understanding—and with love? 'I know that, sweetheart. I love you with all my heart and I believe, I hope, that you love me right back. But your deep loves—your island, your grandpa—they need to come first. If I love you—and I do—then I need to respect that.'

'I...' She was struggling to get her voice to work. 'Marc...'

'Yes, love?' The words were a caress all on their own.

'You blackmailed me,' she managed, breathless, trying so hard to get the words out. Trying to force herself to sound sensible. 'Then you... you threatened me. Now you're trying to bribe me?'

'I am,' he conceded and—reluctantly, it seemed—he closed the box. 'But know, my love, that this project doesn't hang on you agreeing to marry me. I won't be taking my bat and ball and going home if you reject me. For me this will be a challenge, and I hope I'm up to it. But Elsa, with all my heart I want you beside me as I work on this.'

'I can't...'

'Hear me out.' He put a finger on her lips and brushed another kiss onto her hair. 'Elsa, when I left last year I wasn't really sure what love was. I was fumbling with emotions I'd never felt before, but if there's one thing the enforced wait of this planning has taught me it's that those emotions are true. Elsa, I love you and want you for ever. No matter what else, that's the bottom line. I want to work on this project, but you take precedence. If these plans succeed then I can see work for me here as a cardiologist, but I'll learn to prescribe sugar pills and cope with teenage acne if I must. I'll even give up medicine and learn to fish if that's what it takes. Because, Elsa, my love is yours and, no matter what you want to do with it, I'll love you for ever.'

'Oh, Marc…' She stared up into his eyes, and what she read there… He was speaking the truth. He loved her.

Her Marc.

She was trying so hard to be sensible—and suddenly she knew what sensible was.

'Then you'd better give me that ring right now,' she managed, her voice a wobbly whisper. She reached for the box and struggled through tears to undo the clasp. 'I love you so much. I know you won't be happy fishing…'

'Hey, I like fish and chips,' he told her, his eyes smiling down into her teary ones. 'That has to be a start.'

'It's a great start,' she managed. 'But Marc, the way I feel about you, the way I've been feeling all this year… The way I've been missing you… Even if this medical scenario turns out to be too good to be true, whatever happens, I know that I want you as my husband for the rest of my life.'

There was a long silence at that. A silence where everything changed. Where everything settled.

Where the pole stars became truly aligned and would stay that way for ever.

'Then I guess that's pretty much perfect,' he said huskily, and somehow the box was unfastened again and the ring was slipped onto her finger. It was a trace too big, but there was all the time in the world for them to set that right. 'So this means that you and me…'

'Us,' she whispered. 'Us.'

'Definitely us,' he agreed—and then there was no space for words for a very long time.

How did Christmas come around so fast?

How could so much be achieved in so little time?

Another twelve months, a score of enthusiastic medics, a government badgered by Marc, whose extended circle knew people who knew people who knew people, islanders who were prepared to throw everything they had to give the island group a medical service second to none... Twelve months had achieved a miracle.

The extension to Gannet Hospital had opened in October but even before that the medics had been working in what had essentially been a field hospital. Most had come for that initial month and simply refused to go home. Bob Cruikshank's holiday cottages had been full to bursting, and there were now a dozen permanent homes either planned or partly built across the island chain.

There were enlarged clinics now too, on the outlying islands. A dedicated boat. Marc's chopper plus a pilot who'd also had paramedic training.

A miracle indeed.

Bob Cruikshank was playing Santa this year at the island's Christmas dinner. He'd pleaded for the job and Elsa had gracefully conceded.

In truth she hadn't felt at all confident she'd be able to carry it off. For the last week her tummy was letting her down at odd intervals.

Hmm.

But she wasn't thinking of her tummy now. She was watching Marc play Santa's helper. He was giving a pair of elbow-length leather gardening gloves to the very elderly Rina Ablett who loved her roses above all else but struggled with thorns against her paper-thin skin.

Rina opened her parcel and beamed, and Marc swept

her up into a bear hug before setting her down again and heading back to get the next gift from Santa.

But not before glancing towards Elsa and smiling that smile that warmed her heart, that said no matter how much he was starting to love the islanders, his heart was all hers.

As hers was his. Her Marc. Her husband.

Their wedding had been one special day in November, a ceremony on the bluff overlooking the sea, a celebration that couldn't be held in the island church because every islander and then some had to be present. Every islander had contributed to the celebration in some way. Every islander had been part of it.

It had been a day she'd remember all her life.

Robert had given her away, with pride and with love. Maggie had played matron of honour. Sherlock had been ring-bearer—sort of. He'd been roped pretty firmly to Maggie. There was no way they wanted their ring-bearer scenting a rabbit halfway through the ceremony.

Not that it would have mattered, Elsa thought mistily, fingering the slim band of gold that sat against her gorgeous engagement ring. Not that any of it mattered, the ceremony, the words, the festivities. Not even the glorious honeymoon they'd just spent in St Moritz. She'd felt snow for the first time and it had been magical.

She'd felt married from this day last Christmas when Marc had proposed.

Her Marc.

Home.

'That's the end of them.' The last present distributed, Marc headed back to his seat beside her and kissed her. 'All done. No more presents until next year.'

'There's just one more,' she said serenely.

'Yeah?' They'd exchanged gifts this morning, small, funny things because so much had been given to them this year they could hardly think of anything more they could want.

'I have one more gift for you,' she told him and she took his hand. In private, underneath the loaded table, her hand pressed his downward onto the flat of her belly. Or not quite flat.

His gaze flew to hers, questioning, but as his hand felt what she wanted him to feel she saw his eyes widen with shock.

And then blaze with joy.

'Elsa! Oh, love…'

'Happy Christmas,' she breathed, and it was too much. Surrounded by a sea of islanders and medics, by a Christmas celebration to end all Christmas celebrations, this took it to a new level.

He stood and swept her up into his arms, whirling her around in joy. His was a shout of gladness, of wonder, of the promise of things to come.

And then, as he lowered her so he could kiss her, as he gathered her into his arms, as he held the woman he loved with all his heart, the hall erupted into cheers around them.

They weren't too sure what was happening, but they knew one thing.

Their island doctors were where they belonged.

With each other.

They were home.

* * * * *

MIDWIFE UNDER THE MISTLETOE

KARIN BAINE

For Catherine, Chellie, Julia and Laurie,
who helped me get this book into shape,
and a shout out to Aunt Sadie and Nigel.

A donation has been made to an ICP charity
on behalf of my sister Jemma's 'little itch' – Maisie.

CHAPTER ONE

'ANYONE WOULD THINK I had baby brain,' Iona muttered as she retrieved her perfectly good pen from the bin, where she'd tossed it along with the wet paper towel.

'Are you sure you don't?' Della, her heavily pregnant last appointment of the day, enquired with a grin.

'I'm one hundred percent positive on that score.' You needed to have had *some* sort of relations in order for that to happen and Iona had been a born-again virgin since moving to the tranquillity of the Scottish Highlands. A serious relationship was the last thing she wanted to get entangled in when she was just beginning to get her life together at last.

Although baby brain wasn't an actual recognised medical condition Iona did believe the to-do list for mothers and mothers-to-be could easily push other thoughts from mind. Her lapses in memory today were more likely to be new-house brain. She'd received the keys to her first non-share, non-rented flat this morning and couldn't wait to finish work and go home for the first time.

'That's a shame. I was hoping for a buddy to go to mother and baby club with at the church hall.'

'Sorry to disappoint. Maybe when you're planning baby number three we can co-ordinate our schedules.'

Iona took the teasing with a pinch of salt because a child

of her own was never going to happen. She loved the innocence of a newborn and the pure joy they brought to families and had her personal experiences been different she would've loved to have been a mother herself.

Unfortunately, having a baby meant tying yourself to the father for the rest of your life, with no escape, and she wouldn't trust another man enough to make that sort of commitment again. She'd seen her parents caught in that trap, persevering with a long-dead marriage for the sake of their child, until they'd ended up resenting each other. In her effort to escape the toxic atmosphere she'd attached herself much too young to the dashing Andy, marrying him straight out of school. Only to find herself in an abusive relationship that she knew she would never have left if children had been involved too. It had taken her long enough just to get herself out of it.

No, Iona was happy to remain on the spectator side of pregnancy as a midwife. She was keen to help and support mothers until their babies had been safely delivered and monitor them for as long as they needed it, but her obligation didn't go beyond a medical capacity. At the end of the day the babies went home with their mothers and she wasn't beholden to anyone but herself and her job. She hadn't gone back to school and spent years retraining as a midwife to throw it all away for another man.

Della laughed, clutching her beachball belly. There was definitely a glow in the women who came to the clinic to see Iona and whilst she might experience a pang of regret she'd never get to go through the joys of pregnancy herself, she'd accepted it. Conventional motherhood dictated a lifestyle she wasn't prepared to give up her newfound freedom for.

She dipped the test paper into her patient's urine sample and checked it against the colour chart for analysis. 'Hmm, there's a slight trace of protein. Excess protein can be a sign of a urinary tract infection so we'll have to keep an eye on that in future appointments and if you experience any other symptoms, let me know straight away. Other than that, I'd say pregnancy is agreeing with you.'

Protein in the urine could also be an indicator of kidney damage or other disorders, including pre-eclampsia, but since Della's blood pressure was normal and this was the first sign of a problem, Iona didn't deem it necessary to worry her. If repeat tests showed similar readings she would send a sample to the lab for testing.

She tossed the used stick in the bin and gave her hands another wash. After Dr Irvine's retirement she'd been temporarily upgraded to using this room to treat her patients. Although she was glad of the extra space, she had been sorry to see him go. The senior GP partner—whom she suspected had been practising medicine when Highlanders had still roamed these hills—had made the decision to take her on here at the clinic permanently. It was a position for which she'd be grateful for ever when it had provided her with the financial independence she'd long dreamed about.

Jim, as he'd insisted she call him, had been a true gent with an old-school approach to treating his patients. He'd known everyone in Culcranna by name and had always had time for those who'd needed him. As a result, he'd been well loved and respected. Only time would tell about his replacement, Dr McColl, who'd taken over as senior partner now Jim was content to spend his retirement on the golf course.

Although Fraser McColl was closer to her age than his predecessor, there was a stern quality in his manner that put her on edge and had caused a few run-ins between them. The latest had been his decision to cancel the staff Christmas party usually held on the premises out of hours. He'd called it unprofessional, made noises about it not being covered by insurance and she'd fought him on the issue because she'd been so looking forward to experiencing the tradition she'd heard so much about. Her colleagues had made the annual shindig sound so much fun she'd imagined it would be the perfect way to mark her first Christmas in the village.

Fraser had refused to back down, probably because he'd never understand how much her new job and new home meant to her. By all accounts he came from a family of means, with land and a title to boot, so a tiny flat and a steady income were probably inconsequential to him when they were everything to Iona.

Despite her rallying cry to the rest of the staff to protest, Fraser had imposed so many restrictions on the celebrations they'd been forced into a staid dinner at the nearest restaurant instead. Iona thought his stance on the matter was more about him letting the power go to his head than any insurance issues and had told him so in a fit of pique.

Since then they'd had a few minor rows, more to do with their clash of personalities than to any professional discourse. Iona didn't appreciate anyone imposing unjustified restrictions on her after enduring a lifetime of that with her ex, and apparently Fraser didn't gel well with people who didn't fall into line. Which was tough luck for him because she was no longer prepared to tailor who she was to suit the needs of others.

There was no doubting Fraser's skills or popularity as one of the practice doctors but his tendency to take over certain situations wasn't a character trait she was keen on these days. With his dark, wavy hair and piercing green eyes he certainly cut a dashing figure in the sleepy village that even Iona wasn't immune to. Whilst he had some of the local ladies hot under their cardigans, he reminded her of the men in her past who'd tried to stunt her personal growth. There was too much apparent control freakery about him for her to drop her defences, or any item of clothing, and she hated herself for finding him remotely attractive.

Perhaps if he kept his mouth shut she could enjoy the view at least, without having her hackles raised along with her pulse.

'You wouldn't be saying that if you saw me in the wee hours of the morning, running to the loo every five minutes, or when my insides are on fire with heartburn.' Della shuffled her bottom to the edge of the chair before attempting to get to her feet, trying to balance the extra weight she was carrying around her middle.

Iona gave her a hand rather than watch her struggle like a turtle flipped onto its back, trying to right itself.

'Well, you haven't long to go now. I'll see you in a couple of weeks if you don't go into labour before then.' They'd discussed Della having to be induced if she went too far past her predicted due date but as this was her second pregnancy with no previous complications, Iona wasn't expecting she would require medical intervention.

'Thanks. I can't wait to have this little bundle in my arms.' That tender belly-rub every mother-to-be performed in here made Iona think about her own mum and the excitement she must've felt before her impending birth. A woman didn't carry and protect her baby for nine months expecting they'd both end up trapped in a life neither of them wanted.

She swallowed the rising sob in her chest. They were both free from those soul-destroying relationships now. It was just a tragedy it had come at the price of her mother's death.

'Your daughter will be here soon enough.' Iona handed Della's antenatal notes back to her with a smile. This was supposed to be a happy time for both of them. She had her own baby to get back to—her shiny new flat—and since they were three-quarters of the way through December she'd even treated herself to some new Christmas decorations. Some might say she'd gone overboard but she had enough to brighten up this dreary place too and really mark her first Christmas in the village.

'I need these bloods sent off to the lab, there's a pile of hospital referrals that need to be chased up, and this is Mrs Robertson's prescription. Her husband's going to call in before closing. I've informed him we usually require forty-eight hours for repeat prescriptions and we can't keep on doing this.'

'But she is eighty-three and we have to make allowances,' Sheila, Fraser's secretary, reminded him as she took the stack of paperwork from him with a nod and set it on her desk.

'It doesn't mean I have to be happy about it.' He had enough to do without these last-minute requests to deal with too.

Taking on the role of senior partner brought with it a lot of extra form filling and bureaucracy but it was a position he revelled in. It gave him an extra say in how the practice was run and that would make him infinitely happier in his work. Structure and boundaries gave him a sense of security, an assurance he was doing things right. It was when he strayed from the rules that things fell apart. Okay, so he was no longer that over-active little boy whose parents had sent him to boarding school so he wouldn't disturb his sick mother, but he'd learned his lesson since then. If he played by the rules there was a place for him and things would work out fine. Now he simply had to get everyone else to fall in line with him.

Not all of Jim Irvine's practices adhered with that idea of running a smooth clinic. Now, there was a man who hadn't bothered too much about form filling or adhering to schedules. That kind of reckless approach had led to inevitable chaos and caused a run-on effect that could have seen the practice run into the ground if not for Fraser picking up the slack to keep the place afloat.

At least Sheila, his second-in-command, who'd been here since the year dot, appreciated how hard he was working to make these changes a success and could be relied on to keep on top of things. Sure, some of his forward-thinking ideas were going to rub a few members of staff up the wrong way. One particular community midwife with chestnut-coloured curls, who thrived on challenging his authority, sprang to mind, having made it clear she preferred his predecessor's slap dash ethos to his.

When Iona had first started working at the clinic Fraser had been pleased they'd drafted in some new blood to bring some modern thinking into the outdated practice and lower the average age of the village population at the same time. There weren't many single, young women in the vicinity but if he'd harboured any nonsensical ideas about finding someone else to settle down with again, Iona had put paid to that with her rebellion against his attempts to bring some structure to the practice.

She refused to attend his weekly meetings regarding the cleaning rota for the staffroom on the basis she ate her meals in her car and was solely responsible for its upkeep. Then there was the argument they'd had over the clutter Iona seemed to accumulate in her room. She'd told him in no uncertain terms that it was her territory and as long as it was clean and functional it was not Fraser's concern.

It seemed Iona preferred to tackle problems as they came in rather than pre-empt them. He'd been there with Caroline, his last girlfriend, and wasn't prepared to go through it again. Caroline had let him imagine they had a future together, planning that happy family with him he'd long been denied. Only she'd decided at the last minute it wasn't what she wanted at all and had blamed him for apparently not being true to her, or himself. Whatever that meant.

So he'd ploughed all of his energy back into work instead of the domestic bliss he'd been promised. He wasn't going to let another flighty woman steal his dreams from him when a new efficient way of working would better serve patients and staff alike.

Whether Iona Munro liked it or not, his new system was getting results. His last patient had been and gone and he was finishing for the day bang on time. Simply by sticking to the ten-minute time slots for each appointment, everything was running like clockwork. He'd say that was a resounding success and a score for all of the Type A personalities out there.

'I'll get on to these straight away, Dr McColl,' Sheila called after him since he'd already left the main office to check all patients had left the premises. At this time of the evening, as the working day was winding down, the hubbub outside the treatment rooms had usually died down, but there were still a few voices ringing out from the reception area. Any out-of-hours emergencies now should have been referred to the hospital or the doctor on call for the area.

The notion that his perfectly executed schedule had been thrown into disarray ploughed grooves across Fraser's forehead even before he was met with the debacle in the waiting area.

'Lift your side up a little higher. Left a bit. How does that look now? Is it straight?' Iona was balanced on a chair, trying to pin a gaudy gold-foil garland to the ceiling, with Victoria, the receptionist, as her partner in crime.

'What the—?' Fraser stopped dead in his tracks at the sight of Iona, barefoot and on tiptoe, breaking every health and safety rule in the workplace. He was in danger of hyperventilating as he did a quick risk assessment of the scene.

'Oh, hi, Fraser. I thought we could brighten the place up and make it look less sterile in here.' Unlike the rest of the staff, who quickly made themselves scarce, Iona carried on decorating as though she was perfectly entitled to do as she pleased. It was one thing managing her own caseload but she didn't have any authority outside that.

'It's supposed to be sterile!' Fraser didn't want to lose his temper when that would be a sign he wasn't in control. Although the garish garlands draped across every available space, transforming the beige room into an eyesore of gold and red, hinted he hadn't asserted his authority here as much as he'd believed.

'Lighten up, Fraser. It's Christmas. If you're worried about the cost, it's coming from my own pocket, not yours.

'Fraser.' This was exactly why she rubbed him up the wrong way. Iona gave no thought for the rules or decorum in the workplace, or anywhere else for that matter. The patients loved her easygoing persona but for Fraser that free spirit vibe was unsettling, as was anything that didn't fit into his idea of conformity. It upset that safe environment he was trying to set up here, and quite frankly he didn't know how to handle it.

Fraser had mistakenly believed Caroline had been the one person who'd understood him when they'd made their plans to get married and settle down into quiet family life, but when his father had died and he'd inherited the family estate he'd discovered the truth. Once Fraser had the means to make those dreams a reality Caroline had confessed they'd been nothing more than an idea she'd been paying lip service to, not a legitimate option. That level of deception had ultimately ended their relationship and Fraser's hope for the future.

This was different, though. Iona wasn't a love interest, so her casual attitude to life shouldn't bother him on a personal level, but she was a staff member and they had rules in place here for a reason.

'I appreciate the gesture,' Fraser said diplomatically, doing his best to remain calm. Iona didn't know him personally so wouldn't understand the issues he had with the whole palaver at this time of the year.

They'd never gone in for the whole over-the-top lead up to Christmas at boarding school and the death of his mother on Christmas Eve had cemented Fraser's dislike of the season. It was a reminder of the childhood he'd lost and the family that had never recovered from the devastation of cancer. Now he dreaded that last week in December more than ever since it was also the anniversary of his break-up with Caroline.

He'd made the mistake of trying to embrace Christmas last year in an effort to make it special for her with an over-the-top marriage proposal, including a horse-drawn sleigh and carol singers serenading them along the ride. Only she'd turned him down on the basis that he was 'being fake'. Fraser couldn't win and was now even less likely to get caught up in the fuss, reverting back to his true Grinchy self, unwilling to be one of those people who lost their minds for the sake of one anti-climactic day.

On the rare occasions his parents had retrieved Fraser for the holidays it had been a non-event anyway. They'd gone through the motions without ever getting bogged down in the sentiment. Whilst he'd yearned for this infantile nonsense as a child far from home, he'd learned to live without it.

Iona carried on making her mark on the recently painted ceiling, humming Christmas carols and reminding Fraser what a very long month December could be when you weren't in the festive spirit.

'As I said, I appreciate the gesture but we can't have all

of this cluttering up the surgery.' He would've told her that if she'd sought his permission in the first place.

'I think the patients will love it. It gives them something to focus on other than their aches and pains.'

Sure. They'd all end up with tinsel blindness on top of everything else.

'I'm sorry, it'll all have to go. It's a health and safety hazard.' Fraser began to detach the string of fairy lights from the reception desk.

'Okay, I'll give you the lights. They haven't been assessed by a registered electrician but they are bonny. Perhaps I could bung more tinsel there instead. I have some neon pink somewhere...' Iona clearly wasn't going to give this up without a fight and, as had become the custom, Fraser would have to get tough to have his opinion heard.

He ripped down the cardboard Father Christmas she'd stuck to the counter and hoped it wouldn't leave any sticky marks behind. 'It's all going to have to come down.'

Iona stopped this time. 'You're kidding me, right?'

'I don't kid.' He reached his hand up and tugged the large blue and silver foil star dangling from the ceiling until the tack holding it in place dislodged and pinged to the floor. This was exactly what he was talking about. One drawing pin in the wrong person's foot and they could be facing a lawsuit. Luckily for them both he spotted the gold pin glinting on the dark carpet and retrieved it before it damaged more than his peace of mind.

'What harm can a few decorations do?' Iona faced him, her displeasure flaring in her big brown eyes and her full lips pursed into a tight line. It didn't thrill him to note he was the one with the power to steal away the twinkling smile she wore for everyone else.

'They're a breeding ground for germs with so many sick people coming and going. Then there's the dust. Think of how many asthma patients we have. Our appointment list is full enough without putting it under more stress.' Deep down Fraser knew he was grasping for excuses but coming into the clinic every morning and being reminded of the worst days of his life was too much for him to bear.

'Okay. Okay. I get it. I was only trying to do something nice. Talk about dampening the mood,' she muttered as though he wasn't there, and began dismantling her ceiling display.

'I know, but perhaps next time you could check with me first instead of going rogue?' Fraser understood her intentions had been good and would've preferred not to fuel this animosity between them, but Iona's spur-of-the-moment actions were infuriating when they impeached on his carefully laid plans and tugged on emotions that needed to remain dormant for the remainder of this dreaded month.

'Yes, sir.' With her anger clearly still bubbling away, Iona yanked down the bunting she'd only finished hanging.

Fraser watched in horror as she tottered on the chair, clearly off balance, her arms freewheeling in the air as she fell.

With lightning-fast reflexes he rushed over and caught her in his arms before she hit the floor. Iona's yelp softened to a gasp as he hooked a hand under her knees and one under her arms. Instinctively she latched her arms around his neck but that contact and the strong grip she had on him almost startled him into dropping her again.

The adrenaline rush was making them both breathe heavily and in that moment, holding her in his arms, their faces almost touching, it was easy to forget what they'd been fighting over, or even where they were.

She weighed very little, reminding him how delicate she appeared to be beyond the bravado. Despite her petite frame, she projected herself as a larger-than-life character but, with their clashing personalities stripped away for the time being, he was reacting solely as a man with an attractive woman pressed against him and was too stunned to do anything other than enjoy the sensation.

Iona blinked first. 'You can put me down now. I think I'm safe.'

'Sure.' Fraser abruptly set her back on her feet and tried to compose himself. 'Like I said, a health and safety nightmare.'

He ignored her tutting as she tore down the rest of the decorations, thankful that this moment of madness had passed, letting normal, tense service resume between them. It was easier to view her as a threat to his plans for a new, improved workplace than through any inappropriate romantic haze.

CHAPTER TWO

As SHE DID every morning, Iona arrived at the clinic with plenty of time to spare before she was officially on the clock. Due to the unpredictable nature of midwifery, scheduled meal breaks were impossible and she often had to eat on the road, if she managed to eat at all. So having a quick cup of tea and a bowl of porridge in the morning as she checked her schedule for the day ensured Iona had at least one proper meal in peace.

Today she was especially keen to get on the road as she'd booked the afternoon off. It was moving day and she was bursting with the excitement of transferring her belongings from her rental to her very own home. It wouldn't take more than a few runs in the car with the meagre possessions she had, and some of her male colleagues had volunteered to give her a hand with the heavy lifting. The sooner Iona got around her patients, the sooner she'd get settled into her own place.

Except as she lifted her first spoonful of thick, oaty goodness to her mouth, a note in the blood results of one of her patients immediately threw her plans into chaos. Iona shovelled in her breakfast as quickly as she could while digesting the news that had come in.

At around five days old, babies were offered newborn blood spot screening, or a heel-prick test, where a small amount of blood is taken to screen for certain genetic disorders. In this case, the baby had tested positive for one of the listed conditions—phenylketonuria, or PKU for short. Although Iona had done some research into the illness during the course of her training, it was a rare metabolic condition she'd never personally come across before, with approximately only one baby in ten thousand in the UK a sufferer.

The genetic mutation for phenylketonuria was passed on by both parents who might not even have been aware they were carriers. PKU patients, unable to break down the amino acid phenylalanine, a building block of protein, could have a build-up of protein leading to brain damage without adherence to a strict low-protein diet. It was imperative the child be referred to the metabolic unit at the hospital as soon as possible to begin treatment and prevent any long-term damage.

Although modern advances thankfully kept the condition under control with the restricted diet and amino acid supplement to ensure normal development, Iona was aware the news would have a great impact on the family. Every new mum wanted to believe her baby was perfect and to be told otherwise could be difficult to accept and overwhelming.

She took a gulp of tea before pouring the rest down the sink and gave the dishes a quick rinse. There wasn't liable to be a spare minute today but she had one more thing to do before she could hit the road and she wasn't looking forward to it.

Every time she had thought about Dr McColl since last night her blood had boiled, sure his intense dislike of the season was to spite her. She'd made no secret of her desire to make this Christmas one to remember but Fraser seemed determined to thwart those efforts at every turn.

Iona told herself it was this battle of wills that made

her react so passionately when she thought of him and nothing to do with whatever frisson she'd imagined when he'd caught her in his arms yesterday. She was no longer the kind of woman who let common sense be overridden by such a romantic cliché. It would take more than being swept off her feet and a handsome face for her to fall for another dominant male. Her sense of self was now defined by her home and her job, not by some fool idea of romance, love and that non-existent fairy-tale ending.

With a deep breath and a sharp knock on the door, she entered Fraser's room out of courtesy rather than a desire to see him for the first time today. In too much of a hurry to waste time on pleasantries, she didn't wait for him to acknowledge her.

'I thought I should give you the heads-up on one of your patients, Marie Gillen. Her baby has tested positive for phenylketonuria.'

There was a slight rise of Fraser's eyebrows before surprise was overtaken by furious typing on the computer keyboard.

'Is this something you've encountered before?' he asked over the sound of the printer whizzing into life.

'Not first hand.' The discovery of rare conditions always brought a range of emotion to the fore, with sympathy for the family at the top of the list. As a medical professional, though, Iona became curious to learn as much as she could to pass on to the parents so they were equipped to deal with whatever challenges were thrown at them. It had to be the same for the GPs who would go on to treat these patients, probably for the rest of their lives.

'Nor me.' Fraser ripped out a handful of printed pages, stapled half together and passed them to Iona, keeping the remainder for himself.

'I'm going to speak to the metabolic unit before I see Mrs Gillen. She'll need a referral straight away.' Since

Marie and her newborn were Iona's patients, she would be the one to oversee the initial handover to the hospital.

'This is some basic info on PKU you can give to her. I'm sure you have it all in hand but it will do us all good to reacquaint ourselves with the challenges ahead.' The way Fraser said it made it sound as though he expected her to make a home visit straight away when she'd intended to wait until she'd spoken to a consultant.

'You know I'm on a half-day? I'm only here until lunch-time because I'm moving house today.' Iona didn't know if he was aware of her time off so she gave him the benefit of the doubt that he wasn't deliberately trying to antagonise her again.

'You can see her first and put the rest of your appointments back. The family need to know and this kind of bombshell is best delivered in person.' When Iona didn't respond immediately, stunned that he was pulling rank on her, Fraser added, 'You know this is a time-sensitive condition and we need to begin treatment as soon as possible.'

She knew he was right and if she hadn't been so caught up in her moving plans she would have suggested the same. As the only midwife at the practice, she didn't have anyone else to delegate to so the responsibility was solely hers to deliver the news to the family. That didn't mean she couldn't be irritated at losing her time off.

The slightest brush of his fingers against hers as he handed her the information started that prickling sensation beneath her skin she'd experienced for the first time last night when he'd held her in his arms just a fraction longer than necessary.

That spark of awareness in Fraser's eyes said he'd felt it too but it only served to annoy Iona more. The GP who'd stolen Christmas was now dousing cold water on the plans for her afternoon off so she shouldn't find anything remotely attractive about him.

'I'm sorry for yesterday but, you know, we have to have a code of conduct in the workplace or all hell would break loose.'

She stared at him, unblinking, wondering if he was trying to justify nixing her time off by blaming her for making a move on *him*. Her cheeks burned all the more when she realised he was talking about her dalliance into interior decorating and she was the only one whose thoughts had strayed elsewhere.

'It's all sorted now. Don't worry about it.' Although Fraser deserved more flak over his over-the-top reaction to a few baubles, it would keep until she'd got over this bout of madness.

'If you need an appointment for me to see Mrs Gillen, let me know and I'll fit her into my schedule.'

There were a lot of things about Fraser that frustrated Iona no end but she couldn't fault his devotion to his patients. Their mutual patients were a shared interest. Somehow that didn't give her any more comfort. Iona greedily snatched at more reasons to dislike him to erase the memory of the tenderness she'd felt in his touch and the desire she'd seen in his eyes when he'd held her close.

In that brief moment she'd understood those defences she'd built up against this man were because she was afraid of liking him too much. She had enough physical and mental scars to be wary of any man, especially the bossy kind, but she worried even that mightn't be enough to save her.

'I'll let you know. I guess moving day will just have to wait.'

Fraser nodded and with her last obligation here taken care of, Iona was able to make her escape from the claustrophobia of these four walls.

There was nothing akin to driving out on the open road, radio blasting and singing along at the top of your voice where no one could hear. Iona loved her job. Sure, it was challenging, the hours long with no discernible time for breaks, but it was rewarding. Not only did she get to accompany these women throughout their pregnancies and sometimes get to welcome their babies into the world herself, she was able to enjoy her independence on a daily basis.

She was free to drive out here in the beautiful Scottish countryside, often travelling for miles between each of her appointments. It gave her that sense of empowerment over her destiny, even though she was still technically an employee.

Her freedom was everything to her after her marriage, during which Andy had practically held her prisoner. She'd been blinded by love in those early days, unable to see how he was slowly isolating her from friends and family, insisting he was the only one she needed in her life. Cut off from anyone who could've helped her, she'd been at the mercy of his temper when it had shown itself. He'd used any excuse to lash out at her—if the dinner had been overcooked or she'd been wearing too much make-up—but towards the end he hadn't even bothered making excuses to beat her it had become so commonplace.

Iona flinched, almost able to feel those blows raining down on her after all this time. It was then she had understood why her mother had endured her own loveless relationship for so long. She'd been worn down, cut off from the outside world with no means to support herself financially when she'd sacrificed everything for her family. It had been Andy's talk of babies and her mother's death that had finally galvanised Iona into action. She could never have brought a child into that toxic atmosphere when she'd grown up in similar herself and had followed the pattern into adulthood.

It had taken death to enable her mother to leave her own

marriage and Iona hadn't been prepared to wait for the same fate. The strength she'd found to walk out on Andy and file for divorce had carried her on to university and to carve out a whole new life for herself.

Placements during her training had seen Iona working in hospitals and birth clinics but that environment had been a conveyor belt of women passing through her hands with no room to get to know them on a personal level. Life as a community midwife gave her much more of an intimate connection, visiting the patients at home and being on hand as they settled into family life.

She took a bite of the pre-packed sandwich she'd bought at the garage on the way back from Mrs Gillen's. Car picnics were Iona's speciality, if not the hearty dinner she'd been hoping to have in her own place tonight. Now all she wanted was to get back and collapse into bed.

It had been a tough day all round with having to deliver baby Gillen's diagnosis. The family had been rocked by the news and it would take some time to come to terms with what it meant for them but they had family close to provide a good support system.

With some liaising with the hospital team she'd managed to arrange a meeting for them tomorrow morning so hopefully that would ease their minds that their son would still live a full and active life with proper guidance.

She'd talked them through the basics of PKU, as outlined in Fraser's printouts, leaving the experts to discuss the day-to-day realities. There had been no need to panic them by overloading them with information when they couldn't do anything until they'd seen the metabolic consultant and dietician who'd be overseeing the treatment.

The circumstances, however, dictated Iona had stayed with the family much longer than she'd anticipated and she'd been forced to push the rest of her appointments back. It wasn't something she was happy doing to people waiting in for her but given the cold weather her patients had assured her they'd no intention of venturing outside today. She didn't blame them. Given half a chance, she'd have stayed indoors with a mug of hot chocolate and a cheesy Christmas film on the TV.

Of course, the extra time had meant not only had she missed out on her afternoon off but the surgery would likely be closed by now and she'd wanted to stop by to grab a few things for tomorrow.

After eight months in the village Iona knew the area pretty well but in the dark, with the first flurry of snow visible in the car headlights, these remote roads were daunting, to say the least. When she saw the lights on at the clinic ahead she breathed a sigh of relief that she'd made it back in one piece and she could stock up on supplies for tomorrow's excursions.

It would be an early start tomorrow again in order to keep up to date with all of her patients and paperwork. Being a midwife required stamina and not for the first time she was glad she didn't have to go home and go straight into wife and mother mode to keep others happy. As soon as she was done here she could go home and slip into the guise of knackered singleton guilt-free.

'Hello. It's Iona. Can you let me in?' She rapped on the clinic window, hoping whoever was here, cleaning or catching up on last-minute paperwork, would open up.

'I hope you're not expecting overtime.' Fraser's dour tone almost tipped her over the edge into a rant about putting her patients above financial gain and her own plans, until she saw the tease playing on his lips. In her exhausted state Iona wasn't sure she was prepared to deal with the sight.

'I just want to restock with supplies for tomorrow morning.' Iona didn't rise to the bait, not willing to prolong her working day any longer than necessary. With his large frame filling the doorway, she chose to duck under his arm as he held the door open, rather than take the chance of touching him again by pushing past.

'How is Mrs Gillen?' Unable to take the hint that she didn't want him near her, Fraser followed her into the stockroom. Iona should've known he'd want a full account to analyse if she'd handled the situation correctly, no doubt concerned he'd be the one to pick up the pieces if Marie fell apart.

'Shocked, obviously, but reasonably calm. I passed on the printouts you provided.' He could give himself a pat on the back that he'd participated in some way if that's what he was interested in.

'Good. Good. Would you like me to make an emergency appointment to discuss any concerns with her?' With his arms folded and resting casually against the shelves, Fraser left scant breathing space in the small room. There really was no reason for them both to be crammed in here so Iona forced her way past into the corridor so she wasn't suffocated by his spicy aftershave.

'No, I've made arrangements for her at the metabolic unit. The consultant and dietician will take over from here.'

She doubted he'd be one hundred percent happy about being out of the loop but there were areas even out of his expertise.

'They know best,' he conceded politely.

'How come you're here so late?' Usually you could set your watch by Fraser, who tried to keep office hours when he wasn't on call. He'd never have made it as a midwife.

The idea of him in blue scrubs, tootling around the countryside in her small car, made her grin and she had to turn away so he wouldn't see her amusement.

'I thought I'd swot up on PKU while I was waiting for you.'

The admission made her do an about-turn. 'Me? What on earth for?'

Their contretemps over the decorations immediately sprang to mind, along with that back-of-the-neck tingling sensation. Her pulse apparently thought she was in a sprint and other parts of her were reminding her it had been a long time since she'd been with a man and she should simply acknowledge this growing attraction for her colleague. If the opportunity arose to get close again, she couldn't be certain common sense would get any say in the matter when her hormones were currently doing all the talking.

'I thought you might need help moving in.' The expression on Fraser's face displayed concern rather than an intention to seduce her. He was the innocent party in the lurid fantasies her overtired mind insisted on conjuring up.

'I'll just have to reschedule for the next time I'm free. Whenever that might be.' Her need for sleep now was more vital than assuaging Fraser's apparent guilt that she'd been held up and she wished she'd never broached the subject with him. It put her in a no-win situation. Saying no to him wasn't going to help their already strained relationship but letting him trespass into her private life wasn't going to be comfortable for either of them.

'Call it my apology for yesterday. I could've handled things better.' Hands in pockets, he gave a shrug and appeared even less of a tyrant than ever. None of that was helping Iona maintain that wall of steel she tried to surround herself with at the merest hint of a too-alpha male. Sincere apologies and taking responsibility for anything weren't traits often associated with such domineering personalities. She should know.

On this occasion Iona had to consider the possibility she might have been mistaken in her assessment of Fraser McColl. Then she could stop being so hard on herself for being drawn to him. Unfortunately this humble side of him decreed a compromise on her part lest she become the sort of obstinate-to-a-fault twit she despised.

'Me too. I should've asked before I did my sugar-plum fairy act. I got a bit carried away.'

'Really? I hadn't noticed.' There was that grin again and Iona wondered if it was reserved for the privileged few or it only made appearances out of working hours. It was unnerving that she even wanted to know what her relevance was to the rare sighting.

'It's my first Christmas in my own home, free from demanding family members, messy flatmates and fussy co-workers. Excuse me for being a tad over-excited.' It spoke volumes that the first purchases for her new place had been an abundance of Christmas paraphernalia instead of essential household appliances.

'I can't say I understand the need for the fuss but each to their own as long as it doesn't leak onto the premises again.' Fraser verbally slapped the back of her hand but she'd had much worse from other men she'd inadvertently ticked off in the past.

'What do you have against Christmas anyway?' Since they appeared to have embarked on a truce, Iona thought it best to find out as much as she could about the elusive doctor before the clock chimed and he transformed back into his monstrous alter-ego.

She could see the inner struggle he was having as to whether or not to share the reasons behind his anti-Christmas stance in his hesitation to reply. He was watching her as though judging if she was trustworthy enough to keep his secrets.

Eventually Fraser sighed and said, 'My mother died on Christmas Eve. I was six when they first discovered she had breast cancer. I haven't really celebrated since, packed off out of the way to boarding school when she first became ill. Come to think of it, I don't remember ever celebrating even before I associated her death with Christmas. It's just not a point in my life I'm keen to relive every year.'

The heartfelt explanation shook Iona to her core—she had never expected such an honest and bleak insight into his background. As someone whose job was all about families and protecting young children, it was only natural Fraser's story should get her choked up. She knew how traumatic it was to lose a mother but at such a young age he must've suffered dreadfully.

It explained a lot about his negative outlook on the season and she winced at how tactless her actions now seemed with hindsight. The shock of seeing those decorations would've brought those painful memories flooding back to him and it was no wonder he'd been angry at her. She was sorry that he'd been denied the joy in sharing Christmas with family but she didn't want to pry too far into his personal life and jeopardise their ceasefire. It wasn't as though she was keen to discuss Christmases gone by either.

'I understand that and I'm really sorry for your loss but if you ever need someone to sprinkle a little Christmas magic, you know where to find me.' It wasn't a serious offer when it was probably too late to change his opinion on the subject but she did manage to get him to smile.

'I certainly do but don't let my hang-ups encroach on your obvious enthusiasm. You're perfectly entitled to celebrate however you choose, in your personal life.'

'It is a big deal for me this year,' Iona said apologetically, understanding his point of view but also determined to go all out for herself.

'In that case, we should start with getting you moved in properly.' Fraser turned off the lights and ushered her towards the door so he could set the alarm.

Ready or not, her new best friend was coming home with her for the night.

CHAPTER THREE

'LET ME GET that for you.' Fraser made a grab for the door while balancing a heavy cardboard box in his other hand.

'It's fine. I can manage.' Iona, who could barely be seen over the top of the stacked boxes in her arms, insisted on doing it herself.

'No problem.' He took a step back so she wouldn't think he was trying to crowd her. Iona was so independent Fraser always felt he was in her way somehow, even though she would never have managed to move all of this on her own.

None of this had been in his plans tonight. He had, instead, been anticipating another quiet night in with nothing but the clock chimes echoing through the house to disturb him. It had been his guilty conscience preventing him from walking away from the whole situation when he'd heard from other staff members how excited she'd been about moving in tonight.

Iona nudged the door open with her bottom but he wasn't sure how they were going to manoeuvre her belongings up the narrow staircase leading to the flat above the shop.

'Sorry. I didn't mean to snap. It's just…this is a milestone for me.' The apology was as much of a surprise as the tears he could see making her eyes shine like glossy chocolate. It was clearly an emotional moment for her and probably for more than the reasons she'd given him. He'd experienced something similar when he'd taken over the family home after his father had passed away, believing it was going to be the start of his new life with a wife and children, surrounded by love for the first time. Before then, being on his own had been something he'd simply taken for granted because he didn't remember life before it.

Even if he hadn't had his hands full, Iona didn't give him a chance to pry any further as she made her way upstairs. Clearly the sharing of personal information was only coming from one direction tonight. Fraser had surprised himself by telling her about his mother's death. It wasn't something he usually told people and certainly not those he had trouble getting along with. However, he did want to explain his behaviour surrounding the Christmas issue so she wouldn't hate him too much. Since she hadn't slammed the door on him, Fraser had assumed he'd made the right move.

He'd kept finding excuses to stay behind at the surgery tonight—paperwork, the weather, waiting for news on the Gillens—but as soon as Iona had arrived he'd realised he'd been waiting to see her again so he could make it up to her for spoiling her plans. He had been sure she would come back to make preparations for the next working day and he suspected his overtime had been driven partially by curiosity over that frisson between them last night. It had definitely been attraction on his part, unexpected and somewhat inconvenient since they were co-workers and not harmonious ones at that.

Wandering the empty corridors of his family home, Fraser had little else to focus on other than his work and now that it had become entangled in his personal life it was impossible not to spend the night thinking about Iona.

He didn't know what he'd expected to come of seeing her after hours but he certainly hadn't imagined going home with her. With their history he'd never thought she'd actually agree to let him help.

It wasn't immediately obvious if her concession was for purely practical reasons or if she, too, was keen to explore that new chemistry between them. He wasn't about to ask when any possible answer was sure to unsettle him more. A dalliance with a colleague was totally out of the question, too disruptive, too close to home, and it had disaster written all over it. He couldn't afford to have his love life screwing things up at work when he was just beginning to get things the way he wanted.

'I know what you're thinking.'

Fraser nearly dropped Iona's belongings at being caught having inappropriate thoughts about her.

'What's that?' He aimed for a neutral 'I have no idea what you're talking about' tone as he stacked his box on top of the ones she'd positioned on the floor. There was still a car full of bric-a-brac outside but he reckoned he could unload it into the hall in double-quick time if he incurred her wrath.

'Why would I leave a pretty chocolate-box cottage for this only a few days before Christmas?'

Once it became clear his thoughts remained private, Fraser deemed it safe to engage in conversation again. 'It's none of my business.'

Since she'd pointed it out, the contrast between the homely bungalow he'd helped her empty to come to this shell of an apartment did raise questions.

'I mean, Mrs Dunlop said I was welcome to stay as my rent is paid up until the New Year.'

'But you're excited about having your own place? I think you mentioned that.' Fraser could tell how happy Iona was. Her smile was warm enough to heat the whole building—which was just as well because he doubted the central heating had been on since the last tenant had vacated the property.

Personally, Fraser couldn't see the attraction but, given how Iona had no qualms about making her mark at the surgery, he was certain she'd quickly make it a home. As soon as she bought some furniture. Unless this was one of those futuristic, space-saving apartments where the fixtures and fittings popped up from the floor at the touch of a button, she really didn't have any furniture of note.

Iona's quirks were in danger of bringing Fraser out in hives, her inability to plan ahead making him itch. When he'd transferred his stuff from his bachelor pad to the family home he'd allocated a specific timescale for completion, with all his things boxed and labelled accordingly for the removal company. Iona had randomly chucked things into cardboard boxes and bin liners with no forethought given to how she expected to find anything again. Even if she hadn't got caught up at work, there was no way she'd have managed to get things in order in the space of one afternoon.

'I do have a bed, well, a mattress, and there's a kettle here somewhere.' She began rifling through everything, unwrapping the contents until the floorboards were littered with bits of newspaper and kitchen paraphernalia.

'I'll go and bring the rest in.' Fraser couldn't stand back and watch this level of chaos without wanting to fix it. Something he knew Iona wouldn't appreciate. This wasn't his mess or responsibility and he had to get used to the fact Iona had chosen to live this way.

By the time he'd lugged the rest of her trash chic luggage into the flat Iona had moved into the kitchen. It would be generous to call the space open-plan, it was more in keeping with a student bedsit or, in its current state, a squat.

He shuddered as he set the bags down in the one space he could find amongst the mess she'd already created.

'If that's everything, I'll head home.' Back to his pristine house, which didn't look as though it had just been burgled.

'Look what I found!' Ignoring his plea to be released back into civilised society, Iona held up the elusive kettle and two mismatched mugs.

'Great,' Fraser muttered through clenched teeth, accepting his fate. It wouldn't help relations between them if he declined her hospitality when she was trying to be friendly.

'For a job well done.' Iona clinked her mug to his once she'd completed her task, oblivious to his discomfort in the corduroy beanbag serving as his seat during their tea break. The chipped cartoon cat mug he was drinking from was a world away from his mother's fine china he'd become accustomed to.

'So, er, what are your plans for the place?' The old outhouse, long forgotten somewhere on the family estate, was more inviting than these four bare walls, yet Iona was so pleased with it Fraser wondered what kind of place she was used to.

Iona shrugged and slurped her tea. 'I'll get some paint to freshen it up a bit for Christmas and I'll pick up whatever bits and pieces I need along the way.'

Fraser snorted in disbelief at her *laissez-faire* attitude to being a homeowner. For someone so fastidious about her work and keeping track of her patients, Iona was very blasé about her own personal life.

'We're very different creatures, you and I.' Fraser supposed she would be as ill at ease with his set-up—with the family heirlooms giving it that look-but-don't-touch vibe that made people hover nervously—as he was here.

'I thought we'd figured that out a long time ago.' She

was teasing, even though there'd been nothing funny about their previous arguments.

'We've had our moments.' This insight into Iona's chaotic world, such a contrast to the one Fraser had created around himself, made sense of their feisty exchanges. They were completely different people and living up to that adage about opposites. Last night they'd finally recognised the attraction even if they hadn't acted on it.

Somewhere across the room Iona cleared her throat and he knew her mind had ventured into the same dangerous territory as his.

Fraser drained the last of his tea. He'd become too comfortable in Iona's company, if not her new dwelling. 'Time to go.'

'Thanks again for all your help.'

He struggled to clamber out of the shape-shifting cushion trying to swallow him whole, which didn't help the growing sense of panic clawing at his chest. He had to get away from here, be somewhere safe and orderly where he wouldn't be ambushed by the furnishings or unexpected emotions.

'Perhaps I'll start my purchases with a chair or two.' Iona came to his aid, holding out her hand to hoist him out of the man trap.

'Not on my account,' Fraser insisted. He had no intention of coming back here and certainly not to relive those distracting feelings he kept experiencing around her. If only he'd stuck to his schedule, all of this could have been avoided. This kind of havoc was exactly what happened when he didn't abide by his own rules.

'You never know who's going to drop in and, as I've just witnessed, not everyone's used to slumming it on beanbags.' Unlike his, Iona's place was the sort people would be dropping into whenever the notion took them. She wasn't the type to be governed by social etiquette outside work, which made her home so much more appealing than the formal invitation one would require to gain admittance to his. Fraser couldn't remember the last time he'd even had a house guest but that isolation was part of the charm as far as he was concerned.

Fraser negotiated his way through the detritus on the floor, waved goodbye at the door, but for the entire journey home he couldn't help worrying on Iona's behalf about her lack of preparation for the move. Neither could he put out the thought of the contents of his own apartment sitting in storage now he had no use for them. Iona was so pleased with so little but she really deserved better, and with a small effort on his part he could provide it for her *and* have her think of him a tad more fondly. He didn't know why her acceptance had suddenly become important to him but it might have had something to do with her smiling at him instead of the usual scowl he elicited.

It warmed him on the inside, reaching parts of him he'd thought frozen in time along with the contents of his family home.

Even though he was worn out after his impulsive house removal, he knew he'd be returning to that compact residence before the night was over. Whatever spell had been cast on him the minute he'd taken Iona in his arms Fraser couldn't seem to stay away from her and that definitely didn't fit in with his plans for a carefully organised life.

Iona sank back into her bubble bath and closed her eyes. This was just what she needed after such a fraught day. Okay, so she'd had to wait for a while for the hot water to come through but like everything else wrong in the flat she was happy to put up with it when she was now the proud owner of all she surveyed.

A secret smile played across her lips as she thought of Fraser's reaction on seeing the place. The outright horror on his face had been comical and she'd admit to intentionally pushing his buttons by leaving everything lying around to see if he'd try to tidy her up outside work. Iona knew he preferred everything spick and span as he was forever rearranging things in the waiting room, but since he'd insisted on stepping into her personal life, this was her way of marking her territory, creating a boundary. There was a chance she'd also been trying to rile him so he would overstep the mark and criticise her so she could stop thinking of him as anything other than her tyrannical boss.

To his credit, he hadn't risen to the bait, proving there was some restraint and positive qualities behind his fussy, bossy exterior. He'd been generous with his time and support for her tonight and, coupled with yesterday's revelation that her urges towards him weren't only of a violent nature, she was losing track of the reasons to give him a wide berth. At least he'd made it clear he wasn't in a hurry to come back any time soon so she wouldn't have to worry too much over the consequences of inviting another man into her life.

It was easy to recall the feel of Fraser's hands, strong and capable as he'd cradled her after the fall, and imagine how they might feel on different parts of her body. Iona soaped a flannel up her arms and across her chest, startled that her thoughts of Fraser had turned so…carnal.

She let out a groan and covered her face with the cloth. It wasn't as though she'd become a nun on leaving her abusive ex but she'd put her career ahead of any notions of settling down again after being bitten, and a relationship of any kind had been the furthest thing from her mind. As far as she'd discovered, they only brought pain and heartache to everyone involved and she'd had enough of that to know she was better off unattached.

Now she'd settled into her position here and got her foot on the property ladder, it seemed her neglected libido was making a bid for freedom too. Its untimely reappearance around a man with the uncanny knack of riling her temper was entirely inconvenient—a weakness in the armour she'd built around herself since her reinvention. This warrior queen no longer needed anyone to give her life meaning.

Iona ducked her head under the suds, letting the hot water envelop her whole body in a warm hug. It had obviously been way too long since she'd enjoyed the physical benefits of a relationship of any description when her mind was dragging her towards that riptide with the potential to pull her back under.

In her watery cocoon Iona thought she could feel a dull vibration coming from somewhere beneath the flat. She sat upright, listening to the rhythmic drip, drip, drip of the tap, which almost lulled her back down into the depths of soapy luxury until the shrill ring of the doorbell and more thumping noises downstairs prompted her to action. Someone was desperate for her attention.

'I'm coming!' she yelled, pulling on her dressing gown with no heed to the water sluicing onto the bathroom floor. There was no time to dry or dress if she was to get to the door before they left so she simply belted the robe around her naked body to protect her modesty.

Fraser was the last person she expected to find on her doorstep.

'What's wrong? Did you forget something?' She couldn't think of any other reason that would have brought him back again so soon.

'No. I…er…thought you could use these.' He glanced over his shoulder towards the stack of chairs Iona hadn't noticed currently blocking the path.

'And they couldn't wait until tomorrow?' Although it was a nice gesture, it hadn't warranted an immediate return visit tonight. The impulsive act was so out of character she was thrown by his possible motive. Was this intended to impress her or an attempt to impose his authority in all areas of her life?

Iona folded her arms and did her best to make Fraser realise she wasn't impressed that he'd interrupted her 'me' time for the sake of a couple of chairs so he wouldn't get used to the idea of dropping in at will. It did the trick as he grimaced and gave her his best game-show-host impression in trying to sell her the quality of his wares with a flick of his hands.

'I couldn't bear to think of you here in this empty flat when I have a load of furniture sitting in storage.' He gestured to the vehicle behind him, having apparently exchanged the practical car he drove to work for a gas-guzzling four-by-four packed with other household goods.

'Really? This has absolutely nothing to do with you trying to *fix* me? I know you, Fraser, and how much my empty apartment was probably keeping you from sleeping.' Her cynical eyebrow took on a mind of its own as she searched for a dark ulterior motive behind the selfless offer. He'd made it obvious he had issues with her laid-back approach to her interior décor but she hadn't realised it was to the extent he'd empty the contents of his home to spruce hers up.

'Sorry. I was trying to do you a favour. I probably should've asked first.' Fraser took a step back, shoulders slumped with such dejection Iona may as well have told him never to darken her doorstep again. It was a trick she'd seen her ex use time and again to garner her sympathy and she'd always fallen for it, believing she'd been judging him too harshly and accepting an apology for whatever misdeed he'd committed against her. Only for him to exploit that weakness, lull her back into a false sense of security and strike even harder next time around.

She was less trusting these days but she had absolutely no obligation to Fraser so if he did overstep the mark in any way, she wouldn't hesitate in bouncing him back down the path.

'I'm not dressed for company, or furniture delivery.' Standing here in the cold, face to face with the subject of her recent fantasies, made her aware that she was clad only in a layer of terry towelling.

'No problem. If you want to put some clothes on, I can bring the stuff inside for you then I'll get out of your hair.' There certainly didn't appear to be any sign of anything untoward going on behind his earnest expression and she could use the items he was offering. This would be no run-of-the-mill second-hand furniture either, having probably been vacuum packed in plastic wrap to prevent it being spoiled.

'If you insist.' She left the door open and scarpered back upstairs to put some clothes on. Things were awkward enough without hanging around him semi-naked and partially aroused.

Iona did take her time getting ready, going as far as drying her hair before venturing out of her bedroom again. Fraser deserved a hard time for trying to organise her life for her so she let him sweat for a while. Literally.

When she walked back into the living room he was breathing heavily, the sleeves of his once pristine shirt now rolled up and her flat looking as though someone actually lived in it.

Not only had he carted all the heavy furniture up a flight of stairs single-handed, he'd arranged it all and tidied up the mess she'd left on the floor earlier.

'You really didn't have to do this,' Iona protested, tightening her grip on that theory Fraser was only doing it to exert some control over her. Yet, amongst the seats and the table he'd set up, there was also a small electric fire and a television solely provided for her comfort and not any obvious ulterior motive. Perhaps he deserved some credit for his thoughtfulness but that meant accepting she'd been on his mind tonight too and she certainly didn't want to contemplate the implications of that.

'I wanted to,' Fraser said simply, and continued unpacking a bag onto her kitchen worktop.

'What are you doing?' As far as she was aware, she was the only one named on the mortgage and she hadn't advertised for a lodger but here he was, making himself at home.

'I didn't think you'd had time to do a shop so I picked up a few essentials for you on the way over.'

Bread, bacon, butter, eggs, milk and a huge chocolate bar lined the counter as though he knew her shopping list off by heart. Although he was providing the means to christen her new home with all her favourites, Iona didn't want him to think she was a pushover, someone who could be trained with titbits of chocolate. She was in charge of her life now and didn't need anyone making decisions on her behalf. It would be easy to take all his efforts at face value, and as much as she wanted to believe he only had the purest of intentions at heart she had to protect herself by assuming the worst. Andy had made it impossible for her to trust anyone, especially handsome men who seemed too good to be true.

'You really didn't have to. I'm quite capable of going to the shop myself, thank you.'

'I know. I just thought—I wanted you to feel more at home. Sorry.' He started to pack the groceries back into the bag and the waver in his confidence about being there had guilt gnawing at Iona's insides that she'd got him wrong. Perhaps Fraser *was* simply trying to do something nice for her after all. Learning to trust new people was a long and difficult journey every time, no matter how hard she wanted to speed up the process.

'No, it's okay. Leave them.' Iona reached out and touched his hand to get him to stop and show him the gifts were appreciated. His sharp intake of breath and her reluctance to move back out of his personal space drew them back into that fizzing awareness of attraction to one another.

This thing between them was nothing either of them could control but she knew Fraser didn't want to act on it any more than she did. They were complete opposites; they'd drive each other crazy.

Every nerve ending in her body was drawing Iona closer, telling her to submit once and for all. Yet, with Fraser refusing to succumb too, she held her ground. A rejection now would be humiliating every day for the rest of her working life here. If he declined her advances now, it would give him the perfect excuse to undermine her the next time they clashed at the clinic, blaming her hurt feelings for her next bout of stubbornness. A risk she wasn't willing to take if it could jeopardise any future decisions regarding her patients' welfare.

Eventually Iona forced herself to return to the less dangerous task of putting the groceries away in the cupboards.

'How did you come to have so much spare furniture?' She kept her tone casual, even though her heart was pounding with as much adrenaline and arousal as if they had kissed because she'd imagined it so vividly.

There were a few beats before she heard Fraser move away. As though it had taken him that time to shake himself out of the daze too. 'My dad died a couple of years ago and I inherited the family home. I sold my apartment and moved back but I haven't decided if it's what I want on a permanent basis.'

Keeping hold of the contents of his place if he'd sold it didn't make much sense to Iona, but she understood the death of a parent was such an emotional upheaval it brought about huge life changes. It had been her mother's death that had prompted her to strike out on her own regardless of not having anywhere to go or anyone to help her.

'Sorry for your loss.' It was a sentiment she'd heard so often herself yet seemed so inadequate when it passed from her own lips. Those four words could never hope to comfort someone who'd suffered such a devastating event. She'd never known how to respond to it either. It wasn't the done thing to burst into tears or go off on a rant about how unfair it was so she'd learned to graciously nod and thank people for their condolences.

'We weren't really close. Not since Mum died. Or ever, really.' Fraser was disarmingly frank about his relationship with his father and Iona was shocked to discover they had more in common than either of them had realised.

'I know the feeling. It's hard to bond with a parent in those circumstances. Almost as though you're being forced into a relationship you never had because the one you were closest to has gone for ever.' In those early days after her mother's death Iona had done and said all the right things expected of a dutiful daughter trying to make sure her dad wouldn't feel the loss as acutely as she did, filling that role of caregiver left empty by the woman who'd sacrificed everything for her family. None of it had come naturally and she had soon come to realise it had been fear and grief fuelling her actions, not love. She'd rather be alone than submit to another man's whim again.

Fraser was such a strong, confident individual she didn't imagine he'd been in quite the same position with his family but it would explain that frostiness he exuded at times. She knew she'd erected a lot of barriers to keep herself safe when she'd moved away. It had taken a lot of time to make herself accessible to people again, and only because she'd wanted to work in such a people-friendly environment. She was still working on the walls she'd barricaded around her heart, which weren't dismantled so easily. She wasn't sure she'd ever be ready for them to come down again.

Fraser's loss and the anger and sorrow that surely had been part of that were relatively recent and raw. Something he would have to work hard to get past. It wasn't so unbelievable that it formed part of the reason he hadn't moved in for that kiss when the opportunity had arisen. That lessened the sting slightly but also flashed more warning lights that this complex man was the last one she should set her cap at.

'I can't say I was really any closer to my mother but it's all in the past. We're supposed to be celebrating your future.' Fraser smiled but there was a sadness behind it that touched her heart so deeply she couldn't tell if she wanted to reach out and hug him or rip off his clothes.

His decision to move back to the family home rather than stay in his own place seemed all the more bizarre if it held such dark memories for him. Given the same opportunity, she'd prefer to slum it in her Borrowers-sized flat than move back to a house echoing with tears of the past. A clean break was the only way to leave those ghosts behind.

'You didn't think about selling up?' A senior partner in a thriving GP practice with no discernible dependants that Iona knew of should've had the means to live wherever he wanted. Unless he had some debilitating addiction syphoning off his pay packet but she couldn't picture Fraser with any vices that would have seen him spiralling into that kind of desperation.

'It—it's complicated. Walking away isn't really an option, being the last of the McColls.'

She'd heard the rumours that he came from a wealthy background so there was a chance his father had written a clause into his will that Fraser would only inherit if he remained in situ. The kind of emotional manipulation that made it difficult to leave an abusive relationship. Including one from beyond the grave, it would seem.

Iona was lucky that she'd had her mother in her corner, trying to provide some sort of stability, when her father had made no attempt to hide the fact he'd rather have been anywhere than at home with his family. If both of her parents had been demanding and continually messing with her head, she would never have survived this far.

'What about you? No other family or friends nearby who could help you out?' Fraser turned his back on her to go and play with the heater he'd provided, an orange glow flickering in the fake fire screen at the touch of a switch providing a cosier atmosphere already.

'I see a lot of my ex-patients but they've got young families to take care of. Then there's Katherine, but she's not in any condition to do anything but waddle these days.' Katherine was her recently widowed, pregnant colleague currently on maternity leave and probably Iona's only real friend here. She didn't mind her social calendar being pretty much empty when this was supposed to be her new start away from the demands everyone else put on her time.

'I meant outside work.' Given Fraser's usual gruff demeanour, it was difficult to picture a queue of people lined up at his door, waiting to take him out for a night on the town either, so this interest in her out-of-hours activities seemed unnecessarily intrusive.

'I'm a long way from home and, as you know, our line of work can be very demanding. It's not a typical nine-to-five job. Colleagues, and patients to some extent, are my friends.' Iona became so involved with the families it was impossible to sever ties completely and she often received calls in the middle of the night, asking for advice. There wasn't space for her to be lonely and she happened to enjoy her own company. Having anyone in her home, especially of the male variety, was a novelty and not something she wanted to get used to.

'Now you're in the centre of the village I'm sure you'll get to know everyone very well.'

Iona got the impression he was encouraging her to socialise to get himself off the hook from having to bail her out again. Which wasn't a bad idea if it limited those sparky moments between them, although he'd been a great help tonight. She couldn't pinpoint the exact moment when they'd moved from foes to making cow eyes at each other, or which one was more damaging to her well-being. Particularly when she didn't want him to leave.

This was one of those occasions when Fraser was grateful for his bolthole in the hills. There had been many times when he was on call or the roads were treacherous with snow and ice that his location was a nuisance. Tonight, however, it would be good to put some distance between him and Iona.

They'd become too close, too soon, in the space of twenty-four hours for him to be comfortable. Not that the effort of the drive had put him off coming over for a second time tonight. The sight of Iona fresh out of the shower, hair wet and wearing nothing but a robe, had made the trip worth it. He'd fallen over himself to install his long-neglected furniture, which he'd retrieved from the converted barn at the back of the main house.

If he got her set up tonight, spread the word that she'd moved into the centre of the village and needed a few friendly faces to come and welcome her, he'd have no more excuses to make himself available.

He crouched down by the heater to demonstrate and relay instructions so there was no confusion on how to operate it and no need for him to worry about her shivering here.

'It's very straightforward. This is the on switch—'

'And, let me guess, this turns it on?' Iona knelt beside him, their thighs almost touching as she made fun of him.

They were back to where all this trouble had started, locked in that lustful gaze, battling between their libidos and common sense, desire pulling them closer than the world's strongest magnets, their mouths and restraint venturing into the danger zone.

That red-blooded male trapped inside the body of a man described by his ex as 'too buttoned-up to love' was screaming out to kiss her. Well, for once Fraser wasn't going to hold back and would be true to himself and his feelings instead. If that's what it took to be with Iona, he was willing to change from the stuffed shirt he had a tendency to be.

He kissed her. Hard.

Her hands cupped his face and she returned the kiss with equal abandon.

Fraser couldn't remember the last time he'd felt so alive, so aware of his every breath, every beat of his heart, quickening with each flick of her tongue against his. If this was what he'd been missing out on by playing by the rules all this time, he'd be throwing the etiquette book right out the window.

Iona fell back onto the floor, bringing him with her until he was splayed across her body, every soft curve of her lush body hardening his. He wanted her to the point where nothing else mattered except exploring this walk on the wild side with her.

Somewhere in the depths of his hormonally dazed brain Fraser registered her hands pushing against his chest and he wasn't so far gone he'd ignore any hesitation on her part. He immediately rolled away and apologised.

'I'm so sorry. I thought you wanted this too.' He'd never forgive himself if he'd made an unwanted advance.

Iona sat up looking every bit as dazed and confused as he was about what had just happened. Or had almost happened. 'I do, I did, but let's be honest, this isn't me and I'm fairly certain this isn't you. Thanks for your help with everything but I think we should call it a night. We have work in the morning.'

She got to her feet and headed towards the door without looking back at him, leaving Fraser in no doubt that she wanted him to leave now so they could revert back to solely work colleagues tomorrow. He didn't blame her when he was at a loss to explain what had come over him other than pure lust. That didn't make the rebuff any easier to take when he'd put himself out there in a way he hadn't done in a long time. If only he could rewind the clock back to earlier in the night when he'd first left the premises and avoided taking another blow to his confidence and their working relationship! Then he wouldn't be returning home with an even worse opinion of himself than if he hadn't tried to help her.

The irony of this was, of course, that Fraser was trying to be himself, acting completely on impulse without moderating himself as he usually did, or trying to be the person he imagined people wanted him to be.

Yet Iona had rejected him just the way Caroline had when she too had accused him of not being true to himself. Perhaps he simply had to face facts. There was no one willing to love him for who he was, or who he tried to be for them.

CHAPTER FOUR

IONA WAS LOATH to leave her new flat the next morning, wishing she had some time off to fully immerse herself in unpacking. The task itself wouldn't take her more than a couple of hours but she could spread that out to last a full day with a chance to binge-watch some of the DVD box sets she had waiting for her.

Since she'd decided to keep her days off for the Christmas period Iona had to carry on her working day as usual and save her solo housewarming party for then.

Her unusual reluctance to get to work might also have had something to do with Fraser's unexpected late-night visit and their nocturnal shenanigans.

She'd finally conceded that his attempt to furnish her flat had been thoughtful, generous and more than appreciated, but it was the re-ignition of that heat between them that had made the night especially unforgettable. Every time she thought of Fraser now, her blood boiled for more than their clash over the Christmas decorations in the clinic. It wasn't a secret they had a clash of personalities but who knew it had been the build-up of such immense sexual tension between them? That kiss, and her reaction to it, had been as much as a surprise as the wild passion Fraser had apparently been hiding under his buttoned-up shirt.

A fluttery sensation started in the pit of her stomach and

quickly spread throughout the rest of her body as she recalled the intensity with which they'd dived on each other. As though they'd tired of pretending the chemistry didn't exist and had abandoned themselves to it instead. Desire for Fraser had hit Iona so hard it had literally knocked her off her feet and she could have given herself completely to him at that moment.

Their time together last night proved that first encounter hadn't been a one-off and it scared her half to death. Iona wasn't so damaged by her ex that she believed every man who crossed her path was going to physically abuse her but she remembered how it was to have to constantly think about the other person in a relationship—their moods, their feelings, their needs—and how exhausted it made her. There was little joy in it for her and on balance there was more benefit for her to remain single.

Although she couldn't shake off the knowledge that chemistry between them would be equally as explosive in the bedroom as it was in the workplace. Fraser's kiss alone had had more heat and passion than she'd experienced in her marriage or any college dalliances since but she wasn't going to get burned again. This was the same man who liked to 'take an interest' in her patients, as he put it, whereas she thought of it more as checking up on her. Enough reason for her to give him a wide berth.

If she ever got involved with another man it would have to be with someone who was content to let her be herself, without a desire to bend her to his will. Fraser McColl would never settle until she'd come to heel. The food and furniture delivery was proof enough he was incapable of letting her run her own life without his interference.

Going into the surgery this morning, Iona's stomach was tied in knots wondering how he'd respond to her after her epic rejection and if his bruised ego would make life more difficult for her at the clinic.

'Morning, Victoria,' she called to the receptionist, not stopping for her usual chat in the hope she would manage to dodge Fraser on her way through the clinic.

She knew he was there on the discovery of his labelled, neatly stacked plastic containers in the communal staff fridge. The sight always gave her the urge to mess up his arrangement out of sheer badness. This morning, however, she resisted targeting the regimented meals and fruit snacks since he had gone out of his way to help her before things had spiralled spectacularly out of control.

This morning she had her antenatal clinic so it wasn't unheard of for her to run into Fraser at some point, or indeed consult on the treatment of mutual patients. On walking past his room, she noticed the door was firmly closed, a sign he didn't want to be disturbed by anyone. Fraser didn't normally shut himself off from the outside world until his first patient of the day had taken a seat. It was going to be awkward facing each other after that wanton display they'd put on in her living room but they'd have to get over it when they still had to work together. Regardless of how difficult it was going to be to put the thought of that spine-tingling kiss to the back of her mind.

Her day was taken up with the usual pre-pregnancy checks keeping her too busy to dwell on what was going on behind Dr McColl's closed door. It wasn't her business to know what was going on in his head but it was her job to be professional and supportive to every mum-to-be and make sure her ladies and their babies were progressing as they should.

'Roughly how often do you feel the baby move?'

'Have you given any thought to breast-feeding?'

'How are you feeling generally?'

There'd been no complications or referrals so far today

so that meant she'd get out for her home visits on schedule. There was no better way to leave Fraser and that lapse in judgement behind than to get onto the open road and put the vast rural Scottish countryside between them. At least her next patient was bound to close her clinic on a high.

'Katherine!' Iona rushed to give the heavily pregnant woman a hug, or as close to it as her protruding round belly would allow.

'Having a rough day or are you just happy to see me?' Katherine backed herself into the nearest chair and sat down with all the grace of a reversing truck, leaving her other two charges hovering nervously at either side of her.

Hamish and Poppy were too old to be pacified with the box of toddler toys here to entertain the children who often accompanied their mothers, yet were too young to be left unattended in the waiting room for the duration of this appointment.

'Both.' Iona helped Katherine with the shoes she was struggling to take off and pulled a couple of extra chairs over for the little ones.

Iona handed out the lollipops she kept for restless children and improvised some art supplies with printer paper and whatever pens and pencils she had lying around in order to keep their minds and hands occupied so she could have a proper discussion with their mum. Once they were ensconced at her desk she helped Katherine up onto the bed and pulled the curtain partially around her for at least the illusion of privacy.

'Sorry. They've been playing up this morning and I didn't want to send them to school only to get a phone call to drive back and collect them again. They're complaining about tummyache, but as you can see…' Katherine indicated the empty lolly wrappers and the hands dipping into the jar for seconds '…it comes and goes. I think they're just missing their dad.'

'It's only natural.'

Katherine was one of their own, a practice nurse at the clinic who'd taken Iona under her wing when she'd started. The excitement over her new pregnancy had been matched with that of sharing it with her new friend.

Neither of them had expected she'd lose her husband so early to brain cancer only weeks after his diagnosis. The loss and grief had caused Iona to keep a close eye on Katherine, providing a shoulder to cry on and her mobile number for whenever she needed to talk. They'd become firm friends over the course of these past months, especially because neither of them had any other family close by to rely on. The bond they'd developed had gone beyond a work or a patient/midwife relationship.

'Noel did all the decorations at this time of year. He went all out until you could probably see our house from space with the number of lights he put up outside the house. It's not the same now. It's never going to be the same again.' Iona could see Katherine was trying hard not to get upset for the sake of the children, including the one who was due in the not-too-distant future.

'No, it's not, but that doesn't mean it can't still be good. You're a strong woman with two beautiful children and you'll get through this, I promise.' Iona's heart went out to the family. They had moved here from the city with the intention of providing a better environment in which to raise their kids, unaware their future would be cut short and leave Katherine to cope on her own with them.

Iona couldn't in good conscience turf Katherine back out to her husbandless home after a ten-minute check-up when she was this low. Her mental health was as important as the baby's welfare at this point; any distress could impact on the pregnancy.

'Listen, I have some time before my home visits. Why don't I go and make us a cuppa before we take all your measurements? I think we might even have a few chocolate biscuits stashed somewhere too.' An image of Fraser's rectangular plastic tub with his biscuits counted to the last crumb came to mind. This was an emergency. He'd understand, and if he didn't, well, he'd just have to come and tell her so.

'Fraser's?'

'He's a medical professional. He knows chocolate cures all ills.'

Iona returned with a tray of sweet tea and biscuits for the two adults and glasses of milk for the children.

'Now, tell me how you're really feeling.' Iona made sure the kids were distracted enough not to eavesdrop on their conversation before she dug deeper.

That head start on her visits wasn't going to happen after all but it was more important for Katherine to be in a good frame of mind before she left here. Iona worked mostly on instinct and her gut was telling her she needed to be here.

'Stressed. Knackered.' Now she'd let the façade drop, the bags under Katherine's eyes were more noticeable and she was slumped against the pillows, crumpled under the weight of her woes.

'Let's start with the source of your stresses at the minute and we'll see if we can't tackle them one by one.' Tiredness wasn't unusual at this stage of pregnancy when the baby bump was so large it was impossible to get into a comfortable position for a good night's sleep. However, depression could also be a factor and given recent events in Katherine's life it would be surprising if her mood hadn't been affected. The important thing was to recognise and acknowledge it so she could get help. Being a counsellor was one of the many unofficial roles a midwife was prepared to undertake to ensure a happy, healthy mother and baby.

'Apart from the obvious, there's all of the practical

things I'm left to deal with now Noel's gone. I mean, I was expecting him to pick up the slack with the shopping once I was at the whale stage. I can barely carry my own body weight, never mind lug bags of shopping around, even if I did have time, what with the school runs and the housework I've to do too. I can't keep on top of any of it and I've still to get the place ready for the baby coming.' Katherine let out a long, ragged sigh then helped herself to a biscuit and ate through the rest of her feelings.

'First things first, is there anyone who can give you a hand until the baby comes?' A good support system played a huge part in any pregnancy but here, with a grieving family heading into their first Christmas without their husband and father, they were going to need people around them more than ever.

'My parents are on a cruise over the holidays. They'll be back nearer my due date to help with the children but we're on our own until then. They weren't going to go but they've been so looking forward to it and I persuaded them we'd be fine. Unfortunately, Noel didn't have any family.' Katherine crammed another biscuit into her mouth.

'At least you'll have someone around when you're in hospital. Until then you know I'll help out wherever I can, and I'm sure everyone else in the village will want to offer a helping hand.' Everyone was fond of Katherine here and though she would never want to impose on people, Iona knew they'd fall over themselves to do what they could for her.

'Thanks, I appreciate that but I know we're not exactly local and everyone has their own family to focus on.' There was that note of resignation in Katherine's voice that everyone would be too caught up in their own lives and Christmas preparations to even think about driving out into the wilds to do a bit of vacuuming. She probably had a point.

Everyone except Iona had a life outside work and mightn't
be as readily available as she was.

'You could put an ad in for a cleaner for a couple of
weeks. I know it might seem like an extravagance but you
don't want to be wearing yourself out. You should be taking it easy. It doesn't matter if your house isn't pristine in
the grand scheme of things. You've done an amazing job
of keeping your family going these past months so don't
give yourself a hard time over a bit of dust. Order take-
aways, let the kids decorate with cut-out snowflakes and
finger paintings. Whatever it takes to get through the holidays. Remember Christmas is only one day and you've got
a much more significant one coming up. Trust me, you'll
all be more excited about welcoming a new baby into the
house. Until then, stick a DVD on for these two and get a
nap when and where you can.'

'That feels like such a copout.'

'No, it's called self-care. Your little ones are much more
likely to remember you spending time with them than what
decorations they did, or didn't, have this year. Speaking of
which, did you hear Scrooge McColl enforced a ban on any
festivities here so I have an overflow of garlands and sparkle? I'll come over and blitz your place with some magic
fairy dust next time I'm passing if you want.'

'Ah, yes, I'd heard Fraser had put his foot down this
year about the staff party too. I suppose he has a point.
The drinking has had a tendency to get out of hand. It's
better to keep these things separate so they don't muddy
the waters at work.'

Iona couldn't help but being piqued at her friend for
taking Fraser's side, no matter how on point her insight
was, but she'd rather stay mad at him than think about that
amazing lip-lock and the effect it had had on her last night.
With his mouth on hers, his body pressed close, she'd been

close to throwing away everything she'd worked towards, and walked away from, in a rush of hormones.

'Mu-um. I'm bored.' The first rumblings of discontent sounded from beyond the blue curtain as the children tired of their improvised art session.

'We'll be done in a wee minute or two. Get my phone out of my bag and you can play that game you like on it until I'm ready to go.' Katherine shouted instructions to her offspring and handed Iona her now-empty mug. 'See? I wouldn't get a minute to relax.'

It was probably true but at least those few minutes of normalcy over a cuppa with her friend had evened out the frown lines on her forehead. A chat seemed such a small thing but it could do wonders for mums, or anyone else feeling low or isolated. Once the baby came Katherine could socialise at the mother and baby club in the community centre but Iona would provide her company in the days leading up to the big event so she wasn't completely on her own.

If nothing else, this brief respite should have given Katherine some time to de-stress before she had her blood pressure checked, along with everything else. 'In that case, we'll get on with what you came in here for.'

'Sorry. I didn't mean to turn this appointment into a counselling session.' The small laugh was an improvement on the near-tears mood when Katherine had come in and proved Iona's theory that a listening ear could make all the difference.

'That's what I'm here for, to make sure you and bump are all right. You can call me anytime you need a friend. Now, do you have a sample for me?'

'Yes.' Katherine handed over the bottle with her urine sample for her to test.

'If you just pop on the scales, we'll make a wee note of your weight.' Increased weight was expected, indicating that baby was thriving, but as Iona plotted the digits on her chart they became cause for concern. Compared to the reading from the week before, Katherine had put on five pounds.

'I don't think I want to know.'

'You are growing another human being in there.' The dipstick she used to test the sample indicated the presence of protein and, combined with the excess weight, called for action.

Unbidden, Katherine lay back down on the bed and uncovered her belly so Iona could check the baby's size and position.

'Have you noticed any unusual swelling lately in your hands or around your ankles?' As Iona felt around the bump she could tell the baby remained in the head-down position and, compared to the last measurement, the growth seemed normal. If the baby appeared too big or too small she would need to order an ultrasound for a more accurate evaluation of its growth and check the levels of amniotic fluid.

'My ankles are puffier than they have been but that's not surprising with all the extra weight they're carrying.' With some help from her midwife Katherine took off her socks so Iona could see for herself.

The alarm bells were deafening now Iona could see the oedema causing the ankles to balloon and Iona was sure the skin around her patient's eyes were puffier than usual too.

'Any headaches, nausea or problems with your vision?' All the symptoms so far were pointing towards a diagnosis of pre-eclampsia that, if severe enough, could potentially cause serious, sometimes life-threatening problems and often warranted early delivery.

It was constriction of the blood vessels that caused the high blood pressure and this reduced blood flow could affect the liver, kidneys and brain. Such changes caused small blood vessels to leak fluid into the tissues, resulting in the swelling, and these leaks in the kidneys caused the protein from the bloodstream to spill into the urine. Although it was normal to have a small amount of protein in the urine, more than that signalled a problem. Less blood flowing to the uterus could lead to growth problems for the baby or placental abruption, where the placenta separated from the uterine wall before delivery. Early delivery was often needed to protect the mother's health and prevent a stillbirth.

'I suffer from migraines anyway and nausea comes with the territory. I just assumed it was the stress of the holidays. Why? Should I be worried?' If Katherine had had her nurse head on and not her busy mum one she would've recognised the signs for herself. Then again, all symptoms individually were common enough during pregnancy and it was only when they were added together they suddenly became something sinister.

'I'm going to check your blood pressure.' Choosing to avoid the question until they knew for sure there was a need to worry, Iona wrapped the cuff around Katherine's upper arm to take the reading.

With the tea and chat she'd had time to settle so elevated blood pressure now would solely be down to medical reasons and not outside influences.

A blood-pressure reading was considered high when the systolic upper number was greater than one-forty or the diastolic lower number was higher than ninety. Katherine's readings far exceeded acceptable figures. One high reading in isolation might not give an accurate picture, and results could fluctuate throughout the day but, combined with the other symptoms, Iona wasn't content to wait longer than necessary. The same reason she was willing to go with her gut instinct on the initial urine screening instead of waiting for the requisite twenty-four-hour sample collection.

'It's high, isn't it?' There was such resignation and understanding of the consequences in Katherine's question Iona didn't even have to answer it.

'Do you have any errands to run in town, or anywhere you could leave the kids for a while? I'd like you to come back this afternoon so we can do more readings. I think another urine test might be in order.' In place of twenty-four-hour monitoring there was another one-time test that could be carried out on a random sample. The protein-creatinine ratio could show signs of pre-eclampsia if it showed at least point three of a milligram per decilitre in results, creatinine being a waste product the kidneys should have filtered out.

'I was going to get a few groceries while I was here.'

Iona unfastened the cuff and noted the readings, which had cemented her suspicions. 'You go ahead and do that and I'll nip in and have a chat with Fraser about the next step.'

'If it's pre-eclampsia, we could both be in trouble, right?' Katherine lowered her voice as she stroked a hand over her bump, illustrating exactly where her fears lay.

'At the minute I'm simply being cautious. We need to do a few more checks but since you're not yet at thirty-seven weeks and your baby's developing well, it could be we just need to monitor your blood pressure closely for the rest of your pregnancy.'

If Katherine had been at the end of her term they would have had to think about inducing her but Iona didn't want the complications of an early delivery for any of them unless absolutely necessary. In certain situations a Caesarean section would be performed if there were signs mother or baby wouldn't be able to tolerate labour, but that would create more difficulties for Katherine when she had to cope back home alone with two other small children after the birth and the impossible task of resting.

'I'll see if I can find a babysitter for a few hours.' Katherine set her mind to practicalities and Iona was grateful for her calm acceptance as anything else could have exacerbated the condition.

'Good idea but don't over-exert yourself and I'll see you again in a couple of hours.' With the most reassuring smile she could give her, Iona helped Katherine down off the bed.

An official diagnosis was going to plunge the family into even more chaos over the festive period but this baby had to be delivered safely wherever, or however, that might happen.

'Right, kiddos. What do you say we go and get some comics and sweeties?' As most mothers were prone to do, Katherine hid her own worries so as not to upset her children and did her best to carry on as normal, so strong on the outside whilst inevitably crumbling on the inside. A widowed single mum with another baby on the way, facing a potentially life-threatening illness, couldn't help but draw compassion.

Before the family trooped from the room Iona threw her arms around her friend and hugged her close. 'We've got this, okay?'

She meant every word of the promise, even if that entailed having to consult Fraser on the case.

Fraser closed the door after his patient, even though there was no real need for continued privacy after he'd completed his paperwork and made his triage calls. On any other day he'd have been content to have an unimpeded view of clinic life but he wasn't ready to face Iona, or whatever new feelings he'd developed for her over the course of the past forty-eight hours.

Even when he'd been loading his old furniture into the

vehicle last night he'd known it was a mistake to return. That hadn't stopped him. Going against his own judgement was never a good idea and not an oft-practised one for this very reason—acting without considering all potential outcomes that could affect those around him was what drove everyone away from him in the end. Somehow he had to find a way to exercise some damage control with Iona for the sake of their working relationship. For his own peace of mind in future, one of their hot-tempered arguments would be preferable to the attraction that seemed to be drawing him closer and closer to her.

The knock on the door was a reminder he had more pressing matters to attend to than a romance that could never happen.

'Come in.' Fraser brought up the notes for his next patient on the computer screen to maintain a modicum of professionalism.

That pretence lasted merely seconds as Iona strode into the room full of purpose and Fraser's heart lurched at the first sighting of her this morning. With her uniform on and her hair tamed into relative submission, she was a different woman from the one who'd greeted him on the doorstep fresh out of the shower, but she had no less of an effect on him, his pulse leaping with the recollection of how she'd tasted on his lips.

'I…er…' Fraser had spent half the night and most of the morning in between consultations trying to construct a speech to excuse any behaviour that could have been misconstrued as inappropriate or an opening into a budding relationship. Only now, seeing Iona again, those words eluded him. He was fighting a losing battle when his better judgement was overruled at every turn by that primal need she'd unleashed within him.

'Katherine was here for her check-up and she's showing signs of pre-eclampsia. I know this is my jurisdiction but I wanted to consult with you on the matter since there could be certain complications for her family if she's admitted to the hospital.' If thoughts of their time together was on her mind, Iona didn't show concern for anything other than her patient. It was a serious enough condition that she was prepared to let him in on the case, not for his opinion but so they could work together on the best outcome for the family.

Fraser sat back in his chair and gestured for her to take the seat across from him to discuss their colleague's situation. 'How so?'

If she wasn't going to acknowledge what had transpired last night, he was more than happy to follow suit. He didn't need to give himself to another woman who had no qualms about rejecting him. It was a mercy in a way that it had happened before any notion of a romance had got off the ground, instead of waiting to deliver the blow when he'd invested everything he had emotionally in a relationship.

Iona cleared her throat, showing an uncertainty that he'd never seen her demonstrate before. She fidgeted with the hem of her skirt, unable to sit still, making her discomfort obvious.

A silver dagger engraved with guilt stabbed at his insides with the thought that stepping out of his regimented way of life and into hers had somehow caused her apparent distress. Although Iona would be the first to say not everything had to be about him.

'You know she lost her husband not that long ago and they have two other children?'

'Yes, we were all devastated for her.'

Fraser wasn't heartless and as the doctor who had treated Katherine's husband he was acutely aware of the loss she'd suffered. The death of a patient always stayed with him, in this case not only because the family was known to Fraser but because of the sense of powerlessness a terminal illness brought to everyone involved. Even doctors weren't immune to that frustration when all they could do was make the patient comfortable and pain-free where possible before the inevitable end. Any death felt like a failure on his part when his job was to treat illness and save lives, regardless that in such tragic circumstances no one had the power to stop fate in its tracks.

The conversation stalled with Iona waiting expectantly for him to say more on the subject than merely expressing sympathy. She didn't give him long to figure it out before she rolled her eyes and tutted at him.

'There's no one to mind the kids if she goes into hospital.' Iona spelled it out to him with a heavy dose of exasperation.

'Right. Of course. That's the last thing Katherine needs. She already has so much to deal with.' The family had had more than their fair share of bad luck and tragedy recently and it seemed it was going to continue for now.

'I've asked her to come back in a couple of hours for further blood-pressure and urine checks before I make the hospital referral. I thought that would give us some time to make a few phone calls to see what options are available so we can present her with the facts when she returns.'

'There are definitely no friends or family members she can call on since this is an emergency? I'd hate to think of the children being sent away to strangers when they are still grieving for their father.' Fraser wouldn't wish that on another young soul, having been through it at much the same age. Bereavement was such a confusing concept for children to deal with and they needed guidance and security—something that had been sadly lacking from his own father when he'd needed it most—to help them get through it. More upheaval and stress would have long-term consequences for the family unless someone was able to step in and find a way to smooth their path.

Unfortunately, Iona was shaking her head. 'Her parents are in the middle of the Caribbean somewhere on a cruise and not expected back before the New Year. Katherine might be able to hire a babysitter for an hour or two but there's no one close enough for her to ask to care for them long term. Two small children is a lot for anyone to take on in a village where nearly all the residents are over retirement age and those that aren't have young families of their own. With the exception of present company, of course.'

'So, that only leaves…'

'Temporary foster care.'

A solution they both knew would only upset Katherine more and terrify the children at the prospect of being sent away from the only person they loved to be at the mercy of strangers. That frightening journey into the unknown was something Fraser had been through himself when he'd been sent to boarding school away from everything he'd ever known. He'd much rather the children were able to stay with a familiar face, and together, if possible, to make the experience less traumatic.

It was difficult for a child to see the necessity of such actions, often blaming themselves for events as though they'd done something wrong and the decision to banish them from home was a form of punishment.

Although Katherine had no other options here, unlike his parents who'd simply decided they preferred not to have him around, Fraser doubted her little ones would understand it any better than he ever had.

'I hope it won't come to that and we might be able to sort things out for her. That's not something a member of our staff, a friend, should have to consider for her children. Have you broached the subject with her yet?' It wouldn't be the first time he'd had to contact social services regarding the welfare of children he suspected were being neglected, but it was a different story dealing with someone he knew personally was a fantastic mum going through a rough time.

'Not yet. I wanted to be clear in my own head about what would happen first before I overwhelmed her with information. Katherine isn't some addict or neglectful parent who doesn't deserve her children and I don't want her ever to be made to feel that way.'

'I'll do whatever I can to prevent that.' Not that either of them would sleep easily if her children were taken into care at all. 'Her parents really can't get home any sooner?'

Fraser didn't know what type of people they were but most parents, with the exception of his, would rather cut short a holiday to care for their daughter and prevent their grandchildren going into care.

'I'll try and convince her to contact them today. Perhaps I'll have more chance if she knows the alternative but even then, it's doubtful they'd make it back before she's admitted to hospital.'

Fraser could see why she'd brought the matter to his attention. Katherine was one of their own and they had to explore every available avenue before succumbing to the inevitable conclusion. He intended to do whatever he could to help.

'Have you spoken to the consultant at the hospital?' Fraser was already going through his list of contacts to see who he knew that could assist them in the matter.

'I'm going to phone now and get her booked in.' Yet Iona wasn't making any move to leave and start the ball moving.

Fraser lifted the phone on his desk and began punching in numbers. 'You do that. I have a friend who's a social worker. I'll ask her advice off the record about what can be done before we make anything official.'

It was a long shot but he was willing to try anything if

it would ease Iona, Katherine and the children's suffering in some small way during this difficult time.

Her soft, 'Thank you for understanding,' and slight upturn of the mouth was sufficient payment.

How he wished someone like Iona had fought his corner for him to remain at home when his mother had become sick, and after her death, when his father had seemed to find his presence even more unbearable. If the McColls had had a family friend close enough to persuade them their son would be better off at home, his life might not have been ripped apart, never to be the same again.

CHAPTER FIVE

BY THE TIME Katherine arrived back at the clinic alone, Iona had already made arrangements for her to be admitted to hospital. The specialist Iona had spoken to was keen to monitor Katherine closely and try to get her blood pressure lowered.

'One pregnant lady reporting back with a full bladder as requested.' The humour wasn't quite covering up Katherine's fear and she was even paler than she'd been this morning.

'If you want to pop into the bathroom, we'll get another sample for testing.' In the meantime, Iona would call on Fraser for his input and find out if he'd heard anything from his social worker friend.

It was strange lapsing straight back into professional coolness towards each other after the heat they'd generated in her flat last night but it probably was best they didn't acknowledge anything had gone on and set aside their personal entanglement to focus on Katherine. Fraser had been very sympathetic to her predicament, most likely because of what he'd told her about his own childhood and losing a parent himself. Still, he didn't have to get personally involved and it said a lot about his character that he wanted to help get them out of this situation. His empathy with Katherine and the children was all the more remarkable given the cold relationship his parents had apparently fostered with him.

There'd been a couple of other things that had surprised Iona about their earlier meeting in his office. First, that he'd suggested making the call off the record, which was unusual as he wasn't known for going against procedure. In all likelihood it was his familiarity with the patient and the situation the family were in but there was a part of her wishing he'd done it for her sake too.

She'd also been rattled by the mention of his friend, a *she* by all accounts. A casual phone call to chat about the situation suggested he was acquainted with this woman on more than a professional level and that thought burrowed so far under Iona's skin to possess her soul that not even a priest with his Bible and crucifix could have driven it out. Obviously the upheaval of these past few days must've messed with her head if she was seriously thinking of herself as the spurned lover when she'd been the one doing the spurning. She had no right to have her claws out for his other potential suitors.

Iona's green-eyed imagination might have had something to do with the way she burst into his office. 'Katherine's back. Did you manage to speak to your *friend*?'

Fraser did a double take but didn't comment on her intrusion or her surly tone. 'I did get hold of Sandra, as a matter of fact.'

So he was on first-name terms with her.

'Iona?' An unusually timid Katherine appeared behind her and she cursed herself for not closing the door behind her.

Fraser rose from his chair and ushered them both in. 'Come in, Katherine, this concerns you too.'

He pulled another seat over so Iona could sit next to him and they could discuss this together.

She leaned forward so she was closer to her patient.

'As you know, there are some concerns about your current symptoms. The high blood pressure, protein in your urine and the nausea are all adding up to a possible diagnosis of pre-eclampsia.'

Katherine broke eye contact with him to focus on the hands clasped in her lap as she fought to hold it together. 'You still have the other test to do, though?'

'I've already spoken to the consultant at the hospital and they want you to come in. This afternoon.' There'd be more blood tests and if her uric acids were high, they might have to induce her.

The tears dripping down Katherine's face were a silent acceptance.

'They need to keep an eye on that blood pressure and treat it with whatever medication they deem necessary to bring it down to acceptable levels.'

'How long for?'

'As long as it takes. If things settle down they might permit us to monitor you at home but if they think you or the baby could be at risk there's a possibility they could keep you in until you're full term.'

This was out of Iona's hands now and solely down to the severity of the condition. She didn't want to scare Katherine any more than she wanted to give her false hope she could be home by dinnertime, but Katherine was in the profession so she knew the score and that they didn't have all the answers immediately to hand.

'What about the children?' As the implications of her impending hospital stay finally hit, Katherine fidgeted more and more in her chair, panic setting in. Iona should've taken her blood pressure before scaring her half to death.

'Where are they now?' It wasn't as though they were going to spirit her away without letting her say goodbye, as though she was going into witness protection.

'I managed to get Mrs McAdams to watch them for an

hour at the coffee shop but I couldn't possibly ask her to do that indefinitely. I can phone my parents but they'll have to arrange flights. What am I going to do, Iona?'

Iona had to swallow several times to prevent her airways closing as her friend implored her to help. 'There's a possibility they'll have to go into temporary care. Just until you're discharged or your parents get here.'

'No. No!' Katherine rose along with the pitch of her voice.

Tears were pinching the backs of Iona's eyes too as she attempted to calm her down. 'Social services will have to get involved once you're admitted. They have to make sure there's someone to take care of them.'

'I can do that. You said it yourself you can monitor my blood pressure at home. I can come here every day if I have to but nobody is taking my babies away from me.'

'We don't want to do that but you need to go the hospital for the sake of the baby. You'd never forgive yourself if something happened.' It wasn't a threat, it was a truth Katherine had to face. They weren't about to handcuff her and frogmarch her to the hospital but it was in her best interests to let them do comprehensive checks and begin the necessary treatment.

'I will never forgive myself if I have to put my children into care.' With her head now in her hands, she was sobbing so hard Iona was afraid she'd go into labour.

'It'll be okay, Katherine. Come on, sit down.' Fraser guided her back into her chair. 'I put in a call myself to a social worker friend of mine for some advice. Now, there's a chance we won't have to get them involved if you can come to an agreement with a family member to take care of the children.'

'It's not an option. I told you, there's no one until my parents get here. I need someone in the interim.'

'To be honest, Sandy confided in me that it's going to

be difficult to place them in emergency care so close to Christmas. If there's anyone you trust to mind them, I'm sure you could come to some arrangement with the local authority.' Reading between the lines, Iona could sense that it wasn't going to be easy keeping them together. Two young children who were still grieving for their father were a lot to take on when most people had already made their Christmas plans. Even those without family had an idea in their minds of how the festive period should pan out.

Katherine's children had done nothing wrong to find themselves in this situation and they deserved a better end to such an awful year. They needed to be spoiled and having so much fun they didn't have time to think about who was missing from their dinner table. Once their mother went into hospital they were going to be even more afraid and confused than they already were, and being split up and shipped off to strangers was going to make it harder to recover from for them.

All those horrible childhood experiences stayed with you long into adulthood, as Iona knew very well, and it was about time they had some positive memories of this year to cling to.

'I'll take them.' She didn't know who was more shocked by her outburst, Katherine, Fraser or herself. There'd been no thought to the practicalities of the suggestion, merely an emotional reaction to a situation she couldn't bear to witness without trying to do something about it.

'Are you serious?' The minute Katherine's face lit up with hope, her fate was sealed. There was no way she could back out now, even if the practicalities would have to be ironed out. She had no experience of raising small children but she could remember what it was like to lose a parent and it was that empathy that was making this decision for her.

'You need time to think this through.' Fraser was staring at her as though she'd gone mad, but why recommend a close friend should help if he didn't expect one to put themselves forward?

'Sometimes we just have to go with our gut feelings, and mine's telling me to do the right thing here.' Such was the common theme of their clashes, Fraser wanting to do everything by the book when she was happier to trust her instincts. Iona was usually justified in her actions and she hoped this time would not be the exception. Katherine literally had no one else and she certainly wasn't going to start analysing the pros and cons of her decision in front of her. This was one argument she wasn't prepared to give him.

'Can we really do this? I mean, the kids know Iona and it will only be for a few days…'

Damn Iona for giving Katherine this hope without proper consultation. Fraser didn't want the two mites to enter the care system any more than she did but he didn't want her to rush into something else without thinking, only to regret it. These were small children with real feelings who couldn't be picked up and set down on a whim. He was an adult and even he was having trouble keeping up with Iona's changeable moods.

Yet he couldn't deny he'd be happier to see the children go to Iona than imagine them spending Christmas without fun and love, the way he had too often.

He sighed and assumed the position of chief negotiator in the deal. 'There is the possibility of short-term foster care but you will have to notify children's services and request they assess you as a foster carer as soon as possible.'

'That shouldn't be a problem, surely? Iona is acquainted with the children and she's a medical professional. What more could they want?' In Katherine's mind at least, it would be the perfect solution to her current crisis.

Fraser wouldn't deny her peace of mind but it was going to involve more than signing a few pieces of paper. Thanks to Sandy, he was aware of some of the scrutiny Iona would be subjected to in order to assess her suitability as a carer. 'They don't know Iona as well as we do and they'll want background information for the social worker to submit a report for approval.'

'What sort of background information?' For the first time since riding to the rescue, Iona was frowning and perhaps thinking seriously about what was being asked of her. It sparked the embers of suspicion that there might be something she wasn't keen to share in her past. Maybe she wasn't as much of an open book as he'd assumed.

'Stage one will go into detail about your health, marital status, employment and accommodation.' They exchanged glances, fully aware her flat was barely adequate for a busy midwife without the addition of two small children.

'That could be a problem.' Despite her previous pride in her new home, even Iona could see the unsuitability of the premises for the purposes of raising children.

'They won't turn you down on the grounds that your flat's too small or you don't have a garden. I think it's more about ensuring the children have their own space.' It was going to be tight for sure, but Fraser could see Iona whipping the furniture back out if it would secure a place for Katherine's little ones to stay.

'Couldn't you just stay at our place?' It was natural Katherine would want to keep things as normal as possible but that didn't take into consideration the day-to-day practicalities of Iona's job.

'It's too far out for me to commute from every day. They're forecasting one of the worst storms of the year next week and neither I nor my expectant mothers can afford for me to get stranded up there. I don't think it would make practical sense unless you have a snow plough I can drive to work?' Not even the usually optimistic midwife could salve the crushing blow of disappointment falling on the plans of everyone in the room.

Crazy as this plan was, it was the only one available to save the children from going into care. It didn't matter to either of them where the children stayed as much as who they were with. They needed someone familiar enough that they felt safe and that could only be Iona, regardless of how unprofessional that was for a member of staff.

Fraser was acquainted with Katherine in much the same capacity as Iona. She'd been at the clinic longer than both of them, yet after these past couple of days he felt closer to Iona. Perhaps it was down to the time they'd spent together outside work, or because he'd already done her a favour he wouldn't have dreamed of doing for anyone else, but he was compelled to get involved. If only to make sure she wasn't taking on too much.

The kids deserved the best Christmas ever but her empty flat wasn't the right background to frame that happy scene.

As a child Fraser had seen both sides of the coin during the holidays. Either left at boarding school with those whose parents had lived abroad, going through the motions without any of the sentiment supposedly attached to the holidays, or at home, where his parents hadn't bothered about making a show for his benefit any more.

He'd always told himself that if he'd had a family of his own, they'd know they were loved, have all the joys most other children took for granted. After his disastrous attempt at a relationship this could be the closest he got to make that dream come true for some other frightened youngsters who didn't have a clue what was going on beyond missing the stability of a family home.

That big house, full of furniture and possible adventure, had always been missing the laughter of children and this could be one way to exorcise the loneliness there. It was vast enough to provide a solution and a home for the holidays. He could give Iona and Katherine a gift money couldn't buy.

He took a deep breath, contemplated getting a fellow doctor to prescribe him anxiety pills before he said what was on his mind. 'They could come to my place.'

The two women swivelled around to stare at him, mouths agape.

'Pardon?' It was Katherine who found the words to speak first. 'I could've sworn you just offered to take my kids in.'

'My house is closer to the clinic than Katherine's and bigger than yours, Iona, with a garden and rooms for each of the children. It makes more sense. On the understanding that Iona moves in too as their primary carer.' That covered all bases and though Fraser didn't have much experience of children outside the clinic, he was sure he'd do a better job than his parents had. Iona had made it clear in no uncertain terms that she didn't want to get involved with him on a personal level so that was the end of that issue. The focus would solely be on doing the right thing by this family and he wouldn't let any personal conflict impact on that.

'Iona?' Katherine turned to Iona for approval of this new radical plan.

The decision now rested with her and if she fought him on this it would be for more personal reasons than any excuse she could come up with.

'You'd have to go through an assessment too.' If she thought that would unnerve him, she didn't know him at all.

'Not a problem. I've got nothing to hide.' Even if they brought in a crack investigative team, all they would dig up on him was a list of disappointed exes who hadn't been fans of his regimented approach to relationships.

'You're really prepared to do this? To have me and two children move into your house indefinitely?' Iona was challenging him in front of Katherine to deliberately put him on the spot but he'd made up his mind.

'I don't say things I don't mean, Iona. Katherine needs someone for the children, you need a place for all of you to stay, and this way I can make sure you get to your shifts on time. It sounds logical to me.'

It wouldn't be beyond the realms of possibility for her to believe he was only doing this to ensure the running of the clinic wasn't affected by this madcap scheme. That was safer than letting her know he wanted to help her when he was doing that way too often to go unnoticed by anyone, including himself. He didn't understand what made Iona different from any other colleague that he put himself out to this extent, and he couldn't say he was happy about the disruption, but he'd become a slave to his conscience. Along with other parts of him he didn't wish to acknowledge.

'I'm sold. I'll be much happier having them in such capable hands. I can't thank you enough.' He'd managed to convince Katherine that his intentions were honourable, even if Iona continued to eye him with a certain scepticism.

'If we're all in agreement, perhaps I should put a call in to Sandy and see if we have to make this official?' He directed that at Iona, prompting her to give him a response confirming she was on board.

'I guess so. Katherine, you'll need to pack a bag for the hospital and get some of the kids' belongings together.' Hopefully as a sign of things to come, Iona was on her feet and setting the plan into motion. Since this was work-related-*ish* she would put more thought into this than she had over her last house move.

'Do I have time to take Hamish and Poppy somewhere first so I can break the news to them? I don't want to scare them by just disappearing in case they think the same thing's going to happen to me as their daddy.'

'We'll make time. The longer we take explaining to them what's happening, the better they'll understand it and make it easier for all concerned.'

As Katherine disappeared out of Fraser's office to get things organised, Iona hung back.

He supposed they weren't going to get far if he didn't deign to give away the keys to his kingdom again. He pulled out his desk drawer and retrieved his spare key, scribbled down his address on a scrap of paper and slid it across the desk towards her. 'If you put the postcode into your satnav, you should be able to find it.'

Iona closed the door and sat down again, clearly wanting a private conversation with him. Fraser braced himself to hear her regret over what had happened between them the previous evening and prepared to give her assurances it wouldn't happen again.

'Is there something else I can help you with?'

'It's about this background check for social services…'

There was a restlessness about her as she alternated between wringing her hands and rubbing her palms on her knees. He'd thought she'd seemed uneasy when he'd mentioned it but now he was worried that whatever she was about to tell him would jeopardise the whole plan, maybe even her position here if it was as serious as it appeared.

'Is there something bothering you, Iona?' Fraser couldn't begin to imagine what it was she was about to tell him but he knew it wouldn't leave the confines of these four walls if she trusted him enough to confide her secrets.

She stared at her hands, avoiding eye contact, her shoulders rising and falling with each shuddery breath, her usual confidence deserting her. 'I…er, I was in a difficult relationship a few years back. Married, in fact. The police were involved.' She took a deep breath. 'There are hospital records too.'

Fraser knew what she was trying to tell him, yet he didn't want to accept it.

'Iona,' he said softly, 'did he—did he hurt you?'

She lifted her head, the haunted look in her eyes breaking his heart. The idea that anyone could lift a hand to harm a curl on her head was as devastating as the thought of her cowering under the threat of violence. It took a special kind of coward to hit a woman and a worse one still who'd feel the need to crush her spirit. Someone obviously threatened by strong women who needed to exert some sort of power over her. Someone who'd never deserved to have her in their life.

'Andy exerted his control in physical form but he also inflicted mental torture on me too until I was a prisoner in my own home. It took a lot for me to leave him and retrain as a midwife so I could get my life back.'

In his position as a GP Fraser had witnessed a lot of domestic abuse cases, knew how quickly they could escalate into physical violence and how emotional abuse could cause as much damage. He'd referred countless patients to counselling as a result and treated many others for depression. For some the scars never healed but Iona was one of those rare survivors who'd used that trauma to become stronger and more powerful than the man who'd tried to dominate her through fear. It explained the mystery that had surrounded her move to the village as well as her habitual defiance against any form of control.

He was completely in awe of her strength. 'You're an amazing woman anyone would be proud to have in their life.'

With a swipe of her hand Iona erased any trace of the tears he'd seen forming. 'Anyway, I'm only telling you this because I'm worried it could affect my suitability as a guardian for Hamish and Poppy.'

There was no evidence of self-pity in her words when goodness knew she'd be entitled to it. It must've have been a serious domestic situation for police involvement and injuries to warrant hospital treatment. His urge to track down the person responsible for hurting her and give him a taste of his own medicine was almost as strong as his wish to hug her and comfort her when she was having to relive the nightmare. Neither of them would endear him to her. Instead, he did his best to allay her fears.

'I'm sure that will have no bearing on your current situation. You're not in contact with this individual any more, are you?'

Iona gave an emphatic 'No. We're divorced', letting him know she'd cut all ties with her abuser and giving him some peace of mind that there was no chance she'd let herself be dragged back into that nightmare again.

It was a very personal and painful matter she probably wouldn't even have shared with him but for her concerns over Katherine and her family. Fraser was thankful she'd been brave enough to walk away and start her life over again here in Culcranna.

'You've done nothing wrong and you have absolutely nothing to be ashamed about.' He wouldn't call her a victim when he knew she'd hate to be thought of in that way but that's exactly what she'd been. Now she was a survivor, a warrior who'd fought the battle for her life.

'Perhaps you could ask your friend if she thinks it could cause any problems down the line.'

'I can certainly do that if you want or we could ask Katherine about keeping this as a personal favour, without getting social services involved?' He knew fostering wouldn't be a problem, after all Iona wasn't at fault for an error in judgement. If that was the case every person who'd ever fallen in love with the wrong person would be barred from the process, himself included. Although this would go against proper procedure, he knew they'd all be happier with a more informal arrangement.

'Thanks, Fraser. I'll have a talk with her.' She didn't have to say any more than that as she left for him to understand how momentous this was for her, and him.

'No problem.' Fraser felt honoured Iona still trusted him enough to share the deeply personal information even after last night. Perhaps it was meant in some way to explain her reaction. She'd been hurt in the worst possible way and her fierce fight for independence had been her survival strategy up until now. It helped him understand her a little more and, just like that, he knew he'd been thrown back into the path of oncoming chaos.

CHAPTER SIX

'IT'S NOT TOO late to change your mind, Iona. I don't want you to feel obligated to do this because I have no one else.'

Iona and Katherine were sitting in the hospital car park, the children chattering away in the back seat at the prospect of their adventure in Fraser's grand house, with Katherine expressing her last-minute doubts about the arrangements.

'Definitely not. You heard Fraser. Between us we've got it all sorted.' Iona was still trying to get her head around his involvement in all this. Not only had he assured them they could manage this without outside interference, he'd managed not to treat her as a victim when she'd confided in him about her abusive past. He had been sympathetic without suffocating her, understanding that she didn't need a white knight to ride in and rescue her, offering help only when she'd asked for it. That alone was a big step for Iona after all this time of going it alone.

Fraser was full of surprises today. When he'd first suggested they stay at his house she'd nearly fainted. That wasn't in his senior partner's handbook and made him more human beneath that starched shirt.

'I thought I sensed some tension between you two and I wouldn't force you into a situation you're not comfortable with.'

Katherine was twisting the handle of her bag, which reminded Iona that the prospect of spending the next however many days in residence *chez* McColl was creating the same mass of knots in her stomach, but she couldn't let Katherine fret. Whatever was going on with Fraser, it certainly wasn't going to happen in front of the children. She'd shut down any notion of something happening between them and she'd never drag innocent minors into a potential messy relationship when she was proof of the damage that could do.

'Hey, neither of us would do this if we didn't want to. It's not in our DNA. Fraser's not that bad once he's off the clock. He helped me move into the flat and brought me some furniture to fit it out.' That was when the trouble had started and now she tended to forget he was a danger to her sworn singleton status.

'Maybe I really did read the signs wrong. Is there something else going on I don't know about?'

'No!' The denial came too fast and felt so wrong it was obviously a lie, but so much relied on this plan neither of them questioned it. 'Honestly, there's nothing to worry about.'

Although Iona veered between wanting to kiss or strangle Fraser at times. It was a blessing now that they hadn't fully given in to temptation when they were going to be shacked up together as stand-in parents for the foreseeable future.

She couldn't actually believe she was moving out of her home only a day after she'd moved in to live with another man. So much for the quiet Christmas she'd planned for herself but she could always do that next year, or the one after that. Katherine and the children certainly weren't having the jolly time they'd anticipated this time last year and they took precedence over Iona's self-indulgence.

'You will bring these two up to see me, won't you?'

Katherine reached around the back of her seat and fumbled to find the hands of her precious babes.

'Every day if I can.' It would be the only way to convince them that, unlike their father, their mum would recover and come home again.

Iona got out of the car to retrieve Katherine's things from the boot, allowing her some privacy to say her goodbyes. Understandably she was teary when she did eventually step out to join Iona.

'Take care of them,' she sobbed before swamping her friend in a hug.

'We will. Now, are you sure you don't want me to come in with you?'

Katherine shook her head and wiped her tears on the back of her hand. 'No. I'll be fine. Take them back to Fraser's and get them settled in. I'll call as soon as I can.'

'I promise I'll do everything I can to make sure they're happy.'

Things would work out fine if Fraser could straddle the line between senior partner and the guy she could rely on. If he swayed too far into the realm of either persona, their new arrangement could be in serious trouble.

'It won't be long now, guys,' Iona shouted into her rearview mirror to the bobbing heads of the children, who couldn't sit still. Thank goodness they were comfortable enough around her to see this as a holiday of sorts rather than something to fear.

It was Iona's nerves that were stretched tight enough to snap at any second in the unfamiliar surroundings. The night was creeping in and as they drove further and further into the wilderness there was a sense of being swallowed up by the darkness.

The lack of lighting out here wasn't helping. All it

needed now was for the car to break down and this would have all the markings of a horror movie.

Eventually they came to a set of gothic black wrought-iron gates, which opened on their approach. The security cameras mounted either side of the gates turned and followed her progression up the long, winding driveway. The security measures were good for the children's safety but not exactly a warm welcome to visitors.

Iona's jaw almost dropped into the footwell of the car as Fraser's fortress loomed into view.

'Is it haunted?' Hamish leaned forward between the two front seats to peer through the windscreen.

'Don't be daft. It's just a lovely big house with plenty of room for you and your sister to run around in.' The huge mansion sitting in the moonlight was the sort of place she imagined a gang of pesky kids and their Great Dane might come to solve mysteries but this was no cartoon, this was their real home until further notice.

The trio made their way to the front door and as it creaked open Iona half expected a tall, deathly pale butler, who'd probably been spying on them since their arrival at the gates, waiting to greet them. She was more surprised to find a hunky doctor in casual wear on the other side, imagining Fraser would have employed someone else to answer the door rather than have his usual routine disrupted by meeting his guests personally.

'You're here?'

She hadn't expected Fraser to be home, having thought he'd wait until they were in bed and less likely to disrupt his usual routine before he came back.

'I finished up earlier than expected and it occurred to me I didn't give you the security code for the gates.' There wasn't a hint that he'd come back for anything other than practical reasons. Yet the faded denim jeans and soft sage-green wool jumper he was sporting projected a friendlier image than his formal shirt and tie ensemble. He'd taken the time to change and since he wasn't expecting any other visitors she had to assume it was for their benefit.

'Can we come in?' The wind was beginning to howl around them on the doorstep and she pulled up the collar of her coat to act as a barrier against it.

'Yes. Sorry. The heat's on and dinner's in the oven. It's only chicken and chips, I'm afraid. I'm not much of a cook.'

'That makes two of us.' Iona followed the children, who'd run ahead, into the house, the idea of someone making dinner for her heavenly. He'd picked a child-pleaser too and although Fraser could deny it all he wanted, what mightn't be a complicated meal was something he'd gone out of his way to do for his house guests when undoubtedly he was more of a gourmet diner.

Hamish stopped dashing in and out of the rooms long enough to address Fraser. 'My mum says I'm the man of the house now and I have to take care of my wee sister.' He puffed out his chest in an attempt to appear bigger and braver than his young age portrayed.

'That's right but Iona and I are here to help out if that's all right with you?'

'Sure.'

Fraser played the big brother role perfectly, instead of barging in and taking over as he was prone to doing at work, so Hamish was suitably reassured Fraser wouldn't usurp his position.

'This is some place you have. I didn't know you ran a hotel business on the side.' They followed Fraser through the halls of his home, Iona as mesmerised by the elaborate décor as the two little ones.

'Very funny. I told you, it's my parents' place. I inherited it and I'm not entirely sure what I'm going to do with it yet.' When anyone else would've been jumping for joy over the riches bestowed upon them, Fraser didn't seem particularly happy about it. Up until yesterday she might have believed his resistance had something to do with being beholden to someone else's plans but he'd indicated there'd been some bad blood between him and his parents. On his part anyway. She couldn't imagine him inheriting the family fortune if they'd held a grudge.

'Complicated, you said. I can sort of see why. It's not everyone who has a couple of million spare to buy you out.'

'Not self-funded, I'm afraid. It's the family business.' He gestured towards the stern portraits lining the walls whose faces bore some resemblance to their casually dressed descendant leading the way to the kitchen.

Places were already set around the farmhouse-style table in the middle of the floor, which wasn't in keeping with the opulence on display elsewhere. The children were directed to their seats so Fraser could dish up dinner.

'This is cosy. I would've expected one of those mile-long dining tables in the Great Hall where you need a megaphone to be heard from one end to the other.' Iona poured drinks for everyone from the water jug on the table and watched Fraser's cheeks stain red at the joke.

'I prefer to sit in here.'

This old house had every cliché in the book and if she went exploring she'd be sure to find servants' quarters and maybe a housemaid or two hidden away. If he'd owned up about his status, he could have saved them a lot of trouble and provided a live-in nanny.

Whether from habit or a conscious decision to fit in, Iona noticed he didn't sit at the head of the table and pulled up the chair next to her. 'Tuck in, everyone.'

In an effort to set a good example to the other guests, Iona lifted her knife and fork and helped herself to the first hot meal of the day or, in her case, the week. She couldn't remember the last time she'd had a home-cooked meal and this didn't taste as though Fraser had tipped a couple of bags of frozen chips and chicken strips onto an oven tray. The giveaway was that it tasted of the food it was purported to be. He'd made them from scratch and added corn on the cob to their plates in an attempt to get the children to eat some sort of vegetables.

'This is lovely, thank you, Fraser.'

'Have you got loads of money?' Hamish, obviously taking a keen interest in the new surroundings, blurted out what anyone would've assumed on setting foot in the house.

'Hamish, it's not polite to ask that.' Iona scolded him, although it was human nature for that to cross a person's mind. There was no reason for Fraser to work at all as far as she could tell from the house and land he'd inherited. He was clearly dedicated to his profession since he could've retired at any point since his parents' passing. She was sure he could spend many happy hours alphabetising and arranging every expensive knick-knack here, instead of tending to the sick.

'It's all right,' Fraser said placatingly as the young lad leaned back on his chair, arms folded, potentially gearing up for his first showdown with authority.

'Hamish, please sit on your chair properly so you don't damage it.' If Iona had been aware this place was full of priceless antiques she wouldn't have taken responsibility for two small children and the damage they could do running amok here. It was surprising that Fraser had agreed to it at all. Along with being a babysitter, she was going to have to be a disciplinarian too. Neither she nor Fraser were parents to these children and there were going to be times the kids would no doubt push the boundaries so they had to set them early on.

'For the record, I'm not rich, but I do own the title of Laird and the land. As for the house, I'm trying to decide whether to break centuries of family ties and tradition and sell up. Anyway, if you're all finished, I'll show you up to your rooms.'

They traipsed up the grand staircase and along a carpeted hallway until Fraser stopped at a door on the landing. 'I thought Hamish would be comfortable in this room.'

The plush bedroom could've come straight out of a five-star hotel brochure but it wasn't very homely. Hamish set his superhero backpack on the bed. It was lost in the furnishings of a very adult room.

'It's very grown up, isn't it, Hamish?' Iona acknowledged Fraser's effort in preparing a space for Hamish and at the same time tried to convince the boy this was all one big adventure.

'There's plenty of space for you to put your things away and your bathroom is through there.' Their host gave a whirlwind tour, pulling out drawers and opening doors. An en suite bathroom was a luxury for Iona, who was used to house-sharing.

'You could put your pyjamas on, Hamish, and we'll come back when we get our own rooms sorted out.' They left the door slightly ajar so he wasn't completely abandoned.

'Poppy, you're next door to your brother.' The second room was less intimidating, smaller and decorated in neutral tones. Once they'd dotted Poppy's toys around and covered the bed with the favourite fluffy pink bunny blanket she'd insisted on bringing, it would be more child-friendly.

The door creaked behind them and a worried little face peered out at them.

'Come in, Hamish. Don't be shy. You're free to come and go as you please.' Fraser was usually so meticulous about everything being in its proper place it was strange to hear him being so welcoming to the boy. It was clear he wanted the children to be comfortable here, a magnanimous gesture on his part when Iona had the impression he never had been before.

'It's just a thought, Fraser, but could we bring another bed into this room? Perhaps Hamish and Poppy would prefer to stay together as he's promised to look after her for his mum.' She didn't want to embarrass the boy by suggesting he might be scared in that big room alone but wanted Hamish to think she was doing this to keep his sister safe.

'Sure. I'll show you to your room before I start shifting the furniture around,' Fraser said, striding out of the room at breakneck speed.

Iona took some pleasure in seeing Fraser disconcerted at the suggestion because it reminded her this congenial host act could be a façade and she shouldn't let her guard down just in case.

'This was my mother's room.' Fraser didn't give her the same warm introduction as the others into her new living quarters and she didn't dare enquire why his mother had had a separate room from his father.

'It's beautiful.' The scene before her was straight out of every little girl's fairy-tale. A four-poster bed and closet space big enough to fit her flat in, not to mention the rolltop bath in an alcove, was a fantasy come true. The floral wallpaper and thick pink carpet underfoot weren't to her taste but fitted perfectly in here.

'And where's your room?' She'd have to know in case of emergency, not because she was curious where he spent his nights.

'I'm down the hall.' In the other direction, she noted as he spun away from her.

'Thanks for this, Fraser. You didn't have to do this.'

'Neither did you.'

'No. We're a regular couple of heroes.' Iona laughed, not seriously fooling herself she was doing anything more than any other decent human would do.

'Or two people with nothing better to do over the holidays,' Fraser muttered, and left her to her own devices.

Iona heaved her bag onto the bed and unpacked the few things she had. There had been no way to predict how long they'd be here so they'd only brought the essentials for now. If anyone needed anything else, they could call home and get them. She eyed up the tub, wondering when she'd get an opportunity to use it. It wouldn't be tonight. She was exhausted and in danger of falling asleep and drowning in it and she had to get the children tucked up in bed at some point too. Although, judging by the thumping and banging coming from down the hall, they'd no intention of sleeping tonight. She had visions of them using the antique bed as a trampoline and Fraser presenting her with an extortionate bill for damages at the end of their stay.

'Hey, guys, can you keep the noise down in there?' Putting them into a room together might have been a bad move after all.

There was another loud thump against the wall, followed by the sound of muffled voices.

Iona sighed. She'd have to put her foot down tonight or they'd never get any sleep. She whipped the door open, fully prepared to read them the Riot Act if they carried on wrecking the place, except it was the Laird himself making all the racket and being reckless with the furniture. He had a bed base tipped on its side and was sliding it through the door, so focused he didn't appear to see Iona peeping at him. That's exactly what she was doing here, watching him as he stripped off his jumper—being a peeping Tom.

Fraser tossed his knitwear aside, revealing a tight white T-shirt layer. Iona scrunched up her face at being denied a sneaky glimpse of what lay beneath. Her stealth, however, was rewarded seconds later when he lifted the hem to mop the sweat from his brow.

Darts of lust targeted Iona's erogenous zones, the sight

of his taut stomach and that sexy V where his jeans rode low on his hips hitting bulls-eye after bulls-eye. When she realised the heavy lifting had ceased and she dragged her eyes back up his body to find she'd been caught ogling, she forced her buckling knees to carry her forward.

'You didn't have to do this on your own. I would've helped.' The belated offer of assistance should've been enough to deflect the fact she'd been gawping where she oughtn't, but the smirk on his face suggested otherwise.

'It's no problem. I can see you're busy.' He flipped the bed upright and manoeuvred it adjacent to Poppy's, mesmerising Iona with every flex of biceps she hadn't known he possessed under those buttoned-up shirts. Then he was on his hands and knees, tightening all the nuts and bolts and giving her a good view of his taut backside.

'I'll bring the mattress in.' She excused herself from the sight and the too-hot room to drag the mattress in from the hall.

Unfortunately her muscles weren't as well developed as Fraser's and she had to employ a combination of shoulder charges and kicking to move it.

'Let me try.' A large hand rested on her shoulder and almost collapsed her into a puddle. She hoped this hormonal mess incapable of functioning would return to her normal competent self soon once she got used to seeing a man around the house.

'Right, you two, into the bathroom to brush your teeth.' Leaving Fraser to the manly bed-building, she shut herself away to compose herself and remember who she was and who he was.

'Why's your face all red, Auntie 'Ona?' Poppy's scrutiny made her blush harder so she was forced to splash herself with cold water at the sink.

'It's hard work, moving furniture.' That was plain to

see from the trickle of sweat making Fraser's hair curl at the back of his neck.

Another splash of water and Iona kicked the door shut. She was too young to start getting hot flushes and needed her brain to compartmentalise this man back into his 'unsuitable dating material' box. The best way to stop daydreaming about his body was trying to wrangle two small kids into bed in a strange house but she knew once she did that the adults would be left alone and there were no guarantees her mind wouldn't start to wander again.

Fraser made up the spare bed and exited sharply back to his own room, collecting the jumper he'd cast aside along the way. Iona could put the kids to bed while he took some time to cool down.

He tugged his shirt over his head and tossed it into the laundry hamper in the bedroom with the rest of his clothes. At the last minute, before he stepped into the shower, he locked the bathroom door. He was going to have to remember he was no longer living alone.

His mind flitted back to Iona standing in the doorway, watching him so intently he may as well have been naked. The first blast of ice-cold water took away his breath along with the mixture of manual labour, anger and lust making him sweat.

While he lathered his body with soap, it was easier for him to fixate on never being able to please her than the memory of her predatory gaze sweeping over his body or he wouldn't leave this cubicle until he'd found some satisfaction.

He didn't want to be assigned a significant role in this scenario that he wasn't ready to accept. He was, however, considerate of the children's plight, and how they'd left the warmth and familiarity of home to be here. This wasn't a school full of stern masters and other frightened children but it could be equally as imposing. As an adult, and the owner, there were times it scared the hell out of him too.

Fraser had done everything he could to make them comfortable by cooking dinner and preparing their rooms, all the time wishing he'd retained some of the household staff after his father's death.

His best hadn't been good enough for Iona and though he'd shifted things around to suit he didn't think she'd find favour with anything he did. Ordinarily it didn't bother him if people took to him or not but he was sharing more of himself than ever with Iona and he wanted her to see the best in him. If he'd had any sense he would've volunteered for on-call duty this weekend and avoided crossing paths as much as possible then he wouldn't have to be constantly under her scrutiny.

Fraser slammed off the shower and towelled down before throwing on a clean shirt and jogging bottoms and padding barefoot downstairs to the kitchen. It was odd expecting to hear the chatter of other people when at any other time he imagined every creak and murmur might be the ghosts of his past come back to haunt him.

The house was quiet except for the sound of the kettle as he waited for it to boil and he assumed the others had all gone to bed after their fraught day. For the umpteenth time he wondered how he'd got himself into this mess. Iona. His life had been thrown into turmoil from the moment he'd held her in his arms and fried the logical side of his brain. How was he supposed to sleep now when the same woman was only down the hall from his bedroom?

'Oh. Sorry. I didn't realise you were down here. I fancied a cup of tea before bed.' Iona's unexpected arrival made him spill the hot water over the kitchen worktop and he had to move quickly before it scalded his feet too.

'Great minds…and all that.' Fraser grabbed some

kitchen towels and crouched down to mop up the mess he'd made on the floor.

Iona reached for another mug from the cupboard he'd left open.

'Sugar?' she asked, and it took him a few seconds not to respond with an equally sweet nickname to the one he'd imagined she'd bestowed on him.

'Not for me, thanks. It's in the container there beside the kettle if you want some.'

'I didn't mean to disturb you but you should know I'm a night owl.' Iona justified her appearance so late, even though this was to be her home too for a while.

'I'm more of a morning person myself but I suppose we should take the quiet times when we can get them, huh? Are they both down for the night?' Actually, Fraser didn't usually sleep long enough to have a preference, only catching a few hours in between when exhaustion finally overwhelmed whatever problems or memories had been keeping his brain awake. New people in the house were bound to bring him additional thinking time in the small hours.

'Out for the count.'

'We can take this into the lounge if you want. If we leave the door open, we can hear any little feet wandering around upstairs.' If they took their tea in there they'd have extra room to spread out and create much-needed distance between them.

'Are you sure you trust me not to spill anything on your antique rugs?' Iona was teasing but she didn't realise how close to the mark she was—Fraser was still afraid of causing damage to the family heirlooms. It had taken a long time to get used to being in charge around here and this was an act of defiance against the house rules for the sake of those he'd invited to treat his home as their own. It was just difficult for him to understand what that truly meant.

Not long ago he'd thought that was having a wife and children and now he didn't know if he'd ever have the right to the deeds without either.

'It's okay, I'll have the staff come in and clean up after you leave.' Fraser's deadpan delivery made her almost snort her tea back out.

'Do you actually have people who do that?'

'My parents did but I didn't see the need. Most of the time I only use the lounge and the kitchen, which I'm quite capable of cleaning myself, as you know.'

Iona's giggle, which came at his expense, nonetheless lifted his spirits. If they could find the funny side in his compulsions they were making progress.

Iona sat in the chair opposite him, her legs curled up under her. 'I know you have very valid reasons for not celebrating Christmas but you don't even have a tree.'

Which, apparently, was the crime of the century. It suggested his life was in some way lacking because he hadn't bothered chopping a tree down to stick in a bucket in his front room.

'Last year wasn't a great Christmas for me either. My… er…girlfriend left me. Just after I proposed to her. I wasn't in a hurry to be reminded of it.' It hadn't crossed Fraser's mind to decorate because he was supposed to be the only soul in residence. When he'd had a partner, a vision of a future together and there'd been something to celebrate, he'd done the whole festive frivolity along with everyone else, but, as in his childhood, it had turned out to be fake and a waste of time pretending Christmas was something special.

Talking about it now wasn't as painful as it once had been. It was a positive sign that he was beginning to move forward and not letting either event define who he was. That should probably include no longer allowing bad memories to taint future holidays.

'I'm so sorry. I don't want to make you uncomfortable in your own home but the children could be here for Christmas. It's only a few days away and I'd like to try and make it special for them. Would you mind if I decorate? I could limit it to their room if you'd prefer and you wouldn't have to do anything except say yes. They're still little enough to believe in the magic and I don't want to spoil it for them. Your house is beautiful but it's not very child-friendly.'

Didn't he know it. When he hadn't been at school, abiding by the rules there, he'd been restricted by the list of dos and don'ts at home. Don't make too much noise. Don't leave toys where people could trip on them, dress smartly, don't talk back… He'd never been free to explore childhood without a scolding. There hadn't been much reason to change anything in the house once he'd found out a family was off the table for him.

'This has never been a fun environment for raising children.' He'd been more of an intruder when he'd been home, having to be careful not to disturb his mother, who had invariably been in bed, exhausted at the very thought of having him here. These walls echoed with the loneliness of his childhood and he'd have changed everything in a second if Caroline had accepted his proposal and set up home with him. After she'd left there hadn't seemed any point in changing anything.

'My mum used to put on the whole show with the tree, the presents and the big family dinner. It was wonderful. Except for the ever-present threat of my dad's temper, which would explode when he found fault with the smallest thing. Then that lovely tree, the thoughtful gifts and the dishes of food would end up smashed on the floor.' Iona clutched her tea close to her chest and looked smaller than ever.

Their constant battle over power seemed to be about

asserting their right to be heard when they'd both been nothing but casualties of their past.

'I guess a domineering father is as damaging as a disinterested one,' Fraser mused aloud, although Iona's experiences of ruined celebrations had taken her in the opposite direction from his attitude.

'So you can see how important it is we get this right?' Iona didn't have to guilt-trip him. Fraser had accepted that responsibility when he'd agreed to host them here. That's why he was so afraid of getting it wrong. He trusted Iona had enough experience of at least one loving parent that she had more clue than he did about how to do this.

'You have free rein. Go tinsel crazy around the house with my blessing.' He was sure he could stomach it for a few days.

'Are you serious?' As soon as he said it her eyes lit up like fairy lights and she dropped the defensive body language.

Fraser winced as she set her cup on the floor, flattening a circular patch of the deep-pile carpet, but let it pass since she looked so happy. He didn't want to be another man to make Iona miserable. Her enthusiasm was contagious, his smile growing to match hers. What harm could there be in letting her loose with a few ornaments? The house wasn't governed by the health and safety rules of the workplace or even those set by his parents. As he had to keep reminding himself, he was free to do as he pleased and now so was Iona.

'I'm serious. Honestly, I'm not the monster you think I am.'

She bounced out of her seat and launched herself at him. 'Thank you. Thank you. Thank you.'

She landed a smacker of a kiss on his cheek before she whispered, 'I've never thought of you as a monster.'

In that second all his icy edges melted and he would've

let her redecorate the whole house if she'd asked. There was something about her and her quest to fix everyone that made him think she might be able to fix him too.

'Let's try and keep it that way,' he eventually managed to get out after the shock of her touch and his need to please her ebbed away.

He ignore the urge to nuzzle into the cloud of soft curls falling around his face and waited until she backed off before he could breathe again.

'I'll make a list of everything we have to do. I've never planned a family Christmas before.'

'Neither have I.' Fraser had never even considered he'd truly been part of one and now there was a possibility he'd always be of the opinion it should include Iona and a kid or two.

CHAPTER SEVEN

'I HAVE TO make a few patient calls then I'll pick the kids up from their after-school club.' Iona checked in with Fraser after ensuring he didn't have any patients in with him.

'Should I expect a lorry load of fake snow and a herd of reindeer to meet me on the drive when I get home?' He spun around in his chair, arms folded across his chest and giving her that bright smile that was fast becoming a familiar fixture. They'd come such a long way since the day they'd fought over the decorations here at the clinic and she was glad of it. Now she was comfortable enough to walk into his room and plant her backside on his desk.

'Unfortunately, it was too short notice to get the reindeer. They're fully booked until the New Year. You might get the snow, though—I hear they're predicting a white Christmas this year.'

'I'm sure the kids will love that. Not so good for the rest of us who still have to work. Speaking of which, I've managed to get cover in for Christmas week in case we're still playing happy families.'

That's exactly how it had seemed this morning as she and Fraser had teamed up to get the children ready for school. She'd made sure they were washed and dressed before they all sat down to a Fraser breakfast special of freshly made French toast and bacon. He'd also packed lunches for everyone as they headed out on the school run. There was definitely something to be said for being organised when they were all benefitting from it and starting the day calmly instead of the chaotic mess it could've been, left to her.

'Oh, good. I'm not planning on going anywhere but babies have a habit of not sticking to the schedule. With you at home that means we've got things covered.' She high-fived Fraser.

Home. How quickly she'd come to think of that huge house and the inhabitants as somewhere she'd every right to be and wanted to be. Not every housemate was someone to dread, just as living alone didn't have to be everything. Last night, chatting with Fraser, had reminded her there wasn't always something to fear from sharing her personal space. It could actually provide a sense of well-being to have someone to unwind with and talk to. Until now Iona hadn't realised the extent to which she'd isolated herself. Outside work and patients she didn't have anyone to call on for a chat or a shoulder to cry on if she needed one, and there was something reassuring, therapeutic even, in having company other than her own.

For too long she'd associated any form of relationship as a hassle, something to be endured or avoided at all costs. Simply having someone who understood her, who was willing to compromise his needs to accommodate hers, showed her there was something different out there if she wanted it.

'Should I bring something home for dinner?' He'd swivelled around again and tossed that word casually over his shoulder, which made her shiver every time she thought of him waiting there for her.

'That would be great. I've promised Hamish and Poppy we'd make it to the hospital for visiting later then we can start decorating. I'll get some Christmas supplies with them after school.' They'd have more than enough to keep them busy until bedtime and hopefully seeing their mum would help settle them. According to the staff member she'd spoken to this morning, Katherine's blood pressure remained high and they weren't prepared to send her home yet.

Fraser stopped typing momentarily to glance at her. 'Is there anything else I can do for you?'

Iona was aware her continued presence, sitting here, was disturbing his otherwise perfectly arranged desk but she was enjoying this new easy atmosphere between them too much to leave.

'Um, no, I don't think so.'

'You're sitting on my notepad.'

She shifted her position slightly so he could retrieve his precious notepad but hadn't anticipated the effect his hand brushing against the curve of her backside would have on her. The joke had well and truly backfired and her attempt to provoke him had succeeded in raising her own temperature.

She leapt off the desk as though someone had started a fire beneath her, things suddenly feeling too hot for her to handle.

'I'll see you at home,' Fraser called after her, and now she really couldn't wait to finish her shift.

Iona phoned around her patients to give test results and check in with her ladies before she clocked off for the day. Once she'd finished her shift, any emergencies would be down to the duty midwife. The midwives from neighbouring clinics took turns at covering nights and although it was a large catchment area they weren't overly stretched with callouts.

She was already putting her coat on as she dialled

Angie, one of her first-time mums, so she could get started on her evening plans as soon as possible.

'Hi, Angie, it's Iona here. I'm just calling to tell you your last test results were all clear. The antibiotics seemed to have cleared up your UTI so there's nothing to worry about.' She turned off the light and grabbed her car keys from the desk.

'Thanks, Iona, that's a weight off my mind. It's been one urine infection after another lately.' The heavy sigh was a standard response from most of her patients in the later stages of their pregnancies as they struggled to even tie their own shoelaces. Although she'd never been pregnant, Iona could understand the frustration of not having a say in what happened to you. Andy had taken that right away from her with the physical and emotional torture he'd put her through until she had been too frightened to make any decisions for herself in case he disagreed. Thankfully, those days were long behind her and she was a different person now from who she had been then.

'How are you feeling otherwise?' It had only been a couple of days since Iona had seen Angie at the clinic but it was a question it was always necessary to ask in case anything untoward crept in between appointments.

'Some heartburn at night and I don't know if this is anything but my hands and feet have been really itchy. It could be an allergic reaction, I suppose, but I haven't changed my washing powder or anything recently. It's probably nothing.' While Angie was talking herself out of the significance of any symptoms, the comment managed to stall Iona's exit.

'What about the baby? Is he still moving about plenty?' Adrenaline was rushing through her system at the prospect of what this could mean for her patient but she didn't want to scare her.

'Not as much today but I was up late last night because

I couldn't get comfortable at all.' There was a yawn to illustrate the lack of sleep.

'The itching was more noticeable at night?' Iona retraced her steps back into the office, turned the light on and retrieved Angie's file.

Mild itching itself wasn't uncommon during pregnancy as the skin stretched to accommodate a growing belly but it could be symptomatic of a more serious condition.

ICP, intrahepatic cholestasis of pregnancy, was a potentially serious liver disorder, often characterised by itching when bile acids, which should have flowed from the liver to the gut to aid digestion, built up elsewhere instead.

To get a conclusive diagnosis they would need a variety of blood tests to check liver function and measure bile acid levels but time would be of the essence, especially if the baby's movements had reportedly slowed. There was a high risk of stillbirth for those with an elevated BAL. There was no cure and with Angie in her thirty-seventh week of pregnancy it was possible the hospital would want to induce labour to prevent the worst from happening.

'Angie, is Chris there with you?' This would go much easier if she had her husband there to support her.

'No, he's at work. Why?' That element of fear Iona hated hearing in her patients' voices when she had to deliver distressing news was there, turning her own blood to ice.

'I don't want you to panic but I would prefer it if you went to the hospital to get checked out and make sure everything's all right.'

'Why? What's wrong? Chris won't be home for hours—he's working in Aberdeen. Is my baby in trouble?' The panic gradually picked up pace and there was only one thing Iona could do.

'Everything's going to be fine. I'm being cautious but

I'd prefer to get you to hospital for a scan to make sure the baby's not in any distress. I'll drive you myself.'

'Should I have my overnight bag ready?' Angie sniffed back the tears but she already sounded calmer that she wouldn't go through this alone.

'That mightn't be a bad idea.' Not only would it give her something to distract her until Iona got there, the obstetrician might decide to keep her in.

'I'll phone Chris and let him know.'

'I'll be with you as soon as I can and, Angie, please don't worry.' Words were never enough to soothe a scared mother-to-be but the presence of an experienced midwife often put her mind at rest that someone knew what they were doing in the circumstances.

Iona was in the car and on her way before she'd hung up. Technically the call should have gone to the duty midwife, who probably would've told her to phone for a taxi or rung straight through for an ambulance, but Iona thought there was more chance of keeping her calm by doing it herself. She would do the handover, of course, leaving Angie in the care of the consultant lead team at the maternity unit, but having a familiar face for most of the journey could make all the difference to a woman's first experience of pregnancy in such difficult circumstances. On speakerphone, she managed to call ahead and let the hospital know she was bringing Angie in.

This kind of crisis was the reason Iona could never be a normal wife and mother with responsibilities. It would only take her back to those dark days of having to account for her every move outside the house until it was easier to simply stay put.

Wait. This week that's exactly what she was supposed to be and she'd failed at the first hurdle. Not only was she going to be late for the school run but she was going to have to renege on the promises she'd made to her surrogate children.

The steering wheel took the brunt of her temper as she lashed out and swore. It was going to be harder to juggle motherhood and work than she'd imagined, as she'd become so accustomed to doing what she wanted when she wanted. Iona wasn't used to thinking about other people outside work or relying on anyone but herself.

Now she was going to have to depend on Fraser, her pseudo-husband, to jump in and save the day. It was going to take hours to get to the hospital and back, by which time she'd have missed visiting time, dinner and Christmas decorating. She wasn't looking forward to disappointing the children or putting in an SOS call to Fraser. Already she could see there was a fine line between controlling and being in control when it came to family obligations, and she was a long way from both. Fraser might have the better temperament for taking care of children after all. Gut instinct was all well and good but she had others to think about now and a flaky parent was as damaging to the bonding process as an overbearing influence. She prayed he'd step up to cover her inadequacies until she could make it up to everyone later. If she made it back at all before bedtime.

'You're rubbish at this.' Hamish provided the harsh critique as Fraser lifted the tray of charcoal that purported to be the walls of their gingerbread house.

'I'm doing my best.' He dumped the charred remnants on the draining board along with the other gingerbread rubble from their last attempt. They'd managed to stick three walls, and Fraser's fingers, together with the icing before it had collapsed on itself.

'It's yummy.' Poppy helped herself to a broken piece of the front door and wandered off again. It was nice to know it hadn't been a complete waste of time.

'My mum makes good gingerbread. I wish she was here.' Hamish kicked the leg of the kitchen table with the toe of his scuffed shoe, which ordinarily Fraser wouldn't have stood for but he understood that feeling of being let down by Iona tonight.

How many times had he stood waiting at the school entrance, bag packed and ready to go home, only to be told at the last minute no one was coming for him after all? Enough to stop him trusting a word his parents had said. Young children didn't understand the reasons you flaked out on them, they didn't care about anything except the fact you didn't stick to your word. Once that trust was lost it was difficult to get back. These two had every right to be annoyed. It wasn't as if Iona couldn't have arranged for someone else to provide a taxi service, no, she'd chosen who'd deserved her attention and it certainly hadn't been the master gingerbread builders here. Still, it wasn't going to help lift the mood if he let rip at Iona when she did come home. Parenthood was new to both of them and they were learning on the job.

Fraser pulled over a chair and sat down so he was at eye level with the disgruntled seven-year-old. 'Listen, this isn't easy for us and I wish it was your mum here baking for you, and she will be, soon. I know you're disappointed you didn't get to see her but I'll do my very best to get you there tomorrow.'

'Sure...' Hamish didn't look up from his feet, already cynical about trusting the word of an adult.

It took Fraser to physically tilt his chin up to make him look at him. 'Hey, I mean it.'

Hamish didn't seem convinced but he did stop taking out his anger on the furniture and ran off to find his sister.

Tonight had been tough, thanks to the last-minute change of arrangements. By the time Fraser had finished at work and picked up their new dependants it had been too late to make it in time for visiting at hospital. Hamish had been in a foul temper since and Poppy much too quiet for a five-year-old.

Fast food hadn't managed to lift their spirits and neither had the impromptu art class he'd set up. The lack of decorations they'd been assured would be up today hadn't gone unnoticed by the children so he'd persuaded them to make their own. Although their paintings were colourful, they weren't enough to brighten up the huge room.

He'd let them stay up well after their bedtime in the vain hope Iona would show up before they retired for the night. The kitchen massacre could be dealt with after that.

'I think it's time you put on your pyjamas and brushed your teeth.'

'Iona said—' It was Poppy's turn to protest.

'I know, Iona promised we'd decorate but she got caught up at work.' In her brief call she'd told Fraser she was driving her patient to the hospital but, knowing her, she'd stayed on for moral support too. A quality he'd admire in her if it wasn't for the two disappointed faces staring at him.

It was better for him to imagine she was hand-holding a frightened pregnant woman than that she'd been in an accident on that dark, potholed road back to civilisation. Like it or not, they were a makeshift family as a result of their recent decisions and apparently that entailed worrying about all members, every minute of the day. It wasn't a responsibility anyone should take lightly and, in hindsight, it had probably been fortunate Caroline had changed her mind about the prospect of family life before they'd married or he could've been left as a single father.

As Fraser began seriously contemplating reporting Iona as a missing person, car headlights slowly made their way up the drive. Although relieved she was safe, he was going to have to confront her about the childcare situation.

Hamish and Poppy ignored his request, watching Iona through the window with him. When she turned the key in the front door there was a posse waiting for her.

'Hello. Sorry I'm late, everyone. I had to take a very poorly patient to hospital and I didn't want to leave her on her own.'

'Hi. How is she?' Fraser rammed his hands in his pockets after he noticed they were covered in icing and glitter.

'They're keeping her in to do a trace but her husband is with her now.' Iona flung herself into a chair and kicked off her shoes.

'I hope everything works out all right.'

'Me too.'

'There's some dinner left in the oven if you're hungry.' He'd saved some leftovers as he'd never seen her take a proper meal break in all the time she'd been at the clinic.

'Starving. Thanks. How did you get on today?'

'We did some painting and tried our hand at building gingerbread houses. It didn't go very well.' An understatement she'd see for herself next time she stepped into the kitchen but it was important she knew he'd done his best to keep the children entertained in her absence. Despite the fact that they were still upset, he'd genuinely wanted to get involved with them and had shaken off any notion he'd be as bad a parent as his own. Far from putting the idea of fatherhood far from mind, he was afraid it was strengthening the case for having children of his own. Unless he found a partner who was completely committed to the idea with him, it was a non-starter anyway.

'Sounds fun. Sorry I missed it.'

'Did you get Christmas stuff?' Poppy piped up with the question that had prevented her from going to bed, afraid of missing something.

'I didn't get to the shops in time, sweetheart. I stopped off at the petrol station but this was all I could get for now.

We'll get more tomorrow.' She handed a bag to Poppy, who proceeded to sit cross-legged in the middle of the floor and empty out the contents.

One by one she held up the items—strands of silver and gold tinsel, a packet of foil-covered chocolate tree decorations, plastic mistletoe and a tree-shaped car air freshener.

'You said we'd have a proper tree.'

Iona attempted to hug the little girl but was brutally shrugged off. 'We'll get one tomorrow after school.'

'Unless you have something better to do.' Hamish gathered up the unwanted gifts, stuffed them back in the bag and dumped it at Iona's feet. Fraser was beginning to feel sorry for her. She hadn't intentionally hurt them, had simply tried to do the right thing by everyone. The last thing she would've wanted after a long day, and evening, was to face more stress at home.

'You heard Iona, we'll do everything tomorrow. It's late and we're all tired.' He gave his child-minding partner a hand up so they were both imposing their authority together from a higher vantage point.

'We couldn't see Mum tonight because of you,' Hamish spat, and caused Iona to flinch.

'Enough, Hamish. Tomorrow, you were told. Now, go up to your rooms and get ready for bed.' It went against all his instincts to scold the children but he couldn't let them attack Iona. It would undermine their position as the adults in charge if they didn't set boundaries from the start.

Unfortunately, it also put him into the doghouse alongside Iona as far as the sullen child was concerned.

'You're not my dad and you're not my mum. I hate you both.' Hamish stomped out of the living room and up the stairs. Fraser's heart ached for him as he was clearly missing his two parents.

Iona stared open-mouthed as Poppy trotted after him

and the sound of the bedroom door slamming echoed through the house. 'Now what?'

'Let him cool off for a while then I'll go and have a talk with him.' Fraser had never wanted to get emotionally involved but since he had some understanding of what the boy was going through he might be in a better position to talk him round.

A dazed Iona sagged back down into the chair.'

'I really didn't mean for them to feel like an afterthought but Angie had suspected ICP and this is her first baby. I'm an idiot for thinking I could get away with postponing their evening and making up for it with a bag of tat from the garage.'

'Don't be so hard on yourself. We're dealing with two vulnerable young children. They're scared and have had such upheaval they need to lash out at someone and, unfortunately, that's you tonight.' Fraser put an arm around her shoulder and gave her a squeeze to let her know he was on her side.

'You heard Hamish, he hates me, and I'm pretty sure Poppy's right there with him. Even if he hadn't said it I could feel the animosity in the atmosphere as soon as I stepped into the room.' Years of walking on eggshells had finely tuned that skill, anticipating shouldering the blame for whatever perceived misdemeanour she'd committed to justify Andy's foul mood. Although, in these circumstances, the anger directed at her was understandable.

'Now, now, don't go getting all sorry for yourself. I do believe he said he hated us both. Something I'm choosing not to take seriously or personally when he's clearly upset.'

Iona appreciated Fraser's attempt to make her feel better but so far it wasn't working. 'Nice try, but we both know this is my fault. I just hope you won't hold it against me. I'm trying, I really am, but it's difficult for me too. I'm not used to factoring anyone else into these last-minute decisions, or trusting anyone other than myself. That's why I felt the need to take Angie to hospital myself and why I'm struggling to work as part of a team here with you. It's going to take time, Fraser, for all of us. I've relied only on myself for so long none of this is coming naturally to me.'

She was bone weary, leaning into him and making him wish they could put the whole saga behind them and relax until tomorrow, when they had to do it all over again.

'For me neither. They'll forget all about it once they get to see their mum and they have a lovely sparkly Christmas tree to stare at.'

'I hope you're right.'

'Always,' Fraser said with a grin. 'Look, I can identify with the kids but that doesn't mean you should be punished for doing what you thought was the right thing. My parents sent me to boarding school at an early age and let me down time and time again, telling me they were coming to pick me up, getting me excited, only to change their minds at the last minute. At that age you're left feeling as though no one cares, that your feelings don't matter, even when there's a perfectly reasonable excuse.'

'Gee, thanks for making me feel better.' Now she had the added guilt of making Fraser relive his abandonment issues too.

'I'm simply trying to explain the fear hidden behind the surface anger. As long as you follow up on your word tomorrow, I'm sure they'll forgive you.' Fraser's wounds obviously still ran deep from his experiences but that was probably why he'd bonded with the children so quickly.

Iona was afraid her actions would somehow exclude her from the circle of trust they'd been working on together.

'What about you, Fraser? Will you forgive me?' She'd hurt him on several occasions and eventually she'd run out of lives with someone who'd obviously been so let down in the past.

'I did, the moment you came home safe.' Fraser tilted her chin up so she was looking into his eyes, and seeing the truth of his words reflected there made her heart melt. The knowledge that he cared enough about her to worry made her want to wrap herself up in his arms and the warmth of that beautiful sentiment.

He dropped his hand away so quickly she thought she'd imagined the whole exchange. 'Now, come on and we'll get you some dinner.'

It was obvious he wanted to keep things light between them so she simply had to file away the moment along with all the other ones they couldn't talk about. 'I wouldn't say no. I didn't dare stop for any on the way home. The wind is picking up out there and I had visions of my wee car being blown into a ditch or a tree falling on my roof.'

'In that case, we should get your dinner on in case there's a power cut. You start reheating and I'll hunt for candles and torches.' They made their way to the kitchen, where Iona picked at the gingerbread ruins lying around as she waited for the microwave to ping.

From now on they had to work as a team. It was the only way they'd survive.

The reheated pizza and fries were no substitute for Fraser's home cooking the previous night but Iona's rumbling belly was past point of caring.

She'd expected disappointment and guilt about not following through on her plans with the children but the full blast of Hamish's rage had almost finished her off. Judging by the bomb-hit worktops she wasn't the only one who'd had a tough day.

'Thanks for covering for me,' Iona said after swallowing a mouthful of the wine Fraser had poured for her. He hadn't had much say in the matter but he hadn't tag-teamed the others to point out the extent of her failure so she was grateful.

'What did you think I'd do? Leave them somewhere with a sign around their necks saying, "Please take care of me"?' Fraser was trying to make her laugh and he succeeded.

She'd been expected an 'I told you so' once she realised what a great undertaking this whole thing had been. If they'd been in this position a month ago she'd have been horrified at the thought of leaving Fraser in charge of the children. It wouldn't have been a stretch to imagine him marching them around the house in regimented fashion, issuing commands. Since getting to know him properly, she'd almost become too complacent that he was up to the job.

The paint-splattered surfaces and baking attempts showed how hard he'd tried to cover for her without expecting, or receiving, a gold star for his efforts. Thank goodness he was in this with her because it was clear now she'd never have managed them, and work, on her own.

'Maybe you should do that to me.'

'Something tells me you wouldn't be willing to let anyone take care of you.' Fraser's insight was spot on but she was willing to let him clear away her dirty dishes for her.

'Take care of me, yes. Take charge of me, definitely not.' It was a warning shot that he shouldn't dare to try but as she locked eyes with him he didn't look away. As if he was telling her he was up to whatever challenge she set him.

CHAPTER EIGHT

AN ALMIGHTY CRASH interrupted Iona's late supper, so loud it made her jump out of her seat. 'What the hell was that?'

She'd seen plenty of horror films to know big houses were playgrounds for ghosts, ghouls and everything else that went bump in the night.

'That was the front door being slammed.' Fraser bolted in the direction the noise had come from but his explanation didn't put her any more at ease. The solid wooden door didn't open and close by itself. Either someone had come in, or gone out, and both scenarios sent chills through her cold enough to freeze her bones.

'I'll go and check on Hamish and Poppy.' She left Fraser walking out into the night and took the stairs two at a time in her haste to make sure they were safe.

On opening the door, she was relieved to see Poppy was fast asleep. Hamish's bed, however, was empty and his backpack missing along with the few personal possessions he'd brought with him.

All the blood seemed to drain away from her body until she was sure her empty Iona shell might collapse at any second. It was only the fear of Hamish being outside alone in the dark keeping her upright and propelling her downstairs.

She ran out onto the porch to locate Fraser, not taking

time to find her shoes when it was her fault the child was out there somewhere exposed to the elements. 'Hamish is gone and he's taken all his things with him.'

'There's no sign of him out here. I'll grab a torch and head down to the gate. He can't have gone very far.'

'Let me come with you,' she begged, cursing herself for not keeping tabs on him when he'd been so upset. Katherine had told her she'd need eyes in the back of her head to watch the children but she'd seized the quiet to wallow, not realising it had been the calm before the storm.

'Not unless you put on some warm clothes first.'

Iona complied without fuss, fetching her coat and shoes before meeting him again at the door.

'We'll lock the door behind us and if we don't find Hamish soon, you come back here and I'll carry on the search myself.' Fraser handed her a torch and pre-empted her fears about leaving a second child alone.

Hamish would never have entertained the idea of leaving the comfort of the house to venture out into the wilderness if he'd been happy, and she was accountable for his current state of mind regardless of anything Fraser said to the contrary.

'Hamish!'

Every now and then they caught a glimpse of beady eyes watching from the edge of the trees, which turned out to be woodland creatures curious about who else was out here with them. With each crunch of the undergrowth in the distance, every creepy sound of forest wildlife, she drew closer and closer to Fraser's side, sure he'd protect her from any assailant who might come from the shadows. Goodness knew how a small boy was coping out here when a grown woman was letting her imagination scare her half to death.

'What was that?'

'It's an owl.'

'Did you hear that? Anything could be lurking out here.'

'It's the countryside, Iona. You have to expect some noise from the neighbours. We are sharing their habitat after all.' Fraser was right, she'd been brought up in the city with a soundtrack of speeding cars and emergency sirens, not living, breathing creatures. Unless you counted the drunks who had sometimes serenaded her outside her bedroom window. This relative peace took some getting used to.

'What are we going to do when we find him, Fraser?' *If* wasn't an option. They had to find him but they also had to get him to come back with them and to want to stay with them. Otherwise social services would have to get involved and it was disheartening to think Hamish would rather do that than spend another night under the same roof as them.

'Get him into the heat as soon as possible before he ends up with hypothermia, tell him off for scaring us, then have a talk about the position we've all been put in.'

'How come you're so sensible about all this?' Fraser was managing this all so much better than she was and more than she'd given him credit for. Anyone would think he'd had experience in caring for children it came so naturally to him. The total opposite of the father figure and domineering partner she'd assumed he'd make.

'It might be difficult for you to accept but I was a boy once too. One who found himself in a similar situation. Except my parents chose to send me away to live with strangers.' The explanation didn't make it sound any less heartless. Unlike Katherine, his parents had had a choice. It was gut-wrenching to picture any child in that predicament but more so of Fraser as that lost little soul when he was such a source of strength to her now.

Iona had been afraid and unhappy too but she'd had her mother to remind her she was wanted and loved, even if her parents hadn't demonstrated it to each other. It was no wonder he gave off that defensive vibe that made it difficult to get close to him. She counted herself lucky he'd let her see the real Fraser, who was warm and caring and everything his parents apparently hadn't been for him. Instead of launching herself at him and forcing a hug on him, she cleared the ache in her throat and simply said, 'Childhood sucks.'

'But it makes us who we are today. You want to know why I'm such a stickler for the rules and doing everything by the book? It's because I thought, by being the perfect son, my parents might love me more and want me around. I thought I'd been too wild, too unruly for them to have at home. Clinging to the rules, projecting that perfect image in the hope people will like me has become my way of life. I don't know why when it's never worked.' He gave a bitter laugh but there was nothing remotely funny about what he'd shared with her.

Iona knew that kind of loneliness and uncertainly intimately, along with that constant worry about trying to please people who neither deserved nor appreciated it. Yet, since coming here with the children, she'd never had any sense he'd been pretending to be anyone else other than himself. It might be because he'd abandoned his rule book for their sakes.

It was proof of his strength that he'd become such a success yet had retained that compassion that endeared him to his patients, and now her too. A lesser mortal might have rebelled against the idea of school and authority but Fraser had turned it to his advantage and applied it to his career to get him to the position of senior practice partner. Every day revealed new layers to Dr McColl, making it impossible for her to deny her growing affection for him. The longer they were under the same roof, the closer they became physically and emotionally. It was lucky they had two small children to act as a buffer between them. As long as they remained safe, she was sure her heart would too.

'Listen. Do you hear that?' Fraser stopped beside her.

'Don't you start. I thought I was the paranoid one here.'

'Shh. Listen.'

She was about to tear strips off him for shushing her when she heard the faint cry for herself. They stood motionless, holding their breath, hoping to locate the source.

'Help.'

The plaintive cry was so full of pain and exhaustion she cursed the McColl family for not having the foresight to install floodlights out here for such emergencies.

'Hamish? Where are you?' Fraser's voice carried easily through the night, ensuring the boy would hear it no matter which direction he was in.

'At the gate.'

They sprinted the last few yards to reach him, their torch beams picking out a crumpled figure lying on the other side of the metalwork. Iona clamped her hand over her mouth to smother her gasp. 'What on earth happened? How did you end up down there?'

'He's tried to climb over the gate.' Fraser jabbed the security code into the control panel and they waited for an eternity for the gates to open and allow them access to the child.

'Where did you think you were going out here?' Iona knelt down beside him and brushed the dirt from his face, glad to see him again.

'I want to see my mum.' Hamish's face was streaked with tears and mud and Iona had to catch her own sob before it escaped with his.

'Can you stand?' Fraser was focused on the injuries Hamish had sustained during his not-so-great escape. Shock was probably the least he'd be suffering from the height he'd fallen.

Hamish sat up and Fraser attempted to disentangle the backpack from around his shoulders only to prompt an ear-piercing scream.

'My arm hurts so bad.' The unearthly squeals subsided into equally disturbing whimpers. Each agonising sound was like a fist in the gut. Hamish would never have been hurt if Iona had come home as planned.

'He might have broken it.' Fraser tossed her the backpack and scooped the boy up into his arms, careful not to jar the arm he was cradling.

It wasn't a life or death emergency but they took him back to the house with no less urgency, guided by one torch now that Fraser had his hands full.

'The key is in my pocket.' He turned to her in the porch lights and she stuck her hand in to fumble for it, trying not to acknowledge the solid muscled thighs beneath her fingertips.

Once back in the house Fraser laid Hamish gently on the sofa and Iona switched on every light and lamp she could find so they could examine him.

'We're going to have to get your coat off so I can check that arm, Hamish.' Fraser didn't want to hurt him any more than he already had been, but he had to assess the damage to prevent further injury. Hamish was responsive and breathing and Fraser didn't want to think about what could've happened if they hadn't found him out there.

Hamish wasn't his son but after a couple of days of taking care of him Fraser worried just the same. It was impossible not to draw comparisons with his own parents and their apparent lack of compassion for their only child when the severity of Hamish's injuries was taking priority right now.

Iona put her hand to the boy's back to help him upright and between them they managed to remove his outer layer with the minimum of discomfort. Hamish peeled his sleeve back to expose the skin, every whimper reminding him this was more than a scratch. Although Hamish's complexion was grey from the shock, there was no blood and the bone hadn't broken the skin, minimising the risk of infection.

Fraser confirmed that Hamish could move his fingers with no sign of numbness or blue tinge to suggest otherwise. The swelling, bruising and tenderness around the deformed area he was protecting so vehemently did, however, suggest a fracture of some description.

'I think you've broken your arm, Hamish. We need to stabilise it here, support it so there won't be any further damage done until we get you to the emergency department.'

'It hurts.' The fear and pain wasn't just from Hamish's arm—it was clearly also about not having either of his parents here to comfort him when he needed them.

'They'll put a cast on it at the hospital, you know.' Iona leaned over the back of the couch, trying to find a silver lining in this for him.

'They will?' Hamish stopped crying to mull that over.

It occurred to Fraser that those unfortunates who had come to school with broken bones encased in plaster had suddenly become the most popular pupils there. 'Yeah, and everyone will want to sign it.'

Fraser winked at Iona for her quick thinking as it could keep Hamish distracted from his injury for a while and get him to co-operate.

'Will it hurt?' he asked, narrowing his eyes, suspicious they were conspiring against him.

'Not at all. They'll just want to protect your arm. As I do.'

'I think your mum packed some liquid paracetamol for you so that should help with the pain. Fraser, do you have ice in your freezer to bring that swelling down?' Iona, satisfied that Hamish was going to let them help, took the first step to stabilising the injured limb.

'Yes. Top drawer. You'll find towels and tape in the bathroom.' Fraser was going to have to improvise a splint for the journey. There were a lot of household items they could utilise, such as rolled-up newspapers, but towels would provide some padding and relieve some of the discomfort.

'Hang in there, pal, we'll hit the road as soon as we get that arm supported.

'Then I can visit my mum?' Whether this injury had been a deliberate attempt to get Hamish to his mother, or an unfortunate coincidence as he'd tried to run to her, there was no question of his desperation to see her.

'I'll see what I can do.' Fraser couldn't bring himself to be angry about it. If he'd had an inkling his parents would've welcomed the sight of him at any given moment he'd have broken out of boarding school in a heartbeat.

Before Fraser was forced into making any promises that might be beyond his ability to carry out, Iona returned with supplies.

'Would you believe Poppy's still fast asleep?' She shook her head as she deposited the ice, towels, bandages and tape on the coffee table and administered a spoonful of medicine to Hamish for the pain.

'Thank goodness for small mercies.' With the smallest one of them safe and sound, they could concentrate on the one they'd failed. Parenting was hard and they weren't perfect by any means but the important thing was they were doing their best.

With some manoeuvring and cajoling they managed to get Hamish to lay his arm down on the folded towel, covering the distance from his fingertips to slightly past his elbow. Fraser tied the towel around the arm, making sure it was completely wrapped and snug, tied at either end and avoiding any pressure on the injury site.

'Can you wiggle your fingertips for me?' He rechecked circulation, sensation and motion to make sure he hadn't tied it too tight but the arm remained immobilised.

When Fraser was satisfied Hamish was as comfortable as could be expected, Iona fashioned a sling from the bandage to cradle his arm, fastening it around his neck to make it secure.

'That's not too tight, is it?' she queried before backing off.

'Thanks.' Fraser could've handled this on his own but it was reassuring to have her here, backing him up. They were a team, and for the first time in forever he no longer felt alone. This was how he imagined a family would be, all pulling together to make life more than bearable for one another. He wasn't looking forward to the time when Iona and the kids moved out and he was back to rattling around the house on his own with no one to think about but himself. It did much more for the soul to be around people, helping when and where he could.

Iona draped Hamish's coat around his shoulders, presumably to stave off some of the cold facing them on the other side of the front door.

'If you're happy to stay here with Poppy, I'll drive Hamish myself.' It wasn't that he wanted to leave her but it was more practical than waking the little girl to make the long journey Iona had already done once today.

'Sure. Let me know that you've got there safely.' That made him smile. He wasn't used to having someone worry about him and to know he'd impacted on her in some small way meant the world to him.

'I will.'

It wasn't easy getting Hamish into the back of the car but eventually they got the seat belt around him so it wasn't jarring his forearm. He had more colour in his cheeks now and he'd stopped whimpering. In fact, he was having trouble staying awake, so the car ride could put him over into sleep soon.

'I'm sure you're exhausted after the day you've had. Get yourself to bed and we'll let ourselves back in. Whatever time that might be.'

With the car door closed on Hamish to keep the wind off him, they were left facing each other in the driveway.

'I'm sure yours has been equally as eventful. Thanks for taking him. Just make sure you take care.'

'I will,' he assured her. He had a lot to come back for.

Iona threw her arms around him for a hug and kissed him on the lips as though she was afraid she'd never see him again.

Fraser embraced the contact, catching her around the waist and finally admitting to himself that he was fast falling for her. He lost himself in the kiss, fuelled with the desire which had been rising in him for days.

Her warm mouth on his, her tongue seeking his, turned the goodbye peck into passionate foreplay. There was nothing he wanted more than to sweep her up in his arms and carry her off to his bedroom and close the door on the rest of the world but it would have to wait. They had responsibilities and he wasn't the sort of man who'd put his wants before the needs of a child.

With great reluctance Fraser pulled back while he could still think straight, rested his forehead against hers and waited for the white noise in his head to subside.

'I'll see you when I get back.' His voice was thick with emotions he'd long thought dormant.

They extricated their limbs from each other until they were only holding on by their fingertips and they finally had to let go or he'd never get in the car.

Kissing Iona went against all the restrictions he'd imposed in order to protect his heart. Yet it was one of the best moves he'd ever made.

He set off for the distant city lights with a spark of hope in his soul that he might not be alone for the rest of his days after all. Unlike the little boy so often shunned by his parents and the adult orphan forced to return to the ancestral home alone, Fraser was finally excited about coming back. That was down to Iona being there and for once he didn't want to have his future all laid out for him. It excited him more to wait and see what could happen.

Iona stumbled back to the house in a daze and gave one last wave at Fraser driving away before going back inside. She touched her fingers to her softly swollen lips, which were throbbing from Fraser's tender kiss. For days they'd been fighting that recurring desire for each other but there was no denying it was there and she had no will to fight it any more either.

On a day when everything had gone wrong, Fraser had ended it on a high for her. Who knew where that kiss would lead to? But she wanted more. Now she was convinced he wasn't the prison jailer she'd assumed him to be there was no reason to keep her feelings for him on ice.

Deep down she'd known he was nothing like Andy even before he'd shared the painful truth behind his need for order in his life. It was his security blanket, as her solitude was hers. These past days, however, had shown her it was no longer enough to simply exist in her safe bubble and to really embrace her new life she had to let someone step inside it with her. She could honestly say so far that living with Fraser had only been positive and those long-held fears about allowing a man to get close to her again were beginning to ebb.

Fraser knew she wasn't a woman who could be pushed around and he seemed to respect that, making her fears about repeating past mistakes redundant. The timing was awkward but a relationship shouldn't affect the children if they kept it quiet. They were going to have enough on their plates anyway with the aftermath of Hamish's exploits.

Not only were there physical restrictions on him now but they were going to have to explain the accident to his mother.

She groaned. It would be a miracle if Katherine agreed to let her continue as his interim guardian after this.

Once she'd peeked in on their younger, less troublesome charge again, Iona stripped the pillows and cover off her bed and brought them downstairs.

With the lounge curtains slightly parted she'd be able to see the others coming back from her makeshift bed on the sofa. Fraser's ancestors wouldn't have approved but the man himself would only want her to be happy and that seemed to overrule his sense of decorum these days. A quality she simply couldn't find fault with, regardless of how hard she'd tried to.

CHAPTER NINE

IT WAS THE early hours of the morning before the travellers returned. Outside it was dark and gloomy, the kind of winter morning when you didn't want to get out of bed, even if it was only a blanket on a sofa. Iona wouldn't have been surprised if Fraser had decided not to drive back until the sun came up but now that she could stop fretting about him falling asleep at the wheel, her tension headache was easing off.

Iona had managed a couple of hours' sleep but she couldn't say they'd been particularly restful, on alert for Poppy upstairs and the sound of the car coming back outside. Not to mention the adrenaline pumping around her body in anticipation of embarking on a new phase of her life with Fraser. Bit by bit he was helping her see relationships didn't have to be toxic. She could have someone by her side, enriching her life with support instead of trying to snuff out her spirit. Perhaps in time she'd get to do the same for him and show him he deserved to be loved for exactly who he was.

Fraser stepped out of the car looking as spritely and alert as if he'd had a full eight hours' sleep and opened the rear car door to emerge with a sleeping Hamish in his arms. Iona smoothed down the crumpled clothes she'd slept in and tried to tame the nest of snakes she called her hair before she ran to the door.

'Is he okay?' she whispered, spying the cast covering most of his forearm.

'He'll be fine.' Despite the possibility he must be running on empty, Fraser summoned the energy to flash her a reassuring smile. Iona couldn't believe she'd ever believed this man to be selfish when he'd shown her a hundred different ways how wrong she'd been, setting his own comfort aside to give them all whatever they needed at any given time. Other than her mother, she'd never known anyone else to do that for her and it comforted her knowing she wouldn't be on her own with whatever the next crisis was.

Out of the blue it occurred to her he'd make a great father one day and made her wonder why he wasn't one already. He had a successful career, a title and an estate, he was drop-dead gorgeous and a natural with children. Unless he had some horrible, dark secret locked away in the cellar, she couldn't understand why his ex hadn't snatched him up, having fallen madly in love with him. A few days in his company and Iona knew she was well on the way there herself.

Perhaps it was his childhood experiences preventing him from settling down. She could empathise when her knowledge of parenting had come from two people who should never have stayed together. Both she and Fraser had to figure out who they were in their own right, away from the influences of the past.

She watched him carry Hamish to bed, her blood pumping so fast in her veins as she acknowledged those strong feelings there was every chance she might pass out. The man was carrying a sleeping child to bed after driving for hours so she could get some rest. Andy had never shown her such consideration from the day they'd married. The problem was she and Fraser had gone past the point where a quick fling would satisfy, too involved in each other's lives now for anything casual. If they acted on that kiss, picked up from where they'd left off, she had no doubt it would be the start of something so serious and meaningful it made the hairs stand up on the back of her neck. Yet she was intrigued by the possibility of something new and exciting to spice up her life.

To take her mind off the shock at the new direction things had suddenly taken, and wanting to thank Fraser, Iona set about making some breakfast in the kitchen. She lifted out some eggs and bacon and proceeded to cook them while waiting for the toast to pop and the kettle to boil. This house had been designed and built to be an intimidating status symbol, yet Fraser had made her feel part of it and she was no longer afraid of breaking something or forgetting proper protocol. There'd been a marked change in Fraser's behaviour since they'd moved in and it showed how hard he was working to overcome his hang-ups rather than force them all to conform. Something she appreciated to a level he couldn't possibly understand.

'Something smells good.'

Iona's stomach flipped along with the bacon and eggs at the sound of Fraser's voice and she wondered how they were going to be able to work together again when she went gooey inside every time he spoke.

Viewing the scene through the eyes of a third party, it could be construed as the very picture of domesticity, sharing a quiet breakfast together after a rough night with the kids, and she couldn't find a thing wrong with it.

'I'm starving. All I had was a curled-up sandwich from the vending machine and the dregs left in the coffee machine. It's so nice to come home to a cooked meal and good company.'

The compliment was likely born primarily from his

hunger but Iona knew herself it was much preferable to returning to an empty flat and a microwaveable meal for one.

'So, no complications with Hamish's arm?' Normally she'd refrain from bringing up medical matters at the table but he was a doctor and wouldn't be as squeamish as the average person.

'A small fracture. It should heal in no time.'

'That's good news, I suppose. We'll still have to tell Katherine about it, though.' It wouldn't say much for their ability to take care of her children if Hamish had broken his arm already and Iona wouldn't blame her if she decided to discharge herself to do the job properly herself.

'It's all sorted,' Fraser said once he'd swallowed his huge bite of toast. 'I managed to sneak Hamish in to see her while we were there.'

'How on earth did you manage that? On second thoughts, maybe I don't want to know.' It wouldn't take much for a handsome doctor to sweet talk his way in anywhere and she didn't want to hear the details of him charming some other woman who wasn't her.

'Katherine was awake, she's still not sleeping, so I explained what had happened. She understood, had a chat with Hamish and he's promised to behave. He's much happier now he's seen his mum.'

'I'm glad. I trust you told her how sorry we are?' The development lessened the burden of guilt lying heavily upon her.

'I did and it only succeeded in making her cry and thanking us again for taking them on.' Fraser shrugged then proceeded to clear his plate and drain his cup.

'I suppose you'll want to get some sleep?' After last night they were all entitled to a lie-in. Everything else could wait until they had clear heads again to think about where they were headed next.

'I managed a nap when Hamish was getting X-rayed

but I'm probably better staying up now or I'll end up with night-lag. Actually, I was thinking about Christmas here.'

'Oh?' In all of yesterday's drama Iona had forgotten about the very event she'd been building up to and which she'd done a very poor job of preparing for so far. Unforgiveable for someone who'd promised not only herself but two young children she'd make the Yuletide special.

'I think we need a make-over. Especially with Hamish. Perhaps if we give them Christmas we could all learn to forgive and forget the mistakes of the past twenty-four hours.'

'What do you suggest?' He'd obviously been concocting some sort of plan to bring it up now.

'Well…' He shifted in his seat, appearing restless to get on with it as soon as possible. 'Christmas here was never the jolly family fun time most people associate with the season. Even when my parents did deign to bring me home for it, we merely went through the motions. I always knew their heart wasn't in it but that doesn't mean we didn't decorate accordingly. The house made a picture-perfect Christmas-card scene if it didn't go beyond the superficial exterior.' His description of his strained family time tugged at her heartstrings for the young Fraser who'd been denied a childhood.

The way he'd looked after her and the children made it clear he was someone who had so much love to give and deserved buckets of it in return. To feel unwanted, unloved and confused by what was going on in the adult world around him must have been frightening for him. Each time he did something to make them feel safe here, Iona knew it was because he wished someone had been around to do the same for him at that age. For all the money and land he'd been surrounded by, his life sounded as lonely and messed up as hers had been and the emotional damage done in those formative years wasn't easy to shake off even as an adult. They had more in common than anyone would've guessed from their vastly different backgrounds.

'In that case, what are we waiting for?' Iona was wide awake again and ready to get started now he'd put the thought in her head that they might actually be having their first proper Christmas. Together.

After all he'd been through, Fraser was offering so much by opening his home to them and Iona wanted to show him the best of the season along with the children. It would have been easier for him to lock himself away here on his own for the holidays, the way she'd planned to. Or, worse, taken out his pain and dislike of Christmas on those around him. He was better than that, stronger, and if he was prepared to stand up and reclaim his life back from fear, it gave her the impetus to do the same.

Opening the door to the attic made Fraser's heart pound just as much now as it had when he'd been a bairn. That creak giving away his location to anyone who happened to be searching for him, that blast of cold air bringing goose-bumps to his skin and the dust filling his nostrils as he disturbed the family mausoleum of memories.

The only time he'd been up here as an adult had been shortly after his father had passed away to store boxes of his personal papers and belongings until he decided what to do with them. He'd been alone then, Caroline playing no part in his actions then, when Iona was the very reason he was up here now.

'Watch your step. There isn't much light up here, I'm afraid. We didn't spend much time in this part of the house.' Fraser took Iona's hand in his and guided her steps with the aid of the single light bulb hanging in the middle of the vast space. A scary place for a child with a vivid imagination. Scarier still for a grown man who hadn't fully dealt with his father's death and the unanswered questions he'd left behind.

Once she was on a firm footing he had to let go of her hand even though he liked the feel of it there, soft and warm and comforting that he wasn't here alone.

'Where should we start?' With her sleeves rolled up, Iona was gung-ho about tracking down these vintage decorations he'd told her were here. Hands on hips, ready to excavate, she could've been standing at the entrance of a pharaoh's tomb, ready to create history, she exuded such excitement. It was refreshing to see her embrace that inner child when he'd gagged and bound his long ago.

The contrast of her exuberance in the midst of this stuffy environment helped Fraser see it was possible for the two to exist together here. If anything, her sense of freedom brightened the whole house and Fraser wondered if by stifling his childish enthusiasm back then he hadn't done his family a disservice. Perhaps if he'd been allowed, by his parents and himself, to explore the boundaries more he could have brought light into the place to combat the sombre spectre of his mother's illness.

He kicked out at one of the boxes but there was nothing could be done now to salvage his relationship with his parents. All he could do was focus on those people who were important in his life now.

'What about here?' He headed to the far side of the room where neatly stacked boxes were labelled for convenience. An act he doubted either of his parents had undertaken. His father would've deemed such manual work demeaning to a man of his standing, and his mother had never ventured far from her bed for much of his childhood. Yet he recognised her handwriting on the containers, tracing his fingers over her elegant letters and wondering when she'd handed over responsibility to the staff instead of sharing it with her only child.

'Let's see what we've got,' Fraser said, dismantling the tower to place the boxes side by side on the patchwork carpet underfoot, comprised of offcuts and old rugs his father had refused to throw out.

'May I?' Iona sat cross-legged in the midst of the display, itching to unwrap whatever treasures she imagined they'd find.

'Go for it.' Fraser didn't have any sentimentality for any of this stuff and if he needed the space he wouldn't think twice about getting rid of everything. If they could fulfil one promise to the children, though, and create the sort of wonderland Iona had envisaged all along, he was willing to finally sort through it. With the children fast asleep in their beds they had plenty of time to do it.

It had been on his mind the whole way to the hospital and back to do something that would lift everyone's spirits. After all, they'd all been orphaned in one way or another for the holidays. As the adults, it was down to him and Iona to make the place feel like less of a foster home when none of them had planned to be here.

Of course, that hadn't been the only thing on his mind. Kissing Iona had ensured he stayed awake and alert for the entire journey. He didn't know why he'd done it any more than why he'd brought her up here with him.

Only that it felt right. There'd been no faking the concern she'd shown for Hamish when he'd gone missing, or her willingness to co-operate with him when it had been desperately needed. No more reason to keep hiding from his growing feelings for her.

'These are beautiful.' Iona reverently unwrapped a box of vintage baubles, each decorated with snowy scenes on their fragile glass shells.

'We should have a tree somewhere to hang them on.' Behind another stack of boxes he eventually found the artificial Christmas tree that, at some point, had replaced the real pine they'd once picked out together.

Flashing images of those times flickered at the back of his mind when they'd been happy, together as a family, which he'd long forgotten. He couldn't figure out if it was better or worse to discover the atmosphere around the season hadn't always been as strained as he remembered in those early days before it had turned into such a chore for all of them.

'Your handiwork, I presume?' Iona dangled a pipe-cleaner reindeer complete with googly eyes and a tiny red pom-pom nose from her finger, delighted with her find.

Fraser took the handmade decoration and stretched out beside her, fighting back the emotion suddenly trying to burn a hole in his chest. 'I remember making this with Mum.'

He pulled up his legs and laid the reindeer on his knees to see it better.

'You did have some good times with her, then?'

'When I was very small—I hardly remember—I think we used to have craft days. We made silly animals and space rockets out of whatever she had in this big wooden art chest. It was full of cards and stickers and glitter, and all sorts.' The memories came flooding back, almost drowning him with images of them playing together, actually going out as a family, his mother and father either side of him, swinging him by both arms and laughter ringing out all around.

'That's lovely, Fraser. She sounds as though she really loved you.'

'At one time. Then she got sick and no one seemed to want me around any more. After she died, well, Dad was old-fashioned and he didn't know how to raise a child on his own, he'd left all of that to Mum. I suppose it was eas-ier to let the masters at boarding school do his job for him but we were never close again. He paid my school fees and put me through medical school but we were more acquaintances than father and son.' Tears were burning the backs of his eyeballs for that boy once surrounded by love who had somehow ended up abandoned miles from home and for the relationships he'd lost with his parents.

He spotted a rare family photograph lying at the bottom of the box and lifted it out. It had been taken at Christmas, these same decorations hanging downstairs in the background. He couldn't have been any older than Poppy—it was before he'd been sent away from home. They were all smiling, opening presents under the tree like any other normal family. Fraser's insides flipped over at the sight. There were probably no other happy snaps of them together after that and with both parents now gone there wouldn't be another.

Fraser could feel the warmth of the tears falling down his face but he didn't wipe them away, finally letting the emotions of the past run free. It was Iona who softly brushed away the evidence of his pain, stroking his face and giving him the comfort he desperately needed.

'Is it possible they might have sent you away because they thought they were protecting you in some way from your mother's illness? Neither of us can know for sure what their reasons were but when I look at that photograph and hear how much your mother loved spending time with you it does make me wonder if they thought it was best for you. We both know the toll cancer takes on a family and they might not have wanted you to watch her decline.' Iona clasped both of his hands in hers, trying to make him look back on the time from an adult standpoint instead of as that confused little boy.

He'd blocked out those happier times because he'd had tunnel vision about being to blame for being sent away. Deep down he must have known they'd loved him at one time but he'd spent more of his life with stern strangers so those memories had gradually faded. The only vivid recollections he'd had were the traumatic ones because they'd had such an emotional impact on him. Perhaps he'd perceived the separation from his parents as neglect because he'd been angry at them for leaving him.

It wasn't surprising he'd become an afterthought to his parents with the surgeries and treatments that had gone hand in hand with the breast cancer and the later, secondary cancers that had spread throughout his mother's body.

This new theory that they'd tried to protect him, not cause him pain, didn't lighten his heart, only made him sad for the time with his parents stolen from him. These days they would have had counselling, talked through their feelings and had other help to pull them through the sickness and bereavement. Instead, illness had devastated the whole family piece by piece, the same way cancer had taken his mother. It was such a waste.

'I suppose it's possible but it can't change what happened or how I felt.'

'Can't you find it in your heart to forgive them?' Iona rested her forehead against his, their hands still clutched together between their chests.

'I can try.' Fraser didn't want to hold on to a grudge or remain trapped in this guilt any longer. It would be time and energy better spent focused on the future.

'It might help you find some closure. I know it sounds hypocritical when I've come out here to escape the people who were supposed to love me most in the world. I lost my mother too but my father's still alive. I can't say he ever showed me any such affection. If he had I might think more kindly towards him and might not have let myself get swept up into an abusive relationship myself.'

Fraser knew how much her experiences must have impacted on her given that he was still in recovery from his last break-up. But Iona had been married, physically hurt by the man she'd intended to spend her whole life with, and that wasn't something easily forgotten.

'You're the strongest woman I've ever met.' While he'd remained locked in the house with his resentment and anger, Iona had moved on and somehow managed to leave the issues of her early life behind to focus on her future. Not only that, she'd devoted herself to helping others and proving she was better than the man who'd claimed to be her father.

'I've had to be. I don't have anyone else.' She turned away from him and busied herself with putting the decorations back in the box, including his prized reindeer, but she didn't fool him. That tough façade was protecting a fragile heart identical to his.

'Hey.' He caught her chin between his thumb and finger and turned her head so he could drop a soft kiss on her lips to let her know he wasn't going anywhere. 'You've got me.'

'Have I, Fraser? I don't want to get into something I'm going to regret. Do you promise you're going to be here for me?' The question was so full of residual pain he knew she couldn't bear to have it inflicted on her again.

Right here, talking about and raking through the remnants of his past with her, the wind rattling the old bones of this house, it was the only place he wanted to be. She'd messed up yesterday but she'd owned it, wanted to make amends, and that was more than anyone who'd wronged him in the past had ever done. Being with Iona, he didn't have to think about the next step, free to do whatever came naturally without fear of being judged.

He was beginning to see what Caroline had meant when she'd accused him of not being true to her, or himself, when he'd been unwittingly projecting an image of the man he imagined he *should* be, instead of the one he was around Iona. He needed to embrace every part of who he was to fully enjoy life, including that inner child who'd been stifled for too long. He had nothing to lose and everything to gain.

'Always,' he promised, and kissed her again. It was the sweet reward he'd been waiting for since last night, the thought of which had got him to the hospital and back without incident, knowing she'd be at home, waiting for him.

He felt her soften at his touch then she kissed him back with such urgency and desire he didn't want to think about anyone other than the woman back in his arms where she belonged.

He shifted her onto his lap, never breaking the seal between their mouths because he couldn't get enough of her. She unbuttoned her blouse and Fraser helped tug it over her head to reveal her full breasts cupped in wisps of black lace. Every part of his body tightened to attention, begging to be freed with her.

He pulled off his sweater and Iona stood up to remove the rest of her clothes, leaving her breathtakingly naked before him. He barely had a chance to drink in the beautiful sight or unzip his trousers before she straddled him again and lowered herself onto his straining erection.

The immediacy of the act jolted him, body and soul, every nerve ending ready to explode with satisfaction. The intimacy wasn't purely physical as they stared into each other's eyes, rocking together in search of that place of utter peace. They needed each other, needed to find a release for all of those pent-up emotions and replace the pain with something much more enjoyable.

Iona bore down on his shoulders, riding him with relentless urgency, her breasts bouncing as Fraser thrust ever upwards to meet her. He caught her tight, pink nipple in his mouth, sucking hard enough to make her gasp and contract her inner muscles around his shaft. The sensation urged him on to tease the other pinched bud but she arched her back, increased the pace of her hip grinding and drove him to the brink of insanity much too quickly.

With one swift movement he flipped over so she was on her back and he was deep inside her, his movements no longer restricted between her thighs. Unencumbered, he drove deeper and harder inside her, Iona lifting her hips to accommodate every inch of him. Bodies slamming together, Iona's nails clawing his back, each of them making those animalistic noises that only came with raw passion, Fraser knew they were out of control. Neither of them held back about what it was they wanted, or demanded, from each other.

He prided himself on being a considerate lover, aiming to please his partner as much as himself. Yet, with Iona, he was acting on pure, carnal instinct. As she was. At the end of this no one would be left wanting.

Iona knew exactly what she wanted, him, and he was more than happy to oblige. Their chemistry hadn't been a figment of his imagination when they were living out the hot, frenzied truth of it together.

As the wind picked up outside, so too did the ferocity of their coupling. Iona's moans grew more frequent and higher pitched, her muscles tightening to let him know she was almost at breaking point. With every bit of strength he had in him, Fraser drove into her again and again and pushed her over the edge, tumbling with her into that all-enveloping ecstasy of release.

He'd never lost himself so utterly with a woman before and he knew this was more than great sex or physical attraction. It was love for who she was, how she made him feel, and who he was when he was with her. The sort of connection a man was lucky to find once in a lifetime and would be a fool to ever let go.

* * *

Iona curled her naked body around Fraser's, certain that was all the activity she was capable of for the foreseeable future. He'd reached parts of her she hadn't known still existed, the most significant of which had been her heart. Sure, this was, and would probably remain for a long time, the most erotic and passionate encounter of her life but she wanted this to be the start of something between them, not simply the culmination of all the drama and emotion they'd been dealing with.

Fraser had shared a lot with her, including those poignant memories of his parents. Then there was all the passion she'd somehow unlocked from within him. She shivered, the feel of him so new, so recent and so very pleasurable.

'Are you cold?' He mistook her goosebumps for something entirely different and wrapped his arms and legs around her to share his body heat. She wasn't about to complain. This was the most content she'd been in an age and if it wasn't for their sleeping babes downstairs she'd happily stay locked in here for the rest of the day.

Every now and then Fraser kissed the top of her head, reassuring her he was there, all the while she was wondering if he'd become distant, lost in his thoughts. She was confident that he wasn't regretting the tryst but if there was something else bothering him she wanted to put his mind at rest.

'I...er... I'm on the Pill. Thought you should know.' In her line of work she'd seen plenty of women caught out by the same rush of lust causing them to lose common sense and gain a surprise bundle nine months later not to take precautions herself. Although she'd never been so carried away before that the idea of contraception had never entered her head. Fraser wasn't the sort to overlook something as important as protection either but apparently the buttoned-up Dr McColl was just as hot-blooded as the next male. More so, judging by her limited experience.

'Oh. Right. Good. Sorry. I should've taken care of that.' His embarrassment at being ill prepared was as obvious as the fact that wasn't the subject monopolising his thoughts.

'Is there something wrong? You seem so far away.' She rolled onto his chest so she could look into his face and see for herself if he was having second thoughts about getting involved. It wasn't in her nature, or her plans, to be the needy, clingy girlfriend. She simply preferred to know where she stood. There was nothing to be gained for either of them by embarking on another sham of a relationship.

'I'm right here.' He deliberately misinterpreted her comment and tried to distract her with another one of his swoonworthy kisses, which, although gratifying all the way down to her toes, didn't answer her question.

She let him distract her a while longer, until she was in danger of not caring about what had snagged his attention as much as the new yearning he was awakening inside her.

In between smooches and desperately pretending she hadn't noticed the hand tangled in her hair and the one caressing her breast, she asked the question again.

'Where did you go, Fraser?' *Without me*, she wanted to add.

She lifted her head off his chest as he drew in a ragged breath.

'I was just thinking…the kids will be up soon.' He wasn't telling her the whole truth but he was back in the present with her and thinking about the future. Even if it was only the immediate one.

'I know but I don't want to move.' She drew her fingernail around his nipple, teasing the sensitive skin and watching it pucker with arousal.

'Neither do I but we, uh, came up here for a reason.' He grabbed her hand and gave her a half-hearted scolding, his ever-darkening eyes and swiftly recovering libido telling her what he'd much rather be doing. Unfortunately, he was all about doing the right thing, not always necessarily the most fun thing, but on this occasion she had to concede he was right. They'd had their quality time together, which, if all went well, they'd get to repeat somewhere more comfortable and at a more convenient time. That didn't give her any more motivation to move.

'Spoilsport. Don't you have house elves who come in and do all the work while you're asleep?'

'We call them staff, sweetheart, and, as you know, I don't employ any here. It doesn't sit well with my conscience.'

'Damn you and your principles. With one ring of a bell we could've summoned someone to bring us a bed up here and sent a nanny downstairs to see to the children.' She burrowed further into Fraser's side.

His chuckling eventually ended with an abrupt 'Up!', and her clothes landing item by item on top of her naked body. There was something sexy about when he was being bossy, especially when he was naked and she'd had experience of what it was like letting him be on top.

For once she did as he asked.

CHAPTER TEN

IONA HAD A renewed burst of energy once they'd transported their festive finds down to the living room. Running on pure adrenaline since she'd had next to no sleep, she set to work creating a sophisticated winter wonderland as much for Fraser as the children.

He might not have been invested in the aesthetic design but she set him to work where his height was an advantage.

'Hang that garland from the ceiling...

'Drape that bunting around the lintel...

'Find somewhere to put the mistletoe...'

That last instruction drew a lascivious grin from her co-worker as he held the plastic spray somewhere that would make a Christmas angel blush. 'I think custom dictates you're supposed to kiss me under this.'

He'd grown bolder now they'd shared intimate knowledge of one another but she knew he was joking. For now. The next time they had the place to themselves she'd call his bluff and kiss him everywhere south of his impressive sprig.

'You wish.' She tossed some tinsel at him and set his mind back to the task rather than the contents of his trousers. Although that was easier said than done for her too.

'Wow! Did you do all this while we were sleeping?' An

animated Hamish walking in on them soon extinguished all explicit thoughts circulating in the atmosphere.

'Iona did most of it. What do you think?' Fraser credited her with the display when it had been his idea to work through the morning in an attempt to get her back into their good books.

'It's cool. Thanks.' Hamish was back to being the good-natured boy they'd first met, thanks to Fraser's uncharacteristic bending of the rules at the hospital. She trusted he was beginning to see the benefits of acting on instinct and not always following the rules. Making love on his attic floor wouldn't have been scheduled into his daily planner and it was all the more memorable for it.

'It's so pretty.' Poppy came to stand beside her at the tree, marvelling at the delicate baubles and tartan bows.

'Do you want to put the fairy on the top of the tree?' Iona handed over her favourite task to the bleary-eyed child in her pink pyjamas, imagining her mother doing the same thing with her every year.

The McColl fairy was altogether different from the Munro one, which was a chubby-cheeked, soft-bodied angel. She wore scarlet felt trimmed with gold and berries instead of white netting and Poppy was enchanted with her as she placed her carefully on the tree.

'Look! It's snowing.' They all followed Poppy's gaze out of the window to see snowflakes falling like confetti outside. It was the perfect backdrop to their Christmas scene but the snow was always more welcomed by children than the adults. Especially out here where there were no road gritters to clear a path for people who had to get to work in a hurry. Thank goodness they had no plans today beyond keeping the children entertained.

'Can we go out and play?' Hamish had his nose pressed up against the glass with longing.

'After breakfast. What would you like?' Fraser took a

turn at being the grown-up and temporarily put the fun and games on hold.

Poppy tugged on his jumper. 'Can we have pancakes?' she asked, as tentatively as though she'd asked for diamond-encrusted cereal. Her plea caught Hamish's attention back from the snow to stand beside his sister.

'They won't be the same, Pops.' The scowl on his face aged him beyond his young years and the scolding soon made Poppy's head drop too.

'I can make pancakes. It's no problem.' Fraser was quick to put any fears to rest and Poppy beckoned him down so she could whisper in his ear. He nodded, took her hand and led her to the kitchen.

'Dad made them shaped like Christmas trees for us.' Hamish's chin wobbled as he explained the significance to Iona.

She put an arm around him and followed the other two. 'Then I'm guessing you'll have to show Fraser exactly how to make them.'

Breakfast was a raucous and messy affair as they all got involved in trying to re-create the perfect tree pancake. This apparently included decorating with a combination of maple syrup and chocolate chips. It wasn't the healthiest start to the day but the sound of their laughter was glorious to hear after last night's unpleasantness.

The sugar rush soon had them bouncing in anticipation of a day playing in the snow and by the time they were bundled up in appropriate layers, Fraser and Iona included, the snow had formed a thick white blanket as far as the eye could see.

They were heading outside when Poppy spotted the mistletoe Fraser had stuck above the door at the last minute.

'You have to kiss Iona!' She clapped her mittened hands together while a disinterested Hamish—with his cast wrapped in a plastic bag so it didn't get wet—went on to make the first footprints in the snow.

To the squealing delight of their little matchmaker, Fraser planted a kiss on Iona's lips and, satisfied he'd fulfilled his obligation, Poppy ran out to join her brother.

Iona tried to follow her out the door, only to be pulled back under the mistletoe.

'Where do you think you're going?'

'Out-outside,' she stuttered, seeing that glint in Fraser's eye that took her right back to what they'd been doing, rolling about on the attic floor.

'Not until I get a proper kiss.'

With the two mischief-makers busy piling snow into the beginnings of a snowman Iona saw no reason to deny herself. Fraser kissed her long and hard and passionately enough that her knees wobbled when she did finally make it outside.

The four of them worked together, rolling and patting mounds of snow into a head and body shape.

'He needs eyes.' Hamish pulled off his glove and used his finger to dig two eyeholes into the blank face.

'Put that back on before you get frostbite and lose the use of that hand too.' Iona wasn't willing to take any more chances when there'd be no clear roads back to the hospital now.

'Can we use these for his mouth and nose?' Poppy opened her hand to display a selection of small shells and stones.

'Where on earth did you find these?' The nearest beach was miles away and they certainly hadn't had the weather recently for a leisurely stroll around the coast.

'They're her lucky finds. She used to collect them when we went beachcombing with Dad and she carries them everywhere.' It was clear Hamish didn't want Poppy to part with them and Iona wouldn't want to deprive her of her link to such precious memories either.

'We could use those, or you could put them back in your pocket and we'll find something else from around here.' She left the decision to Poppy, who stared at the handful of mementoes before stuffing them back into the pocket of her duffel coat, much to Iona's relief.

'Poppy and I are going on a nature hunt, we'll be back soon,' she called to the boys as they headed off to excavate body parts for their new creation. They weren't paying attention, too engrossed in dressing Mr Frosty, as Hamish had named him. Fraser took off his woollen hat and perched it on Frosty's head.

'He needs a scarf too.' Scotland's latest fashion expert stared pointedly at Fraser's neck covering, which he untangled with a sigh. If Iona and Poppy weren't quick he'd be stripped bare and in danger of hypothermia. Only half of that thought was appealing so she grabbed the first things she found and, along with Poppy's new finds, they trudged back.

'There. Excellent job, everyone.' With his twig arms and pine-cone features, Frosty was finally complete, providing a much-needed bonding session for her and the children.

'High five!' It was Fraser who led the call for self-congratulations with the others. When he got to Iona, it wasn't a high-five she got but a face full of snow.

'I. Am. Going. To. Kill. You!' she spluttered through the icy face mask.

Fraser was bent double, laughing with his co-conspirators. Not to be outdone, Iona scooped up a handful of loose snow and stuffed it down the back of his trousers. The snow-in-the-pants dance was the best form of revenge she could have wished for as she watched Fraser trying to get it out without mooning at his impressionable young audience.

Taking their cue from the adults, Hamish and Poppy took off screaming and throwing snowballs at each other.

'I suppose you think you're funny?' Fraser advanced on her, eyes narrowed and lips pressed tightly together.

'Hilarious.' Iona folded her arms, determined to stand her ground, but the second she clocked him scooping up more ammunition she took off, shrieking.

He reached her in seconds to launch another icy attack, this time down the back of her neck. She screamed with shock and the weight of Fraser bundling her down onto the ground. They landed together, panting and laughing and so carefree she didn't care about the cold soaking through her clothes.

Her heart fluttered with the possibilities that lay ahead with this man who understood her need for space and provided a little order in the midst of her chaos.

The sound of a vehicle crunching through the snow interrupted this new discovery and had them scrambling back onto their feet.

'I'll go and see who it is.' The weight and the heat lifted from her chest as Fraser jogged off to open the gates. Their future was on hold so they could deal with whatever new guests had arrived. With the bad weather closing in, there was no way this was a casual visit but Iona had the uncharitable thought she wanted them gone already so they could continue with their Christmas fantasy.

'Hamish! Poppy!' she called to get them back inside the house to get warmed up again while Fraser established what was going on out here.

They were wrapped up in front of the fire in the lounge when he returned with the visitors.

'Mum!' The children flung themselves at Katherine as she walked in, accompanied by an older man and woman.

'Easy.' Fraser stepped in before they knocked her off her feet.

'They didn't tell us you were getting out this morning or we would've had the children ready for you.' Iona was as gobsmacked as the children to see her since they hadn't said anything other than she was improving on her last check. Whilst she was happy for their sakes that they were reunited, she did feel as though she'd been caught out rolling around in the snow with Fraser when they'd arrived.

'My blood pressure's down and Mum and Dad managed to get a flight in this morning. They agreed to let me out as long as I rest, but I wanted to surprise these two.' The colour was back in the young mum's cheeks at having her children back again and Iona wouldn't have denied her a second with them.

'I think you did that all right but you should be taking it easy. Have a seat. Can we get you something to eat or drink?' At least Fraser remembered his manners, playing the host and introducing himself to her parents. Iona was glad the children were going to have their Christmas after all but she had a horrible premonition hers had come to an end.

'I really just want to get home. I'm sure you understand, Iona.'

She did but it didn't make it any easier for her to say goodbye. 'Of course. I'll go and get their things.'

It was silly to get upset when this was the best present the family could have received but it didn't stop the tears falling as she folded their clothes and packed their bags to leave. It marked the end of their pretend family and she didn't know what that meant for her and Fraser.

Iona composed herself when the time came to see them off. It wouldn't have been fair to spoil their moment when they were so happy to be going home together.

'Thank you for everything.' Katherine insisted on hugging her and Fraser as tightly as her huge pregnant belly would allow and Hamish and Poppy followed suit. Iona managed to keep her quivering smile in place until they finally drove away.

'You'll see them again.' Fraser slipped an arm around her waist and held her close.

'I know. It's just…' If she was honest she didn't know why their departure was hitting her so hard other than the absurd notion that he mightn't want her now they weren't part of the package. As if having a ready-made family to fill his house was the only reason he'd fallen for her.

'You got used to having them around? Me too.' Given the noise and disruption two small children managed to make, his admission would've been surprising once upon a time but not any more. Not since she'd seen the tolerant, nurturing side of him that she'd fallen for.

He closed the door on the outside world so there was only the two of them left to fill the home.

'This is our time now and as the lady of the house I wonder if you might care to join me in the master bedroom?'

Her heart wasn't the only part of her flourishing back to life with the promise he was making her. Time alone with him wasn't a luxury she had yet explored to its fullest potential.

'I'm not really looking my best after rolling around in the snow. Perhaps the Laird would prefer to wait for me to freshen up before he ravishes me?' A girl wanted to look her best for such auspicious occasions. Even those where her clothes wouldn't be required for too long.

'The Laird would not. He does, however, think it would be more fun to freshen up together.' He wiggled his eyebrows in a comically suggestive manner, totally unsuitable for a laird or a doctor, which made her laugh and practically run into the master bedroom along with him.

* * *

The Laird's Chamber was as grand and masculine as Iona had imagined, with swathes of tartan and the family crest everywhere to tell the tale of Fraser's heritage. Yet if it had been cast entirely of gold and diamonds she would still have been more impressed with the sight of Fraser undressing in the room.

Without saying a word, he stripped naked, the sound of a bath running the only prompt Iona needed to mirror his moves. There could've been some awkwardness standing here staring at each other's naked bodies but Fraser watched her with so much admiration and desire that any inhibitions were quashed before they had time to manifest themselves. With such a fine body himself, Fraser had nothing to be ashamed of and clearly wasn't, striding confidently to the bathroom.

Iona felt more of a queen than a lady stepping into the cloud of bubbles in the tub, the warm water inviting her to sink deeper. Fraser's long legs enveloped hers and she relaxed back against his chest, letting the water and her lover wash over her.

She couldn't remember the last time anyone outside a salon had washed her hair but he did so, unbidden. He lathered the shampoo in her hair, his fingers massaging her scalp with a tenderness that made her want to weep. By all accounts, no one had ever taken care of him, yet here he was expressing his love for her by touch alone.

She closed her eyes as he rinsed out the suds and though she was content to remain where she was, she was obliged to give him the chance to experience this bliss too. 'Do you want me to wash your hair for you?'

'In a minute. I'm enjoying taking care of you without you trying to bite my head off for it.'

Now she knew there was no call to rebel against him through fear he was trying to get the upper hand over her,

Iona had to admit it was nice having someone look after her. She'd been on her own for so long, untrusting and suspicious, she'd forgotten simple pleasures like this.

Fraser took a flannel and began to wash her body with long, sensual strokes across her neck, over her breasts, slipping further down between her legs. She closed her eyes and gave herself over to his ministrations. After giving so much of herself these past few days, she figured she was entitled to some pampering.

Under the water he continued to move the cloth along her thighs, teasing across the part of her so desperately aching for his touch. She let out a whimper as he abandoned the flannel and carried on, using only his fingers to stroke her.

He kissed his way across her shoulder to that sensitive spot at her neck that automatically increased her arousal tenfold. It was then he pushed inside her, drawing a gasp and a groan as he soothed her ache.

She writhed against him as he stretched and filled her with his fingers, the swell of his erection pressed into the small of her back turning her on beyond measure. He wanted her but he wasn't going to have her until he'd driven her to climax first. A selfless lover was the best aphrodisiac known to womankind.

With one hand pushing her towards the brink of oblivion, the other was at her breast, pinching her nipple to provide that oh-so-pleasurable pain. Her orgasm slammed into her, the blinding flash behind her eyelids and shudder of gratification taking her breath away with the sheer force of it.

She was so lost in that spiralling bliss she didn't realise those erotic cries echoing around the walls were coming from her.

'Are you okay?' Fraser whispered in her ear, his hot

breath sending another aftershock of rapture rippling through her body.

'Uh-huh.' Apart from having lost the power of speech, her mouth dry and her brain having exploded with the sensations he'd drawn from her.

'In that case, let's get you dried off.' Water sluiced over her and the floor as he stood up and that weightlessness in her body disappeared at once.

'What about your hair?' Fraser wasn't going to cheat her out of doing something for him in return. She wanted him to experience the same moment of pure happiness he'd just given her.

'It's not my hair that's needs tending right now.' He grinned and held up a towel, waiting for her to get out of the bath.

There was no place for her gaze to linger other than at his manhood standing tall and demanding her attention.

Fraser swamped her in the fleecy warmth of the bath sheet, carried her into the bedroom and laid her down on the covers as though she was the most precious thing in the world. At that moment that's exactly how he made her feel.

He unwrapped her painfully slowly, taking his time to appreciate every inch of her he uncovered. There was no mistaking his desire for her, it was there for her to see in all its physical glory, but so was the love in his eyes for her, and that was her undoing. Fraser wasn't the same as the others, he wouldn't hurt her or try to change her, and he loved her for who she was, regardless of how difficult it was for him at times. In the few days they'd lived together they'd learned the art of compromise. Learned to love and live in harmony.

It was an unconventional match but it kept things so exciting and passionate between them that Iona never wanted to leave his bed.

Anticipation was throbbing through her body with that

one look promising all the things he was going to do to, and with, her.

She pressed herself tightly into him, teasing them both as her nipples rubbed against his chest and Fraser groaned, his erection grazing where she craved him most. He swallowed her breathy pleas with a tongue-tangling display of desire that did nothing to quench the fiery lust coursing through her veins.

'I need you, Fraser.' She begged him to fill that part of her that was incomplete without him now.

'I need you too.'

They belonged together and now they'd found each other it was unthinkable that they should ever be parted again.

Last night had been the culmination of their pent-up yearning for one another, a frantic endeavour to release that pressure and find ultimate satisfaction as quickly as possible. Being together here, Iona knew, was an expression of the depth of their feelings for one another, tender and loving as they took their time climbing towards that peak of absolute contentment together. It carried them both in quick succession over the finish line, leaving her breathless and euphoric.

She watched the rise and fall of his chest as he lay down beside her and the smile spreading across his face adding his own glowing review of their endeavours.

'Has it—is it—always this way for you?' It was the sort of question one might attribute to a naïve virgin but she'd never experienced this level of impact on her heart and her body.

She'd had lovers and the occasional relationship but none of her previous partners had reached her or taken her to such heights the way Fraser had. It made her question if she'd truly been in love before or if he was simply an exceptional lover. Perhaps he had this effect on every woman who'd ever shared his bed but she wanted what they had to be special for him too.

Fraser rolled over onto his side, propping his head on his hand, and reached out to brush a tendril of her still-wet hair from her face. She turned her cheek into his palm and closed her eyes, afraid to know the answer in case it ruined this for ever.

'Never.' His soft voice reached in behind her closed lids and travelled all the way to her soul. He was hers and hers alone and if every time was like this she never wanted to wake up alone again.

CHAPTER ELEVEN

IT WAS DARK when they finally decided to leave bed in search of sustenance. Iona walked over to the window to close the curtains and found the world outside glowing with a fresh fall of snow.

'Winter has well and truly arrived.' The night was so peaceful and still, they could've been perched atop their own private glacier, miles from civilisation, and content to be so.

'In that case, we should stock up on food supplies to see us through our hibernation.' Fraser jumped out of bed and began to pull on his clothes.

'What are you doing?' She was dismayed that he was hiding his beautiful body back under layers of fabric when it was so unnecessary.

'Er…getting dressed so we can go down and get something to eat.' The absurdity of what he was doing was completely lost on him so Iona took it upon herself to make the point. She walked over to his side of the bed, making no attempt to hide her own nakedness, and began to unbutton his trousers.

'This is your house, Fraser. We're alone and there's no one around for miles. We don't need clothes.' He put up no objections to her pulling his trousers off—indeed, he appeared very happy to let her do so. There was hope yet he'd learn to abandon some of his stuffy ways with her to lead him astray.

* * *

Fraser approved of Iona's naturist tendencies and with her every effort she was making this into a place he was comfortable to be in. It was early days to bring up the idea of her moving in when she'd barely unpacked in her own flat but she was the sole reason he'd decided he was going to stay in this house.

Iona would certainly blow away the cobwebs here and shake things up as she had done for him. A lot of his old habits and compulsions for order no longer seemed important and no longer dictated his daily schedule. They were no competition when pitted against spending time with Iona instead. With her by his side it was as if his brain had been reset, no longer conditioned to worry about the consequences of every tiny action. It could take a while for him to be a live-in-the-moment kind of guy but with Iona's infectious zest for life he would get there.

They stole downstairs, laughing in the faces of his staid ancestors and making him feel like the naughty child he'd never been here. He'd never done anything intentionally to upset his parents or Caroline. His inability to change had inevitably pushed her away but he'd changed for Iona after only a short time together. Deep down he must have known Caroline wasn't the one for him.

'Houston, we have a problem.' Iona flicked the light switch on and off in the kitchen but they remained in darkness. It was the same in the living room, their beautiful Christmas tree shrouded in shadow instead of twinkling fairy lights. The only light was coming from the fireplace, which would also be their only heat supply too until the power came back on.

'The storm must have brought the lines down. Not to worry, we have plenty of candles.' All those elaborate candelabra around the house would come in useful after all.

'I take it the oven's out of use too?' The desperate call

for food from Iona's rumbling belly was the only downside to the situation but Fraser was used to stocking up for those late nights when he came home and couldn't face cooking.

'Ah, but we do have a selection of cheeses and cold meats. Speaking of which, as much as I appreciate the view, without central heating there's a danger of us contracting pneumonia.' Fraser stacked plate upon plate and loaded a tray up with goodies to take into the lounge and spread out their makeshift picnic in front of the fireplace. Iona snagged the throw from the back of the couch and draped it around their shoulders as she sat down beside him.

It was moments such as this, wrapped up with his lover, feeding each other sustenance after a day spent in bed, that were worth more than money could ever buy.

'Is it wrong of me to want the snowstorm to last for ever so we can stay holed up here?' Iona took a sip from the bottle of water he'd taken from the fridge and a trickle of condensation splashed onto her chest and over her now erect nipple.

'I'd say that sounds perfect.' He leaned down and lapped the droplet with his tongue, thirst quickly overtaking his hunger.

Since having Iona here, he'd decided to make this his permanent residence but it only felt like a home with her in it. If she'd taught him anything over these past days it was to stop over-analysing everything and do what made him happy. He knew they'd only been together a short time, most of that accompanied by two minors, but it was sufficient to know this was right. It wasn't fair to keep ignoring his feelings any more when it had already cost him so much wasted time. 'Why don't you move in?'

Iona's brow knitted together in an expression that showed anything but enthusiasm for the idea. 'I know it's a big house but in case you haven't noticed, I've been living here for a few days now.'

'Well, I didn't think it was the Christmas elves who'd taken over... Seriously, though, think about it, but not for too long. I don't want to waste any more time. I want to be with you, Iona, share this house, and my life, with you.' He'd been here before with Caroline but this was different. He was being truer to himself than he'd ever been, putting everything he was on the line for Iona when he'd never done it for Caroline.

Sweat broke out over his skin the longer he waited for an answer when he'd thought the idea was a no-brainer. They were good for each other, anyone could see that, and their time together in the bedroom, and on the attic floor, had been every bit as exciting as the emotional connection they'd made.

'Fraser...that's—that's...' She was clearly as overwhelmed as he was, struggling to find words.

He knew he was risking a lot on what was primarily a gut instinct they would make this work. The opposite strategy from how he usually lived his life. Iona wasn't the kind of person to be blinded by the expensive trappings that came with him and he trusted her enough to base her decision on the strength of her feelings for him alone.

She stood up, wrapping the blanket around her to cover her nakedness, and Fraser rose with her for the warm hug he anticipated along with her acceptance.

'That's a ridiculous idea.'

He'd stepped towards her before the words slammed into his chest, causing serious internal damage. Optimism and a pitiful hold on the last vestige of hope he could rescue the situation and his heart prevailed. 'I know it's a bit out there but it seems like a natural progression to me when we already know we make a great team. You can ditch that dingy flat, move in here—'

'Quit my job, pop out a couple of kids…' Her tone definitely wasn't in keeping with his earnest endeavour to show her how he felt about her.

'I would never ask you to leave work but I won't lie, I'd like to be a father someday.' He hadn't been thinking quite that far ahead but since she'd brought the subject up he wanted to be honest about his dreams for a family. It had been the deal breaker for Caroline but the way Iona looked after all the children who came into her care hadn't gone unnoticed. He could see a future with her or else he would never have asked her and risked another rejection.

'Fraser, I've only just moved into my own place. You know what it means to me to have my independence. If you're expecting me to sacrifice everything I am for your benefit then you don't know me at all.' Despite everything they'd shared, it appeared Iona was still unwilling to compromise anything for him. Clearly he'd completely misjudged the situation and the baggage she had yet to unpack from her previous relationship if she didn't warrant him worthy of a permanent place in her life. A common theme unfortunately being played out again by someone he loved.

'I was merely asking if you wanted to move in. I've got my answer. That's fine. It was just a thought. Forget I said anything.' Fraser didn't want to cause a row or make her think he was anything akin to her ex when all he'd done was act on impulse. An area in which he apparently still had some work to do.

'No, Fraser. I can't forget it. This is exactly what I was afraid would happen. One small opening into my life and you try to bulldoze through everything. I think we've probably got caught up in this fantasy life we've built around the kids. Let's be honest, before them we didn't really have a lot in common or much to say to one another that wasn't an insult.

'Now they've gone I think we're clutching at straws in

an attempt to keep the fairy-tale going by jumping into bed. But it's not real. I think we've both been too damaged to ever make this work. You need someone here to give you that security you've missed and I can't give up my freedom when it's all I have. I'm going to pack my stuff and go and we'll keep this time together as a fond memory.'

She turned away from him and he knew this was more than a lovers' tiff, she was serious about leaving him and was trying to reduce what they had to a casual fling.

Fraser willed his feet to move, to run after her and beg her to stay but his body was uncooperative, shut down in a complete state of shock. The whole scene was a re-enactment of last year with Caroline, except this was so much more traumatic. Although he hadn't been with Iona long, he knew beyond doubt he was in love with her in a way he'd never loved anyone before. The rejection was not only of him in his truest form but the idea of a future together. Now he'd seen a glimpse of the family and home they could've had together here, he'd never want it with anyone other than Iona.

Nausea undulated through his body as his whole world collapsed around him once more. He reminded himself he was a grown man now, not that little boy who'd been parted from everything he loved without a say. Although Iona's decision to walk out felt very much like being abandoned all over again.

Iona was breathing heavily, her chest tightening with every step she took upstairs to escape the life Fraser was trying to create around her.

Yes, she fancied him like crazy and was maybe even falling in love with him, but the second her defences were down he'd swooped in and tried to exploit that weakness. Living together? Babies? That was a one-way ticket back to that prison she'd broken out of once already.

Iona needed to get back to her own place, her own space, where she could think clearly without abject terror clouding her judgement. Cooped up here, fostering that idea of family with Fraser and the children had messed with both of their heads. Once she was out of the picture again he'd realise that himself. Hopefully by the time they were back at work after the Christmas break they'd remember who they were.

Iona dressed quickly, gathering her belongings as she whipped around the bedroom. If she didn't leave now there was every chance she'd end up back in bed with him at some point and completely forget why her 'dingy flat', complete with borrowed furniture, should be more appealing than Fraser's bed.

It was far too tempting to ignore the distant sound of her phone ringing but she was never really off duty and a call this late could be an emergency.

'Hello.' Her response to whoever was on the line may as well have been an expletive she said it with such aggression but she wasn't in the best of moods, having just ended a relationship with a man she'd come to care for deeply.

'Iona, this is June Lowe, the community midwife on call. I'm sorry to phone out of hours but I understand you're staying with Dr McColl at present and we have an emergency out there. Claire McKenzie is desperately in need of assistance but the main roads there are blocked with fallen trees and downed power lines. We're trying to get an air ambulance out but with the storm… Anyway, we were wondering if you could get through from your end to check on her?'

Iona didn't want to spend long analysing what scenario the rumour mill had dreamed up for Fraser and her being shacked up here together when they would be correct in all of their assumptions. They were consenting adults and it shouldn't matter to anyone else what they did in their private lives as long as it didn't impact on their professional duties. Which it would have done had she not just called a halt to everything.

'Give me the details.' She grabbed a pen and paper from the bedside table and jotted down everything June told her.

Fraser appeared at the door but she didn't have time to feel bad about the forlorn look she'd put on his face.

She put her hand over the phone to let him know what was going on. 'There's a patient in trouble. Claire McKenzie's in advanced labour and her last child was stillborn. I have to get to her. She's not far from here anyway.'

Once she hung up, she forced on her boots and prepared to brave the outdoors.

'Geographically, yes, but we're under several feet of snow in the middle of nowhere. It's not easy terrain to negotiate.'

'I do this for a living, don't forget.' She grabbed her coat and bag, fully aware of the dangers she faced as she walked to her car but nothing was going to stop her from getting to her patient.

'You can't go in that. You'll never make it down the lane.' Fraser insisted on following her outside, criticising her every move.

The compact car was ideal for village life, although probably not conducive to extreme weather conditions, but she didn't have a choice right now.

'Please don't tell me what to do when it comes to my job.' It was easier to leave him when he was trying to undermine her and she started the car regardless of his concerns.

She could see him give chase in her rear-view mirror as the gates opened and she drove away with tears in her eyes and lead in her stomach.

Even at a snail's pace the car tyres slipped and skidded down the lane, gaining no traction at all on the ice, and she was helpless as the vehicle veered off the road and into a ditch.

Before she'd had time to assess any damage to the car, or her pride, she heard the sound of Fraser's four-by-four making its way down the road towards her. Given the circumstances, Iona was going to have to set aside her personal differences with him in order to do her duty to her patient. She'd make sure he didn't take that as a sign she was willing to give him another chance when that was a weakness that had seen her burned too many times.

Once they'd transferred her equipment from the boot of her car into Fraser's I-told-you-so-mobile, Iona got in the passenger side and slammed the door. 'Don't say a word.'

She was in a bad enough mood without another lecture. In the space of fifteen minutes she'd been reminded none of this fairy-tale romance was real, that this relationship couldn't survive reality.

CHAPTER TWELVE

THEY HAD SOME hairy moments during the journey to the patient's house, despite Fraser's careful and methodical driving. There were times when even he couldn't control what happened as the car hit a patch of black ice but the lack of other vehicles in the area at least prevented any serious accident.

If pushed, Iona would have admitted his jeep was better equipped for the road conditions than her runabout, but she didn't think the choice of driver made a difference regardless of Fraser's opinion on the subject. He could have easily handed his keys over to her and gone home but that apparently wasn't something he had been ready to do.

'That's the McKenzie place up there.'

They were forced to stop at the bottom of a particularly hilly stretch of road, their journey brought to an end by the huge tree and assorted debris strewn across their route. The McKenzies' car had been abandoned halfway between the obstacles and their house.

'Could you help me carry my equipment up to the house, please?' Iona could have been churlish and insist she manage on her own, leaving Fraser freezing down here, but that wouldn't achieve anything. By giving him a task, it was also asserting her position in this situation. She was in charge.

'No problem.' He fell into line and Iona loaded him up with any kit she might need. Only time would tell how long this compliance would last once they were confronted with whatever was going on behind that front door.

Mr McKenzie met them at the door, wearing the panicked face of a father-to-be. 'Thank goodness you're here. The baby's on its way. We can't get out and after last time…' He didn't have to say any more as he ran a shaking hand through his hair. Claire had recounted to her the trauma the family had gone through in her last pregnancy, which had ended in the stillbirth of their precious baby. Despite reassurances there was no medical reason the same would happen again, the couple had been understandably anxious for the duration of this pregnancy and this setback wasn't going to allay any of those fears. That was her job.

'Where's Claire? I'll have to examine her and see what stage we're at.' Nothing else could be helped now and the importance of mother and baby's welfare had to come before anything. If they were trapped up here for the entirety of her labour, Iona had to be prepared for any eventuality.

'She's up in the bedroom. Said she was in too much pain to try and get out again.' The understandably anxious birthing partner led them up to what was about to become the delivery suite, but he was so tense Iona wasn't convinced he'd do anything to put his wife at ease.

Regardless of the urgency in the situation, Iona took the time to knock on the door and introduce herself. 'It's Iona. The midwife.'

It was important patients maintain some dignity and privacy where they could so they weren't made to feel little more than a baby-making machine in the process.

'Come in. I'm so glad you're here.' Claire's fears were evident as she welcomed her into the room. Iona didn't know any more than the rest how this was going to play out but she had to act as confidently as she could manage to keep Claire calm. Stress could cause more complications if her blood pressure spiked now and there was only so much Iona could do without the conveniences of a hospital labour ward.

'You've got a midwife and a GP on hand so there's no cause for alarm. Now, how far apart are the contractions?' She left the two men hovering in the doorway to come and examine her patient.

'It feels as though they're constant.' Claire groaned as her belly tightened with another.

'Every two minutes. I was timing them before you came,' Craig chimed in.

'In that case, baby shouldn't be too long.' Iona wasn't worried about delivering the baby at home, she'd done it plenty of times, but she usually had more time to prepare. Especially if there'd been complications in previous pregnancies.

'What if the same thing happens again? Instead of bringing our baby home last time, all we had was a memory box. If something goes wrong here...'

Iona understood Craig's concerns and she'd had the same thought herself but there was nothing they could do but deliver the baby into the world. This constant reminder of their loss was going to prevent Claire taking any good memories from this labour and she had to get him out. He could be a part of the birth experience when the time came but for now it was better for all concerned if he took a back seat.

'We'll have it covered. Fraser, why don't you go and stick the kettle on for all of us? There's a gas cooker downstairs if you don't mind making it the old-fashioned way. Craig can fill you in and I'll get Claire comfortable here.' The message to Fraser was twofold, get Craig out of here and if I need your help I'll ask for it.

As one might have predicted, he wasn't prepared to relinquish the medical lead as easily as that.

'Craig, if you could do the honours, I'd like to have a word with Iona first.' His lips were drawn into a tight line, such a contrast to the soft mouth that had covered her body with tender kisses only hours earlier.

Iona trusted he wasn't so blinded by ego he couldn't see the serene atmosphere she was trying to create here, but she did step out onto the landing to have the conversation in private.

'What's up? I'm kind of busy here.' She kept one hand on the doorknob, making it clear she wasn't going to be detained long.

'I know you're ticked off at me but please let me help.' He could have called her out on the fact she'd relegated him to tea boy, put on some display of anger towards her based on the way she'd treated him since he'd asked her to move in with him. Instead, she could see he simply wanted them both to work together for the best outcome.

'I know what I'm doing but if I need you I promise I'll call.' Thinking of Claire lying behind the door, already afraid of what was going to happen, she knew she couldn't let her personal problems jeopardise the labour should anything go wrong out here.

'Thank you.'

She couldn't resist one last needle before she went back into the bedroom and closed the door. 'Mine's milk with one sugar, thanks.'

At least now she couldn't see or hear him she could get on with her job and bring this baby safely into the world.

'Okay, Claire, I'm just going to do a wee check and see how dilated you are.'

Dismissed from the scene, Fraser was forced to join the anxious Craig downstairs, cursing Iona for her pigheadedness. All he wanted to do was protect her, not that he could tell her that when she'd made it clear she thought he was trying to take over her life.

'Tea or coffee?' Craig greeted him at the bottom of the stairs, clutching a jar of coffee and a teabag.

'Neither. Have you got a snow shovel or heavy chains or something?' Fraser wanted to be more pro-active than simply sitting here, sipping tea.

Rather than rushing off to source essential tools to dig them out of here, Craig was still staring at him blankly, choice of beverages in hand.

It was tempting to try and shake some urgency into him but there was no need to see another display of his headless-chicken routine. He needed clear direction and something constructive to keep him occupied.

'Teatime can wait. We could be doing something useful, such as trying to move that tree. Your wife and child are going to need a clear path out of here at some point.'

That evocative reminder of why they were all here galvanised Craig into action. He turned back into the kitchen and tossed the tea things on the worktop. Iona probably wouldn't have liked the way he made it anyway.

'I'll take a look in the shed and see what I've got.'

'Great. At least then we'll feel as though we're doing something to help.' Iona mightn't want him here in a personal capacity but he could still be useful. With any luck they would all come out of this unscathed then he could set his mind to trying to win her back.

The sounds of scraping and revving car engines outside weren't going to distract Iona. Whatever Fraser was up to, at least it was keeping him out of her business. She had enough to deal with here, without dealing with Fraser's ego too.

It had become clear Claire's contractions had been going

on for some time with little progress. On examination she'd detected a problem that could explain the delay.

'Claire, I think the baby is in what we call the asynclitic position, where baby should come into the pelvis and rotate into position but in this case the head hasn't engaged properly. That's putting pressure on your pubic bone too.' There were certain positions with the foetal head that couldn't be delivered vaginally, which would be grave cause for concern here without proper intervention They were going to have to go back to basics to try and get the baby moving to where it needed to be.

'What do we do?' Claire's sobs were a mixture of fear and exhaustion, her hair stuck to her face with sweat, labour taking its toll. There were still a few tricks Iona could try to get junior to move before there was any reason to start stressing.

'I can tell you what we're not going to do, we're not going to panic. I'm going to go and see what's keeping your husband with the tea and get him to give us a hand to direct baby to the way out.' The attempt at humour took some of the focus off potential danger. Whatever happened, Claire was going to need the support of her husband to get through it, and despite Iona's resistance to engage Fraser in proceedings she would require his assistance if the baby was in distress.

She didn't waste any time locating the men, following the racket outside.

'Both of you come upstairs, now.' She had to yell to get their attention they were so engrossed in clearing the snow from the road.

'Is something wrong?' Craig came running first, with Fraser close behind, his cheeks so pink with cold it made her yearn for that time they'd spent wrapped up in front of the fire. It was too bad she'd learned the hard way there was no point in looking back.

'Baby needs some encouragement to move into place so Claire's going to need some assistance to get into a better position. She's a bit emotional right now so it would be good if you could just reassure her and support her through the contractions in the meantime.'

Fraser hung back to discuss the matter out of Craig's earshot. 'We've cleared a path down to my car. We could try to get her down.'

Iona shook her head. 'We're way past that stage. You're going to have to take my word for it, she's not going anywhere. Unfortunately, neither is the baby. Now, if you really want to help you can come up and run her a nice warm bath.'

She wasn't going to hang around to argue the point. The baby was dictating what happened here, not her and certainly not Fraser.

'We're going to move you so you're on all fours, Claire. It might help tilt the baby's head forward. Craig, can you give me a hand here to move the pillows and get her more comfortable?'

Between them they manoeuvred Claire onto her hands and knees, with the pillows to cushion the front of her body. She was too exhausted to put all the weight on her arms, panting through each contraction with Craig rubbing her back and making encouraging murmurs. It must be nice to have a supportive partner willing you on through such a momentous event but Iona doubted she'd ever experience it through any stage of her life.

'How's she doing?' Fraser wandered in, drying his hands on a towel, having actually followed instructions and drawn a bath for Claire.

'Working hard. Claire, could we get you into the bath for a while? It's not the traditional birthing pool but it might relax you and encourage our long-awaited arrival to drop down.'

Once the next contraction passed they had a small window to make the move before the next one hit. They encouraged her to lean over the edge of the bath in much the same position as she'd been on the bed. It was a tight squeeze with the four of them in the bathroom but they were all working towards the same outcome.

'You're doing great, Claire.' Iona reached down with the Doppler device so she could listen to the baby's heartbeat, which was still fast and strong.

Craig was holding her hand and helping her to pant through the contractions and Fraser was scooping warm water over her back so she didn't get cold.

As the contractions became more powerful it became increasingly clear the baby was finally ready to make an appearance. They had to wait for that brief respite again before transporting her back and in the end the birth was quick, Iona catching him before he slid onto the bed.

'Daddy, would you like to cut the cord?'

'We did it, Claire. We have a son.' Happy tears were streaming down the proud father's face as he did the honours.

Iona placed the baby on the mother's chest so they had that precious first skin-to-skin contact, welling up herself now that the danger had passed and he was finally here. It was always a privilege to be part of people's lives and follow their journey, more so to see it through to a happy end.

'Congratulations. All of you.' Fraser's praise was welcome but it was also tinged with a little sadness for Iona because when this was over she was faced with the prospect of going home. Alone.

Once she was sure the baby's Apgar score determined it was in good health they could leave the couple to enjoy the new member of their family until the next check-up.

A low score now would suggest baby needed extra medical care but indications so far were good.

'Iona?' Fraser no longer sounded full of the joys of a new baby but concerned as he drew her attention to the scarlet stain spreading rapidly across the bed covers, enough to suggest a post-partum haemorrhage.

She nodded an acknowledgement, trying not to scare the McKenzies, but the amount of blood being lost constituted an emergency. Even when births seemed to go to plan they were notoriously unpredictable. These days a woman was very unlikely to bleed to death giving birth, but this hadn't been a planned home delivery and currently they had no way to get her to hospital where they would be best equipped to deal with all eventualities.

'Okay, Claire, you're losing quite a lot of blood and we need to find the source so we can deal with it as quickly as possible. Craig, could you go and phone for an ambulance again and see what's happening out there?' She remained calm and in control of the situation for the benefit of the new parents, who were currently wide-eyed with fear, even though her own pulse was hammering away with the implications of the situation.

'Do you need me to take the baby?' Craig dithered by the bedside, ignoring her request. Thankfully Fraser had his mobile in his pocket so he went ahead and phoned in the emergency. In hindsight it was probably best to have him chasing up some medical support when he understood the severity of the situation.

'It would actually help contract the uterus if we could get the baby to breast feed. Do you think you could try that, Claire?'

She nodded, and with her husband's assistance they tried to get the baby to latch on, leaving Iona the important job of finding out why this had happened using the *T*s—tissue, tone, trauma and thrombin. She hadn't needed stitches so that ruled out trauma, and thrombin, an issue with blood clotting, was rare and would've been known prior to birth. Although the placenta had been delivered there was a chance a bit had been left behind or that the uterus didn't have enough tone to contract and stop the bleeding.

They might not be in a conventional hospital setting but she would follow the same steps regardless. She encouraged Claire to pass urine so she didn't have a full bladder and massaged the top of her uterus to stimulate it to contract, but blood was still gushing at an alarming rate.

'They're on their way. What can I do?' Thank goodness Fraser was here, offering another pair of hands where she desperately needed them.

'I'm going to administer an oxytocic drug but if that doesn't stop the bleeding we should put up an IV. Everything we need is in my bag.' Ordinarily the drugs were enough but if they had to transfer her to the hospital they needed a vein open and ready for easy access if necessary. Any issues with clotting would need to be treated and blood products administered.

With Fraser available to set up the IV, Iona was able to continue to massage the uterus in the hope it might help expel any retained tissue preventing good uterine clampdown.

'You're doing great.' Fraser was doing a good job of reassuring Claire everything was going to be all right, then Iona felt the warmth of his hand on her back and she realised he was talking to her.

That unexpected support when she was so accustomed of weathering the storm alone almost made her cry at his kindness after the way she'd treated him today. She knew in that moment that no matter what happened between them romantically, he'd always be there, supporting her. It put her earlier rant into perspective and her hysteria that he was somehow trying to railroad her into another painful relationship. Fraser would never hurt her. She'd simply been projecting her own fears onto him because she was so afraid of making another mistake.

She couldn't bring herself to respond to him, afraid she'd burst into tears and never regain her composure at a time it was needed more than ever. Instead, she continued bi-manual compression, continually pushing on the uterus externally and internally until they heard the sound of the ambulance siren in the distance and she nearly collapsed with relief.

'I couldn't stop the bleeding, Fraser.' Iona was beside him, watching the ambulance make its way cautiously back down the path he and Craig had shovelled, with the McKenzies loaded up inside.

'You did everything possible. You were amazing. I'm sure she's going to be fine, thanks to your actions.' If Claire required a blood transfusion or surgery to remove any remaining placenta, it was down to the hospital staff now to continue her treatment. Iona had done her best given the circumstances and he was proud of how she'd handled everything in such a potentially life-threatening situation.

It was easy to take midwives for granted when he wasn't actively involved with their practices every day, but having now seen first-hand how fraught a home birth could be, Fraser respected her even more. Especially since she didn't seem to have the confidence in her actions that she'd portrayed to the worried couple. He was sure her calm exterior had prevented them all from losing it and making matters worse, even if her own stress levels had been through the roof.

'I'm glad you were there with me. I couldn't have done it without your help.' After their earlier parting, Iona's words meant more to him than ever. He hoped in some small way he'd shown her he'd never do anything to interfere in her life and only wished to be part of it in some way.

'I'm pretty sure you could. You've managed all this time without me. Now, let's get back to my place out of this cold.' He understood where she was coming from. They were both perfectly capable of doing their jobs on their own but there was something reassuring about having that extra body nearby in case they were needed. It took the pressure off when you were able to share the experience with someone who understood the situation on the front line of medicine.

Neither of them had to go through life alone, if only they'd open up and accept they deserved the kind of love and support they could offer each other. It was something they really should discuss back at his place if Iona was willing to hear him out.

'Well, my car is still in a ditch there so I suppose I'll have to go with you.' That hesitation remained but she did lift her bag, indicating she would follow him.

He saw her legs begin to buckle as the enormity of the day seemed to hit her all at once. She wasn't as immune to the stress of the ordeal as she pretended. Not that anyone else would have known as she'd waited until her patient was safe before she'd given in to her own feelings. On this occasion at least she didn't have to go through it alone. He swooped down and scooped her up into his arms, just like that first time they'd found themselves thrown together.

'What are you doing?' Iona put up a half-hearted protest but he could tell she no longer had the strength to fight and that in itself was cause for concern.

'I don't care if you hate me for it but someone has to look after you. You're exhausted and in need of a strong cup of tea.' Everything else could wait until he was certain she had recovered from the trauma of the birth herself.

The drive back was as quiet as the outward journey had

been but the atmosphere seemed more of a comfortable silence than the frosty drive out to the McKenzies' place.

'I'll get your car fixed up for you later,' he promised as they passed her abandoned vehicle.

'I can do it myself. I was just in a hurry to get to Claire earlier.' Even in her current state she was asserting that independence at any cost.

Fraser sighed. He couldn't understand why she didn't see he only ever wanted to help but he wasn't going to get into another argument with her now.

They pulled up outside the house and he went around to Iona's side of the car to help her out.

'I can walk, thanks.'

'Sure.' Glad she was coming inside at least, Fraser gave her some space and went on ahead.

The scene greeting them in the living room was like something out of a tragedy. The power was back on, the Christmas tree twinkling in the corner of the room and illuminating the remnants of their post-coital picnic on the floor. It was a reminder of the happy times they'd had together and those they could still have together.

Everywhere he went in the house Fraser would be faced with more painful memories. Except now they'd be full of Iona's smile, her kiss and the sense of having her close to him.

The room smelled of Iona's sweet perfume and Christmas and he knew packing away those decorations she'd so lovingly hung for the children would kill him. All the fairy-lights and mistletoe would now become symbols of loss and regret.

Fraser thought of the pain caused by his parents never truly opening up about their feelings to him. If only they'd been able to talk things over, at any stage of his life, it could have saved them all a lot of heartache. He understood now they had been trying to protect him in their own way, but by shutting him out he'd only imagined the worst. They'd missed out on so much, all for the want of better communication. Such a waste of precious time that could have been spent together in his mother's last days. Perhaps he would've even been reconciled with his father at the end of his life too.

He didn't want to make the same mistakes with Iona when she meant so much to him, and he wasn't prepared to give up on love without a fight. This house was a shell without her in it and he could never be happy here alone.

'Please don't go, Iona. Can't we just start again?'

'We're so different…' Instead of the definitive no she'd given him earlier, she seemed to be mulling over the idea of a second chance. Perhaps the visual reminder of their time here had had a similar impact on her too.

'We've known that from the start. That's what makes the sparks fly, remember?' Life would never be boring between them and he wanted to remind her that their personality clashes could be a whole lot of fun at times.

Iona managed a wistful smile. 'Passion might disguise the real problems for a while but they show themselves in the end. I can't be with someone who thinks they can run my life for me. I'm never getting into that kind of toxic relationship again.'

'I would never try to control you. In my clumsy way I was trying to show you how much I cared for you.' Fraser's stomach rolled as he realised his misplaced faith in rules and order had fed directly into Iona's fears about everything she thought he represented from her past, and he didn't know how to fix it. Nothing meant as much to him as Iona and he'd give up anything for one more chance to prove it.

Previous experience had shown Iona that controlling men didn't change their behaviour for anyone. They might pretend for a while to be charming and contrite but that was all part of their manipulation. Their way of maintaining a hold on their victims by showing they were capable of redemption but always under an atmosphere of fear. Her mother had been afraid of her father and Iona would've left her ex sooner if not for the underlying threat of violence. She'd never once been afraid of Fraser. Annoyed, frustrated and downright angry at times with him but never had she seriously considered that by voicing her opinion on anything he would do her harm.

'It took a lot for me to walk away from the last man who tried to control me and it's taken me years to get where I am now. I have no intention of going back there.' Despite how desperately she longed to rewind time back to when they had been wrapped up here together with the world at their feet.

'I'm sorry. Did your ex ever say that to you and mean it? I'm truly sorry.'

Iona had heard the words before but never with the genuine remorse she saw shining in Fraser's eyes.

'I'm afraid to put myself in that position again when my life is very much my own now.'

'And you're not willing to share it with me at least? That's all I'm asking, Iona. I love you. If nothing else I want you to know that and believe it.' The catch in his voice gave away the truth of what he was saying and though hearing it made her heart soar and gave validation to her feelings for him, it couldn't completely heal her scars.

She wasn't used to having someone looking out for her unless they were trying to use it against her for their own means.

'In case you missed it, I'll say it again. I love you, Iona. I want us to be together.'

She was afraid that if she told him how much her heart

was swelling with love for him too she might start ugly crying again and he might change his mind about loving her.

'Asking you to move in here, I suppose, was symbolic. I was offering my heart along with the key to my home. I mean, we can forget the whole living-together thing. I know you just moved into your own place. Just tell me you feel the same about me and it'll give me hope I haven't totally messed this up.'

His rambling was endearing and she knew he'd never try to force her into doing anything when he was doing his best to give her her own space. Today had shown how much he loved her even before he'd said it out loud. Not only had he been there to assist her during Claire's labour in a professional capacity, but he'd been an invaluable source of emotional support to her. Something she hadn't realised she'd been missing until he'd rubbed her back and reassured her she was doing everything right.

His kindness in the face of her hostility towards him said everything about his character that she needed to know. It made her see her reaction towards his offer had been because she'd feared the strength of her own feelings for him, brainwashed by past experiences into thinking it meant she was opening herself up to get hurt again. She was still letting Andy isolate her from people who really loved her.

Iona would never love anyone the way she loved Fraser for everything he'd done for her, and how he loved her. He'd gone against all his own fears to open his house up to her and the children, had decorated for Christmas regardless of his own personal issues and had abandoned his rule book so they had all been comfortable here. He'd sacrificed a lot to try and make her happy.

So she had two options. She could throw herself wholeheartedly into a relationship with him and take the risk along with him that love would win out and make everything worthwhile. Or she could walk away now and protect what was left of her heart, back to the safe life she'd left behind in her one-bedroom flat. If she wanted to live life to the fullest she could no longer hide away from everything it had to offer.

She leaned in to whisper in his ear, 'I love you too.'

As the truth left her lips that veil of suspicion finally lifted. She loved him with every fibre of her being. Fraser McColl was the part of her she hadn't realised was missing until she'd tried to walk away from him.

He gathered her up in his arms and peppered her with kisses. 'You don't know how happy that makes me.'

She had a fair idea with the grip he had on her and the size of the grin on his face. 'Is that offer to move in still on the table?'

He stopped hugging and kissing her long enough to stare. 'Does this mean—?'

'Yes. I want to live with you. I want to spend Christmas here with you and every day after that if you still want me.' There was that slight wobble in confidence that he might have grown tired of her drama.

'Always,' he said, and planted one of those delicious long kisses on her lips.

Fraser McColl was the best Christmas present she could ever have wished for.

EPILOGUE

'Okay, the tree's up, the dinner's in the oven and we have cover for the holidays. Is there anything we've forgotten?'

Fraser had his hands on his head, searching his mind for things they might still have to do, but Iona was certain they'd made provision for every possible eventuality.

'Relax. They're going to be here soon and we don't want you stressing them out. This isn't our first rodeo, remember?' Iona handed him some fresh towels to set out in preparation for their new arrivals so he had something to keep him busy other than driving her mad with his constant worrying.

'No, but it is our first *official* Christmas as foster parents. I want everything to be right for them.' Fraser's compassion for the unfortunate children who'd found themselves in the care system through no fault of their own hadn't lessened over the years and she loved him for it.

'It will be.' She kissed him gently on the lips, hoping it would go some way to settling his nervous excitement. He always gave one hundred percent to the children who came to stay with them, no matter how short their time here, but Christmas was particularly special to him as he wanted to give them the special memories he hadn't had as a youngster. After their experiences with Hamish and Poppy they'd both been keen to offer the same safe environment to others and it had given him a reason to keep on the family home other than through obligation alone.

Iona had moved in shortly after their first Christmas together, shipping her barely opened boxes from her beloved apartment, but Fraser had never put her under pressure to do anything she didn't want to. When it came to those big decisions they always had a lengthy conversation so there was no room for misunderstanding and it had worked out pretty well for them so far. They'd taken their time with their relationship, only committing to marriage when they had both been ready, and doing it on the quiet because it was for no one else's benefit but their own.

Since then it had been a whirlwind of activity in the big house, redecorating and turning the place into a home where everyone was welcome. A family remained on the agenda for both of them but for now they were content to parent on a temporary basis for those who needed it.

'Here they come.' Fraser set the towels on the hall table to open the door for the terrified little faces peeking out from the back of the car pulling up in the drive. He wrapped a hand around Iona's waist and pulled her close, their united front to put the eight-year-old twin girls at ease as they ventured towards the strange new house. His heart was so full of love to give to these children for whom it had been so lacking, Iona knew it wouldn't be long before they started their own family. Fraser had proved time and time again he'd make as good a father as he did a husband. For now, though, these children were theirs to look after and nurture until their circumstances improved, and they'd devote all of their time and energy into doing that.

'Have I told you how much I love you?' she whispered to her husband, doting on him more every time she witnessed his devotion to helping others.

'Not in the last five minutes.' He grinned and left one

last, lingering kiss on her lips before their visitors came to meet them.

'Welcome.'

'Merry Christmas.'

They greeted their new family with warm smiles and a desire to make some new, cosy Christmas memories with them to last a lifetime. It was only right they should share their happiness with those less fortunate when they had so much of it to give.

* * * * *

COMING SOON!

We really hope you enjoyed reading this book.
If you're looking for more romance
be sure to head to the shops when
new books are available on

Thursday 24th October

To see which titles are coming soon, please visit
millsandboon.co.uk/nextmonth

MILLS & BOON

FOUR BRAND NEW STORIES FROM
MILLS & BOON MODERN

The same great stories you love,
a stylish new look!

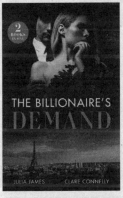

OUT NOW

MILLS & BOON

LET'S TALK
Romance

For exclusive extracts, competitions and special offers, find us online:

- **MillsandBoon**
- **@MillsandBoon**
- **@MillsandBoonUK**
- **@MillsandBoonUK**

Get in touch on 01413 063 232

For all the latest titles coming soon, visit
millsandboon.co.uk/nextmonth

afterglow BOOKS

 Sports romance

 Sports romance

 Workplace romance

 Workplace romance

 One night

 Spicy

OUT NOW

Two stories published every month. Discover more at:
Afterglowbooks.co.uk

OUT NOW!

Available at
millsandboon.co.uk

MILLS & BOON

OUT NOW!

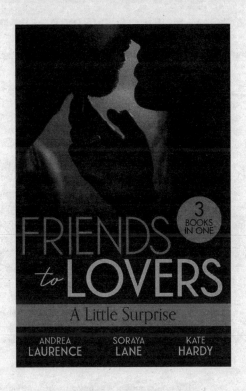

Available at
millsandboon.co.uk

MILLS & BOON

MILLS & BOON

THE HEART OF ROMANCE

A ROMANCE FOR EVERY READER

MODERN

Prepare to be swept off your feet by sophisticated, sexy and seductive heroes, in some of the world's most glamourous and romantic locations, where power and passion collide.

HISTORICAL

Escape with historical heroes from time gone by. Whether your passion is for wicked Regency Rakes, muscled Vikings or rugged Highlanders, awaken the romance of the past.

MEDICAL

Set your pulse racing with dedicated, delectable doctors in the high-pressure world of medicine, where emotions run high and passion, comfort and love are the best medicine.

True Love

Celebrate true love with tender stories of heartfelt romance, from the rush of falling in love to the joy a new baby can bring, and a focus on the emotional heart of a relationship.

HEROES

The excitement of a gripping thriller, with intense romance at its heart. Resourceful, true-to-life women and strong, fearless men face danger and desire - a killer combination!

From showing up to glowing up, these characters are on the path to leading their best lives and finding romance along the way – with plenty of sizzling spice!

To see which titles are coming soon, please visit

millsandboon.co.uk/nextmonth

MILLS & BOON
A ROMANCE FOR EVERY READER

- **FREE** delivery direct to your door
- **EXCLUSIVE** offers every month
- **SAVE** up to 30% on pre-paid subscriptions

SUBSCRIBE AND SAVE

millsandboon.co.uk/Subscribe

GET YOUR ROMANCE FIX!

Get the latest romance news, exclusive author interviews, story extracts and much more!

blog.millsandboon.co.uk

MILLS & BOON

HISTORICAL

Awaken the romance of the past

Escape with historical heroes from time gone by.
Whether your passion is for wicked Regency Rakes,
muscled Viking warriors or rugged Highlanders,
indulge your fantasies and awaken the
romance of the past.

Five Historical stories published every month, find them all at:

millsandboon.co.uk

MILLS & BOON

MODERN

Power and Passion

Prepare to be swept off your feet by sophisticated, sexy and seductive heroes, in some of the world's most glamorous and romantic locations, where power and passion collide.

Eight Modern stories published every month, find them all at:

millsandboon.co.uk

MILLS & BOON

HEROES

At Your Service

Experience all the excitement of a
gripping thriller, with an intense romance
at its heart. Resourceful, true-to-life
women and strong, fearless men face
danger and desire – a killer combination!

Eight Heroes stories published every month, find them all at:

millsandboon.co.uk